SHUBHI AGARWAL, born family in Kanpur, Utta. person, Shubhi is an avid writer, blogger, content creator and poet. She loves discussing mental health which she pursues in her free time, even though she is very young. Besides this, she loves to help and counsel people who have lost hope in life. "I know how important it is to lend a helping hand and a listening ear to people who feel alone or depressed," Shubhi says. A Class 12 student of DPS Kalyanpur, Kanpur, she is preparing for her IPMAT examination to pursue a degree in business management.

At 14, Shubhi began to write *Lakshmila* and by the age of 15, she started up with her own freelance company, SA Writing Services, to write, edit and create content. Having read almost every version of the Ramayana in this world including the Purans, she is well-versed with facts about them. She was a former Wikipedia editor and a national-level debater and won several medals for the same.

She began blogging on her website www.shubhiagarwal.in where she post blogs related to religion. She is a girl with fierce attitude, who doesn't care what society thinks. She speaks on social issues and raises those about which very few speak of. Check her out on Instagram@shubhi.agarwal29, on twitter@shubhi2901 and on Quora at Shubhi Agarwal148. She blogs at www.shubhiagarwal.in and can be reached at shubhiagarwal229@gmail.com

Lakshman-Urmila Mandir, Bharatpur, Rajasthan, the only temple dedicated to Lakshman ji and Urmila ji, the only place where one finds their idols together.

LAKSHMILA

THE ETERNAL LOVE STORY

SHUBHI AGARWAL

Om Books International

First published in 2022 by

Om Books International

Corporate & Editorial Office
A-12, Sector 64, Noida 201 301
Uttar Pradesh, India
Phone: +91 120 477 4100
Email: editorial@ombooks.com
Website: www.ombooksinternational.com

Sales Office
107, Ansari Road, Darya Ganj,
New Delhi 110 002, India
Phone: +91 11 4000 9000
Fax: +91 11 2327 8091
Email: sales@ombooks.com
Website: www.ombooks.com

ISBN: 978-93-92834-21-9

Printed in India

10 9 8 7 6 5 4 3 2 1

My Godparents, my Lakshman *ji* and my Urmila *maa*.
This is for you. I hope it provides complete justice to you.
And my dear You...

शान्ताकारं भुजगशयनं पद्मनाभं सुरेशं
विश्वाधारं गगनसदृशं मेघवर्णं शुभाङ्गम्।
लक्ष्मीकान्तं कमलनयनं योगिभिर्ध्यानगम्यम्
वन्दे विष्णुं भवभयहरं सर्वलोकैकनाथम्।।

(I meditate on Lord Vishnu who has a serene appearance which fills our
inner being with peace; who is lying on the bed of serpent Lord Shesha
representing the eternal Primal Energy or Mula Prakriti; from whose
navel is springing up a lotus which is the source of all creations through
Bramhadeva; and who is presiding over the various elements of those
creations as the Lord of the Devas,
Who is the Substratum of the whole universe as consciousness; and boundless
and infinite like the sky Chidakasha; with a form bluish in colour like the
cloud, the form which is radiating auspiciousness which fills our inner being
with bliss,
Who is the beloved of Devi Lakshmi with beautiful eyes like lotus petals; who
is attainable by the yogis only through meditation,
I worship that all-pervading Vishnu who removes the fear of worldly existence
by making us realise that we are not isolated beings internally but are eternally
connected to him; I worship that Vishnu who is the one lord of all the Lokas.)

Aryavarta in Treta Yuga: Lakshmila Landmarks

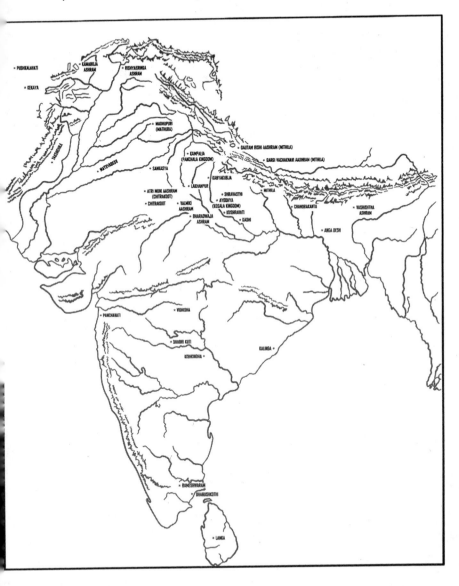

Author's Note

Hello my dear readers,

How *Lakshmila* came into being is an interesting turn of events and to be honest it is no more than a miracle for me to have written *Lakshmila*, I would say. I believe that Narayan chose me as his way to let people know about the story of Lakshman *ji* and Urmila *maa*.

The foundation of *Lakshmila* dates back to my childhood. The Ramayana and I have been inseparable ever since then for I've grown up listening to the glories of Lord Ram and his family every day from my family members, especially my Baba. Instead of lullabies and fairy tales, I used to listen to tales of the Ramayana at night. During my Dussehra holidays, Baba used to take me to the very famous Parade Ramleela which was held in our city for about 10 days. My Baba himself is a great devotee of Lord Ram and an active member of the Parade Ramleela Society, Kanpur and hence I have grown up watching Ramleela sitting on my Baba's lap, playing with bow-and-arrow and sword.

Though I loved and respected each and every character it was always Lakshman *ji* and Urmila *maa* who ruled my heart. Unknowingly, over the years, the morals of the Ramayana became an unconscious part of my soul and began to govern my life in a sublime way. I started to find solutions to my problems as Lakshman *ji* or Urmila *maa* would have solved them.

I remember, when I was 4 or 5, I expressed my desire to visit Ayodhya as I wanted to see Lord Ram's Raj Bhavan. I wanted to see those corridors where Lakshman *ji* and Shatrughan *ji* played their pranks on Bharath *ji*.

But when I reached Ayodhya, I learnt that Lord Ram's palace had been demolished. I was heartbroken. It was unbelievable for me and I became upset. But a priest there told me that God resides everywhere. Even my heart is also his home. I came back from Ayodhya and something had changed. Maybe I brought back Lord Ram and Lakshman with me. Little did I know then that the curiosity to seek Lakshman *ji* and Urmila *maa* and Ayodhya would become the foundation of this book! I came back and started with my research.

It has been almost 12 years now. I am currently 18 and I have been researching about Lord Ram and people associated with him ever since that incident. I began recording my research in a book. I have read almost every single version of the Ramayana in this world which includes my favourite Valmiki Ramayana and the Purans also.

The Valmiki Ramayana and the Kamban Ramayana are my favourite versions of the Ramayana amongst all other versions of the Ramayana, the Padma Puran and the Vishnu Puran became my best allies during the structuring of this book. Every single *shloka* provided me information as well as solutions to real-life problems.

Another incident that propelled me to write *Lakshmila* was the loss of a dear friend owing to some misunderstandings. His words, "Tell Shubhi to come to me the day she achieves something big in life," motivated me to prove myself to him and to the world. His words became my motivation mantra and I began to write. *Lakshmila* is possible because of him. I thank him for this. I guess I would not have been able to complete *Lakshmila* if he hadn't said those words. His words encouraged me to do this.

I made my day and night one and started working on my *Lakshmila*. And at every step of this beautiful journey, my Narayan's guidance and my godparents' blessings protected me. I literally used to spend 12 hours a day on it! I used to meditate for long hours to take myself to the era of my Lakshman *ji* and Urmila *maa* in order to portray their feelings.

As my involvement became deeper, I decided to leave school to write *Lakshmila* full time. I was in class 10 and I decided to opt for private schooling for a year. Maybe it was destined by Narayan as he wanted me to complete my *Lakshmila*! And later on, in class 11, after completing my *Lakshmila*, I rejoined my school.

Writing *Lakshmila* wasn't easy. People discouraged me and made fun of me. They said that rather than concentrating on my boards, I was writing a novel. They even laughed at me and called me mad to consider Lakshman *ji* and Urmila *maa* my godparents. But I ignored their jibes and concentrated on my Laksh.

But my parents stood by me like a rock. They motivated me to write it after they saw my dedication to it.

It took me two years to write *Lakshmila* and every single day has changed my life.

During my research tours, I visited every single place where my Lakshman *ji* and Urmila *maa* went. I was hurt by the behaviour of people towards my Lakshman *ji* and Urmila *maa*. I believe that Narayan chose me to let the world know the story of my Lakshman *ji* and Urmila *maa* and bring justice to them. I hope to change their perspective with *Lakshmila*, and see recognition of their sacrifice in every person's eyes. This book, however, is primarily a work of romantic fiction woven around the beautiful love story of Lakshman and Urmila, mostly untold, found in the fine prints of the different versions of the Ramayana.

Happy reading, folks!

Contents

PROLOGUE
Vaikunth Plans

*This narrative commences much before the earth was created by the Big Bang;
when the sun tore itself apart to create its solar retinue. The love story was made
in the cosmic deep, known as the great cosmic universe. It was ordained to enact
on earth, a billion years later...*

The abode of the gods in the clouds of divine happiness is in a
tizzy because the earth is in danger of being overrun by the armies
of the rakshasas – the demons. The Treta Yuga– the second and
the best of the four eras in the Hindu mythological calendar – is
under siege by demons, including Raavan, the mighty king of
Lanka, who is plundering Aryavarta, the land of the Aryans. As
unrest, mass slaughters and barbarism intensify and the sages are
eliminated one by one, the terror-struck people of Aryavarta call
out to the gods above for help. The deities gather their flock and
put together a delegation to meet the ruler of Vaikunth, Vishnu,
the preserver of the universe and a fierce warrior, to rid the earth
of demons.

The gods and the goddesses, including Shiva, Parvati, Bramha,
Saraswati, Indra, Surya and Agni – foremost in their positions of
importance in the divine order of powers and invocation, stand
before Vishnu in apprehension, fear evident in their voices as they
chant, *Om Namo Narayan,* in oblation to Vishnu-Narayan, who is in
calm repose on Shesha, the serpent with 1,000 hoods.

A boyish smile lights up the deity's beautiful face even with his eyes closed. Vishnu-Narayan is in a light slumber, but he knows why the gods have flocked to Vaikunth. "Save us, O, Narayan, else Raavan will destroy everything in his arrogance," the gods implore. Vishnu slowly opens his eyes and looks at their distressed faces.

Vaikunth, the white land and the home of Vishnu stands magnanimous in its unblemished beauty. Ksheera Sagara, the Milky Ocean that swirls around Vaikunth, flows gently in concoction to the hum and chirp of the birds. The majestic gates of Vaikunth adorned with flowers open the path to the splendour of Narayan, resting on Shesha, with Lakshmi tending at his feet. Unperturbed by their anxiety, Vishnu-Narayan says in a calm voice, "This had to happen, but I have a preconceived a plan. I have to take birth on earth in human form."

Bowing with respect, the gods look at him with hope and curiosity.

"I will be born in Ayodhya soon to Maharaj Dashrath and his eldest queen Maharani Kaushalya as their eldest son Ram. My companion, Shesha, will accompany me as my younger half-brother Lakshman and Sudarshan as Lakshman's twin Shatrughan. They will be born to Maharani Sumitra, the second queen of Maharaj Dashrath. I cannot leave my *panchajanya* – my *shanka* (conch shell), behind. He will take birth as Bharath, son of King Dashrath and his third queen Rani Kaikeyi."

Shiva and Brahma exchange knowing glances. They have complete faith in Lord Vishnu-Narayan, yet they push for an answer to satisfy their curiosity, "Why Ayodhya, Narayan?"

The avatara smiles and continues, "The city will be Ayodhya because it has been the most pious land in Aryavarta for the past many epochs. And, I also have to fulfil a promise I made to Maharaj Dashrath in his previous birth. My dear sister Yogmaya, an avatara of Goddess Parvati, has already been born to Maharaj Dashrath and Maharani Kaushalya as Shanta but the time has not come yet to disclose the how or the why of her earthly incarnation. Keep patience and wait for the events to unfold."

In his previous birth, Dashrath was a poor man but a great devotee of Narayan. Moved by his tough penance, Narayan granted him a boon that he shall be born as Dashrath whenever he takes birth as a mortal on earth.

Om Namo Narayan, the gods cry out in jubilation. "And, since I am incomplete without Lakshmi, just like Shesha is without Ksheera, Lakshmi will become my biggest abettor in bringing down Raavan, the demon king."

"Narayan, how will this happen?" the gods are piqued.

"A few years after my birth, Lakshmi will be found in a field in the kingdom of Mithila. Maharaj SeerdhwaJanak Videhraj, the king of Mithila, will adopt her as his daughter and she will be known as Sita. But Aryavarta will not know that Sita is the infant who Raavan and Mandodari had cast off at birth."

The gods draw their breath sharply, but Narayan continues without pausing, "To accompany Shesha, my younger sister Ksheera will be born as Urmila, the blood daughter of Maharaj SeerdhwaJanak and his wife Maharani Sunaina. Lakshmi's *shanka* will take birth as Mandvi. She shall be born to Maharaja SeerdhwaJanak's younger brother Kushadhwaja and his wife Chandrabhaga. Gomati, the *chakra* of Lakshmi and the wife of Sudarshan will be born as Shrutakeerti, Mandvi's younger sister."

The cascading Ksheera suddenly becomes quiet. Lord Vishnu watches as Shesha silently entwines his hand with Ksheera's, but cannot say no to the call of duty. Sensing their concern for their five-year-old daughter Sulochana, Vishnu calls Shesha's younger brother Vasuki and his wife Yakshi. He requests them to take care of Sulochana, till they return to Vaikunth from earth.

Vasuki embraces little Sulochana, "I shall, Narayan, like my own daughter." He gently pulls at her hand that is in Shesha's clasp and looks up to see tears in Shesha's pleading eyes. Shesha hugs his daughter one more time, before putting her hand into Vasuki's, "Take care of her unspoken feelings. Let her grow up free and marry her to the man of her choice. But he should be a worthy man." Vasuki and Yakshi bow in assent.

As Lord Vishnu finishes outlining his plan, a sense of victory permeates among the gods gathered in Vaikunth, and with a unanimous chant of *Om Namo Narayan*, they leave one by one.

Ayodhya and Mithila prepare to embrace Lakshmila.

Birth of Lakshmila

The destination gears up for its tryst with an epic.

The ancient land of Ayodhya, on the banks of the lower course of the Ghagra also known as the Sarayu River, was unaware that the soon-approaching chain of events would change how the world remembered it. The kingdom was despondent, wallowing in its 'misfortune'.

The bloodline was in peril. The king was ageing and he could not think of a successor to hand over the crown apart from the one born of his own blood. The most magnificent and the prosperous city of Aryavarta in the Treta Yuga yearned for a male heir because it feared that its royal line would be rendered barren. Despite being a bustling city, where only happiness prevailed, Maharaj Dashrath, the king of Ayodhya, was heartbroken because none of his 363 queens had been able to give him a son. Some of the queens, who were rejected by Maharaj, the king, for not being able to give birth to a male heir, immolated themselves while others were killed.

Dashrath was so depressed that he began to neglect his only daughter, Shanta. The craving for a male child robbed the king of his sleep and broke down his health. One day, sage Vashishtha, the clan's spiritual guide, visited the king in his palace and noticed the fine lines of disquietude on his gentle face. Concerned, he advised the king to perform *Putra Kameshthi Yajna*, an invocation rite to beget sons.

Dashrath was perplexed because he had not heard of this particular ritual.

The sage explained the ways to perform the ritual and its implications in detail to the king. "If somehow, we can convince sage Maha Rishyasringa to perform the *yajna*, Ayodhya can be blessed with an heir. But it is impossible to reach this pertinacious and persevering sage."

Convincing Rishyasringa to perform the rite as the chief officiating priest was not an easy mission. The sage was elusive and a recluse. He had to be placated with a sop. King Dashrath was worried.

But Vashishtha persisted. "There is a way, dear king. If your daughter Shanta weds Maha Rishyasringa, she can force him to come to Ayodhya to perform the *yajna*."

Dashrath was not sure whether Shanta would agree to live as a seer's consort in a monastic retreat in the icy Shringa mountain. It was too big a sacrifice for a little girl; he did not dare to ask her.

But Shanta's sacrifice was destined. It was an embedded part of Narayan's plan.

Shanta, who stood quietly behind the door of Dashrath's private chamber to overhear the conversation between her father and the seer, decided to fulfil her duties towards her parents and her land. She was troubled by her father's sorrow at not being able to beget a male heir and his sliding health. She believed that her sacrifice was too little, compared to the grace she had been granted by god to be born into Raghukul, the illustrious solar dynasty of Iskhvaku.

When she approached Dashrath's three official queens – Kaushalya, Sumitra and Kaikeyi – with her decision to marry Rishyasringa of her own free will, they were shocked and tried to persuade her out of it. But Shanta gently overrode their authority.

In a few days, she left the kingdom for Maha Rishyasringa's cave in the Shringa Mountain with the help of King Lompad (also known as King Romapada) of Angadesh and his queen Varshini.

Hope knocked at the door of Ayodhya very soon. Weeks later, a messenger arrived with a missive to the court that Shanta and Maha Rishyasringa were due to arrive in Ayodhya and were expecting Maharaj Dashrath to prepare for the *yajna*. As promised, Shanta and the sage came to Ayodhya, where Shanta's husband officiated at the *Putra Kameshthi Yajna* in the Kanchi Kamakshi temple, the temple of the *kuladevi* (clan goddess) of Raghukul, as the head priest.

The *yajna* was so potent in spirit that Agni Dev – the god of fire – was happy. He rose out of the ceremonial hearth and granted Dashrath a bowl full of white *ksheer* – milk and rice porridge – as his blessings and urged the king to distribute it in equal portions among his three queens.

The Maharaj gave the first portion of the 'blessing' to Maharani Kaushalya and was about to give the second portion to his second queen, Maharani Sumitra; when Queen Kaikeyi, Dashrath's third wife, lured the king into giving her Sumitra's share. The king, who was dazed after the long and tiring *yajna*, bowed to Kaikeyi's bidding. Dashrath had a soft corner for the fierce and beautiful Kaikeyi in his heart.

Was Kaikeyi a pawn to fulfil what Narayan had planned or was it actually just a mishap that left Maharani Sumitra bereft of her share of the divine blessing?

Maharani Sumitra, calm, patient and perhaps wisest of the three queens, turned a blind eye to the Maharaj's favouritism towards Kaikeyi. She got up from the mat (on which she was sitting in order of seniority next to Queen Kaushalya), to leave the temple, when the elder queen and Kaikeyi offered her portions from their share to make up for the slight.

Maha Rishyasringa observed the exchange of blessings among the queens and smiled. "Maharaj, you will become the father of four sons. Maharani Sumitra will bear two sons," he blessed the king and returned to his cave in Shringa mountain with Shanta.

In the Satya Yuga, Sumitra was a woman named Driti, who was one of the wives of sage Kashyap. Driti was a devotee of Lord Shesha. Moved by her unswerving penance, the lord blessed her to be his mother whenever he would incarnate as a mortal on earth. In the Treta Yuga, she took birth as Sumitra whereas in the Dwapar Yuga, she was Rohini, the mother of Balaram.

Ayodhya celebrated the *godh bharai* – baby shower ceremony – of the three queens a couple of months after the *yajna* and waited for nine months with bated breath. There were ripples of excitement among the residents.

Maharani Kaushalya gave Ayodhya its first male heir on the ninth day of the *Chaitra Shukla Paksh* – in the phase of the full moon. The delirious king did not have the time to celebrate the birth of Ayodhya's first male child – a momentous event – when he was blessed with a second son by Queen Kaikeyi, the next day. And then, on the auspicious day of *Kamada Ekadashi* of *Chaitra Shukla Paksh* – during the same period of the full moon – Maharani Sumitra bore him twin sons. Ayodhya was fulsome with the arrival of four bonny boys.

The Valmiki Ramayana says that when Lakshman was born, a strange phenomenon occurred. Clouds disappeared and the sun shone brightly, its rays caressing the Suryavanshi flag on the top of the palace.

Sage Vashishtha said, "I believe the prince hates thunder."

Maharaj Dashrath was overwhelmed. He picked up his sons and held them close to his heart. His eyes shimmered with tears. He had waited long for this moment. His voice quivered with pride when he commanded his aide, Arya Sumantra, to shower largesse on the denizens of Ayodhya. It was time to rejoice. Arya carried rubies, emeralds, sapphires, pearls, gold and coins in platters to distribute among the subjects, with heaps of fruits and sweetmeats.

On the 12th day of the birth of the four princes, the king invited sage Vashishtha to conduct the *naamkaran* – naming ceremony – of the infants. It was time for the heirs to be named. Vashishtha read each horoscope, going through their solar and lunar transits very carefully. Taking a deep breath, he began to name the princes on the basis of their personality types and their futures as their birth charts indicated.

"Maharaj, you are truly blessed; your eldest son will give *dharma* – religion – a new definition. He will be sweet and gentle and will be known for his commitment to his promises. Hence, the world shall know him as Ram."

"Just like Ram, this first-born of Maharani Sumitra is unique. He will grow up to be an example of selfless love and honesty. People will remember him for centuries. There will be none like him. He will always get what he set outs to achieve and therefore we will name him Lakshman, another word for auspicious. He will have the power to overcome death, but beware of his volatile anger."

"The second child of Maharani Sumitra, Shatrughan, will be gentle but mischievous. The demons will find a powerful enemy in him," Vashishtha continued.

At last, Vashishtha sifted through the horoscope of Kaikeyi's son and exclaimed, "Bharath, a child with a golden heart. He will be the calmest and the most dutiful among all your sons."

"The bond between Ram and Lakshman, Bharath and Shatrughan will remain unbreakable," the sage prophesied.

As soon as Vashishtha uttered his prophecy, Lakshman began to wail as if on cue. Maharani Sumitra tried to calm him but her efforts were futile. Ram's little fingers curled around Lakshman's and the younger child stopped crying. Such were the ties of brotherhood!

The heavens watched.

Far away in her abode in Vaikunth, Ksheera suddenly felt lonesome. She desperately wanted to meet Shesha. The longing almost tore her soul apart. For the past few days, her daughter Sulochana, who was being brought up by Shesha's brother Vasuki and his wife Yakshi, had been nagging Ksheera with constant letters and messages that she wanted to meet her father on her birthday. The child's persistent pleas made Ksheera feel more helpless and forlorn.

She sought an audience with Goddess Lakshmi in her palace and coaxed a promise out of her that they would leave for Aryavarta together on Sulochana's birthday to meet their consorts, who have taken birth in their human avataras.

Ksheera came out of the milky ocean to earth with Lakshmi and Sulochana. The trio arrived in Ayodhya, a day's journey from

Vaikunth – in their spiritual auras – to meet Shesha and Vishnu-Narayan. Ksheera's eyes were full of tears.

She peered at Lakshman, smiling in his crib, and identified with the spirit of Shesha, who recognised her immediately. He reached out to Ksheera from within the body of the child and the two yearned to touch each other. Yet, they could not. Shesha was in his mortal form and they would have to wait for some more time to reunite.

Ram and his consort Lakshmi observed their anguish from a distance. There was not much they could do and the spirit of Vishnu in Ram wept in silence.

"Lakshmi, it is time for Lakshmila to show Aryavarta a new definition of pious and selfless love," The spirit of Vishnu-Narayan whispered to his consort, Lakshmi, who filled Ksheera with her silent magic.

Sulochana, who was standing at the far end of the palace, was intrigued by the human form of her father – a lively baby boy. She walked to the crib and peeped at her father from behind Ksheera. Lakshman felt a gentle wave of love sweep over him and Sulochana tentatively put out her hand to hold his little finger, "Father, I miss you."

"Wish you a very happy birthday my child." Shesha was almost choked with emotions. A fierce rush of love enveloped him like a warm blanket.

"Sulochana, our family is incomplete without you, and our journey is yet complete. You are a very important part of our journey, especially for your father. But for now, you will have to be patient." Narayan's voice interrupted her silent conversation with Shesha.

Sulochana stopped chatting with the baby. She knew that Narayan was trying to tell her something profound but she was too young to understand the implications of his words. She wondered what kind of new journey he was referring to. She pestered her uncle for an explanation.

"You will know in time. But until then, you will have to live in Naag Lok with your uncle Vasuki." Narayan bade them farewell from earth. Lakshmi, Ksheera and Sulochana left for Vaikunth with a heavy heart. But before leaving, Lakshmi and Ksheera placed their palms on Ram and Lakshman's brows – erasing the memories of their past lifetimes, with the power of yoga.

Princes, they are born, and princes, they will remain in their mortal spans on earth, till it was time to return, Lakshmi swore softly under her breath.

***

After five years, the weather began to change in the lush kingdom of Mithila – the vast swathe of green plains which straddled the riverine foothills of the Himalayas in the Terai region of the upper Ganga headlands.

The beautiful forest-covered plains were cursed with a drought and crops began to wither. Maharaj SeerdhwaJanak, the king of Mithila, could not tackle the dry spell because the rivers had shrunk for want of rain. There was no water to irrigate the fields. He prayed to Lakshmi, the goddess of wealth and prosperity, for rain and also for a child because he was childless. Maharani Sunaina, his queen, could not conceive despite efforts by the best of the doctors in Aryavarta.

Maharishi Yagnavalkya, a sage, advised Janak to make a hoe of gold and plough the fields with his own hands for 'benediction'. He said the goddess would send Janak the gifts of rain and a child. One morning, when Janak was ploughing the fields with his golden hoe, the blade struck a wooden basket, covered with an intricately embroidered cloth. Fearing it was a bad omen, Janak picked up the basket and removed the cover.

He let out a shout of joy. A baby girl lay fast asleep inside the basket.

King Janak gently lifted the girl out of the basket and hugged her. The goddess had granted Janak his prayer. Sensing human warmth, the child opened its eyes – and the distant horizon suddenly lit up with a flash of lightning. The milling clouds began to rumble and soon big drops of rain soaked the cracked earth. It poured.

Maharaj Janak and the natives of Mithila rejoiced, crediting the baby girl for bringing the blessing of rain to Mithila. At the advice of the sages, the court elders and his relatives, Janak sent his men across Aryavarta in search of the newborn's parents, but in vain. No one came forward to claim parentage. Sage Yagnavalkya and *Raj Guru* Shatanand – the advisor to the king – counselled Janak to adopt the child and bring her up as a princess of Mithila. After much deliberation, Janak crowned her the princess of Mithila.

He named her Sita or Bhumija – the one who is born from the Earth. She was also Janaki, the daughter of Janak, Vaidehi, the princess of Videha kingdom and Maithili, the princess of Mithila.

Strangely, Maharani Sunaina conceived the very day Janak found Sita.

Late one night, just before Sunaina was about to give birth, she dreamt of the milky Ksheera Sagara – the vast white ocean – flooding her. Sunaina's eyes sprung open and she involuntarily reached out to grasp the voice that cried from a great distance, "*Maa,* I am coming."

The next morning, the queen went into labour. King Janak summoned the royal doctor and waited outside the room, sweating. Sunaina screamed and ranted for a week as the pains wracked her body, weakening her strength. Finally, on the day of *Jaya Ekadashi* – an auspicious day in the Hindu calendar month of Maghi – the doctors said that she might deliver. The pale queen was laid at the feet of Vishnu to ease her pain.

On coming to know about Sunaina's tortured labour, Gargi Vachaknavi, a healer, oracle and Vedic scholar, rushed to the palace. She sat holding the queen's hand for several hours, chanting from the Vedas, and in the afternoon, a near-dead queen gave birth to a baby girl. There was complete silence in the chamber because the baby was frail and unresponsive.

Maharaj Janak was hysterical with grief. He held the new-born with trembling hands and put the child at the feet of his household deities, Lakshmi-Narayan. Tears coursed down his eyes. "Narayan, Maha Lakshmi, please let my child live. Grant the baby life. I plead with you," the king wailed, stripped of the vestiges of his royal pride. His prayers were heard in Vaikunth, Vishnu's abode.

The child has to live, the gods said.

At that moment, the baby began to cry. Janak sank to his knees and kissed the forehead of his daughter, "Sunaina, you had dreamt of Goddess Ksheera and look, here she is with us today. We shall name her Urmila, waves of passion and meeting of hearts. She will also be known as Maithili – the princess of Mithila, the one who can fight death and come back to life. I will call her my Warrior Princess."

King Janak was still sitting at Narayan's feet cradling his baby girl, when a maid came rushing with a letter from his younger brother Kushadhwaja:

Dear brother, Mithila is blessed ever since Sita came into our lives. I have great news for you. My dearest wife Chandrabhaga has given birth to a girl and we have decided to name her Mandvi. We will come to Mithila soon to meet the queen, you and the princesses. Janak touched his head to the bejewelled feet of the deities.

A year later, Chandrabhaga gave birth to another daughter, Shrutakeerti.

Janak wanted all the girls to live in the palace together as a family. The four little girls soon filled the fragrant gardens of Mithila's palace with their innocent prattle and mischief.

The Kaal Chakra – wheel of time – had begun to roll.

The Clay Statue

The clay cast moulds itself to flesh and blood.

For seven years Ayodhya and Mithila watched their scions grow up. They did not know that this lull was a harbinger of a storm that had already begun to gather clouds and winds.

Urmila had stepped into the sixth summer of her life. The palace was decorated with flowers and *rangolis* – coloured designs. The sun filtered in mottled slivers through the latticed slats on the window.

Edging her way between the retinue of her attendants-in-waiting, Queen Sunaina crept into Urmila's room silently to wake her up to a birthday surprise. She sang a ditty she had composed years ago for the little girl on her birthday, telling her how beautiful and special she was. At the end of the song, she was surprised that the 'girl' was still sleeping like a log – swathed from head to foot in a white sheet and smothered in pillows. She nudged at the bulk only to find it empty. Urmila had set up a decoy to fool her mother.

"Where has this girl disappeared so early in the morning today?" an exasperated Sunaina looked around.

Mandvi, who had followed her into the room to surprise Urmila, laughed, *"Badi Maa* – older mother – you already know the answer."

Sunaina looked at Mandvi blankly. "Where is she?"

"Maa, how could you have forgotten her love for sword-fighting, especially today? I am sure we shall find her near the cockpit – her lair," Sita chirped from behind Mandvi. The sisters were standing in single file.

Sunaina chose to keep quiet. She was worried. At an age, when princesses were supposed to be learning to cook, tend to their elders, manage the palace and learn the rites of prayers and the fire rituals, Urmila was a tomboy, tramping around in the gardens, villages, forests and fields, practising war games. The rebellious nature of her daughter was a source of constant concern to her.

King Janak refused to hear anything untoward about his Warrior Princess. She was like a son to him – the boy that he longed for. "Maharani, you know our Urmila is different. She is the Warrior Princess of Mithila. Let her grow as she is, into a free-willed and fiery young woman. Don't chain her to the false expectations of womanhood."

Sunaina did not agree with the king, but she did not have the courage to stand up to his wishes. Even after sensing her disapproval, Janak smiled and walked away. He was an indulgent father.

Far away from the palace, in the lush green paddy fields flanking the villages, Urmila was busy honing her skills as a sword-fighter. She lunged and twisted, pirouetted and swerved as she took on the unseen enemies, she was fighting. Her eyes reflected the blue of the cloth that was tied to the hilt of her sword. Unnoticed, an old woman watched her from a distance. After a while, she called out to Urmila in a soft voice, "Rajkumari *ji*, your highness."

Urmila looked around in surprise. The old woman could not help but admire her winsome beauty. Urmila's complexion was as fair as milk, her features were as if chiselled by an artist's scalpel and the fragile body was perfectly made. She had the large grey-blue eyes of the monsoon sky that flashed with lights of their own. Her smile lit up the sharp contours of her narrow face that was flushed with the passion of the 'sword' with which she was playing. Her defiant nature was evident from the manner in which she swept back her messy brown curls.

Tucking her sword into her waistband, she ran to the old woman to touch her feet. Dirt stained the fine fabric wrapped tightly over her bodice and shreds of heather and grass stuck to her hair.

"*Dadi Maa* – grandmother, don't call me a princess. Call me prince! I will soon change how Aryavarta looks at stereotypes with my sword-fighting, the land will learn to honour a woman sword-fighter," she announced with an air of grandeur; and then squealed in delight, "*Laddus* – sweetmeats!" The old woman held several yellow sugar balls in her outstretched hands.

"I made them especially for your birthday," she said.

"Then feed me with your own hands," Urmila was touched. The old woman put one in the little girl's open mouth.

A ruckus in the far end of the field distracted her; she almost choked on the sweetmeat that she was chewing with unbridled enthusiasm. A welcoming party was on its way to where she stood with the old woman. The group, made of Mandvi, Shrutakreeti and a small contingent of girls, was led by Sita.

Just like the Raghuvanshi Princes of Ayodhya, the four princesses of Mithila shared a unique bond. Vaikunth lived in them even as mortals.

"How was your practice?" Sita was curious. She wiped the dust off Urmila's flushed face.

The attachment that Sita and Urmila shared was indefinable and was reflected as their strength.

"I loved it. This is the best start I could have to my birthday," Urmila smiled shyly. Mandvi smirked and reminded her that they had a special class with their mentor, Gargi Vachaknavi, for which they should not be late.

The undercurrents of sibling rivalry between Urmila and Mandvi were palpable whenever they met. Sita was angry because this was not the day to quibble over trivia; it was a special day. Urmila, the Warrior Princess of Mithila, had turned six. No fighting, Sita reprimanded in a stern voice.

Mandvi apologised spontaneously, Sita commanded natural respect. Mandvi stopped bickering and the girls sprinted to Maharishi Yagnavalkya's *ashram* to seek his blessings. The old woman watched them with a fond smile. The *laddus* were forgotten in the din and dust of their girlish excitement.

Maharishi Yagnavalkya was a great saint and the chief priest of Mithila. He espoused the Advaita and Sanyasam traditions. According to the Brihadaranyaka Upanishad, Yagnavalkya, a champion of women's enlightenment, had two wives, Maitreyi and Katyayani. He had also initiated Gargi Vachaknavi into Vedic studies.

"May god bless you, my daughter, and give you a healthy and prosperous life with the perfect partner," he blessed her. Urmila stilled for a second, curbing the sudden flare of anger that would have spurred a sharp retort.

"Thank you, Maharishi, for your blessings, but I am sufficient for myself, I don't need a husband." Urmila was confident of her own strength.

"…But marriage for a princess is essential, daughter."

Urmila shot back, "I beg to differ, Maharishi. These are biased opinions. I want to live my life freely without someone controlling it. Moreover, I am a warrior and my sword is my companion. Warriors can survive without a partner, but not without their sword."

Maharishi threw his hands up in despair at Urmila's headstrong views on marriage; the child had it in her head that she did not need a man in her life. Watching the heated exchange from inside the retreat, Gargi Vachaknavi, intervened with her affectionate words of greeting and gentle encouragement, "My dear daughter, you are indeed unique. Always stay the way you are."

Urmila hugged her tightly. She had always felt unusually drawn to Gargi's magnetic personality and wanted to be like her. Gargi sought permission from the seer to begin their special class.

Maata Gargi, also known as Brahmavadini, was an extremely beautiful and intellectually evolved woman whose love for Vedic scriptures overshadowed her desire for anything else in life. A learned scholar, she wrote several hymns in the Rig Veda and is even mentioned in the Upanishad. It was her intelligent debate with Maharishi Yagnavalkya held by Maharaj Janak that made her an integral part of Mithila. She was the most respected spiritual mentor in the kingdom.

The class began with the chanting of a hymn to honour the Vedic goddess of learning, Saraswati. The princesses looked at Gargi with curiosity in their eyes. What she would teach today? Every week, she opened the wonders of Vedic knowledge to the little girls.

They held their breath. Gargi coughed and cleared her throat; she was reviewing her lesson plan for the day in her head. The mentor had planned something new for her students. Gargi looked at them tenderly speculating how to reach out to them to make them understand the responsibility they had inherited as 'future queens', and the strict codes of conventions queenship brought in its wake.

"Today, our class is special because we will learn more about your inner desires. I want each of you to share with me the kind of personality you would want for your future husbands. Sita, will we begin with you?"

Peeved, the girls stared at each other and then glared at Gargi, whose eyes crinkled with mischievous laughter. The princesses were tight-lipped. After several minutes of gentle coaxing, Sita described the man she would want to marry, followed by Mandvi and Shrutakeerti.

"Mother, I have already said several times, I don't want to marry. I want to stay in Mithila as its protecter," Urmila sounded irritated.

Gargi looked at her for a long moment, the girl somehow touched a deep chord in her soul, and the vein was familiar. She felt protective about this stubborn, willful and yet soft-hearted and innocent girl. Life exacted a heavy price from courageous ones, such as these, Gargi mused, her thoughts drifting from the study module of the day.

Gargi had to speak to Urmila alone. She asked Sita, Mandvi and Shrutakeerti to leave the class because she wanted to have a word in private with the warrior princess. Shutting the door of the hut after them, Gargi sat on the floor, next to Urmila and patted her head.

"My daughter, I know that you don't want to marry and I also know that everyone makes fun of you when you air your hostility about marriage. But love is a beautiful emotion. Give it a chance. Don't set boundaries around yourself against a feeling you do not understand yet. Do you know, people mocked me when I told them I was in love with my *Prakriti*, my Vedas, my texts? But I did not heed such criticisms. Wait for love to come to your life, little later. Wouldn't you seek a love as great as the love of Lakshmi-Narayan, Shiv-Shakti, and Ksheera-Shesha? You are a princess. You have to find a suitable match?"

Gargi's counselling hammered at the walls the little girl had built around herself. "What do I do, *Maata*?" Urmila wanted to know like a helpless child.

"Will you do as I say?" Gargi was making headway.

Urmila nodded. Gargi went inside the hut, into her prayer room set in the deep shadows of the thatch, and brought Urmila a lump of sweet-smelling brown clay. "Engrave the man of your dreams as a clay statue," she smiled.

Urmila looked at Gargi baffled, "How?"

"Close your eyes and put your feelings into the clay. The clay is wet, it will mould around your fingers. Shape it with your hands and it will show you the kind of person you secretly think is perfect for you. The earth has magic. If you meet the person in the clay statue ever in your life, rethink about marriage. Can you do this much for me for now?"

"I will make it, *Maa,*" Urmila was suddenly enthusiastic.

She pressed the lump at the edges, thumbing and fingering it in the middle like a chisel. She blanked out all conscious thoughts from her mind – treating the clay like a toy. An image of the man smiled at her in her subconscious mind, *"Maa,* here he is. If I ever fall in love, this is how he will be. A man as fierce as me, who can give me a tough fight with the sword and the word; someone unique, whose personality traits will stand apart from every man in Aryavarta." The clay in her hand had moulded itself into a face.

Gargi looked at the statue and muttered to herself, "Just like her, fire!" She told Urmila to go out and play with her sisters. She put the statue in a small wooden cabinet in her prayer room. "Help my child meet the man of her unconscious dreams. O, Hari Vishnu, lord; a man who will complement her."

Little did Gargi know that very soon Urmila would find the man she had crafted in clay, a shy but charismatic young lad, who would transform her into a true woman!

The Truth of Shanta

The spirit of sacrifice is rooted in sorrow.

Maharaj Dashrath, ignorant of the emotional turbulence that lay ahead, a tornado that would shake the very foundation of his relationship with his sons, greeted the morning of Mohini Ekadashi, an auspicious date in May when Vishnu was invoked in his Mohini avatara – as an enchantress to steal the pot of elixir from the demons.

Hari Kuntha – Maharani Kaushalya's palace – was adorned with red, yellow and white blossoms for the Maha Vishnu *puja* that was held every year on *Mohini Ekadashi.* The princes, in their pre-teens now, were inquisitive as usual. They pestered the Maharani to tell them about the Mohini rituals, but Kaushalya, the loving mother, was quiet that day. She tried to hide the tears that involuntarily filled her eyes but the boys were sharp.

"*Maa*, why do we pray to Mohini every year? Why is this day special?" Shatrughan was determined to find out.

"This day has a special significance for us. It is the most precious and yet the saddest day of our lives," Kaushalya said without smiling. The festivals usually brought out the cheerful little girl in the oldest of the Ayodhya queens, who was a devout Vishnu and a Shiva worshipper.

"But why, *Maa*?" Bharath insisted.

Kaushalya realised that perhaps it was time to tell them about Shanta and the 'ugly truth' behind Dashrath's motive of forcing her to marry Maha Rishyasringa. She looked at Sumitra and Kaikeyi for strength. They moved closer to stand beside Kaushalya to show that they were in it together – in a tight circle of shared sorrow.

Kaushalya picked up the golden statue of a girl from the far end of her room, went to her sons and began in a low voice, "This girl is Shanta…" At their curious looks, she said, "…Your sister."

There was a hush in the room. The boys looked at each other, bewildered. "We have a sister. Where is she?" Ram, the eldest and the most sensible of the brothers, questioned his mother with narrowed eyes.

"Yes, you have a sister, your father's and my first-born child. She is alive. But we did not know where she was and with whom," Kaushalya explained. Ram was insistent. And his mother could not escape his piercing curiosity.

"She had to go, Ram," Sumitra broke down, "Your father took her away from us."

"But why and how did he take her away?" Lakshman's question was poignant.

"It's a long story," Kaushalya continued in a hoarse, almost inaudible voice.

"One day, Maharaj Lompad, the king of Angadesh and my sister Varshini's husband, came to your father. He requested the Maharaj to allow them to adopt Shanta as they were childless. But their real intention was to use Shanta to help rid their land of a famine afflicting it for decades. They wanted Shanta to seduce Maha Rishyasringa with her charms and lure him to perform a *yajna* in their kingdom because it was the only way to fetch rain."

"So, father allowed them to adopt her?" Shatrughan questioned.

"Yes, he agreed." Kaikeyi was calm.

"Why?" Bharath sounded aggressive.

"He agreed because of his own selfish reasons." Kaikeyi knew she had to come up with a plausible story to satisfy the boys.

"And what were the reasons?" Shatrughan's query cut like a knife.

"He sold her to Lompad because he wanted Maha Rishyasringa to come to Ayodhya too as only Rishyasringa could perform the *yajna* to give Ayodhya a male heir," Kaushalya's voice was cold and deadpan.

Maha Rishyasringa was a sage, who lived in Shringa Parvat, a place women were forbidden to enter. The Valmiki Ramayana has it that Rishyasringa's father, having been deserted by his wife had been so driven by anger and hatred that no female, not even animals and birds were permitted to enter Shringa Parvat.

The four brothers looked at Maharani Kaushalya with disbelief on their faces. Kaushalya was relentless in her account, "Lompad requisitioned the services of temple priestesses to inculcate the luscious charms of a woman in Shanta. She was groomed by the tribe of devdasi (dancers of heaven) and thereafter, sent to Shringa Parvat, Maha Rishyasringa's abode, to woo him."

Angadesh heard the lament of Shanta before she was forced to run away to Shringa Parvat. No one knows it but literature says that Maharaj Lompad tried to seduce Shanta himself as she was a rare beauty. She disappeared one night from her palace in Angadesh without informing anyone.

"Why did she agree to marry Rishyasringa, *Maa?*" Lakshman was outraged.

"She was her father's daughter, stubborn and headstrong. She agreed to seduce him only for her father. She knew how your father pined for a son and only Rishyasringa could perform the *Putra Kameshthi Yajna.*"

"Oh!" the boys said together in disbelief.

"As promised, she brought Rishyasringa to Ayodhya to perform the *yajna* at the Kanchi Kamakshi temple, and that was the one of the few times we saw her. She did not return for a long time after that the rite."

A cry of grief escaped Sumitra, "Our happiness walked out the day she left the palace. I don't think she ever forgave us."

The four brothers sat there numb with shock.

"How is she? Can't we meet her?" Lakshman's voice broke. He rarely expressed his emotions; he was shy about showing the softer side of his nature.

Ram looked at his grieving mother and a tear fell from his left eye, "*Maa*, I want a few answers from *Pitaji* – father." The boys walked out of Queen Kaushalya's palace.

Noticing the presence of the young princes in the *Rajya Sabha* which was unusual, Maharaj Dashrath motioned his ministers to depart. Lakshman looked at his father in anger. "Why did you hide the truth from us?" he demanded.

"What truth, Lakshman?" Dashrath was confused.

"Our older sister Shanta *didi's* story," a disheartened Ram said.

Maharaj Dashrath was Ram's idol. The realisation that his father was human enough to commit a folly anguished him, but his sense of duty towards his father did not waver even once.

Lakshman, who was not so partial towards his father, could not bear the thought of his father being cruel to his sister. "Why did you do this to her?" His voice grew louder.

Dashrath began to weep, "I seek forgiveness. I did not know what I was doing at that time. I was blinded by my desire to beget a son. But ever since Shanta left, I have not slept peacefully. I long to set my eyes on her once, but I do not have the courage to face her."

Wiping his tears gently, Ram comforted his father and sought his permission to meet Shanta. "We will like to visit her before we leave for the *Gurukul* – school. Can we, father?" Dashrath approved. The four princes, their mother and the king prepared for a whistle-stop tour of Shringa mountain in the cold northern terrain to atone for their sins. The journey to Shringa was long, winding through the plains, river valleys and finally up the hills to the abode of the snow that walled the northern periphery of Aryavarta.

On reaching Maha Rishyasringa's *ashram* in the idyllic hill resort of Shringa, Ram requested Dashrath to send news to Shanta about their arrival and fetch her, but the king hesitated. "I cannot face her, my son. Why don't you go and tell her to come out of her retreat to visit us. Let her know that we have come to meet her to repent for the wrongs we have done to her."

A reluctant and embarrassed Ram knocked on the door of Shanta's hut, tentatively. The hut, located in the heart of Maha Rishyasringa's hermitage, was surrounded by lush green forests and fruit orchards by a gushing mountain stream.

A stunningly beautiful woman answered the knock and opened the door. "How may I help you?" she wanted to know in a low lilting voice.

Ram touched her feet, followed by the three princes. Shanta looked at them questioningly till recognition dawned on her. The boys resembled her in so many ways. She began to smile and cry at the same time. "My brothers! I can't believe you are here at my hut."

She glanced past her brothers to her parents and ran to embrace them. "*Maa, Pitaji* – mother, father!" Her cries were ones of surprise and joy.

"Please forgive me, my daughter," King Dashrath repented. "I played with your life to fulfil my selfish desires. But never for a moment believe that I did not love you enough. I am a weak man, who once thought that sons carried on their father's legacy." He looked weak and defeated; the pain in his eyes reached out to touch Shanta's tender heart.

She said gently, "I was never angry with you. I love you and respect you greatly, father. What I did was out of my duty towards you."

Kaushalya engulfed Shanta in a warm hug, "My arms have been empty even though I hug Ram every day. Today, they feel complete."

Shanta broke down in her mother's secure hold of love. "Will you not meet your brothers now, *didi?*" Ram asked. Shanta looked at him with pride in her eyes and called Lakshman, Bharath and Shatrughan to her.

Looking at his children bound in firm cords of fraternal love, Dashrath felt a sense of completeness that he had not felt since his daughter had left Ayodhya. Shanta, meanwhile, wanted to catch up on her brothers' lives. After speaking to each one separately, Shanta came to the quietest, "Lakshman, you are as magnetic in appearance as Sumitra *Maa.*" She ruffled the unruly hair of the strapping boy, who was tall, lanky and fair with a sharp profile – and a slightly broken nose that was tilted at an odd angle.

Lakshman clung to his sister crying, "I am sorry you had to face a life as difficult as this because of us."

Shanta was moved by Lakshman's humility. Wiping his tears, she whispered, "No, Lakshman, don't be sorry. I am blessed to have a husband like Rishyasringa and my little Vindhya makes my world complete." She pointed to a little girl playing with stones, away from the hut.

"Vindhya…" she called out. The little girl with black eyes and a mass of wild curls came bouncing to the group of visitors. Shanta ushered her to Dashrath and her three queen mothers.

The queens looked at Vindhya, mesmerised, as she paid her tribute to her grandparents with a mischievous smile.

"She looks like Shanta!" All of them exclaimed together in wonder and picked her up in their arms. Vindhya was naturally drawn to Lakshman; she felt attuned to his calm disposition.

They played through the day, racing each other across the sprawling green valleys tucked between the icy peaks of the Shringa mountains. During one such race, Shanta noticed that Shatrughan was scowling at Lakshman, unobserved. She guessed that he harboured an 'itch' against his twin, probably stemming from a sense of inadequacy or inferiority complex. She took him aside and set his complex to rest with her encouragement and sage wisdom.

"There can be no comparison between two people. Both are different, yet distinctive. Just like you and Lakshman. You are unique in your own way and he, in his. Sooner than you think, you will be known as Shatrughan and not as Lakshman's twin. So remember that your brother is not to be blamed for any lack of recognition," she said.

Shatrughan listened to her without a word, "I will always remember this."

Vindhya eavesdropped on the entire conversation and was put off by Shatrughan's hidden aggression against Lakshman. She instinctively sided with Lakshman because she felt that he was too soft to fend off his brother's animosity and if no one really watched over him, she would.

The visit mended the cracks and Shanta forgave her parents.

As the royal entourage from Ayodhya departed, Lakshman knew that he had found two very special women in his life, Shanta didi and his niece Vindhya.

Over the years Vindhya became Lakshman's best friend, even though she was six years younger than him. After her father, Lakshman was the first man she adored and her empty life found colours in the companionship of Lakshman and Shatrughan.

In the Gurukul-School Years

The teacher does not always impart in words.

Unaware that lessons are not always learnt by the books but sometimes through the emotional battles one wages, the royal family of Ayodhya returned from Shringa Parvat to prepare for the departure of the princes to the Gurukul for higher education.

The queens were desolate. The princes, who lit up the palace, would be away for several years.

"The princes have to leave now, Maharani. Maharaj is waiting for them in the court," the maid announced.

Fighting back their tears, the queens tried to put a leash on their emotions even though their hearts were breaking inside. The boys were still young and were not immune to the fears of parting from their parents. They found it difficult to accept the fact that they would have to live outside the purview of the nurturing love of their mothers, especially Lakshman.

"*Maa*, as your elder son I promise to take utmost care of your younger one. Shatrughan is my responsibility hence on, but I request you to stay calm and happy even after we leave," Lakshman said with bravado.

Sumitra embraced her son with pride and dignity, "Never will I cry, my son, I promise, until you return." The three queens bade their sons tearful farewells.

The Gurukul became the first *karmabhoomi* – turf of action – of the princes, helping them grow physically, mentally and spiritually. Staying with their guru in the lap of nature and learning how to survive without the comforts of the royal palace was a challenge that would shape the strengths of their character. They had to develop skills to overcome enemies, to stand firm and to fight for what was right; while educating themselves in the scriptures, basics of mathematics, warfare, arts and administration.

The princes missed their mothers. They did not drift; they took care of each other while becoming affluent in the skills necessary as princes of one of the most powerful kingdoms in Aryavarta.

How can one change without learning how to fight enemies? The transformation of the princes was gradual as they learnt how foes were made and how friends often back-stabbed.

In spite of being courteous and compassionate, the princes made enemies in the *Gurukul*. Vridhasvaan was one such jealous peer who tried to rip the brotherhood apart with his sneaky tricks. Shatrughan, the most vulnerable of the four, became his target.

Twins are connected to each other through a sublime unconscious energy and unique psychic bonds. When you challenge one, you indirectly dare the other too!

Lakshman was filled with manic rage one night when he found his twin trapped in a blazing fire. It was allegedly lit by Vridhasvaan to kill Shatrughan. Lakshman saved his brother from the inferno and brutally thrashed Vridhasvaan to teach him a lesson. The message was hammered home in the *Gurukul* that Lakshman spelt danger to adversaries. It was best not to hurt his brothers.

No one messed around with the brothers after the scuffle. But the incident reinforced the indelible bonding between the four brothers and brought them closer still, where each brother was a mother, a sibling, a father and a 'guardian angel' to the other.

The boys studied hard during the day and longed for the warm comfort of the palace at night. "We still have another four years to go without our mothers," the princes said, hugging and lulling each other to sleep. Lakshman, the most emotional of them, cried silently at night remembering the fire that could have killed Shatrughan. Ram offered a traumatised Lakshman shelter in his arms.

The day after the fire, sage Vashishtha summoned the princes to his hut. He praised Lakshman for his selfless love, courage and devotion to his brother and revealed an 'unbelievable' tale about Lord Shesha's altruistic nature.

Gurudev was no stranger to the fact that the Ram and Lakshman, who sat before him, were the incarnated forms of Narayan and Shesha.

"Do you know who Shesha is?" Vashishtha asked.

"No, we have no idea. A deity, may be," Lakshman replied with nonchalance.

Gurudev smiled, "He is the *tamasic* – dark – energy of Narayan, the preserver. We also know him as Shankarshana, Adi-Shesha or Sheshnaag. He is everlasting and endless. It is believed that he has been here before the universe was created and will live even after it is destroyed."

Lakshman and his brothers gaped at Vashishtha as the sage continued, "Shesha is the eldest of the thousand snake sons of sage Kashyapa and his wife Kadru. Shesha is followed by Vasuki, Airavata and Takshaka and several more brothers. Most of the snake brothers were barbarous in nature, so much so that they did not even spare their half-brother Garuda, who was Kashyapa and Vinatha's, (sister of Kadru), son."

The princes waited for the tale to proceed. Gurudev got up to drink a sip of water from an earthenware pitcher, before resuming his narrative. "Shesha, a gentle soul, was distressed by the heinous acts of his brothers. One day, he left his father's home and began to undertake penance for the sins committed by his kin. He meditated in places like Gandhamadhana, Badrikashrama, Gokarna, Pushkara and the Himalayas. His penance was so severe that his flesh, skin and muscles withered to merge with his bones."

Was Lakshman aware that he was Shesha who was incarnated as a mortal or he remembered nothing about his divine form as Sheshnaag?

"Brahma, moved by Shesha's penance, asked him to make a wish. Shesha pondered and requested for control over his mind. Brahma granted him his wish and implored him to go to the depths of the earth and hold it steady it on his gigantic hood. Shesha, till this day, is known to hold aloft the underground to keep the earth on its course."

It is believed that Shankarshana created 11 Rudras from his 1001 heads to destroy the universe. Every time the universe neared its end, a new one was created.

The boys were excited and prodded Guruji for more details. "*Paatal* – underground – has been Shesha's perennial residence ever since. It is also said that Narayan, overwhelmed by his nobility of spirit, offered to sleep on Shesha's coiled length. Narayan and Shesha have been inseparable ever since. Shesha is also the king of the Naaga – snakes," Vashishtha concluded.

It is also said that Shesha played an important role in the creation of astrology, the science of fortune telling.

The princes left Vashishtha's hut deep in thought. They were curious about Shesha, struck by his magnificence. Lakshman was the quietest as they walked back to their hostel. He somehow could not shrug off this uncanny feeling that he had come across Shesha before. Somewhere, Shesha lingered in his mind, tempering the days as he ploughed into the Vedas deeper for more knowledge, along with *Vyakarana* – grammar, *Jyotisha* – astrology, *Arthshastra* – economics, *Dharmashastra* – religion, *Sastravidya* – warfare, and *kala* – arts – in the final days of his education.

The royal princes did not know that the tale was as incomplete as Shesha was without Ksheera. They would only have become familiar with Shesha after learning about Ksheera. Time was soon to reveal the story to them.

The boys become adept in sciences, politics and scriptures, but their emotional growth as men was still incomplete. They were caught between adolescence and maturity. Gurudev Vashishtha requested *Gurumaa* Arundhanti, his companion, to conduct a special class in emotional development and 'orientation' for the boys to assess their levels of maturity. As princes of Raghukul, they had to be emotionally matured and balanced.

The boys gathered at *Gurumaa's* hut feeling shy and gawky. They had a faint idea about the implication of the 'orientation' class and it became clearer when *Gurumaa* explained to them about balancing the emotional energies – the *yin* and the *yang*, *prakriti* (female nature) versus *paurush* (male aggression) and anger as opposed to compassion and love.

She acquainted the brothers with Shesha's other half, Ksheera.

Ksheera, the first child of Samudra Dev and his wife Tirangini, was also known as Vimala for her milky complexion and astounding beauty.

She was as gentle a soul as Shesha in spite of being pampered by her parents. She had a younger brother Panchajanya, who she loved like her own child. Panchajanya was not loved by his parents, and kept mostly to himself, feeling aloof and sad. Ksheera felt his anguish as her own and one day she decided to leave home so that her parents would start loving him in her absence. She was only 12 but she was adamant about leaving. She had been praying to Narayan for years, and moved by her meditative penance, Narayan eventually appeared to her.

Ksheera pleaded with Narayan to provide her shelter. At the sight of the beautiful little girl, who had left her home for her brother's welfare, Narayan felt extremely protective about her and requested her to consider him her brother from then on. He also promised that Ksheera would find succour in his home in Vaikunth thereafter.

Gradually, Panchajanya, who was very fond of his sister, came to live in Vaikunth with Ksheera.

It is not a known fact that Lakshmi was Ksheera's youngest sister. She was born as the youngest child of Samudra Deva, after Samudra Manthan, the churning of the milky ocean during the battle between the gods and the demons.

Ksheera, the home, and Shesha, the heart of Narayan, met often.

They did not particularly like each other initially, but slowly their feelings began to change. They looked out for each other, waited at odd corners to meet each other and their sweet-sour fights made them happy. Their arguments brought a smile on every face in Vaikunth.

On one such day, Ksheera saw Shesha in deep agony. His hoods were flushing red and were swollen. Seeing him in pain, Ksheera was moved to tears.

She tentatively touched his hoods, trying to ease the pain with her gentle caress. Narayan explained to Ksheera that since Shesha carried the weight of *Prithvi* – earth – on his hoods; at times, the burden became too heavy to bear. His hoods strained under the great weight.

Ksheera wondered if there was anyone who could carry the weight of the one who held the earth on his head. "Who would carry his weight of the one who carried the weight of *Prithvi*? O dear king of the Naaga, accept me as your wife. Let me become your *ardhangini* – the other half – and carry your weight," Ksheera proposed to the snake lord.

Shesha happily accepted her proposal with tears in his eyes. In Ksheera, he had a partner just like him, expansive and selfless!

With the permission and blessings of the elders in Vaikunth, a grand wedding was held for Lord Vishnu's favourites.

Panchajanya, Alakshmi (the goddess of misfortune) and Lakshmi stood next to their oldest sister Ksheera, whereas Vasuki, Takshaka and Airavata rallied with the eldest in the snake clan, Shesha.

After a few rituals, the *kanyadaan* – giving away of the bride – was performed by the bride's older brother. Since Ksheera was the eldest of her clan, Narayan came up with a solution, "As Ksheera is my adopted sister I have the right to perform the *kanyadaan*."

After the *kanyadaan* and the seven vows, Shesha happily accepted Ksheera as his wife. "Dear goddess of milk, Ksheera, as Shesha is the king of the Naaga dynasty, you will be the Naaga queen. Hence on, you will also be known as Naaga Lakshmi," Narayan blessed.

Lakshman's lashes were wet with tears. He did not understand why he was crying but he felt Ksheera's sadness; a strange emptiness chipped at the innate fulsomeness of his heart.

"Ksheera is Shesha's better half. They work as a team. One is incomplete without the other. Yet, they never come in each other's way when they stand for their duties. This tale is to remind you that when you marry, take care of your companion emotionally and spiritually but don't let love make you weak and constricting," *Gurumaa* put across firmly. And with the parting advice, she bade them to go.

Love doesn't change or fade. It stays, irrespective of time and distance. Lakshman and Urmila or Shesha and Ksheera stayed in love like the king of serpents in his milky ocean – Ksheera Sagara.

A Short Tale of Ayodhya

Six years on, the kingdom fortifies its ramparts.

While Ayodhya welcomed each morning for six years in anticipation of the return of the princes, Mithila watched its princesses thrive and become beautiful maidens.

"Maharaj, the king of Sankasya, Maharaj Sudhanwa is set to attack Mithila," Senani – the commander-in-chief of Janak's army – sounded anxious but the king was unfazed. "It is time we teach him a lesson. Prepare your men to leave at dawn. My brother Kushadhwaja will lead you."

Urmila, who was present in the *Raj Durbar* – royal court – was piqued and sought her father's permission to accompany her uncle. Janak was rigid in his denial.

While the other three princesses were busy in chores more suited to young women, Urmila was unflinching in her determination to become Mithila's Rajkumar. "I am a warrior. Fear and retreat don't exist in my dictionary. You refuse me? Are you not convinced about my fighting skills, *Pitaji*?"

Janak knew his daughter's unswerving determination. "No, my daughter, I am not, but this is not the right time for you to enter the battlefield. Let Kushadhwaja take on the enemy alone this time but you may accompany us the next time," the king said with a smile. Janak, who believed in the 'enlightenment and empowerment' of his daughters and nieces, had been tutoring them in arts of warfare, administration, Ayurveda, humanities, scriptures and house-holding.

Urmila was a virtuoso in sword-fighting at a very young age and her father believed in her enough to agree to send her to fight on the unsparing battlefield.

Kushadhwaja was at war for 10 days. The family fretted about his safety and prayed constantly. Amid fears about the outcome of the battle and the safety of Kushadhwaja's life, the family held on to its sanity by laughing at the silly sibling fights between Urmila and Mandvi.

On one such chaotic day when Urmila and Mandvi had been squabbling since morning, Janak ordered his family to dress regally for dinner because Maharishi Yagnavalkya and his wives – Maitreyi, Katyayani – and seer Gargi Vachaknavi would join them for the meal that night.

The dinner was a silent affair. Concern for Kushadhwaja had killed everyone's appetite. As Mandvi and Shrutakeerti sat with morose faces at the banquet looking at the platters of food, Sita and Urmila noticed their 'torment' and tried to lure them into eating, "*Rakshasi* – demoness (a loving endearment for Mandvi), *chote pitaji* – younger father or uncle – is fighting for Mithila. You are a brave man's daughter. You should eat for him. Moreover, Maharishi has a surprise for the one who finishes her food first." Urmila winked at Shrutakeerti drawing her into the 'game'.

Shrutakeerti swallowed the bait and began to gobble up her food, and within 10 minutes her plate was empty. She had licked the last morsel of rice and vegetables on her plate.

The Maharishi, his two wives and *Maata* Gargi took silent note of Urmila's presence of mind, and smiled. Maharaj Janak was proud when Gargi expressed her apprehension about finding a suitable match for a girl, who had the intelligence to outwit the great Yagnavalkya.

Shrutakeerti looked at Yagnavalkya with a questioning expression after the meal, waiting for him to unveil the surprise. The Maharishi was prepared, "As promised, my surprise is a tale in which I shall acquaint you with the great king of Ayodhya, and his heritage. Ayodhya is ruled by the Ikshvaku dynasty also known as the Suryavanshi or the Raghuvanshi – the dynasty of the sun and Raghu. One of the most powerful yet humble Suryavanshi kings until now, descending from its first ruler Ikshvaku is Nemi, son of King Aja and princess Indumati, Aryavarta knows of him as Dashrath. A man of exemplary wisdom and courage, Dashrath carries on the legacy of the dynasty that never goes back on its promises. A noble man at heart, he has sent several missions to his rival kingdoms, offering either friendship or war."

Urmila, always the inquisitive seeker, was quick to query, "Maharishi, how can a *Rajdoot* – royal ambassador – carry a message of both friendship and war?"

Maharishi Yagnavalkya was waiting for the question. "Daughter, it's possible. Maharaj Dashrath offered friendship to a kingdom and only on their refusal was it considered a war proposition against Ayodhya. This is how he met his first wife, Maharani Kaushalya. One of the most pious and humblest women, she is the daughter of King Sakushal and Queen Amritprabha of Kaushaldesh."

Sita, the more poised and calmer of the sisters, could not help but intervene, "Maharishi, does Ayodhya have more queens?"

Maharishi nodded. "Maharaj Dashrath's second wife is Maharani Sumitra, the princess of Kashi, which is also the kingdom of Mahadev, of whom she is a great devotee. Sumitra is the one of the wisest women I have ever come across. Her intelligence has the potential to stand unwavering before Gargi, too. Selfless and matured, some say she can even sense the most absurd and inexplicable things which are invisible to the naked eye. She believes that everything happens for a reason."

Urmila felt unsettled on hearing about Sumitra, a woman she had not seen or ever heard of before, but she made Urmila feel empathetic! "Maharishi, I would love to meet her," Urmila said.

"Even I would love to," Shrutakeerti joined Urmila in her wish to meet Sumitra.

The girls listened in rapt attention as Yagnavalkya continued. "Maharaj Dashrath's youngest queen Rani Kaikeyi is said to be one of the most courageous and alluring women in this world. She is the daughter of King Ashwapati of Kekeya. They met and fell in love under daring circumstances – Dashrath's abiding romance."

"Dashrath was out on a hunting trip in Kekeya once when a tiger pounced on him. He only had a broken bow in his hand at the time because he had used all the arrows in his quiver killing many wild animals. He stood rooted to the spot in fear, when a passing patrol came to his rescue. The masked leader of the patrol stabbed the wild cat with its sword. An injured Dashrath, who was mauled by the tiger, fell down unconscious. He was taken to the Kekeya palace and nursed back to health.

When he had gained enough strength to ask about his saviour, he found out that his masked protector had been none other than Princess Kaikeyi, the daughter of the king of Kekeya. Dashrath instantly fell in love with the beautiful and fierce Kaikeyi and asked for her hand in marriage. King Ashwapati agreed and they were married."

Janak, who had no knowledge about the personal life of King Dashrath, was surprised at the stories about the king and his queens. Sita and Urmila listened attentively, while Mandvi and Shrutakeerti raved about Urmila's striking similarities with Queen Kaikeyi.

"Would you like to hear further?" a voice broke the spell that Yagnavalkya had cast. At the door of the massive banquet hall, stood a small contingent of soldiers. Vijay, the commander-in-chief of Ayodhya, who had been sent by Maharaj Dashrath to help Kushadhwaja, entered the hall with a broad smile on his face. Mithila had won the war.

***

The courageous princesses reminded Vijay of the princes of Ayodhya. He wanted the girls to know about them. After seeking Maharishi Yagnavalkya's permission, he began to narrate how

Maharaj Dashrath was concerned that the dynasty would die without a bloodline prior to the birth of his male heirs and about the *Putra Kameshthi Yajna* – a tough rite to beget children.

He told them about how the god of fire appeared from the hearth, placated by the rituals, and offered his blessings in the form of *ksheer.*

"But why did he give the second share to Queen Kaikeyi instead of Maharani Sumitra?" Urmila was upset. Vijay looked at her with interest because she brought Lakshman to his mind, something about her was very similar to the way Saumitra queried him about 'trivia' which was of vital importance. Urmila retaliated against the injustice as fiercely as prince Lakshman.

"Because Rani Kaikeyi stepped forward to claim Sumitra's share and Maharani Sumitra, known for her humility and kindness, allowed her to eat it first," Vijay explained.

Urmila looked at him, flummoxed. She could not believe that a queen as fierce and brave as Kaikeyi could be so selfish and 'low'. She was sorry for Sumitra.

Vijay recounted the birth of the four princes, the stories behind their names, their physical traits and their personality types.

Lakshman struck an intimate chord in Urmila. Something about the way Senani Vijay described him made her smile and her heart skipped a beat. No one noticed it except Shrutakeerti.

Shrugging off her wayward thoughts, she urged Vijay to help her hone her sword-fighting skills. Vijay bantered with her, "Ayodhya forbids disclosure of their war techniques. You shall have to become a queen of Ayodhya to learn from me."

Spurred by a naughty whim, Mandvi poked fun at Urmila. "Which of the four princes would you want to slaughter? I am sure it will be Rajkumar Lakshman?" she asked. Urmila blushed.

The sight of Urmila blushing was rare and it made everyone look at her in awe. Urmila recoiled fearing that she had given away her fondness for Lakshman. The mood became teasingly happy till a maid informed Vijay about the arrival of a messenger from Ayodhya. The commander in-chief of the Ayodhya army excused himself.

He requested Maharaj Janak to allow him to set out for Ayodhya immediately as the princes were due to return from the Gurukul the next evening and on his way, he had to collect gifts for them. They had completed their four years of training and education.

The girls felt a strange kinship to the princes even without meeting them. Sita volunteered that Vijay should carry gifts for the princes from the Mithila girls – tokens of gratitude and respect.

Vijay was humbled by the care with which the princesses wrapped the gifts for the princes. Sita packed a 'goat feather', a charm of distraction, Mandvi a peacock feather quill and Shrutakeerti added a couple of dolls she had made. Urmila gifted her favourite sword with a silent prayer that Lakshman should choose it from among the gifts which came from Mithila.

"Be with him as you were with me!" Urmila's unspoken plea was perhaps the first stirring of love that was unknown even to the sender.

A nameless feeling, undisclosed yet eloquent, travelled from Mithila to Ayodhya!

The Return of the Four Princes

The curtain goes up on Raghukul's glory.

Ayodhya sparkled! Amidst the glittering diyas – earthenware lamps, picturesque rangolis, floral decorations and the delicious aromas wafting from the kitchen, a nervous silence gripped the kingdom as it waited for the princes to return after four years.

Maharaj Dashrath paced in his chamber counting the hours impatiently for Vijay's arrival from Mithila. He was scared that Vijay may be waylaid by the asur tribals inhabiting the forests or by highway bandits.

"Maharaj, Mithila's princesses have sent gifts for the princes," Vijay announced, arranging the gifts in front of

Dashrath for approval. The king was relieved that Vijay had returned unharmed.

Dashrath was at a loss for words as his commander in-chief described the princesses of Mithila, praising their beauty and virtues, instead of narrating his exploits on the battlefield as reinforcement for King Janak of Mithila.

"It is as if Rajkumari Urmila is synonymous with Lakshman, Maharaj. She has the same fiery temperament, intelligence, simplicity, honesty, and sword-fighting skills as our yuvraj. An admirable young warrior princess, she most certainly is. People call her as the Warrior Princess of Mithila," Vijay was euphoric in his description, trying to convey a subtle message to Dashrath about Lakshman's future.

The magnificent sword caught Dashrath's attention and he was drawn to the young maiden.

A desire to see them together in life seeped into the Maharaj's thoughts but he curbed it, unaware that the thought was a premonition of what the future held. Arya Sumantra scattered his drift of thoughts.

"The princes have crossed the first entry gate of Ayodhya, Maharaj!" Arya Sumantra was frantic. The king rushed out of his chamber with tears in his eyes, "Run, prepare the queens for their arrival."

Who could understand the anguish of waiting better than mothers? However much you conditioned them, mothers remained desperate until their child was not in their arms.

Maharani Kaushalya cleaned her palace and rearranged the furniture to welcome the four princes. She had planned a special prayer for the welfare of the princes and the dynasty. Queen Kaikeyi's hands shook as she smoothened the creases of her new body-drape and flowing skirts and rearranged her jewellery. She was preoccupied with thoughts about her boys.

Maharani Sumitra was in the kitchen rolling *kshaakh ke laddu –* sweet rice balls – for her sons, especially Lakshman.

Kshaakh ke laddu made by Maharani Sumitra were Lakshman's favourite sweetmeat. Kshaakh in Sanskrit means rice, Lakshman disliked eating rice

hence, to include rice in his diet, Maharani Sumitra made laddus – sugar balls
– of it. The sugary rice balls were found in Ayodhya, Mithila and Kashi. It is
believed that Maharani Sumitra was the simplest among the three queens; she
prepared food for her sons with her own hands.

The sound of trumpets heralded the arrival of the princes. The
four brothers alighted from their chariot and ran to touch their
father's feet. He hugged them each by turn, unable to take his eyes
off their strapping frames. Ram was still attractive as ever with
limpid lotus eyes while Bharath was calm, with a set expression on
his face. Shatrughan, the naughtiest among the four, smiled with a
mischievous light in his eyes. Lakshman was most striking among
the siblings with his broken nose, his imposing height, sculpted
built and ruffled hair. His golden-brown eyes ringed with black
flashed fire – suggesting mirth and dormant anger.

After the customary welcome rituals, the princes wanted to
meet their mothers. The king gestured at his attendants to disperse.

"Mithila has sent gifts for you all. After you meet the Maharanis,
come back, Senapati Vijay will give them to you," Dashrath said.

The boys ran to meet their mothers.

"*Maa…*" they cried together, stepping inside Maharani
Kaushalya's chamber. The queen was chanting the *Maha Vishnu
Stotra* – the Vishnu chant – which was her daily routine. They
did not want to disturb her and sat on the staircase leading to the
Vishnu shrine in her chamber. The queen, who was in a state of
meditative prayer, opened her eyes to look at the boys. Her eyes
filled with tears of joy. She hugged them tightly to her bosom and
ruffled their hair with affection. Pulling at Lakshman's ears, she
wanted to know how many pranks he had played on Bharath in
the Gurukul.

"I only played a few pranks. *Maa*, don't pull at my ears, I am a
grown man now," he said.

Kaushalya burst out laughing. "You might have grown up for
everyone, but for your mothers, you will always remain a child,
my boy," she teased Lakshman. She was protective about Bharath.
"Go and meet Sumitra," she said. "She must be waiting for you."

The boys rushed to meet Queen Sumitra. While Ram, Bharath and Shatrughan rushed to embrace her, Lakshman stood in a corner weeping like a child. He noticed the uncertain smile and the trembling hands of his mother. Sumitra called him to her and he slumped at her feet, "Don't send me away again."

"I will not let you out of my sight even for a moment," she said. It was the time to undo the promise she was tied to. While the brothers watched the exchange between Lakshman and Sumitra, Shatrughan sulked.

"You often forget you have another son too," Shatrughan said with a petulant pout of his lips.

Sumitra went to Shatrughan and held his hand, "I don't. You both are my lifelines but you are my stronger one when it comes to battling emotional turbulence. Now go, *Maata* Kaikeyi awaits you all eagerly."

Kaikeyi's chambermaid Manthara welcomed the princes. She patted their heads remarking how tall they had grown. The queen waited for them in her chambers. Manthara was a like a stepping-stone to Kaikeyi's life, she was the queen's shadow stalking every move in the palace.

Bharath and Shatrughan did not like Manthara for reasons 'unknown' to them. The old maid brought out an intense dislike in the princes for her; the reaction was spontaneous. They tried to dodge Manthara's display of affection, but Kaikeyi chided them.

Ram, however, respected Manthara while Lakshman called her *Dadi Maa*.

Was Manthara, Narayan's greatest pawn in the Ramayana, as scrupulous and austere as Ram and Lakshman thought her to be or was she set up by Narayan to play her part in bringing about Raavan's end? Manthara was surrounded in mystery.

It was time for the princes to connect to Mithila's princesses for the first time! They were doubtful when Vijay, the commander in-chief, showed them the gifts from Mithila. Vijay described the princesses as he laid out the gifts for the four brothers to choose from. Once they picked up the souvenirs of their choice, they felt connected to the senders.

Ram took the 'goat leaf' sent by Sita and kissed it. Bharath took the peacock feather ink pen sent by Mandvi and tucked it away safely. The clay toys made by Shrutakeerti were taken by Shatrughan and Lakshman picked up the sword.

Lakshman felt a sense of peace as he traced his hands over the sword, trying to feel Urmila's imprint on it. Every touch connected him to Urmila for eternity.

A Rajkumari with a sword! He blushed at the very thought of her. Shatrughan noticed his brother turning a deep shade of crimson and wondered why Lakshman was so affected by the sword he was holding or by the 'unseen' princess.

Twins share sublime energy. Perhaps he sensed Lakshman's vulnerability to Urmila long before Lakshman perceived it.

The night stretched on for Lakshman. He felt the presence of fragile yet strong hands that held the sword, in his heart. His hands smelt of her! With an ache to catch a glimpse of the sword girl, Lakshman finally fell asleep.

Was Lakshman drawn to Mithila's Warrior Princess?

Shanta and Vindhya arrived in Ayodhya the next morning to greet the brothers. The visit was a pleasant surprise for the royal family. The family circle was complete with Shanta in the palace, but Shanta was in Ayodhya for a special reason. She wanted Vindhya to train as a Kshatriya and begin with Lakshman as her mentor in war lessons.

Lakshman was taken up with the idea of training his niece in the arts of war and assured Shanta of making Vindhya a master sword-fighter. He began her lessons, with the help of Shatrughan. Vindhya was amazed to see a strip of blue cloth tied to the hilt of Lakshman's sword. Before Lakshman could say anything about the cloth, Shatrughan blurted out the story of the unusual gift to Lakshman from Urmila.

They teased a serious Lakshman about the princess. Lakshman stayed aloof; lost in his own thoughts. Urmila occupied a lot of his mind space. He found his growing affinity to her disturbing.

On noticing Lakshman's strange state of mind, Shanta took him to her room and tried to probe his preoccupation. She began to smile when Lakshman poured out his heart, "I feel her with me, inside me. The more I try to take her out my thoughts, the more she intrudes. I don't know what is happening to me."

Shanta was silent for a few moments. "Let it stay! Let her stay! Time will reveal what these feelings mean," she said, patting his head with affection. Though Shanta did not say anything more, Lakshman had an inkling of what she was trying to express.

"She shall be a part of me until I meet her." Lakshman was determined.

The Ayodhya princes were no strangers to sibling pranks any more than Mithila's princesses were. And in Ayodhya, Bharath was the usual target of Lakshman's pranks. The lizard trick on Bharath had misfired and Shatrughan ribbed Lakshman, "Tell me when you fall in love. You seem to have lost the nifty touch."

"Love is not for me."

But at the mere suggestion of falling in love, Urmila crossed Lakshman's mind unannounced and peeped into his dreams at night. A laughing image unfolded in his head every night, saying, "Here I come!"

Lakshmila instituted its presence the moment Urmila felt the pull while she listened to Senapati Vijay's tales about Lakshman.

The Arrival of Brahmarshi Vishwamitra

The union of strength is the map of an empire.

Narayan's plan was not defunct but it was held back for four long years when the princes prospered and shone in Ayodhya. Then, suddenly it took a stealthy step forward, a step into this world unknown to the members of Raghukul.

Maharaj Dashrath hastened to the court in a state of anxiety to welcome the great sage Vishwamitra. Acutely aware of the venerable seer's intemperate anger, Dashrath felt uneasy about his visit to Ayodhya at such an inopportune time.

Vishwamitra did not heed royal protocols. He hurried into the court in a huff, taking in the distance with rapid strides. He said he wanted Ram and Lakshman to accompany him on a mission to kill the demoness Tadaka, and her evil sons Subhau and Mareecha, who were tormenting the seers in the forest.

Dashrath turned deathly pale, "But *Brahmarshi* – Brahma's seer – they are too young and fragile to fight demons. I will leave with you immediately with my men and kill the demons." But the seer was adamant that the princes accompany him and lost his temper when the Maharaj tried to coax him out of his demand.

"How do you forget your ancestor Raja Harishchandra, who gave up his kingdom, wife and son to pay *guru dakshina* – offering to the teacher?" The sage stomped his foot in anger.

Left with no choice, Maharaj reluctantly agreed with Vishwamitra.

Ram and Lakshman left Ayodhya barefoot with the sage, the next morning. The sage realised that the princes had to be armed with *divya astra* – celestial weapons – to kill Tadaka, the fearsome demoness, and her sons.

Vishwamitra is credited with inculcating the art of using Brahmaastra, Indraastra, Agneyastra, Manavastra, Naagaastra, Nagapasha, Garudastra, Narayanastra, Vaishnavastra and Brahmashira, the celestial weapons named after the gods who created them, in the Ayodhya princes.

Ram and Lakshman were fearless when they faced Tadaka and her sons. While Ram killed Tadaka, Lakshman cut off Sabahu with Urmila's sword. Mareecha was spared by the brothers because he begged Ram to kill him some other time. An elated Vishwamitra urged Ram and Lakshman to accompany him to Mithila to seek the blessings of the divine sword, *pinaka*, which was in possession of King Janak by inheritance.

Pinaka or the Shiv Dhanush: Lord Shiva had gifted his bow to Maharaj Janak's ancestors, considering them worthy of it.

As the trio journeyed to Mithila, *Brahmarshi* told them the story of Bhagiratha and Ganga. The princes were surprised to learn that Bhagiratha, the legendary king of the Ikshvaku dynasty, was their forebear. However, their enthusiasm dissipated into reproach when they sought shelter in Gautam Rishi's *ashram* on the way.

The retreat was a bleak place. The gloom surrounding the *ashram* even during the day perturbed the princes. "*Brahmarshi*, why is everything so desolate here, except for this little basil plant?" Ram wanted to know.

Everything else around the retreat: the trees, meadows and the even the streams had dried up. The forest had changed to the colour of yellow rust, the leafless branches of the dead trees sticking around like the gnarled limbs of shrivelled animals, charred by blistering heat.

Vishwamitra was uncomfortable. He explained how Gautam Rishi had cursed his wife Ahilya to become a stone in a bout of insane rage, but later prophesied that she could return to her original form of a beautiful woman, when a prince of the Raghu dynasty touched her with his feet.

Ram was assailed with benevolence. Driven by a sudden burst of positive energy, he touched the 'Ahilya stone' – a large brown rock shaped like a crouching woman with his feet, but with eyes full of tears. He bowed his head in respect when Ahilya stood before him restored to a graceful woman. Lakshman too bowed in reverence at the sight of the seer's beautiful consort. The visit and the chain of events that followed, for a strange reason, disturbed Lakshman more than Ram, who thought it was his sacred duty to redeem Ahilya.

The hermitage sent out unfriendly vibes, troubling Lakshman's meditative subconscious.

Their next destination was Mithila. On their way, Vishwamitra told them about Maharaj Janak. The Mithila king's virtues found accord in both Ram and Lakshman, fostering in them a soft corner for the kind and pious ruler.

According to the scriptures, Maharaj Janak, the king of Mithila, was intensely drawn towards spiritual discourse and was free from worldly illusions. His interactions with the sages and seekers such as Ashtavakra and Sulabha were recorded in the ancient texts. The late Vedic literature such as Shatapatha Brahmana and Brihadaranyaka Upanishad referred to him as a great philosopher king of Videha, renowned for his patronage of Vedic culture and philosophy and whose court was a hub of intellectual growth with the presence of Brahmin sages such as Yajnavalkya, Uddalaka Aruni, and Gargi Vachaknavi.

Ayodhya thought about its travelling princes with a smug smile. They had finally stepped out of their palace to see Aryavarta and experience its richness.

The First Meeting

Fates decree meetings of kindred hearts.

The reason why Narayan put Mithila as the better half in his plan still remained buried within the folds of time, but life in Mithila was soon to change forever.

Mithila's princesses had grown into alluring maidens, and their warrior princess, Urmila, was not only one of the finest debaters in Aryavarta, having defeated several famous sages, including Atri Muni, Bramahacharini Vasundhara and Maharishi Bharadwaj in verbal duels under the mentorship of Gargi Vachaknavi, but she was also an ace sword-fighter.

At the age of 15, Urmila was offered the sword of Vishnu Nandaki, by Lord Parashuram, for her sword-fighting skills, but she humbly denied being worthy of it. Instead, she requested Parashuram, "My dear Lord, I feel honored but there are several better swordsmen than me in Aryavarta. I am but only a young princess of Mithila. Instead, I seek your blessings for my land to prosper, my family to share love, gain knowledge and the power to protect their dignity and self-respect."

Lord Parashuram was moved by her humility, "Daughter, your wisdom indicates that you have a divine soul. I grant you strength like this Nandaki and bless you to find a companion who has been yours for the past seven births, a husband who is just like you, fierce, selfless and unswerving in his support of you. You shall bear three children. Your daughter will be your replica and your sons will be as knowledgeable as you." The past was slowly giving way to a new present!

Maharaj Janak was feeling hopeless. He considered no one worthy enough to wed Sita, who was 19 now. After deep contemplation, *Raj Guru* Shatanand suggested that the Maharaj organise a *swayamvar* – the rite of choosing a husband – for Sita.

The king was relieved and Mithila began to make arrangements for the wedding rite. One morning, Maharaj received word that *Brahmarshi* Vishwamitra, accompanied by two young princes, was resting under a banyan tree, just within the boundaries of Mithila.

Ram and Lakshman looked around Mithila with wonder. It was undulating and verdant; drained by three rivers and flanked by hills in the north. The kingdom smelt of fragrant medicinal and spice herbs which grew in abundance on the meadows along the banks of the rivers, Mahananda, Gandaki and the Ganges flowing through the east, west and south of the region respectively.

"Mithila is not only a land of knowledge, but I feel it is also the most beautiful kingdom in Aryavarta. I wish I can stay in these lush green fields of Mithila forever. It is so different from Ayodhya." Ram smiled at Lakshman's excitement.

Every eye was on Ram and Lakshman. The people of Mithila beheld the princes as if Narayan himself was walking on Earth with his companion, Shesha. Greeting the *Brahmarshi* with reverence, Janak expressed his pleasure at finally meeting princes from Ayodhya. He invited them to stay in Mithila until Sita's *swayamvar.*

Vishwamitra agreed, recounting how Ram and Lakshman had killed Tadaka and her son Subahu; and freed Ahilya from Gautam Rishi's curse. Maharaj Janak and Shatanand were speechless. Shatanand knelt at Ram's feet to pay his oblation, leaving Maharaj Janak wondering who these fetching boys could be. He was seized with a sudden wish to marry his daughters off to these dashing and virtuous princes – and the desire kept growing inside the king of Mithila's heart as the day wore on. He retired to his palace, immersed in thought.

The royal priest of Mithila, Shatanand, was the eldest son of Gautam Rishi and Devi Ahilya, who Ram had released from the great curse.

Janak was busy with the preparations for the wedding rite, but thoughts about the visiting Ayodhya princes kept coming back to his mind, making him introspective. He was not sure whether the boys would take part in the *swayamvar*. Queen Sunaina looked at his dejected form in silence, and waited patiently for him to confide in her the reason for his anxiety.

"Sunaina, today for the first time in my life, I regret my decision of Sita's *swayamvar* after having met the Ayodhya princes. Ram is perfect match for Janaki whereas Lakshman is destined for our Warrior Princess. I could not take my eyes off their majestic faces."

Sunaina tried to calm him. "If they are meant for Janaki and Urmila, Goddess Gauri will make it happen. Let us pray that Ram takes part in the contest and wins it."

Lakshman was scared as he walked through the ornate corridors of the Janak's palace, the next morning. The thought that he might finally cross paths with his sword companion, Urmila, excited him and yet brought a strange fear of the 'unknown'.

Little did he know that he was soon to meet Urmila, and under the most playful circumstances.

Maharani Sunaina persuaded her daughters to dress in special clothes for the Gauri *puja* – invocation of the young Goddess Parvati – in the Gauri temple. "But why do we need to visit Gauri temple for a suitable husband, *Maa*?" Urmila asked.

"Every maiden who worships the *Param Tapaswini Maata* Gauri – the goddess who is in deep meditation – with devotion gets the partner she desires. She is the chaste form of Parvati who penanced for 3,000 years and 108 births to get Mahadev – Shiva – as her husband," Sunaina said, explaining the implications of Goddess Gauri to the princesses. But she did not accompany them because Gauri was the unmarried incarnation of Parvati. Married men and women were not allowed to visit her shrine.

"*Rakshasi*, will you also join us?" Mandvi teased. "Yes, but only to pray for my *didi* – older sister," Urmila said, picking up a sweetmeat from a platter of delicious yellow *laddus*. "O, Gauri *Maa*, please change my Urmi's perception about marriage," Maharani Sunaina prayed to the goddess silently.

Brahmarshi Vishwamitra wanted to take flowers to Maharishi Yagnavalkya's *ashram* for the ritual morning prayers and he told the princes to pick flowers for him from the royal garden.

As Sita prayed in the Gauri temple, her friends Medha and Chitravali ran in to tell her about the strikingly handsome princes from Ayodhya, who had not only killed the demoness Tadaka and her son Subahu, but had also released Ahilya from her curse.

"They are in Mithila. The kingdom sings their praises. They look like Narayan and Lord Shesha having descended on earth. One of the princes has big innocent eyes, sharp nose and a dusky colour whereas the other one is fair, tall and extremely handsome. He does not look at women. You both may not be able to take your eyes off the princes," Medha gushed.

The princesses were not particularly interested, but at their friends' insistence on how beautiful the princes were, the girls were curious to see them but from a discreet distance. Maybe, Goddess Gauri also wanted them to meet the princes. Shrutakeerti complained that the flower baskets were empty and they would need plenty of flowers for prayers in the temple. Sita and Urmila set out to collect flowers, both in different directions.

Urmila went to the royal garden to pick flowers because she was fond of the big blooms. But along the way, she forgot why she had come to the *Pushp Vatika* – flower garden, heady with fragrances and colours. The scented flowers had a trance-like effect on her senses. She began to dance in joy at the sight of the riotous blooms.

The morning dew glistened on the tender green grass, making the ground slippery.

Suddenly, Urmila tripped as she missed a step and ran into a muscled young man, almost colliding against him. Time ceased to exist as she and the young man looked deep into each other's eyes under an orchid tree. They remained immobile, feelings overwhelming their senses. Unaware that the woman he held tightly by the wrist was Urmila, the Sword Princess, Lakshman felt an intense pull to the maiden.

"Oh, what a beauty she is! Is she an apsara – celestial being from heaven – or some form of the goddess itself or maybe, the Warrior Princess of Mithila? But why will a Rajkumari come to the garden to pick flowers at this hour in the morning?" Lakshman mused. Urmila was not immune to his physical closeness, either. His deep-set golden-brown eyes with black sparks made her heart beat faster.

Before they could disentangle or could even recognise each other, the flowers in the small bucket that Urmila held in her hand overturned and spilled on them. It seemed as if Vaikunth and Aryavarta were celebrating the first meeting of Lakshmila, the reunion of Shesha and Ksheera, with a shower of flowers.

Approaching footsteps slackened Lakshman's hold on Urmila and she fell in a heap on the bunch of flowers and leaves strewn on the ground. Before Lakshman could apologise, Sita and Ram stood before them. Sita was about to ask what had happened when Urmila burst out in anger, "This man does not know how to respect women. He blocked my way and I fell."

Sita and Ram had met in the same manner Lakshman and Urmila stumbled on each other in the royal garden by pure coincidence.

Sita looked at Lakshman who stood there meekly. She was unable to believe he could be this insensitive. Urmila left the garden with her sister, hurt and seeking revenge. Lakshman could only gaze at her in awe as the sisters returned to the Gauri temple to pray.

जय जय गिरिबरराज किसोरी। जय महेस मुख चंद चकोरी।।
जय गजबदन शडानन माता। जगत जननि दामिनि दुति गाता।।
नहिं तव आदि मध्य अवसाना। अमित प्रभाउ बेदु नहिं जाना।।
भव भव बिभव पराभव कारिनि। बिस्व बिमोहनि स्वबस बिहारिनि।।
पतिदेवता सुतीय महुँ मातु प्रथम तव रेख।
महिमा अमित न सकहिं कहि सहस सारदा सेष।।
सेवत तोहि सुलभ फल चारी। बरदायनी पुरारि पिआरी।।
देबि पूजि पद कमल तुम्हारे। सुर नर मुनि सब होहिं सुखारे।।
मोर मनोरथु जानहु नीकें। बसहु सदा उर पुर सबही कें।।
कीन्हेउँ प्रगट न कारन तेहीं। अस कहि चरन गहूँ मै तेरे।।

(*Glory to you O Daughter of the Mountains! Who looks upon Lord Shiva as a partridge on the moon. Ganesh and Kartikey are not your only children, for you are the shining mother of the entire creation.*

You have always been and will exist for eternity. Even the Vedas cannot fathom your depths completely. You are the cause of all existence and its final dissolution. You are the Ultimate enticer, playing with all creation.

O, the one who grants all wishes, divine partner of the Lord, serving you leads us to life's greatest rewards. O Devi, gods, humans, and sages bow at your lotus feet and in doing so they easily gain all that they truly seek.

You know the deepest desires that reside in my heart because within that abode we are never ever apart. It is because of this that I never spoke my thoughts, saying so I bow to your sacred feet.)

The chants rang out of the temple into the garden; floating across the rivers, hills and the forests through the kingdom of Mithila.

The night for Mithila was heavy. Unable to remove Ram and Lakshman from their thoughts, Sita and Urmila were hardly able to sleep a wink. But when sleep finally overcame them, Urmila had a smile on her face and a tentative plan in her mind. She could not let go of the stranger without teaching him a lesson.

Urmila woke up at the first light of dawn and left for the Gauri temple with a pot of wet mud, flowers and a netting cloth like a mesh. She laid a booby-trap with the mud and mesh – sprinkling the flowers on it – on the narrow track running by the side of the temple and hid behind a tree, waiting for Lakshman to fall into the pit covered with the net and wet clay.

"Learn to accept defeat. Over-confidence often leads to failure," Lakshman spoke lightly into her ears. Urmila turned around in confusion which immediately changed into anger, when she saw Lakshman standing before her with his lop-sided, arrogant and yet gentle smile. He had come from the other side.

She was so flustered that she barely noticed his smile. They began to fight again. "You allowed me to fall yesterday and did not apologise. And you have the nerve to call me over-confident. You have no manners," Urmila was very angry.

Lakshman tried to cut off Urmila's rambling accusations by covering her mouth with his hands, "Look, you collided against me. And moreover, I did not let you fall deliberately. I heard footsteps and let you go for your own good. Learn to maintain your balance. I will not be around to help you every time." She glared at him and indicated that he remove his hand from her mouth immediately.

The hand, however, fit on her mouth perfectly, capturing her breath.

Both felt a little empty when Lakshman removed his hand from her mouth. Urmila could not utter a word for some time.

"As if I need you," she was annoyed.

The wittiest debater of Mithila for the first time did not have words to describe what she felt. And destiny too decided not to rest until it intervened in Lakshmila's lives, igniting their need to meet each other, paving the way for closer encounters.

It was afternoon. Urmila was teaching sword-fighting to a group of children, when a little girl came running to her for help. A group of women was misbehaving with the girl's mother and she wanted Urmila to resolve the feud.

Raj Guru Shatanand was crossing the field with Ram, Lakshman, *Brahmarshi* Vishwamitra and Maharishi Yagnavalkya just then. They stopped in their tracks when they saw the princess standing in the middle of a group of women from the village, trying to reason with two warring women. Lakshman volunteered to help

Urmila, but Yagnavalkya forbade him, saying, "She will not need help. Rajkumari Urmila, the younger daughter of Maharaj Janak and Maharani Sunaina is quite efficient in handling such matters on her own. Be patient and watch."

Lakshman stood quietly, trying to get a closer look at the princess in action but she was far away. Much to Lakshman's surprise, Urmila settled the dispute without much trouble.

"Rajkumari *ji*, these people have destroyed my field," the girl's mother, a woman farmer, wailed.

"Yes, we did so because you are a widow. You are forbidden to grow your crops here," argued an older woman from the group. "So I learn a new code of conduct today. Widows are not allowed to live in Mithila but widowers like Vaidya *ji* can. Why?" A composed Urmila countered the older woman, trying to make the group see sense in a quiet and dignified manner, but the steel inside her showed. Her voice was low and cold.

When the women refused to listen to Urmila, she hit out at their narrow-mindedness asking whether such mean women and their families should be allowed to stay in Mithila, known for its just and generous ways.

"How dare you burn the crops of a woman who has no other means of livelihood? Instead of showing compassion, you rebuke a poor woman. You cannot dictate who will grow their crops in the village. People like you don't deserve to stay in Mithila, but before throwing you out, I give you a chance to repent. Apologise to this widow, help her cultivate her crops and share with her a bit of what you have for now," Urmila commanded the older women of the village sternly. Her anger, like a simmering inferno swamped their belligerence in its scorching strands of reason and justice.

The women asked Urmila to forgive them and girl's mother bowed to the princess in gratitude. Urmila smiled and walked away.

On her way back she saw Vishwamitra, Yagnavalkya, *Raj Guru* Shatanand and the two princes watching her from a distance. She walked over to greet them. Everyone looked at her smiling, barring Lakshman, who looked away. He was busy rearranging the arrows in his quiver. Urmila had a feeling that he wanted to avoid her gaze.

The feeling of kinship between Ram and Urmila was mutual.

Finally, Lakshman looked at Urmila with nervous excitement in his eyes. However, he could not hold her gaze for a long time despite the intense longing to know her better.

Ram was intrigued. This maidenly shame was so unlike his brother. As they walked back, Ram looked at Urmila furtively and then at Lakshman, walking by his side, and vice-versa. *They are so alike*, he thought and paused to draw a long breath of expectation …*I will not let Lakshman's ego stand in the way of his happiness.*

At Vishwamitra's request, Urmila accompanied them to Gargi Vachaknavi's *ashram*. Urmila hurried inside to fetch the wise woman. She wanted to be alone with the oracle for a few moments. She wanted to know why Lakshman affected her this way.

She paused inside the door. Gargi, who was sitting on her study mat reading the scriptures, looked at Urmila closely. The seer sensed a restlessness and yet a suppressed excitement in Urmila and held her gaze with a quizzical look in her eyes, but Urmila was evasive.

How could Urmila explain what had changed in her!

Perplexed by the change in Urmila, Gargi left the hut instructing the princess to get some fruits for the guests outside.

As Urmila went to bring the basket of fruits from a wooden cabinet inside the hut, she glanced at the clay statue that Gargi had stowed away, sitting next to the fruit bowl. Urmila picked it up and for the first time looked intently at what she had sculpted. The clay statue reminded her of the young man who sat outside, Lakshman. The icon looked exactly like Lakshman: bold and handsome with a sword strapped to his waist. She released her breath in one long sigh of hopelessness and helplessness – she had met the one of her dreams. An ache wrenched her heart for the man who sat outside.

She placed the fruit bowl in front of sage Vishwamitra and sought permission to leave. But Gargi forestalled her. "As Mithila debates with Ayodhya, on *Brahmarshi*'s request, I want you here to help me."

Gargi put forth several grinding questions to Ram. He stood firm against the onslaught and replied with confidence. Now, it was Lakshman's turn. "Lakshman, despite knowing that entering *Maata* Ahilya's *ashram* will harm your marital life later, why did you go there?"

Lakshman answered without flinching, "I am but my brother's shadow. How can a shadow leave its body? My acts reflect my karma. I am ready to bear the consequences of my actions."

Gargi was taken aback. "*Brahmarshi*, you were right in your assertions. Indeed, the princes of Raghukul are outstanding in wit, intelligence and understanding." Turning to Lakshman, "Years ago, Urmila also went *Maata* Ahilya's *ashram* with Sita and her reply coincided with yours. You both think alike."

Lakshman and Urmila looked at each other without words. But this time, they did not look away, they lingered as if taking in everything about each other. Deep down, they knew something had changed within them forever as individuals.

Sita's Swayamvar – Choosing a Husband

Parting is not always bitter.

Mithila wiped its tears in the shadows of the night saddened by princess Urmila's unspoken anguish. It felt the same sense of abandonment Urmila did.

One morning, a few days before Sita's *swayamvar*, Urmila disappeared into the royal garden to spend some time by herself to find courage to let her sister go when the time came.

As she looked back on those moments when Sita and she had been inseparable, she was unable to control her feelings of despair.

Hiding behind a rock pillar, her secret crying nook in the garden, she broke down into convulsive sobs. Her tears were for her sister, who was her life. The thought of living, laughing, sharing, and breathing without her was unbearable for the Warrior Princess.

A princess, who rarely cried or believed in emotional weaknesses, broke Mithila's heart with her tears. But it could not embrace its Rajkumari. It stood there, numb.

Lakshman, who was strolling in the garden in the morning, heard muffled sounds of weeping coming from somewhere nearby. He strained his ears to identify the source and traced it to a shadowy corner behind the rock that rose steeply like an outcrop in the middle of the lush greenery. He tiptoed to the rock to find Urmila crying her heart out. Before he could find out why she was weeping, Urmila looked at him with a stricken expression, "Please leave me alone. I have no inclination to fight right now."

Lakshman suddenly felt protective. He had not seen Urmila cry before; she had always come across as a fiery Warrior Princess. He wanted her to feel better and teased her, "Is it some plan to manoeuvre me to succumb to your wiles or is it something deeper that hurts you such?"

"I have known you for the last three days, but not well enough to share my emotions with you," Urmila was contrite.

The barb found its mark because Lakshman suddenly felt like a stranger. He was embarrassed to have over-stepped his authority as a visitor to Mithila. "Most certainly, princess. Have a good day," he said abruptly before turning around to walk away.

He had barely walked a yard when he heard her mumble Sita's name. In a flash, Lakshman understood the cause of Urmila's grief. He retraced his steps to stand quietly in front of her, "Sisters are irreplaceable. I have an older sister too, Shanta *didi*. I can relate to the pain of separation. I dread the very thought of living apart from my brother Ram. But you are a warrior and a scholar. Don't break down," Lakshman tried to share in her sadness, her desolation echoing in his heart.

Urmila could feel his sympathy.

"It is not easy for a girl. I will never understand this custom that forces a girl to leave her family and settle with her husband and his family," she blurted after a pause; not sure whether opening up to this 'prince' from Ayodhya was the right thing to do. She did not know him well.

Lakshman smiled at her confession, "You are the daughter of *Rajrishi* Janak, a great scholar. Such rebellious outbursts do not become your personality."

They sat in companionable silence for a while and then left for their respective destinations. Urmila walked back to the palace and Lakshman to his *ashram*. On their way back, the two realised that they were relating to each other much better. Their early dislike for each other – and the irritation that they suffered in each other's presence, were ebbing to make way for a tremulous friendship.

The day of the 'wedding contest' finally dawned amid fanfare and expectations. Sita was nervous because she did not know what her fate held in store, Urmila was scared about her sister's future.

"Don't worry. He will win you," she tried to fill her older sibling with hope. Sita looked at her sister with a composed smile

"I know Raghunandan will. Raghukul does not fail."

Around mid-morning, the members of the royal family of Mithila took their seats in the *Raj Durbar*. – royal hall. The *pinaka* was placed on a raised podium with a short flight of steps leading to it. The *Durbar* glittered with the rank and file of royal suitors – and their entourages – from all across Aryavarta. The kings, princes and noblemen, who had turned out in full royal grandeur, were decked in gold, silver, velvets, silks and colours of countless shades. They came with their trains, retinues and entourages, laden with rich tributes. Maharaj Janak gestured the *swayamvar* to begin.

The musicians struck up a welcome melody and a *sutradhar* – narrator – introduced the aspiring suitors. The *kathakar* – minstrels and story-tellers – sang paeans to the king of Mithila, explaining the mores of the contest to the suitors. Whoever lifted and strung the mighty *pinaka* bow would win the hand of Maharaj Janak's elder daughter Sita in marriage.

Minutes before the first suitor walked up to hoist the *pinaka*, the princesses filed into the court attired in rustling silks with their heads demurely covered in gauzy veils to hide their faces. A long line of maids followed in their trail carrying platters of flowers, wreaths, gold coins and sweetmeats. Urmila darted furtive glances at the throng trying to spot Ram and Lakshman.

Why weren't they here? She was anxious.

They sat behind their father Janak to watch the contest. The prince of Kalinga walked to the podium to lift the celestial bow. Mandvi, who was looking at him intently, suddenly whispered to Urmila that the Kalinga prince had the power to win Sita. Urmila was quick to refute her for she had complete faith in Ram's abilities.

"But where's Ram?" an arrogant and mischievous Mandvi shot back. "He is not around anywhere," she added, looking around.

"Winners make their entry at the opportune moment. I am sure *Sumitranandan* – Sumitra's son – will bring him to the *swayamvar*." Urmila trusted Lakshman.

Initially, the suitors were upbeat. A buzz went around the court that lifting the bow was an easy bet if one used strength, intelligence and followed the rules of archery. But, the excitement soon ebbed as the kings and the princes failed the test one after the other. Most of them could not even lift the bow. The mercury began to rise as the disheartened suitors grumbled, and cursed their luck. Some of them were angry with King Janak. They challenged him to battle for shaming them in public, undermining their strength and manhood.

Urmila was furious at the guests for deriding her father and heaping indignity on her sister with their jibes. Unable to control her anger, she lashed out at the princes who insulted her father saying that Janak had set them up to show them as mildlings.

"Do not hide your weakness and lack of strength by insulting my father. Do not seek refuge in baseless allegations and threats.

If you have failed, you are ineffectual. Not good enough for my sister," Urmila said in a firm voice. Her father and her sister were her dignity, her pride.

The kings were infuriated at the interference of the young princess. They threatened to lay siege to the court when an authoritative voice intervened, "Whosoever wants to challenge the king will have to defeat the princes of Ayodhya here before they attack Mithila." *Brahmarshi* Vishwamitra walked into the court followed by Ram and Lakshman. The princesses were relieved that they were not let down. Their eyes shone with joy and hope.

Janak was disappointed, "Is there no one in Aryavarta who can string the Shiv Dhanush? Shall my Janaki stay unmarried? I feel there is no brave warrior left in Aryavarta." Janak's appeal touched the visitors and a powerful king, who was invited to the ceremony as a guest, volunteered to marry the princess in an attempt to remove the 'taint' of Mithila's unwed daughters.

Lakshman was furious; anger made him reckless.

"Maharaj Janak, you forget the Raghuvansh. These words are an insult to Ayodhya. I understand your disappointment but your words are harsh. To prove you otherwise, I request you to allow the eldest prince of Ayodhya, my brother Ram, to string the Shiv Dhanush."

Lakshman looked at Urmila in the eye and then courtesied to her. An unspoken understanding passed between the two, bonding them closer. Urmila knew why Lakshman was angry.

With Vishwamitra's blessings, Ram picked up the *pinaka* without much of an effort and broke it into two. The court was stunned into silence for a moment, before erupting into cries of joy.

Urmila was elated because the promise had been fulfilled. She embraced Sita in tears, "Your love wins. I am so happy." An indefinable expression of contentment in Sita's eyes turned them into endless pools of brown. Janak slumped on his throne in relief; a weight had been lifted off his shoulders. He would not have to go groom-hunting for Janaki again.

The first ritual was garlanding. Sita picked up a heavy white and red garland from a platter and put it around Ram's neck. With it, she became Ram's. Urmila looked at Lakshman with yearning as he bent down to touch Sita's feet to welcome her into the household.

Suddenly, the sky rumbled with the distant sound of thunder. Lord Parashuram stormed into the court demanding who had the audacity to break the *pinaka* into two. He refused to be mollified. Everyone was terrified except for Urmila, who dimpled into a smile. She had always been Parashuram's favourite child.

"Please calm down, lord. Tell me why does the breaking of the *pinaka* make you so agitated?" Lakshman's voice was hard with rage. He struggled to control his temper.

"You foolish boy, don't you know the difference between a normal bow and the *pinaka*?" the sage thundered.

"We are Kshatriya princes and for us, all bows are the same," Lakshman did not understand the implication of the breaking of the *pinaka*.

"You half-witted fool. You invite death by disregarding the *pinaka*. Don't you know who I am? I am Parashuram, the one who has beheaded many atrocious Kshatriya princes like you," the sage replied.

But Lakshman was relentless in his attack. "O, great Kshatriya Brahmin, won't you confess that you beheaded your own mother *Devi* Renuka with the axe you carry and shed royal blood unnecessarily. It is you who should temper your anger before you are beheaded."

"You all shall witness two deaths here today, one of this foolish boy Lakshman, who insults me and the other of the one who broke the *pinaka*," Parashuram brandished his axe as if he was about to throw it at the Ayodhya scions.

"Until Lakshman lives, Ram lives. No one can harm him. Raghuvanshi men lay down their lives to protect seers, but atrocious wise men like you deserve to be eliminated," Lakshman roared, whipping his sword out of the scabbard.

The two looked at each other in contempt and anger, and began to spar. Urmila stepped in between them to distract Parashuram. "Lord, do you remember me? I am Urmila, Maharaj Janak and Maharani Sunaina's younger daughter, the one you offered Nandaki to. Anger does not suit you, lord. May I offer you a glass of water? And won't you see my sword-fighting? I know how you love to watch it."

Parashuram's anger vanished at her childish plea. Appeased, he blessed her and the court wondered what kind of magic Urmila had woven to calm the raging seer, known for his fierce anger and hate for Kshatriya kings.

Ram stepped forward to disclose his identity. He folded his hands in greeting, saying, "Lord, I am your devotee. You know the reason."

The reason why Ram could break the pinaka was because of a conversation in Vaikunth between Narayan and Shiva. One day, while they were discussing their bows, made by Lord Vishwakarma, the engineer of the gods, Vishnu felt that Shiva's bow was better and challenged Shiva that he would break it one day if he had an opportunity. And hence, he did so in his Ram Avatara.

As Ram stood before him in reverence, the mists in Parashuram's understanding lifted. He realised that the breaking of the bow was the *leela* – magic – of Hari Vishnu, who kept his word in his earthly show of valour as Ram, accompanied by Mahalakshmi as Sita, the 1,000-headed Shesha as Lakshman and Ksheera Sagara as Urmila.

Lord Parashuram's eyes filled with tears of remorse and devotion. "Narayan himself stands before me. He refers to me as lord. What more I could ask for? Ram, hence on *Rajdharm* and *Manavdharm* – the laws of kingship and humanity – will be synonymous with your name. I beseech you to pick up the *Maha Vishnu Sharanga* – the divine arrow – and destroy my anger."

Ram shot the arrow to the left from the *Sharanga* and revealed himself to Parashuram as the *Chaturbhuj Maha Vishnu* – the preserver of the universe with four arms. Parashuram was overwhelmed.

Lakshman glanced at Urmila with tenderness and possessiveness for having saved his life.

Is It Love?

The road to love is not rose beds.

As silence deepened and enveloped the night in its wake, Mithila kept its vigil on the pensive Warrior Princess, who was perhaps trying to solve a puzzling riddle in her head.

Urmila gazed at the sky from her balcony, lost deep in thoughts. Lakshman was on her mind constantly and she was angry for not being able to banish him from her consciousness. Everything about him fascinated her. Prompted by the love-hate relationship with her sibling Urmila, Mandvi wanted to rile her. She sneaked up on Urmila in the terrace.

"Who do you think about at this hour? Prince Lakshman?" Mandvi wanted to know.

Before Urmila could snub her, Shrutakeerti joined in, "Do you wish to follow Sita *didi* to Ayodhya, too?"

Urmila was appalled. "*Sumitranandan* and I? Not ever. It is an absurd presumption. I don't even like that arrogant prince who knows only anger. He does not respect women."

"Then why did you save his life today?" Mandvi would not to let Urmila off the hook.

"Don't read feelings where there are none. Guests to Mithila are the royal family's responsibility and father has always inculcated in us that duty precedes personal feelings, hence I stood for the visiting Rajkumar," Urmila did not wish to continue the conversation further. It was well past midnight and she was sleepy.

Deep within the shadows of a pillar, Sita was silent. Without interrupting, she watched Urmila with an intent expression in her eyes. Somehow, she was aware that something was brewing between her sister and Lakshman much more than met the eye.

The moon gradually disappeared behind a thick blanket of the night clouds as dawn broke over the eastern horizon. The first ray of sun touched Mithila and woke up the princesses for the day that was foretold to be hectic and chaotic, especially Urmila's.

The princesses rushed to the Gauri temple for an important rite early in the morning. On the way, Sita realised she forgot to bring *roli* – vermillion. She told Urmila to fetch it from the children who were playing near the lake.

Another destined meeting between Urmila and Lakshman waited round the corner.

Urmila collected the *roli* from the children and began to run back to Sita, holding the smear of vermillion paste in her clenched fist. They could not afford to be late for the prayer. On the way, Urmila collided into Lakshman head on. The prince, who was carrying a small brass pitcher of water, spilled it into the vermillion paste on Urmila's palm, daubing her red. She scowled at him, but Saumitra looked at her stupefied. She looked so different.

For the first time as was divined; he felt a tug of something irresistible for her not only as his Warrior Princess, but also as a woman. His fiery Rajkumari stood there fuming, but looking utterly gorgeous in red. She walked away in anger, her body rigid with humiliation. She hated her own self for being so careless. Lakshman stared at her.

Watching Urmila's angry body language as she returned with only a bit of the *roli*, Sita had a hunch that Urmila must have met Lakshman on the way. She smiled to herself and decided it was best not to mention his name or even ask what had happened.

Everyone in Mithila was becoming accustomed to their accidental meetings and rounds of fights.

The princesses were resting in their common quarters in the afternoon when Maharaj Janak came in to meet them. He wanted to invite Ram and Lakshman to dinner and asked Sita to organise the feast.

Sita pleaded with Urmila to find out from the Ayodhya princes their choice of fare. Urmila was reluctant to meet Lakshman again, but she could not refuse Sita. On her way to Maharishi Yagnavalkya's *ashram*, where the princes were staying, a group of children spirited her away to play spooks with them. She chased the little revellers wearing a demon's mask in a game of hide-and-seek. Lakshman, who was passing by, took the apparition to be real. He aimed an arrow at the masked demoness, screaming, "You demon, prepare to die,"

Demons in Mithila during the day! Lakshman found the prospect terrifying. The children began to laugh. "She is our Urmila *didi*. Does she look like a *Rakshasi* to you Rajkumar?" a child piped in.

Urmila removed the mask from her face. Lakshman was shocked, "You! What are you doing here?" he said accusingly.

"Why will I tell you? I am here to meet Ram *bhaiya* – brother." She looked around embarrassed.

"Why are you looking for Ram *bhaiya?*" he insisted on knowing. "How do you know I am looking for him?" Urmila was suddenly incoherent. Her thoughts always ran haywire when Lakshman was around.

"I guess someone overspeaks. You said so just now!" Lakshman laughed at her disorientation, but Urmila ignored him.

"Please tell me where he is. I am here to invite you two to dinner at the palace and want to know about your food preferences." Urmila remembered the purpose of her visit.

"*Bhaiya* loves simple food. He hates chillies," Lakshman smirked.

"And why should the food be spicy, if I may ask?" she raised her eyebrows.

"Because the one who speaks to me is like a red chilli may and might only know how to cook spicy food!" he teased. "If I am *mirchi* – chilli, then you are *nakchara* – peevish. Do you even know how to smile? On the day of the *swayamvar*, you unnecessarily riled Lord Parashuram. He would have beheaded you, if I hadn't intervened," Urmila reminded him.

"If you think so, why did you come in between us?" Lakshman was suddenly irritated. His ego bristled.

The blame game between them continued until Ram came out of the hut in exasperation.

Urmila ran to Ram. "Brother, I come here as a messenger from Maharaj Janak to invite you and your younger brother to dinner at the palace. My sister wishes to know your and your brother's culinary tastes so that she can cook food fit for you to eat," she said, pointing to Lakshman.

"I will love to eat anything your sister makes," Ram's love for Sita echoed in his voice.

"And him?" She made a disapproving face at Lakshman.

"How do you find the energy to chatter incessantly? No wonder you are a debater," Lakshman was curious.

"Yet another derogatory observation by someone who doesn't know how to keep his anger in check and his mouth shut, when required," Urmila retaliated in anger.

Before Lakshman could argue further, Ram ordered him to keep quiet. But Lakshman was not the one to be cowed down.

"I will love to eat anything Mithila's oldest Rajkumari makes. But if anyone else has any inclination to help princess Sita in the kitchen, I will like to say that we princes prefer light food because the one who speaks like a red hot chilli pepper. We cannot expect anything else from her other than fiery spices!" Lakshman retorted.

"Mithila will also prefer *nakchara* prince to keep his anger in check when he comes to eat. Not every time will a rajkumari save Ayodhya from having its Rajkumar be headed," Urmila was not a debater in vain. She knew how to give it back to the boys.

While Ram laughed whole-heartedly, Lakshman sulked. Urmila left with a self-satisfied smile on her face.

Urmila returned to Sita's chamber with information about the kind of food Ayodhya princes would like to eat for dinner. She also told Sita in an afterthought about how much Lakshman irritated her.

Sita by now was apprised of the sweet war of words between her sister and Lakshman and ignored her sister's spleen against the Rajkumar. She told Urmila to make *malpua* – the traditional mini pancake dipped in sugar syrup – for dessert. Urmila agreed. The thought of Lakshman eating *malpua* that she made excited her.

In the evening, three of the princesses were ready to greet Ram and Lakshman but they were delayed by Urmila, who was holed up in her room. She was uncertain...

"Urmila is always the first one to get ready, what is taking her so long today?" Shrutakeerti was impatient. Dinner had to be served an hour before the sun set.

The mirror on the wood and ivory dresser was pensive and mute because the princess rarely looked at her reflection in the crystal glass. But that day, for some reason, she stood in front of the mirror for a long time trying to make out whether she looked fair enough in her traditional light pink and blue *lehenga* – the flowing embroidered skirt and bodice that she had chosen for the evening. The mirror reassured her that she looked arresting. Still, Urmila was not convinced.

"Why does he keep calling me *rakshasi*? Do I really look unattractive?" Urmila thought in self-doubt. She looked worried.

The mirror wondered why princess Urmila was so bothered about what Lakshman thought of her appearance. Shrutakeerti's voice cut into Urmila's silent exchange with the mirror.

"Come fast. We are waiting for you," Mandvi shouted from outside the door of her chamber, which was shut. Urmila emerged looking like a diva – glittering in her swirling silken skirts and heavy gold jewellery. She was usually vocal about her dislike for feminine trappings. So, the transformation was puzzling.

Sharp at an hour before the sun set in the western sky, Ram and Lakshman took their seats at the banquet. Sita picked up a silver salver to serve Lakshman first, which was almost unacceptable to Urmila. She fumed in silence. Mandvi, with her critical eye on Urmila, commented in a whisper on how Urmila watched Lakshman like a hawk.

"Urmi, till when will you deny that you are not aware of him?" Mandvi hissed in her ear.

Urmila did not bite the bait, but watched Lakshman from a distance. Her heart began to pound as Sita served Lakshman *malpua*. Conscious of the erratic beat of her heart, she bit her lower lip and looked down at the floor. Suddenly, she felt his intense gaze on her, the gaze she had been trying to avoid throughout the meal. But, now it compelled her to look at him. His eyes touched her softly, tenderly, yet with a piercing look. In that moment, when she looked into his eyes, he made unspoken love to her, inching away her defenses bit by bit.

Lakshman did not let her eyes move away from his. He felt a sense of exhilaration and possessive breathlessness as he watched her blush and then he suddenly broke the eye contact. He looked at the sweetmeats that had now piled up on his plate and began to binge on them.

Urmila felt let down and angry at how he easily he could twirl her heart like a lasso around his little finger with a mere look. Lakshman felt her glaring at him, but was unaffected. Urmila hated his dispassionate nonchalance. After a few minutes, Urmila, who was watching Ram eat with a sobriety beyond his years, began to feel disconcerted. Lakshman was gazing intently at her, challenging her to hold it.

He knew that she had made the pancakes. His eyes said it. The realisation hit like a blow. Urmila lost colour. He had guessed that she had made it for him. Lakshman smirked and Urmila, for the first time, looked away. She was shy.

"The *malpua* is delicious. I loved it. I wish I can carry some with me." Lakshman looked intimately at Urmila; his eyes were speaking much more than his words. A flush spread on her fair cheeks, tinting them scarlet.

The conversation was interrupted by the arrival of Shatanand, the *Raj Guru*, who advised the king on matters of governance. He carried a letter from King Dashrath. Ram and Lakshman were alert. Shatanand began to read the missive:

Greetings Maharaj Janak,

Ayodhya accepts your request humbly. It will be our honour to welcome Sita as our *kulvadhu* – daughter-in-law. Having heard praises about your daughters from our Senapati, especially Urmila, I will love to meet her, too, and watch her famous sword fight. But for now, Bharath and Shatrughan will be in Mithila tomorrow. Guru Vashishtha and I will arrive in a day or two. The queens send their blessings. Best wishes to your family from Ayodhya.

Regards,
Maharaj Dashrath

Ram and Lakshman let out their breath in relief. An overwhelmed Janak embraced Ram. Lakshman came to stand quietly next to Urmila, "Congratulations, *Mirchi!*" he teased her.

"Same to you, *nakchare,*" Urmila was filled with fellow-feeling for Lakshman. She was elated that her sister had been accepted in Raghukul. Sita and Urmila chaperoned the Ayodhya princes to their own quarters for the evening.

Ram stole glances at Sita incessantly and when he could not hold back his excitement any longer, he sought her time, privately. Urmila caught the looks between Ram and Sita and understanding their need to be alone, she shepherded Lakshman away to her palace.

At Lakshman's bemusement as to why Urmila wanted to be alone with him, Urmila was indignant, "They want to be alone so I suggested that you come with me to my palace or else I won't spend any time with you."

Lakshman's smile put off Urmila. Controlling her impulse to wipe the cheeky grin off his face, she stood in front of an ornate mirror to comb her hair.

Lakshman was nervous. He was suddenly all too aware of her femininity. He could not take his eyes away from her long silky hair. The brown lustrous tresses held him under their spell. She yelped in pain as a clump of her hair tangled in the teeth of her comb and tore at her scalp.

In a flash, Lakshman was by her side to help her untangle it. His fingers accidentally brushed against hers as he tried to untwine her hair, "Let me..."

Urmila tried to move away, "I am fine!" She was aware of his presence in the closed space. The intense moment stayed between them and they were powerless to control their desires. Lakshman broke the spell of the moment, "You said you will show me your swords."

"Yes, here they are," she opened the door to a wide hangar-like armoury that displayed her swords. Urmila was quick to get over the physical sensation caused by Lakshman's proximity.

Lakshman stared at the collection. A princess with so many lacquer swords! He traced his fingers over them admiringly and stopped at an empty space between the rows of blades.

At his questioning look, Urmila smiled, "One of the princes of Ayodhya has my favourite sword. I had sent it years ago with Senapati Vijay as a gift from Mithila to Ayodhya."

Lakshman took out the sword from his waistband and handed it to her. A blue ribbon fluttered on the hilt, "I chose it."

Urmila was dumbfounded. She could not believe that he had chosen her sword as his gift from the hamper sent from Mithila. The thought of his hand holding the hilt of her sword with which she had fenced so many times made her stomach flutter with untold anticipation.

"It has been my favourite too. I killed Subahu with our sword," Lakshman's words brought her back to reality.

Urmila felt the sting of tears in her eyes. The word 'our' hung like fragrance in the air. How easily and unknowingly they had been with each other for so many years.

The childlike animosity was suddenly replaced by intense feelings. What was it that they shared? This indefinable completeness they felt in each other's company even when they sparred?

"Shall we go? If *Rakshasi* finds us together, we are doomed." Urmila looked around with a worried expression, but was amazed to hear Lakshman laugh, "Who is *Rakshasi*? I thought Mithila had only one, you!"

Urmila stuck out her tongue at him. This was the first time she had seen him laughing, it made him look vulnerable. She felt her heart squeeze with an inexplicable emotion.

Of the four princes, Lakshman was the quietest. He more or less kept to himself in spite of being the most emotional of them. It was believed that the only person who touched his heart enough to make him laugh was Urmila. And the first time he laughed was also with Urmila.

As Lakshman and Urmila walked back to Sita's chamber laughing together and poking fun at each other in friendly jousts, Urmila looked at him, wondering, *"Is it love we feel?"*

Yes, I Am In Love

Love binds heaven to the earth.

The morning found Mithila content. It could foresee the bliss and the gratification that the princes brought with them. Perhaps, it knew the silent love that stood at the threshold of disclosure, a new beginning for Lakshman and Urmila.

King Janak commanded his subjects to prepare for the arrival of Bharath and Shatrughan. Ram and Lakshman were unable to contain their tears of happiness as they waited in the royal court of Mithila to receive their brothers. Sita and Urmila looked at the play of emotions on their faces and were curious to see the brothers together. They bonded intensely.

Ignoring the presence of the royal family of Mithila, Bharath and Shatrughan rushed to hug Ram and Lakshman upon arriving at Janak's palace. "Did you meet her?" Shatrughan whispered into Lakshman's ears.

Lakshman blushed and looked involuntarily at Urmila. Shatrughan followed his gaze, "So, you have."

Urmila looked from Lakshman to Shatrughan. She sensed that they were speaking about her.

King Janak was drawn to the four brothers instantly. They were so similar to his girls in so many ways. They were still boys, bordering on manhood. The queens loved their spontaneous shows of respect and genuine affection. Without a word, Shatrughan touched Urmila's feet after Sita's, the small gesture did not go unnoticed by anyone, but no one mentioned it. The boys were well-bred and naturally well-mannered. Slow smiles spread on every face in Mithila because the implications of the tributes paid by the Ayodhya princes were clear.

The two illustrious dynasties had forged an alliance and were about deepen it further.

Besides Urmila, the only one person in the royal family whom Shatrughan was drawn to was Shrutakeerti, but he smiled and shrugged off the warm feeling.

Shatrughan though the more expressive of the four brothers was different from Lakshman in his temperament. He perhaps took after his brother only when it came to acknowledging feelings. They were both shy of emotions.

After the introduction, Sita beseeched Lakshman and Urmila to fetch flowers from the garden. Both of them refused to go with each other, "I will not go with him. He irritates me." Urmila's expression showed her 'unwillingness'. "As if I would have agreed to accompany someone who speaks incessantly," Lakshman sniggered.

The war was on again! "What audacity this man has, when he was the one to pick up a conversation with me yesterday," Urmila was furious.

"I was just telling you I do not like spicy food, and moreover food made by you is no less than poison for me," Lakshman said.

"But you like spicy food, only," Shatrughan intervened. Lakshman glared at Shatrughan.

"There you go; he is a liar, too. You should not have eaten the *malpua* I made, then," Urmila said.

Everyone was mute. Bharath and Shatrughan stared at Lakshman open-mouthed. They had never seen their brother misbehave with a woman before. Lakshman and Urmila insulted each other like belligerent children, oblivious to the presence of the members of Ayodhya and Mithila royalties in King Janak's court.

Lakshman suddenly became reticent and looked down, cursing himself. Urmila was in tears and it bothered him. He had hurt her.

The fight ended. Sita was aggrieved at Urmila's behaviour. On their way back to the palace, Urmila made several attempts to speak to Sita, but the latter ignored her. She wallowed in self-pity and in her despair she could not understand how deeply Lakshman was wounded by her self-centredness. He walked beside her in complete silence.

No one understood the light banter between Lakshman and Urmila. What they considered to be a ridiculous fight was actually a way the two connected to each other.

Preoccupied with her thoughts, Urmila tripped on the uneven ground, fell down and injured her foot. She cried out in pain and looked at Sita. Before Sita could help her get up from the ground, Lakshman rushed to pick her up, "There you go again losing your balance. Let me help you up."

"Don't you dare touch me," Urmila hissed in anger. Her foot hurt.

Lakshman's arms fell slackly to his side. "Sorry, but I cannot be more gracious than this." He walked off in annoyance, leaving Urmila to tend to her wounded foot. No one wanted to speak to Urmila after the little scene with Lakshman. She got up, turned around and hobbled into the forest.

Lakshman stopped midway when he heard the princesses shouting after Urmila to stop. "I will find her," he declared despite Sita's assurance that Urmila knew the forest well. He could not let her wander in the forest alone, and he left the entourage quietly.

The woods were not very dense, but full of shadowy corners and deep glens. He called out to her. Urmila did not reply; the silence that greeted his calls was disquieting. Just as he was about to give up his search, he heard the sound of someone munching – the low crunching sound of teeth biting into a solid object. Led by instincts, he went deeper into the forest following the sound. Urmila was sitting on a branch of a guava tree, chewing on a juicy green fruit. Her clothes were muddy but her eyes were sparkling. Lakshman stood, transfixed. She had never looked more beautiful before.

He requested her to return with him, but she ignored his plea. Instead, she challenged him to cross a small pond and sit with her on the tree, if she wanted her to go back with him. Lakshman did not refuse. He swam across the pond and climbed the tree to sit with her on the same branch, "Now it's your turn to fulfil your promise. Let's go."

Urmila looked at his messy clothes, ruffled hair and determined eyes and her heart began to race. She knew she was doomed for life. Taking a deep breath, she offered him a guava, "No *Sumitranandan*, I won't go. No one loves me."

"Everyone loves you. Sita *bhabhi*, Ram *bhaiya* and even I..." he suddenly stopped in mid-sentence. "You?" Urmila caught on to that one word that Lakshman had been avoiding very consciously. "Who would I fight with, tease, if you stay away? Life without you is boring, joyless," Urmila whimpered.

Lakshman suddenly lost his cool. "Enough," he pointed his index finger at her. "Now, you will listen and I will speak. Do we agree on this?" He took charge of the situation. Urmila was intimidated by his intensity and transfixed by the depths in his eyes. But they calmed her in a curious way.

"You are a reflection of your sister. She loves you like her extended self. She scolds you for she wants you to be well-mannered. Don't doubt the love your family has for you. What is not expressed doesn't mean it doesn't exist. They feel lost without you right now. You are their anchor, their strength. I know I was at fault. I used harsh words. But, my intention was not to hurt you. Please consider

my words as a flaw in my character. I don't think before I speak.
I know that you made the *malpua* and trust me, it is the best dish I
have ever eaten in my life," Lakshman admitted, blushing.

"But no one thanked me or praised me or even came to look
for me," Urmila was desolate. Tears streamed down her cheeks.
Lakshman held her hand lightly, "They did not because they
believe in you. I came after you." And he smiled.

"You consider me a fool," she sobbed.

"No, I don't. I think of you are a child, too naive and innocent;
pure and kind. You are on the outside what you are on the inside.
Serene, pure and honest," Lakshman said with tenderness.

"I am sorry for my misbehaviour. You are not that bad," she
pouted looking like an insecure child. Lakshman merely smiled.
He took her hand to help her down the tree. Urmila's heart danced
with joy.

They walked out of the forest as friends.

As they moved towards the Ganesh temple through a secret
path led by Urmila, Lakshman probed her heart. "What do you
think of marriage?"

Urmila was puzzled, "I don't think I want to get married ever.
I am a warrior. Well, what are your thoughts about it?"

Lakshman was quiet for a moment and then smiled, "Marriage
will distract me from serving my elder brother. It may mean making
my wife a priority and for me, my brother Ram is the sole reason of
my existence. So I don't think I will marry."

"But if your companion understands you, allows you to do
your duty and loves you enough to be with you despite your call of
duty, then?" Urmila was curious.

"What if it was you? Would you do that for me?" He needed
an answer.

Urmila was silent. She could not look him in the eye. She could
not confess her love for Lakshman, even to herself.

"No, why would I be interested? I don't want to risk my life
by marrying a man who wears anger like a badge on the tip of his
nose," she jested to take the seriousness out of their conversation.

She sensed his withdrawal like a yawning space between them. She had hurt him. Her mind ticked. Did this imply that she meant something more to him? She yearned to know but was scared of being spurned. Suppose he turned down her love?

The path meandered by a lotus pool near the temple. A single blue lotus bloomed in the middle of the pool. Urmila stopped to look at it. She wanted to pluck it and she waded into the pool to pick the flower. Suddenly, a giant serpent which was coiled among the lotus leaves sprung at her to swallow her. She was petrified.

"Save me, *Sumitranandan*," Urmila screamed, closing her eyes in fear. When she opened her eyes, the snake was nowhere around. Lakshman was shooting arrows at the retreating monster, which was at the far end of the pond. No sooner did the snake see Lakshman than it realised that the king of the Naaga, Lord Shesha, stood before it. The snake bowed to Lakshman and slid away.

Lakshman plucked the blue lotus and gave it to Urmila, "Are you fine?" He was so close that she could almost hear his heartbeats.

"Thank you for saving my life," she whispered against his chest.

"I saved mine," he murmured holding her hands in his. They realised at that moment that they loved each other. A collective sigh of relief greeted the two when they arrived at the temple. The *puja* could not be conducted without them. Urmila hugged Sita and apologised. Lakshman was teased by his brothers mercilessly.

The moments they spent with each other travelled back with them. They felt incomplete without each other.

The family was shocked when Urmila told them how Lakshman saved her from the snake. King Janak and Queen Sunaina expressed their gratitude, thanking Lakshman for risking his life for their daughter.

"I am like your son, *Maa*. It is my *dharma* to save her life," the prince replied, stealing a glance at Urmila.

Mithila bowed to the humility of Ayodhya's Rajkumar, once again.

The sanctum was ready for the rite. A posse of seers – Maharishi Yagnavalkya, Maitreyi, Katyayani, Gargi and Shatanand – sat in a circle around the hearth facing the deity. Katyayani wanted Lakshman and Urmila to light the earthenware lamps in the four corners of the temple, according to Mithila's tradition.

According to wedding rituals in Mithila, unmarried siblings of the bride and groom lit earthenware lamps in the four corners of the Gauri temple. This ensured that the siblings marry well.

The shrine was opulent and Lakshman felt the potent power of the resplendent deity. He lit the lamps with Urmila and placed them in the four corners of the temple. Urmila was unable to take her eyes off Lakshman as they arranged the lamps inside the temple. She was so lost in him that she did not realise that her *chunariya* – drape covering her torso – had caught fire.

"Milaaa..." The terror in Lakshman's voice brought her out of her daydream.

"Why don't you ever heed dangers? Will it be too much to ask you not to be so careless? Had I not been with you, what would have happened then?" Lakshman was frantic; his eyes shone with tears. He pulled out his *angavastra* – body cloth – to cover her bare torso. Urmila knew that she would not ever be able to love another the way she loved Lakshman.

The instant changed her forever. "I am safe as long as you are with me," she confessed quietly. He tried to propel her outside the temple, gently. Urmila resisted. She wanted to tell the deity about her love for Lakshman and seek her blessings. She told him to wait outside; she had to be alone with the goddess.

"Mother, I hide nothing from you. You know my heart's desire. I am in love with him. If my love for Saumitra be true, pure like your love for Mahadeva then, *O, Param Tapasvini Maha* Gauri, bless me so that I get Saumitra as my husband," she sobbed at the altar of the goddess, pouring out her heart to the deity.

The goddess smiled and dropped her garland on Urmila. "May all your wishes come true. My blessings are always with you, my dear daughter. Narad Muni's words will not fail. May you be blessed with the man you truly desire," Gauri blessed her.

Dev Rishi Narad's words held wisdom and always came true. It was Narad Muni who had said that if one's feelings for the other were pure and true, then, despite the obstacles on their way, lovers united in the end.

Urmila wanted to stay back in the temple but she did not want to keep Lakshman waiting for her outside.

The woman that came out of the temple was different. She was replete with her love for Lakshman and she acknowledged her desire for him. Before Lakshman could find out why she was smiling, they were interrupted by Bharath and Shatrughan. The brothers were curious to know what happened to Urmila in the temple.

King Janak and Queen Sunaina invited the four princes to dinner, primarily out of gratitude. When they arrived in the evening, each prince nursed a secret wish deep in his heart. They looked unruffled but their calm disposition masked deep agitation.

Maharani Sunaina told the princesses to serve dinner. Urmila's eyes were riveted on Lakshman, who returned her gaze with an equal intensity. They were oblivious to the presence of others. The two had to tear their eyes away from each other when a maid came with a message for Urmila. "The children are waiting for the princess in the royal garden. They have come for their painting lessons, princess," the maid announced.

Taking leave of the guests, Urmila left for the royal garden. Lakshman was taken aback because he did not know that Urmila painted as well.

"She is an excellent artist," Shrutakeerti said.

"My sword princess is a painter too!" Lakshman replied to Shrutakeerti in a low voice. He wanted to see her teach art to the children. Opportunity arrived when Ram and Janak became engrossed in a discussion about matters relating to governance. Lakshman sought permission to explore the palace. He walked out of the banquet hall and ran to the garden to watch Urmila instruct children in the nuances of fine artistry.

Urmila could not speak to him in the presence of the children. She continued to paint. The portrait that stared back at her from the parchment canvas was that of Lakshman.

Was there anything else that she thought about ever since she met him?

"Who is it you are painting?" Lakshman's voice was like a breath of warm air on her neck. She was startled to find him peering at the portrait.

Her brush stopped in mid-air and her eyes closed involuntarily as his hands wove their magic on hers. She tried to evade his touch, "Why are you here, *Sumitranandan?*"

Urmila and Lakshman were powerless to fight their feelings for each other.

Lakshman held her wrist tightly yet gently, refusing to let go. Urmila pleaded with him but he claimed possessively, "What you ask for is mine." Urmila turned red. "Promise to meet me later, Mila," Lakshman exhorted. His voice was rough with the expectation of the 'delightful forbidden'.

"Tomorrow, I shall," she replied and ran back to the palace, laughing silently to herself.

All the way, the endearment 'Mila' haunted her like the echo of a heavenly melody inside her head. Such a beautiful name! She could not think of anyone else calling her by that name.

'Mila'! She sighed. "I shall never feel like Urmila again."

Only the mirror, her bed, her enhanced heartbeats and the hint of tears on her eyelashes witnessed the overwhelming power of her love at that moment in a mute testimony.

As the brothers returned to the hermitage, Bharath and Shatrughan decided not to let Lakshman off the hook that night; they had to know the deepest secrets of his heart. He had to be 'inquistioned'. It was their prerogative and Lakshman had to 'surrender' – such battles of nerves were not uncommon among the brothers.

Bharath cleared his throat. The sound cut through Lakshman's wayward thoughts. He was distracted; his mind was far away floating with Urmila in a wonderland of blue lotuses, his conversations with her spooling in his head like a thousand blooms. Lakshman winced as his brothers dragged him down to earth – to the reality on the ground.

"Do not terrify him, brother. Someone else has entered his life now and has taken on the responsibility of scaring him," Shatrughan shot a snide glance at Bharath. They both burst out laughing at the indignant expression on Lakshman's face.

"Stop it. You both are enjoying at my expense," Lakshman hit back, hurt.

"Okay, we won't tease you any more." Bharath was the first to relent, even though he did not pass up any opportunity to make fun of Lakshman.

"But tell us what did Rajkumari Urmila paint?" Shatrughan was curious. Lakshman flushed, "My portrait. As beautiful as her."

"Will Ram *bhaiya* help you bring your secret love for Urmila to its fairytale ending?" Shatrughan threw him the final straw.

"No!" Lakshman was uncomfortable. He did not want Ram to know of his love for Urmila. The thought subdued him. "It's time we slept. Let me be. Concentrate on your Shrutakeerti," Lakshman faked a yawn.

The night was long. It watched the princes toss and turn on their mats, waiting for the sunrise so that they could meet their beaus. The agony of missing each other was lethal to their peace.

The Unique Proposal

An offer, a white blossom and the coming of age.

And I want to be the one you walk with in the sun, and the one you search for when your world gets dark. Love begins unannounced but when it progresses, the entire world hears its knock.

Urmila was on her way to Lakshman's cottage at Maharishi Yagnavalkya's *ashram* with a platter of food cooked especially for him, when Gargi Vachaknavi stopped her. She noticed the

serene glow on Urmila's face and knew that she had met the man
of her dreams.

"My daughter is a changed princess. I sensed your destiny was
Lakshman since the day I saw him," she said tenderly, placing her
hand on Urmila's head.

Gargi's gentleness and maternal love touched Urmila. With
tears in her eyes, Urmila held Gargi's hand, *"Maa*, he completes me.
Just like Lakshmi needs Narayan, Shakti needs Shiva, and Ksheera
needs Shesha, in the same way your Urmila needs Saumitra." Gargi
smiled, "You both are made for each other. He will love the food
you have cooked for him. Go, he must be waiting for you."

Urmila believed in Maata Gargi more than she believed in her own mother.
She knew she was on the right path when she had Gargi's approval and blessings.

Watching Urmila from a distance coming towards the cottage,
Shatrughan excused himself on the pretext of running an errand.
He wanted Lakshman to be alone with Urmila.

The awareness between the two was pure chemistry. They
avoided looking at each other inside the cramped room.

"I keep my promise," she said shyly handing him the food.

"Have you cooked it?" he asked softly thinking how innocent
she looked in her blue swirling skirt.

She nodded in silence. He crossed the distance between them
in two large strides, "I had been waiting since morning. Mila, I…,"
he stopped, hearing the footsteps of his brothers.

Ram and Bharath looked at Urmila, surprised. "I cooked
lunch for all of you," she gushed and ran out of the cottage to her
palace without pausing for breath.

Urmila sought refuge in the confines of her chamber, fighting
a new flood of emotions. She slumped on the bed wondering
what Ram and Bharath thought about her, remembering the
frustrated look on Lakshman's face when his brothers walked in
unannounced. She must have embarrassed him.

She was still smiling to herself recalling Lakshman's
embarrassment, when her best friends Chandrarashi and
Malvika, the princesses of Kanyakubja, rushed to her palace

to chat. The conversation soon drifted to Ram and Lakshman. Urmila's friends were quick to note her unusual reluctance to discuss Lakshman.

"Are you in love with prince Lakshman?" Chandrarashi was direct in her query. Urmila feigned disbelief but her friends were no fools. They could see through her facade of 'indignation'.

Irked, Urmila sat cross-legged on her bed. "There is nothing special between us, Chanda. I am the Warrior Princess of Mithila and love is not meant for me. The same applies to him. The goal of his life is to serve his brother Ram. You both are way out of line."

Both Chandrarashi and Malvika looked at the portrait that leant against the wall in a corner of the room.

"We know you since childhood. You cannot fool us. You paint only what you love. Why did you paint a portrait of Lakshman?" They picked up the portrait. Urmila was quiet. Her face changed colour as she looked at the portrait of the smiling prince. "Tell us how much you love him, Urmi," Malvika insisted.

What Urmila did not dare tell her friends was how scared she was. The mere thought of Lakshman rejecting her love and laughing at her vulnerability filled her with dread. But before she could reply, Maharani Sunaina entered Urmila's chamber.

"Maharaj Dashrath is due to reach Mithila any moment now. Your father awaits your presence by his side, get ready to welcome him," her mother commanded.

***

Maharaj Janak stood up to welcome King Dashrath and honour him – the mighty ruler of Raghukul was his benefactor in battle and a strategic ally as well. The king of Ayodhya was escorted into the court by his sons. Janak's daughters stood by him. After blessing Sita, Dashrath beckoned Urmila to him.

"I wanted to meet you ever since I heard about your sword-fighting skills, my dear daughter," he said with a smile. Urmila bowed to him.

"I stand small in front of your majesty. O, illustrious king. I am lucky to be blessed by you."

Watching Maharaj Dashrath's affection for Urmila and her warm response, Shatrughan nudged Lakshman, "Your path to fulfilling your heart's desire has become easy, brother. Father is besotted with princess Urmila. You can now tell her how much you love her."

"I only wish to serve our older brother, Shatrughan. I will not let anything detract from my duty," Lakshman was firm in his denial of love for Urmila.

Shatrughan looked at him sullenly, "Brother, you cannot hide yourself from me. Being your twin, I feel the love you hold for her within. You both are too similar. Your anger daunts all except her. She respects all your relatives and she knows how to make them happy. Before you turn your back on your feelings, find a way to survive without your *mirchi* in Ayodhya. She has changed you."

Lakshman stood quietly, torn between his feelings for Urmila and his duty towards Ram. His stillness touched Urmila, shattering her carefully-crafted calm. She was watching him from where she stood next to King Dashrath and she instinctively knew that something was troubling him; she could feel his confusion.

Janak, in a retinue, guided Dashrath to Maharishi Yagnavalkya's *ashram* and directed Urmila to make arrangements for an elaborate dinner. It was a tall order given the paucity of time, but Urmila was known to pull off stunts in the kitchen. She was a natural organiser.

On her way to the retreat with dinner for the royals from Ayodhya, all she could think of was Lakshman. She scanned the cottage for him but he was nowhere to be found.

She laid out the meal, inviting everyone to eat. The entourage from Ayodhya sat in a row with Maharishi Yagnavalkya, who was effervescent in his praise for Urmila, "King Dashrath, the beautiful paintings you see here have been made by her. Princess Urmila is not only a great warrior, but also a talented artist and a debater; she has defeated me several times."

"Maharaj Janak is blessed to have you as a daughter. I wish my queens were here to meet you." Urmila had made a profound impression on King Dashrath with her multi-tasking persona. She was an all-rounder.

"I wish I could, too, especially *Maata* Sumitra. My admiration for her runs deep." Shatrughan winked, pulling her leg.

"What about her sons, Rajkumari?"

Urmila laughed. "Shatrughan, you are just like my younger brother." Smirking, Shatrughan was at it again, "And *bhaiya?*"

She blushed. "Saumitra is a great swordsman and more than that, he is a nice human being too. He saved my life several times."

The moment Urmila uttered the words, Dashrath came to a decision. He found in Urmila an ideal consort for Lakshman. His decision was in consonance with a cosmic pledge, made long ago.

Urmila could not help but ask, "Maharaj, where is *Sumitranandan?*"

Shatrughan was quick to interrupt. He wanted Urmila to know about Lakshman's secret mission, "Father, Lakshman *bhaiya* has gone to the Gauri temple. He wanted to spend some time alone with the deity." Dashrath was concerned, "But why? Is he okay?"

Shatrughan calmed him. "He is."

Urmila reassured Dashrath with a smile. "Don't worry, Maharaj, I will find out. I was going there to invite the women for tomorrow's *puja*."

Dashrath was relieved. "I am happy as long as you are there, daughter," the king said.

"Then, Maharaj, obey your daughter's orders and eat in peace." Everyone present at the *ashram* burst out laughing.

"This is how Urmila wins hearts. She is truly a gem. Maharaj Janak's wait has been worthwhile. First, he bagged an obedient and virtuous daughter like Sita and then our Warrior Princess, Urmila," Gargi observed in mock jealousy.

Matreyi laughed, "Gargi, you are wrong. She is our prince as she claims."

Urmila did not want to be the focus of their banter. She ran to the Gauri temple, leaving behind a growing bonhomie between the two great kingdoms and their patron seers.

Simultaneously, Dashrath sought Vashishtha's blessings before he sent Shatrughan with word to ask Maharaj Janak to meet him urgently. Janak, who left early to attend to an evening audience in the court, returned in a hurry. On his arrival, Dashrath suggested that Urmila should become a member of the Ayodhya royal household as a daughter-in-law.

"O, father of great daughters, your daughter Urmila is born with excellent qualities. The clan into which she marries will be blessed to have her as their *kulvadhu*. Maharaj, I want you to bless my clan by giving your daughter's hands in marriage to my dear son Lakshman. I wanted her to be my Lakshman's wife ever since I heard of her," Dashrath said, offering Janak yet another alliance.

Maharaj Janak and Maharani Sunaina burst into tears of joy, "We are blessed. There is no one more worthy than Lakshman to claim Urmila. From today, both my daughters belong to Ayodhya."

Ayodhya and Mithila rejoiced at this exchange of commitment and alliance between their kings.

Away from the hectic match-making in Maharishi Yagnavalkya's retreat, Lakshman sat on the stairs of the Gauri temple thinking about Urmila. The sun had set into a cobalt blue twilight. He was caught in a tussle between his natural restraint, commitment to his older sibling and his surge of love for Urmila. Immersed in his own train of thoughts, he did not notice Urmila come to sit next to him quietly.

"*Sumitranandan!*" she called out to him in a soft voice. He looked at her in shock, "Mila, what brings you here at this hour in the evening?"

"I want to tell you something." She was hesitant.

"What?" He was scared to hear what she wanted to say. But he firmly clasped her trembling hands in his when she held them out.

"Not here, let's go to the *Pushp Vatika*," Urmila said.

"Today, the Urmila who stands before you is a princess without the armour of her cruel words. And it is you, who broke it with your chivalry and silent care. I don't know when, how and why you found a place in my heart, *Sumitranandan*, but I know that I belong to you. I love you," Urmila admitted her love with a shy reserve.

Lakshman put his hand under her chin and lifted her face to him, "I have loved you ever since I held your sword in my hand. In spite of that I cannot ask you to be a part of my life." Lakshman's intense love and despair showed in his quivering voice.

But his words diluted the depth of the moment, Lakshman could not commit himself. His confession of love tripped on the stumbling block of his *dharma* – his duty towards his clan. Urmila looked at him, desolate and listless. He gave her the world in a moment and took it away in the very next. The heavens trembled in a brief infinitesimal moment of fear. If that what had been ordained by the gods was undone on earth? "Mila, I am a torn man. I cannot marry," Lakshman wiped her tears with unsteady hands.

As she cringed at his touch, he held her forcibly, "You don't understand. My mother is an ordinary princess of Kashi, who married into the great kingdom of Ayodhya. If you marry me, you may regret your decision for I will not be able to give what you deserve."

"My love stands unchanged for you even on a bed of thorns," Urmila was unshakeable. "My life is life only with you." Urmila could not think of life without Saumitra.

For the first time, Urmila revealed her strength to Lakshman and he looked at her for a long time. How would he be able to live without this fierce yet gentle princess? He knew in that very moment that he could fight the world, fight for her, but could not fight her. He had lost the war he had been preparing himself for.

Lakshman saw hope in Urmila's eyes, remembered her confession of love, her unflinching support for his *dharma* and gradually mustered courage, "Let me hold your hand not to lead you or hurt you but to love and protect you. Will you be my companion for life, Mila? I want to live with you even in the days when we are not together."

Urmila was silent. She had no words. Tears flowed down her cheeks like a deluge and she hugged Lakshman as if she would never let him go. They cried and laughed at the same time. The completeness of their love enveloped them like a warm shroud and they basked in its secure tenderness.

Finding a nook between his shoulders and neck, she lay with him under the moonlit sky, quivering with emotions. He shielded her with his arms, "Your sword has been my undoing. It has brought me to you. I fell for an unseen princess years ago when I touched her sword. Do you know it was my Shanta *didi* who gave me hope that someday we shall meet? She said that when people are destined to be together, fate pulls them to each other."

Lakshman narrated Shanta's story to Urmila.

"I want to meet her. After having heard so much about her sacrifice, I know she must be a strong woman." Urmila snuggled closer. "Yes, she is. I will introduce you to another strong woman in my life, my Vindhya," Lakshman said fondly.

Urmila felt an intense pang of jealousy at Lakshman referring to another strong woman in his life. She was tense. Lakshman looked at her quizzically. She turned away dejected, "Do you have someone else in your life?" He burst into laughter, "Mila, you are jealous if I am not mistaken."

She feigned aloofness, "Jealousy and me, never! By the way, who is she?" He pulled her cheeks, "God! Mila, you look so cute when you get jealous. Yes, Vindhya is a very important part of my life. She is Shanta *didi's* daughter, my niece. She is just a few years younger than us."

Urmila sighed in relief, "You are monstrous." He winked, "Yes, I am, but you know what, Vindhya wanted to meet you ever since she learnt to fence with your sword."

"Oh!" she exclaimed. "I would love to meet your Vindhya," she laughed, relieved. "It's time you went back. The family is waiting for you to return for dinner. I have to leave too," Urmila disengaged from his embrace. "I yearn to feel you closer, still," he kissed her eyelids, pulling her close. "And I can kill the one who brings tears to your eyes. Your eyes are the birthplace of my love. I felt my own heartbeats in them the first time only when I set my eyes on you."

They stood there for moments which felt like an eternity, feeling each other's erratic heartbeats. A film of wetness on her cheeks made her look up. Lakshman did not hide the tears trickling down his cheeks, "Mila, the thought of leaving you even for a moment kills me."

Urmila stood on her toes and kissed his tears, "I am always with you, within you, never apart but we have duties that we have to attend to and we will have to leave."

Reluctantly, they went their way.

Urmila reached the palace just in time for the braid ceremony. The womenfolk in the palace were preparing to tie Sita's hair in the three-strand braid symbolising the divine union – the bride, the groom and god. On seeing Urmila, Sunaina and Chandrabhaga forced her to sit at the dresser to braid her hair in three delicate strands – and teach her how to twist the tresses into tasslelike braids.

"It is Sita who is getting married, not me!" Urmila was confused.

An ancient ritual, it was believed that women of the family taught the bride how to tie her hair just before her marriage. It was known as the braid rite. It was believed that a girl was taught how to tie her hair and was allowed to let it down only when she was alone with her husband, after her marriage.

"No *didi*, you will wed too along with Janaki," Shrutakeerti bounced with excitement. Urmila was numb with fear, "I will not marry."

"Not even him?" Maharani Sunaina removed the red cloth from a large painting. Tears of relief flowed from Urmila's eyes as she looked at the familiar face that stared back at her. It was Saumitra.

Her mother told her about the conversation between the kings concerning her marriage and looked at Urmila for an affirmation.

Urmila nodded her head, blushed and ran to her chamber. Her sisters followed close behind.

Sita enfolded Urmila in a tender hug, "I could always see him in your eyes." Urmila held on to her sister, "I have never known a yearning as deep as I feel for him."

Sita looked at her ponderingly for a few moments, "You are getting married to the man you love and you are still crying?"

"These are tears of happiness. I still cannot believe I am to marry him." Urmila hugged her sister tighter. "*Didi*, Sumitranandan is unique. He is the best. I could not ever imagine I would fall in love. Marriage was not my priority ever. But he made it possible. He has made me someone else."

For a change, Mandvi embraced both her sisters forming a sibling circle. "Prince Lakshman is a perfect match for my *Rakshasi*," she said with a skewed smile.

"You forget me," Shrutakeerti said, putting her arms around them. "Even I knew. Someone told me."

"And don't we all know who that someone is?" The sisters teased Shrutakeerti about Shatrughan, celebrating Urmila's bliss.

***

Lakshman entered his cottage quietly. He had never known such happiness and contentment. He was taken aback to see his father waiting for him, "I am sorry to disappear without informing anyone, father."

Maharaj Dashrath came up to him, "Lakshman, my son. Did you meet daughter Urmila? I sent her to check on you. Are you fine?"

Lakshman embraced Maharaj Dashrath, "Yes, father, I met her and I am fine." The king of Ayodhya gently led his sons to dinner after which they retired to their respective cottages.

Back in the cottage, Shatrughan wanted to know what happened between his brother and Urmila, "*Bhaiya*, did you reveal your feelings to princess Urmila?"

"Yes." Shatrughan jumped in excitement, "Princess Urmila will be my sister-in-law. And I will be her favourite brother-in-law."

"Keep your excitement in check. We have not broken the news to brother Ram and father." Lakshman admonished Shatrughan.

"Your father knows everything! And, he has decided that you will marry her. The match has been fixed," a rejoinder came from the door. Dashrath stood at the threshold of their cottage, smiling, "I am your father, son. Daughter Urmila is the perfect match for you," he said. Lakshman stared at his father in disbelief, unable to reply. Dashrath had fulfilled his duty both as a father and as a king. He walked back to his cottage.

Shatrughan looked at Lakshman with tears of happiness. *Destiny wanted to see you thrive and fulfilled,* he blessed Lakshman in silence.

As Ayodhya's royal family celebrated the alliances, the night looked down at them with benediction and prayers that all may turn out well in their life as they expected.

The Four Weddings

Weddings seal karmic prophesies in the mosaic of destinies.

Mithila was the stage where the play was about to begin, the gods smiled in heaven waiting for the curtain to go up on the divine script.

The guests trickled in since early morning. Mithila was redolent with the colours of happiness and the fragrance of revelry.

The kingdom was decorated with marigold wreaths and at night – earthenware lamps twinkled in every home. Flaming torches lit the street corners. The emblem flags of the kingdom fluttered 'red and blue' in every terrace and garden. The homes had been given face-lifts in the traditions of Madhuvan – intricately painted with motifs from folklore, Vedic scriptures and the religious pantheon.

The Terai hills, bordered by gushing rivers, loomed fresh and green in the distance.

Shanta was in Mithila for the wedding. It was a rare visit. Everyone in the family first bowed their heads in reverence to Shanta and then hugged her. She was the living symbol of 'sacrifice' in the clan.

A sister's love is an extended part of a mother's selfless devotion. Shanta had compromised with her desires for her father's wish to be blessed with male heirs. Her brothers took extreme pride in their sister.

The princes were delirious with joy because weddings were the time to bond, reveal innermost secrets, bare their deepest desires, celebrate and rib each other round-the-clock like any other close-knit happy family.

Shatrughan looked at Shanta and winked at her, "Brother had you not found our sister-in-law, you would have been married to princess Sunadri according to father's wish."

Lakshman was in no mood for such gimmicks. The very thought of his childhood friend in Urmila's place made him shudder in fear.

Soon after Shanta's arrival, the royal family of Ayodhya set out for the *Rajya Sabha* – the court. The wedding date had to be fixed.

As Shanta met the brides-to-be and blessed them tearfully, her eyes lingered on Urmila. She knew how emotionally fragile and yet egoistic her younger brother Lakshman was. Not any ordinary woman would suffice for him because he was special.

Urmila touched her feet, remembering Lakshman's deep spiritual connection with his sister and his niece Vindhya, "I don't see Vindhya with you, *didi*." Shanta looked at Urmila in surprise and yet in gratitude that Lakshman had told her about Vindhya.

"Vindhya is in Dhanvan Rajya at her friend Princess Subramaniya's place. Since she had already left by the time the alliances were fixed, she could not accompany me to your wedding but I will most certainly bring her to Ayodhya, once she returns." Shanta smiled at Urmila's affection for Vindhya – any misgivings that Shanta had about Vindhya's acceptance in Lakshman and Urmila's lives after the wedding faded.

A hush came down on the *Rajya Sabha*.

The time to match the horoscopes had set in; an auspicious hour to fix the wedding dates. Maharishi Yagnavalkya and Gurudev Vashishtha picked up the parchment scrolls to scan the birth charts of the princes and the princesses minutely to decide on an appropriate date for the weddings.

"Maharaj, one aspect which is a cause for concern in Ram and Sita's horoscopes is the complete match of their 36 zodiac characteristics. It foretells of extremities. Their marriage will either be exceptionally happy or end in struggle and loss," Gurudev announced pensively. "Whereas Lakshman and Urmila will enjoy a happier married life because of their 35 matching characteristics."

Fine lines of tension appeared on Maharani Sunaina's face. She dared not think ahead.

"When the very next moment is unpredictable in life, how can their lives after the weddings be prophesied?" Shanta rejected the oracles, refusing to acknowledge the uncertainties. Janak agreed with Shanta and requested Vashishtha to select a date irrespective of the 'predictions'.

"In that case, the most auspicious day for the weddings is the fifth day of *Shukla Paksha* – full moon. Mithila can proceed with the preparations," Maharishi Yagnavalkya proclaimed.

With the announcement of the dates, cries of jubilations rent the court. But Maharaj Dashrath not very comfortable, the words of warning rankled in his head. He sought Gurudev Vashishtha and Bramharishi Vishwamitra's advice once again with Shanta's reassurance. After a brief discussion with them, he smiled and walked to Maharaj Janak, who was sitting with a worried look on his face.

"Maharaj, Ayodhya will be grateful if your younger brother Maharaj Kushadhwaja's daughters Mandvi and Shrutakeerti marry my sons Bharath and Shatrughan respectively, together with Sita and Urmila," Dashrath proposed.

"We stand beholden with your decision. We are blessed that our daughters will remain together," Janak replied, accepting the offer.

"Prepare Ayodhya for the arrival of four *kulvadhu*s," Dashrath ordered his men.

Janak's happiness was also underlined with sadness. "We will not linger on the rituals of parting – *bidaai*," the king of Mithila said, his gratitude shining through the curtain of tears in his eyes.

Mandvi was quiet after the alliances were finalised and dates fixed. She left the court quietly. Chandrabhaga rushed after her without anyone noticing. Mandvi had initially refused to marry Bharath but now Chandrabhaga had to convince her to marry Bharath. Mandvi had put down her own conditions to the 'alliance'.

It was believed that Chandrabhaga had been told that Maharaj Dashrath had given his word to Rani Kaikeyi that her son would become the king of Ayodhya. She thus convinced Mandvi to marry Bharath. An astute Mandvi agreed only after she was guaranteed that Bharath would become the king of Ayodhya.

Ram looked at the joy on Lakshman's face with tears in his eyes. He ruffled his brother's hair and said, "Urmila is ideal for my brother. I can sense it from the peace in his eyes. They are calm."

Lakshman clung to Ram like a child, "I shall forever be your little Lakshman."

Shanta watched the exchange with rush of affection. Sibling bondings made her wistful; she went back to her childhood hunting for the 'fraternity' she had lost out on, the years when she could have basked in the love of her brothers.

The rituals began in Mithila. The first among many was the *Diya Milan*. Katyayani, a Vedic priestess, explained its significance to the couples before they performed it.

Hindu weddings have been marked by significant rituals since ancient times. Diya Milan is an important ritual in which the bride and the groom light an earthenware lamp and place it in the water to understand the drift of their marital life.

With all the four princesses set to marry on the same day, Mithila looked to Chandrarashi and Malavika to perform the duty of the *vidhikari* – official bridesmaids – appointed to oversee the rituals.

The next and the most awaited ritual was the *mehendi* – henna ceremony. Urmila requested Sunaina that she should be allowed to apply the red henna paste on one of Sita's hands as Sita was a mother figure to her.

Sunaina felt the sting of tears. "I won't be there with you both in Ayodhya. Promise me that you will take care of each other and will not let your parents down."

"I will have it no other way, *Maa*," Sita held her mother close to her. "Urmi, will you please put *mehendi* on one of my palms, too. My happiness will not be complete without your touch." Urmila picked up the henna stick, dipped it in the paste and began to draw on one of Sita's palms and then on the wrists – an exquisite mandala with the sun and the moon facing each other in the centre.

Queen Sunaina etched floral motifs on Urmila's hands and then on one of Sita's hands. The three were nostalgic, sharing an intimate symbol of womanhood; a vital bonding between the mother and the daughters bridging the generations and histories of individual lives.

Shanta, on the other hand, drew intricate designs with the henna paste on her brothers' palms and wrists. Lakshman was irritated. He was allergic to the earthy scent of henna and he wanted to sneeze. Shanta laughed. Lakshman was still as innocent as a child.

"The princesses are to leave their home and parents for you, so promise me you will keep them fulfilled emotionally," Shanta was earnest in her request; she was not sure whether the boys were aware of the responsibilities that weddings brought in their trails.

"We will, *didi*." The brothers were unanimous in their reply.

The next on the roster of rites was the *haldi* ceremony.

Haldi or the turmeric-anointing ceremony is an important Hindu pre-wedding ritual. A mixture of turmeric, sandalwood powder and rose water is first smeared on the bridegroom's body and then a portion of the same mixture is taken from the groom's body and anointed on the bride's.

While the ceremonies were underway, a maid ushered Maharani Sunaina away. The royal astrologer was waiting for her in her palace. Sunaina had summoned the astrologer because the marital predictions made by Vashishtha had unsettled her. Sunaina looked at the soothsayer, worried, as he pored over the horoscopes.

"Your older daughter will spend her life in a forest after 12 happy years of marriage and the younger one will be separated from her husband for 14 years after 12 years of happy married life." Sunaina was dumbstruck. She could not believe the cruelty of their fates. She sought the astrologer's advice on whether the weddings should be stopped, but he advised her to go ahead with the alliances because the unions were destined.

Finally, the day of the wedding arrived. Mithila was dressed like a bride, awaiting the groom's procession from Ayodhya.

The grooms' cavalcades arrived in the evening when the sun was low on the distant hills. A golden glow bathed Janakpuri – the capital cluster of Mithila's royalty.

They were welcomed by the womenfolk of the palace and the guru-mothers of Mithila. After the tying of the *raksha dhaaga* – the scared red and yellow protection threads – a pre-wedding ritual, the Ayodhya princes stood up on their respective chariots. They were dressed in wedding finery with their swords strapped to their waists.

The procession of chariots rolled to the palace in a blaze of lights, revellers carried flaming torches and drummers beat the rhythms of 'divine' ecstasy. The princes had come to take home their brides. People from faraway lands, who had gathered in Mithila for the wedding, hailed Raghukul as the processions passed by.

The veiled princesses, dressed in red and gold wedding skirts, richly-embroidered drapes and heavy gold jewellery, waited in their quarters.

Maharani Sunaina and Chandrabhaga, accompanied by two women, Uma and Malini (hailed as Goddesses Parvati and Saraswati), tied the *raksha dhaaga* on the wrist of each of the princesses. Uma and Mailini blessed the royal brides for happy new lives ahead as they tied the threads.

The *baraat* – groom's retinue – waited at the gates of the Mithila palace to be invited inside after an *aarti* – a welcoming oblation with incense, lamps, flowers and vermillion paste. Maharani Sunaina and Chandrabhaga performed the *aarti*. King Janak looked at his daughters with wistfulness as he escorted them to the wedding marquee decorated with flowers and earthenware lamps. This was the last time Janak and Sunaina would call their daughters 'their own'. After the *kanyadaan* – giving away of the girl – they would stand empty-handed.

Tears flowed unchecked in the churning of emotions.

Janak put his hands on Sita and Urmila's heads and blessed them when they bowed to touch his feet. How would the girls ever pay back their parents for the love they had showered upon them? Sita and Urmila bore debts of their 'lifetimes' to their parents.

Slowly, with a heavy heart but with a graceful bent, Janak, Sunaina, Kushadhwaj and Chandrabhaga took their daughters to the grooms.

Lakshman was unable to take his eyes off Urmila. She looked out of this world, almost like a nymph from heaven in her bridal finery. Her black hair flecked brown with *henna* was tied into a bejewelled knot to highlight her sharp features. Of average height and on the leaner side, Urmila was perfect for his tall build.

Urmila looked up. Her face flushed scarlet as she locked her gaze with his. She wished she could tousle his wavy hair further and kiss the sharp bent of his crooked nose. He looked magnificent, tall and handsome!

She would never forget the look of disbelief and at the same time, the expression of peace on his face. Her hands that held the wedding garland trembled with fear. A trickle of sweat ran down her ears, tickling her lobes.

With a bit of playfulness, somberness and love at the beginning of the garlanding ceremony, Gurudev Vashishtha requested the parents of the brides to perform the *Var Puja* – invocation of the groom.

The ritual demanded the legs of the grooms to be placed on a tray of gold and washed with holy water from the River Ganges and milk in a symbol of purification.

Sunaina wiped their feet with a cloth and handed them gold coins as 'purification' gifts.

Maharaj Janak was heartbroken, "How do I give my daughters away like this? I do not have the courage." Sunaina held his hands firmly. "We have to."

Both of them gave away Sita to Ram and then Urmila to Lakshman. Janak placed Urmila's right hand on Lakshman's and put a piece of red cloth, betel leaves, betel nuts and flowers on them.

"I SeerdhwaJanak, king of Mithila, give away my heartbeat, my Warrior Princess to Raghukul Tilak, *Sumitranandan* Lakshman." A tear fell from his right eye.

Lakshman held his hands gently. "Father, your Warrior Princess is my responsibility from now and I will never love her any less than you." Janak blessed him. The queen broke down. Urmila sat at the wedding hearth with a look of utter grief on her face; tears streaming down from her kohl-lined eyes.

Lakshman felt her anxiety. He wiped her tears, "Mila, I am here to live your future with you without taking away your past, your roots from you."

Kanyadaan is the humblest gift to the bridegroom in Hindu weddings. With this daan – gift – parents give away the pride, the joy of their life to another man. The same is said for Saptadi, the seven vows around the holy fire by the bride and the groom, in the hope that Agni Dev, who resides in the fire, will strengthen holy matrimony.

When it was time for the *pheras* – sacred rounds around the ritual fire, each couple was blessed by the king, queens and the royal invitees. The couples circumambulated the fire together.

Even though he was born hours after Bharath, Lakshman was always considered older than him because he was born to the second queen of Ayodhya. Thus Lakshman was married before Bharath.

"My dear daughters, the *sindoor* – vermillion powder, the *mangalsutra* – the sacred black thread, and the *chudamani* – the lotus headdress are the symbols of a married woman. From now on, these are essential adornments for you," Sunaina explained to the girls.

Lakshman took a pinch of vermillion powder from a little golden pot and filled the parting in Urmila's hair. Then, he took the *mangalsutra* chosen by his mother, Queen Sumitra, and tied it around her neck. The little gold pendant gleamed on the black and gold chord. As he tied the *chudamani* around her hair, the ceremony was considered complete.

The four princes, who went through similar rounds of rituals, were finally deemed married in the eyes of god and their respective clans.

Urmila touched her *sindoor, chudamani* and *mangalsutra* with a feeling of elation. She was finally his and she was wearing 'him' on her. *Had Lakshman become imbibed in her soul*, she wondered as she looked at him with contentment.

Maharani Sunaina and Chandrabhaga escorted the couples to the wedding banquet, which was a lavish feast of fragrant rice, bowls of curried vegetables and cottage cheese, lentils cooked in spices, assorted sweetmeats and *ksheer*. Sunaina explained to them the feasting ritual, "I know you have been fasting since morning and now is time to break your fast. Sita, Urmila, Mandvi and Shrutakeerti will break their fast first."

As Urmila was about to put a portion of sweetmeat into Lakshman's mouth, he stopped her hand in mid-air, "You haven't eaten since last night. Let me feed you first." And he put the sweetmeat back into Urmila's mouth.

Lakshman's concern for Urmila moved everyone to tears.

After the weddings, the two cities looked different. Ayodhya sparkled with its new additions while Mithila cried silently. A heartbroken King Janak tried to put off the *bidaii* ceremony of his daughters.

The Ayodhya royals graciously accepted his plea to defer the farewells, but Urmila felt betrayed by her parents' pettiness.

After the princes retired to their chambers, leaving the princesses to speak to their parents in the privacy of their living quarters, Urmila gently reminded Maharani Sunaina and Maharaj Janak about their duty as the brides' parents,

"*Maa*, *Pitaji*, you grieve a loss that is to be borne with grace and calm. You plan your daughter's wedding since her birth yet when it is time for the girl to leave home, you weep for her. You hold her hand and lead her from her past to her future and yet you hurt when your daughter takes that one step forward."

Maharaj Janak enfolded Sita and Urmila in a warm hug and cried, "Urmila, my daughter, my Warrior Princess makes me a proud father today. After the *kanyadaan*, a daughter is *paraya dhan* – another's wealth. A father has limited rights on her thereafter."

Urmila was furious to see her father wallowing in self-pity, "Who can separate Mithila from Maithili, Janaki from Janak? I am your Maithili and *didi* is your Janaki. We will always remain so. Mithila is our heart but Ayodhya is our duty. And you forget Rajrishi – royal monk-king Janak, it is you who have taught us not to flinch from duty for love."

Astute by nature, Urmila understood her father's dilemma but Mithila could not afford to show its weakness and flounder in the face of Raghukul's pride and glory; the two ancient kingships had to meet on equal terms. Sita looked at Urmila with pride.

Both Maharaj Janak and Maharani Sunaina were surprised at her wisdom, "We have indeed been blessed by Maha Vishnu and Maha Lakshmi to have nurtured daughters like you."

Sita was sad. "Bless us that we can fulfil our *dharma* like Devi Ksheera the way she stood by Adi-Shesha through rain and shine," Mithila's older princess appealed to her mother.

Sita and Urmila left for their sleeping quarters after reassuring their parents. Maharaj Janak and Maharani Sunaina were awake for a long time trying to imagine life without the sunny chirping of the girls. The palace felt empty.

Creating Beautiful Memories

Memories make an epic love story, connecting time and narratives.

A day after the wedding, Urmila told Lakshman that she wanted him to become a part of her past moments by reliving them with her and create some new memories with her in Mithila. "I want to see your smile when I look back at my yesterdays and feel your touch when I look at my tomorrows."

Lakshman hugged her, "I will do whatever you say." And they agreed to explore Mithila together before leaving for Ayodhya.

A maid interrupted their moment of togetherness with the message that Maharani Sunaina wanted to see them both in her palace right away. Wondering what could be so important, they followed the maid. All the four newly-weds were in Maharani Sunaina's chamber. They were apprehensive about what was to unfold, but the Maharani was quiet. She did not look intimidating.

"I have asked you all here together to tell you about an important tradition of Raghukul. According to the tradition, as Shanta says, you cannot spend the night together until the *garbhadaan sanskaar*. So, the girls will sleep in their own quarters or in a common room if they so desire and the princes will have to move to the *atithi grah* – guest room," Maharani Sunaina said with a smile.

Having pined for so long, Lakshmila felt let down at the thought of living away from each other, even for a night. They looked at each other in dismay before leaving Sunaina's chamber.

The royal breakfast held a special significance for the newly-weds, the day after. They were supposed to dress in their wedding finery for the morning feast. Urmila entered her chamber where Lakshman was dressing for breakfast. She stood behind him, partially hidden from view, taking her fill of him. She looked at her own attire and marvelled at how the colours of their clothes complemented each other.

Their minds and hearts were in complete harmony. They had picked the right colours to match their clothes and offset each other and to stand out in Raghukul.

He turned around suddenly, "How long will you stand there looking at me?" Urmila came forward. She was shy under his intense gaze and tried to hide it by arranging his *angavastra*. "How did you know?" Lightly holding her by the waist, he pulled her closer still, "Your scent, your presence, your silence reveal you to me, Mila. I hear your breath inside me."

Urmila turned crimson, "We have to be at the breakfast table before someone comes looking for us, please," she tried to persuade Lakshman to let her go. He looked at her deeply for a moment before allowing his hands to fall, "Let's go." She stood there feeling empty where his hands held her a moment ago.

As the family gathered in the dining hall for breakfast at a low table with long rows of silver platters and bowls, Maharani Sunaina explained the breakfast ritual of Mithila to the grooms with a smile, "*Pranaam* Maharaj, Gurudev, sons Ram, Lakshman, Bharath and Shatrughan. A tradition in Mithila says that the husband has to guess the dish which his wife has cooked for the first time as she begins to hold house for him. Thus, today's breakfast has been made by your wives. You will have to taste and identify the dish your wives have cooked."

Amid chuckles and low rumbles of laughter, the princes tasted the dishes placed on the table, one by one. When Lakshman was served chickpeas, he loved the taste of the red spicy curry and immediately declared, "So much spice. This has been cooked by my Mila."

His brothers cheered him for recognising Urmila's cooking; and eventually after much confusion, several attempts by trial and error, Ram, Bharath and Shatrughan too identified the dishes cooked by their wives. The rite left everyone smiling; happiness mingled with the scent of spices lingered in the air.

The royal carriages waited at the gates to take the couples on a tour of the city. The princes and princesses had to greet the people of Mithila, under the watchful gaze of the prime minister.

Lakshman and Urmila's chariot stopped near a big, green field. "A surprise awaits you here, *Swami*," Urmila held out her hand to Lakshman to get down from the chariot, "Wait here until I come back."

And she disappeared into a hut, nearby.

Lakshman turned around to a tap on his shoulder a few dreamy minutes later. He was aghast. Urmila stood before him dressed like a warrior, "Rajkumar Lakshman, I, *Janaknandini* Urmila, challenge you to a sword fight." A ripple of excitement ran down Lakshman's spine.

She looked magnificent, "I take it up."

The sword fight was the brightest gem in the royal wedding crown – the high point of the celebration. Crowds thronged the fields, pushing and jostling for a better look at the sparring couple. The makeshift fencing arena came alive to the clanging of swords and the battle of spirits between two great swordspersons of the era.

It was an iconic moment. The greatest swordswoman of Aryavarta was clashing with one of the greatest swordsmen of Raghukul. Even with his slick pace and sprightly energy, Lakshman was no match for his wife. Eventually he accepted defeat, chivalrously. "This is the first time someone has defeated me."

Urmila smiled, "Learn to accept defeat."

But their clash of wits was not yet over. They left the battle of nerves open to the next round. As they caught their breaths resting against a rock pillar, Lakshman praised her, "You can defeat even *Maata* Kaikayi. How did you learn to be a virtuoso in sword-fighting?"

"As far as I can remember, my sword has always been my first love. I have grown up with only one aim, to protect Mithila from attacks. For father, I am his son, not his daughter. But look where we stand today? It was my destiny to be your wife. I did not have any intention of marrying anyone until you stepped into my thoughts, and my life."

Lakshman held her hands reassuringly, "You are free to pursue your love for sword-fighting even in Ayodhya and protect the kingdom in my absence," he smiled. "I am always with you in every aspiration of yours. You can seek guidance from Gurudev, if you want."

Urmila looked at him, "Dare I say, I am proud and blessed to have found you."

"Not more than me," Lakshman pulled her up from where she leaned against her rocky support. It was time to visit another memory.

The destination was the royal garden. Urmila frisked around in it with mixed emotions because she was sad to leave the sanctuary behind, but happy at the same time that Lakshman could cherish her favourite 'hideaway' with her. They remembered their first encounter under the orchid tree and felt nostalgic.

Urmila took him to the rock, where Lakshman had found her crying twice, "You know *Swami*, this has been my secret crying corner for tears. It began with Mandvi. We were very young and she ridiculed me ruthlessly for my love of weapons and war games, especially swords. We had a huge fight and I pulled her hair in anger. She began howling and since *choti maa* and *chote pitaji* – aunt and uncle – were not in Mithila at the time, I was taken to task by father and *Maa*. Even then, father had been silent for the sake of that *Rakshasi* Mandvi. It hurt me to watch my father scold me for something I hadn't done, and for the weapons, he had taught me to believe in. How could my father, who had never uttered a harsh word to me until then pull me up for someone else's fault? I wanted to be away from everyone at that moment. I found this place and cried my heart out. From that day onwards, this rock shelter has been my favourite retreat when I seek answers in solitude."

The memory was sacred to Lakshman because Urmila's tears could spell his ruin; the premonition haunted him like a nightmare.

"Mila, you are incomparable. Never change. Be proud of who you are." Lakshman felt a tiny stab of anger for Mandvi in that instant. She should not have hurt Urmila.

"I want to know your favourite childhood memory, now," Urmila implored. He smiled, going back in time.

"We were eight years old. The four of us were playing with stones in our garden, pelting them at each other. Bharath, for some reason, had always disliked Manthara *dadi*, mother Kaikayi's chief maid-in-waiting. He once threw a stone which hit Manthara *dadi* by mistake. Manthara *dadi* is a conniving schemer who wanted Bharath to become the king of Ayodhya instead of *bhaiya*. None of us had any sympathies for her. But somehow father came to know of our mischief from her. And when grilled about it, Ram *bhaiya* took the blame for Bharath's prank upon himself and had to bear the consequences. He was jailed in a stable for a week. How could I leave *bhaiya* alone? So, I took another stone and hit Manthara *dadi* deliberately. Father ordered me to stay with *bhaiya* for a week as punishment."

"I would have done the same," Urmila wished she had known him as a child.

"After we were punished, Bharath fell sick. He would not eat without us. Shatrughan also refused to eat and his condition worsened without us. *Maata* Kaikeyi was summoned from Kekeya immediately. And, perhaps that was the first time father broke his word. He called us back to the palace. I asked Reema, *Maa's* chief maid, why he had relented but she did tell us why our penalty was commuted."

They had come closer in their souls, bonding deeper, as they traded childhood memories.

The last place that Urmila took him to was Gargi's *ashram*. The *ashram* had something that belonged only to Lakshman. Maybe fate wanted him to have it now!

Urmila called out to Gargi Vachaknavi on reaching the hermitage. "What do you want here?" *Maata* Gargi was apprehensive. "How could I leave Mithila before *Sumitranandan* met my special and most treasured *Maata*?" her voice broke.

With tears in her eyes, Gargi rushed back inside the hut and came out with a tray of *aarti*, "May you both be blessed, my children." Lakshman and Urmila touched her feet. She took note of the way they complemented each other.

"Your union was destined. You both will remind the world of eternal love. Not even physical separation can separate your souls," the seer predicted.

The Vedas tell how Maata Gargi had awakened her kundli. Thus, she already knew what anguish lay hidden in the future for her beloved goddaughter Urmila.

She guided them into the hut. Urmila looked around fondly. "*Swami*, I fell in love with the Vedas and the Upanishads here with *Maata*. Perhaps, I am who I am because of her."

Lakshman folded his hands humbly, "*Maata*, I shall forever be grateful to you for making my Mila who she is. *Maa* told us about you. She often said that no woman in Aryavarta was as spiritually enlightened and erudite as you."

"*Putra* – son, Devi Sumitra is one of the most humble and wisest persons I have ever known. You had to come today because the *ashram* had to give you something it had preserved with care until now."

Lakshman looked at her with curiosity. She returned with a clay statue in her hand, "Here, take this. It belongs to you."

Lakshman's eyes widened as he looked at the clay icon. The little sculpture was his verisimilitude. "How, why...?" he stammered.

"Urmila made it when she was a child. The girls were asked to craft their dream men in clay and even though Urmi was firm that she would not marry, I insisted that she make a clay statue of a man with her heart's eyes. I said we will try to find the man in the clay idol for her. She made you, so, this belongs to you from now on," Gargi said.

Lakshman's hand trembled because he had not ever felt this connection of souls as he felt then, at that moment. They sat there looking at each other in complete surrender for long moments, holding the statue.

Gargi took two scared threads for protection from her shrine and tied them on their wrists. "*Maata*, was Mila a sincere student or a mischievous one?" Lakshman looked at Urmila provokingly.

"She has been the most mischievous, yet the most honest. She keeps nothing within. My best student, she is exemplary in her meaningful arguments in debates. No one can defeat her except you. I want your children to be as intelligent." Gargi loved to praise Urmila.

"*Maata*, you disown me. You forget I dislike sharing my things with anyone." Urmila's eyes filled with tears. She could not bear the thought of any other child, who was as intelligent and brave as her. The little girl in Urmila rebelled at the idea of 'sharing' what was hers.

Gargi wiped the tears from Urmila's eyes, "I am your mentor and mother. I shall miss you, my child, but you will always remain in my heart."

As Lakshman and Urmila rode back to the palace, they thought about the beauty life held in small moments, in the memories that were stranded in time for years, without fading, hoping for revival.

Bidaii – Farewell

The heart is a fast learner, ending old chapters for new beginnings.

Mithila wiped its tears repeatedly. It knew that the princesses would soon leave its lush headlands. The kingdom grieved at the thought of the morning without their beautiful faces to set its eyes on. But the kingdom had 'unwittingly' gained, consolidating its position in a changing Aryavarta.

Maharaj Janak and Kushadhwaja were disconsolate as they entered Urmila's quarters. "I seek your forgiveness, my daughters. I, the one referred to as Raj Rishi, was intent on breaking my *dharma* had you not offered me your foresight. Your *bidaai* will take place tomorrow. We have informed King Dashrath and Shanta about it," Janak's shoulders slumped in agony.

"My sons," he turned to look at the four princes. "If you all can forgive us," he apologised.

Ram and Lakshman embraced Janak. "Father, we are but your sons. You make us feel ashamed with your apology. It is not easy to bid farewell to daughters. Only a great man like you can do it so humbly."

The news of their departure the next day left the princesses distraught, especially Urmila. The initial bluster with which she had reasoned with her father left her. The mere of thought of leaving Mithila and everything that she had treasured since she was an infant terrified her.

She was caught in a dilemma. She had wanted to be a part of Raghukul with a desperation that she dare not voice to anyone except her sister Sita, but she had not bargained to relinquish all that was familiar – all that went into making her. Suppose Raghukul turned out to be intimidating and inhospitable? Doubts hounded her.

She held herself back with an effort lest she broke down completely.

Lakshman somehow understood her fears. He noticed the haunted expression on her face and her body language. He took her aside to the terrace, gently.

"I know you are a warrior and warriors do not easily shed tears, but Mila, you are a girl too. Let your tears flow, accept your anguish. *Maa* always says that you should let your tears wash away your grief. Allow them to come. By restraining them, you do yourself injustice. This is your last night in Mithila. Relish your moments. Express your emotions. Go to your mother and father. Hug them tightly, visit your favourite places and bid them good bye. Go, Mila! I shall wait for your return."

Urmila looked at him with pride and respect, "Mila stands incomplete without her Laksh." Hugging him tightly, she said, "You are right, *Swami*. I will not let my last night in Mithila go waste." She suddenly felt a calm settle over her.

Lakshman kissed her forehead with love, "That's like my Mila." And he joined his brothers.

The sisters shared the moment of parting with one another in a new camaraderie bred by the grief of an imminent separation and also of union, elsewhere on an alien land. They cried on each other's shoulders. Soon after Mandvi and Shrutakeerti left to bid *adieu* to their parents, Sita held Urmila's face in her hands and placated her.

But Urmila was inconsolable, "How will they live without us, how will we bear being not around them? The mere thought of *Maa* not being present to scold me, feed me and pull my ears makes me feel melancholic and insecure. With father not there to chaperon me everywhere and to fulfil my smallest whims, who will pamper me, *didi*?"

"Mothers are irreplaceable. Their love envelops us in warmth and travels with us wherever we go. *Maa* will always be there but the love of three more mothers waits for us in Ayodhya. We are blessed, Urmi." Sita was wise in her counsel. She held Urmila's hands into a gradual acceptance of the 'new'; the familial patterns were slowly changing with new liaisons and associations in the offing.

Sita and Urmila entered their parents' quarters surreptitiously.

The room looked back at them with sadness. The thought of Janak and Sunaina's daughters not running in and out of their chambers from the next day broke its heart. The room was a silent witness to the parting, foretold aeons ago.

"*Maa*, this is our last night in Mithila," Urmila continued, "Both of us want to sleep with you tonight and hear you sing the lullabies you crooned to us as children." They put their heads on Maharani Sunaina's lap. Queen Sunaina caressed their heads and began to sing a lullaby.

Both the princesses fell asleep.

Sunaina, holding back her tears until now, let them flow in torrents. She felt the tug of their childhood in her heart and the memories of their innocent pranks. Their impending departure tore her soul apart. Maharaj Janak held Sunaina gently, "Let them fly away from your nest, Sunaina. A new life awaits our daughters. We have to stand by them through this." He wiped his own tears with trembling hands.

The morning dawned even before the cock crowed, waking up the palace to prepare for the flurry of farewells. Sunaina came in to wake up her daughters but Sita was already out of the bed. Urmila was not in the room. Sunaina and Sita assumed that she was with Lakshman.

Well-aware of her daughter's disappearing act, she thought it best to check with Lakshman. Lakshman was aware of Urmila's need to be alone, "*Maa*, Mila is not with me. I have not seen her since last night. But don't you worry. I know where she can be. I will go and fetch her."

Lakshman took Sunaina to the royal garden and peeped behind the big rock. She sat there as expected.

"Caught you!" Lakshman teased her. "…Crybaby." She looked at them with her tear-stained face.

"Mila, I have been cheated. Instead of the Warrior Princess of Mithila, I am taking back a wailing child to Ayodhya," he ribbed her. His eyes, however, shone with gentle love for her.

She loathed him when he teased her, "I am but a Warrior Princess, *Sumitranandan*. You dare not challenge me again or else I won't leave you." She rubbed her eyes with the impetuousness of a child caught in a mischievous act.

Sunaina was indignant. She pulled Urmila's ears, "Is this what I inculcated in you? You should not behave this way in Ayodhya. Lakshman is your husband. You owe him respect."

Urmila clutched at her mother's hand, "Who will scold me and pull my ears when I annoy him in Ayodhya, *Maa*?"

"Maharani Sumitra!" Sunaina chided. "You will have three mothers in Ayodhya: Maharani Kaushalya, Maharani Sumitra and Rani Kaikeyi. From now on, you have to listen to them. I received a letter from Maharani Sumitra assuring me of your comforts, and asking me about your likes and dislikes. Indeed, she is the wisest queen of all. Respect her, I shall always reflect in her always."

Urmila whispered softly, "I promise not to let you down, *Maa*." Lakshman, who was watching the emotional exchange between the mother and the daughter quietly, promised to protect Urmila with his life.

"I promise you *Maa* that your Urmila is my life from now on and I shall let no harm come to her. Not even a single teardrop will fall from her eyes."

"God bless you my son. I am privileged to have a son-in-law like you," Sunaina touched Lakshman's lowered head. Urmila sulked. She was so possessive about her mother that the sight of the Lakshman and Sumitra breaking down the walls of formality with amicable conversation made her skin prickle with anger. Lakshman and Sunaina burst into laughter at her childish possessiveness.

In the palace, Urmila looked aournd her bedroom with love and a sense of loss. "I will miss you so much. Don't change until I come again. And remember me with love." Chandrarashi and Malavika wanted to spend time with their best friend before she left. "We will miss you terribly, Urmi." The three of them huddled on the bed.

"I will miss you, too, but remember my promise. My children shall marry yours." Both Chanda and Malavika cried in joy, "We will wait for that day."

A maid escorted Urmila to queen Sunaina's room. Urmila was dressed for *bidaai*. Clad in a traditional red *lehenga* with matching gold jewellery inlaid with rubies and red corals, vermillion and the *mangalsutra*, Urmila caught her own reflection in the mirror. The image that stared back at her was that of a warrior goddess, a bride who combined strength and the beauty of a diva.

"Ready?" Urmila turned around to the sound of King Janak's voice. The king stood there with a look of disbelief in his eyes, "The most beautiful woman in the world stands before me."

She ran to him, "I love you, father."

"I will miss you my Warrior Princess, but it's time to go. With you I send the heart of Mithila to Ayodhya. Mithila stands barren without you."

Urmila wiped his tears, "I shall always carry Mithila in me."

"Let's go," Janak walked with her slowly to the *Rajya Sabha* where the courtiers waited with tearful eyes to bid the princesses farewell. The princes of Ayodhya stood demurely in a corner with their father. They were not unmoved by the grief that smote every heart present in the court.

The princesses had to leave their imprints on the walls of the corridors that had raised them, watched them grow, and nurtured them with love. Sunaina made each of them dip their hands in a bowl of *kumkum* – vermillion – and turmeric paste – and put their palm imprints on the wall.

This ritual preserved the memory of a daughter in her father's house. It was a tradition that implied that she had to leave behind all that the house had given her and take away only memories of it.

Chandrabhaga ordered the maids to fetch a tray full of gold coins, rice and dry *ksheer*. She instructed the princesses to throw a handful of coins behind them as they walked towards the exit with their husbands. They performed the ritual with a heavy heart.

A girl child is said to be an avatara of Goddess Lakshmi in one's house. This ritual symbolises that even after a daughter leaves her parent's home and goes to her husband's, she wishes prosperity to prevail in her father's house.

The couples stood at the threshold of the royal court, ready to go. Urmila embraced her mother and wept. When she sought her father Janak's blessings, he placed his hand on her head, turned around and walked away without looking back. He could not bear to see her go. Urmila walked to Kushadhwaja, Chandrabhaga and Raj Guru Shatanand for their blessings before coming to pause in front of Gargi. She was scared of being abandoned by her spiritual guide – Gargi Vachaknavi was Urmila's pillar of worldly strength.

"Mother, I will miss you the most. Promise me that whenever *Maa* and *Pitaji* will visit Ayodhya, you will accompany them."

"My daughter, whenever you miss me, remember me with your heart. You will find me near you. You are my warrior and I know you will win in life too," Gargi blessed Urmila.

Chandrarashi and Malavika refused to let go of their friend, and clung to Urmila, weeping. Urmila gently withdrew from their embrace, "Remember my promise. We will meet soon." The four princesses stepped into their *dolis* – palanquins – to leave Mithila forever. The bearers picked up the carriages, swaying to the slow rhythm of parting as they moved out of the palace gates.

As Rajkumari Urmila bade farewell to her childhood, sitting in her doli, she looked back at all those fond memories that waved at her as she passed them by and then she looked at the man by her side, her husband, and wondered how in a matter of only a few days, had she changed from Janaknandini Urmila to Lakshman Patni Urmila. She did not understand whether to cry for what had ended or smile for what was about to begin!

The Pranksters

Little laughter, little mischief – heavens measure the depths of love.

Mithila let the princesses go with a heavy heart wishing them happiness and fulfillment. The palanquins veered at the border of the kingdom's riverine lowlands to turn towards Ayodhya across Magadh along the Ganga. Would Mithila ever be the same without them?

The Ayodhya entourage, comprising the bridal palanquins and several horse-drawn chariots, stopped at the Kanchi Kamakshi temple *en route*. It was the shrine of their *Kuldevi* – the guardian deity of the clan – and Maharaj Dashrath wanted his sons and their wives to seek the blessings of Goddess Kamakshi, an incarnate form of Parvati, before they moved on to a new life. Kamaskshi was the foreteller of destinies and the fulfiller of desires.

Dashrath, accompanied by Gurudev Vashishtha and Shanta, left for Ayodhya from the temple itself ordering the princes and their consorts to reach Ayodhya after the ritual Ganga *darshan* – bathing – at the Bhagirathi Tat – the banks of the Bhagirathi-

Ganga. The entourage, which had now shrunk in size, travelled through great swathes of swamps, criss-crossed by narrow *howdah* tracks. The princesses were silent on the way, refusing to warm up to their husbands' overtures.

Shatrughan, who was closely observing the four sisters, decided to divert their thoughts about Mithila and ease the pain of parting. He sought Lakshman's help to play pranks on them to make them smile. Shatrughan and Lakshman waited for an opportune moment.

The convoy halted near Magadha in the evening, where Arya Sumantra, one of King Dashrath's trusted aides, decided to camp for the night. A large posse of servitors pitched big white tents on wooden poles, hundreds of billowing silken shelters for the royal couples and their personal helps to rest for the night.

As the couples sat under a starlit sky to cook dinner, Lakshman set fire to the rocks with a pile of bracken and dry twigs near where Urmila was overseeing the building of an open mud oven. The heat from the fire flushed Urmila's face red.

"Oh, that's like my *mirchi*, red and spicy looking!" Lakshman said laughing. He grabbed Urmila by her arms and wiped her face with his *angavastra*, slowly kissing her neck. Urmila could not stop blushing. He held her hand without taking his eyes away from hers and they began to boil sweet potatoes in a large wok, stirring it together. Urmila was completely lost in this carefully-orchestrated act of intimacy, a prank that threatened to flare into passion. The spell broke. They looked around to find Shatrughan and Shrutakeerti watching them, laughing.

Urmila got up, embarrassed, and joined Sita.

The family was enjoying a light meal of rice and curried sweet potatoes together in the solitude of their surroundings, when a messenger galloped in with an important missive for Rajkumar Lakshman.

Lakshman took the letter and went to his tent to read it in seclusion. It was from his niece Vindhya, who was still at Dhanvan Rajya, not far from where they had camped in Magadha, and she wanted Lakshman to fetch her and take her back with him to Ayodhya.

Lakshman did not discuss the contents of the letter with anyone and while everyone was still asleep, he left quietly for Dhanvan Rajya.

Vindhya was eager to know about the wedding. On their way back, Vindhya expresses her feelings of betrayal, "You broke your promise to me, *Mamashree* – maternal uncle. I was to find a suitable bride for you, but you found her by yourself."

Lakshman smiled fondly, "I tried not to, but she just walked in. She is pure magic. You will also fall in love with her." Vindhya sounded haughty, "That we shall see only after I test her."

"Do let me know what you feel after the test," Lakshman's eyes sparkled with mirth.

***

Back in the camp, Urmila panicked. Lakshman was nowhere to be seen – neither in nor around any of the tents. Ram and Sita tried to calm her but she was nervous like the heaving waters of the mighty Ksheera – the ocean of bliss – stripped of its 1,000-hooded guardian Shesha.

Shatrughan considered it just the moment to set his plan into action, "I know where he may have disappeared."

Everyone looked at him in anticipation. Shatrughan winked at Bharath, "Magadha!"

"Why would he be in Magadha?" Shrutakeerti queried. "To meet Rajkumari Sunadri," Shatrughan let the information sink in. "She has been his best friend since childhood."

Urmila paled, "I do not understand." Shatrughan, though playful in his own way and generally loving, could be a little devious at times. "Rajkumari Sunadri is *bhaiya*'s childhood friend. They were very close to each other, rather, she *was* or shall I say still *is* madly in love with him. *Pitaji* had no objections to their marriage but we objected. I don't like her. He ignores us when he is with Sunadri."

Urmila felt the sudden sting of tears and jealousy. Her fists clenched in anger and her eyes sparked fire. The princesses forgot their grief of leaving home. They rallied behind Urmila protectively, when they saw Lakshman entering the camp with a girl.

Urmila stiffened. Before Lakshman could explain his hurried departure from the camp, Urmila lashed out in anger, "You have the audacity to bring Rajkumari Sunadri here?"

Lakshman gawked at her in confusion. He could not understand her sudden reference to Sunadri. But a glance at Shatrughan warned him about what had transpired in his absence, and Lakshman decided to play an accomplice to the hilt, "Ram *bhaiya* took the one-woman vow, not me, Mila."

Urmila looked at him emotionally distraught, tears filling her eyes, "Don't call me Mila hence on. You lose that right over me." Lakshman sensed trouble and dropped his act. The depth of the hurt his words had caused showed on Urmila's face.

"Mila, wait before you judge me, don't be in a hurry. She is not Rajkumari Sunadri," Lakshman pleaded with her. Urmila looked at him blankly without reacting; her head felt foggy.

Vindhya, who was watching the little scene quietly until now, knew it was time to intervene. She hugged Urmila, "Please forgive him. I am not Sunadri. I am Vindhya, his niece. It was just a silly prank that *Mamashree* played on you at the behest of Shatrughan."

The little prank played to bring smiles on the faces of the princesses became grounded in hurt, bequeathing misgivings and fears. It backfired. Shatrughan stood dejected because he was held as the reason for Urmila's anguish. From the way Shrutakeerti glared at him in disgust, it would be long before he was condoned. The princesses were not yet used to the brash ways of the brotherhood – the princes bonded in their boyish pranks.

Urmila patted Vindhya's head, "God bless you," she said, walking out of the tent. Lakshman watched her go. Bharath and Shatrughan tried to reassure him but they knew that holding her back and forcing her to take part in the family reunion in one of her turbulent moods would be futile.

Urmila would not forgive Lakshman, and he was not ready to give in without a fight.

Urmila ran deep into the forest. She found a secluded cranny between two rocks where she broke down into tears at how callously Lakshman had cut her up with just a few 'meaningless' words. That was a mean trick to play on her. Was he oblivious of the pain the mere thought of him with another woman caused her?

Suddenly, a pair of strong arms held her from the back, "I am sorry, Mila." She tried to disentangle from his embrace but his hold on her was firm. She became limp in Lakshman's arms. He turned her around to face him tenderly, "You are and shall always be the only woman in my life. I love you. I just wanted to make you smile, forget Mithila."

"Mithila is a part of my essence, but you are me. Your smile is enough to make me smile. You could not have loved me ever to hurt me so," Urmila was relentless.

"I can never think of any other woman than you. You consume me and still if you think otherwise, today in the presence of air, water and fire, I, *Sumitranandan* Lakshman, vow that I will always belong to my wife *Janaknandini* Urmila until my last breath. I hereby take a one-woman vow, Mila" Lakshman pledged, almost shouting at the trees, air and the sky to bring them in as witnesses.

"I did not want you to prove your love with an empty promise." Urmila was sad. He let her go. "I understand your anger. All I seek is forgiveness and trust that no other woman has ever existed for me; no one except you ever shall. I shall await your trust in me again." And with that, Lakshman turned around to leave.

Urmila hesitated. Was she too harsh in her jealousy?

Lakshman, in the meanwhile, went too near to a wild clump of the jasmine tobacco flowers in bloom and tried to smell them. He began to sneeze violently and shouted out to her. Disarmed, she ran to his rescue but broke into convulsive laughter as she looked at the flowers. "*Sumitranandan*, don't you know smelling this tobacco flower brings on sneezing fits? And look at your nose, it is red. No wonder the moniker *nakchara* suits you so well."

"For a moment there, I thought I would die of sneezing, Mila," Lakshman had a forlorn expression on his face.

"I will never let anyone take my Saumitra away from me." Urmila hugged him. He slowly kissed her neck again, "Am I forgiven?" Urmila closed her eyes and breathing his scent in, whispered under her breath, "I love you."

"I will always be sorry, Mila, for what I did today," Lakshman's voice shook with emotion. Urmila put her hand on his mouth. "I am sorry too, *Swami*, for doubting your love. I forget that there is no jealousy where there is true love." She rested her head on his chest.

Suddenly, they heard whispers and muffled laughter from somewhere behind them. Shatrughan and Vindhya were standing with broad smiles of relief on their faces. "You forgive him too easily, *bhabhi maa*," Shatrughan teased them.

While Lakshman chased him to teach him a lesson, Vindhya and Urmila bonded over a heartfelt exchange. Shanta's daughter sought reassurance from Urmila that her uncle would not be put to the grindstone of house-holding and royal duties so that he would be left with no time to devote to his niece, once they were back in Ayodhya.

Urmila assured the girl that she would ensure that Lakshman devoted enough time to her.

Shatrughan asked Urmila to forgive him, "I stand as your culprit, *bhabhi maa*. Forgive me. I failed to understand the pious love you have for my brother."

"You are like my son. I cannot be angry with you," Urmila replied. Shatrughan touched her feet.

Vindhya watched as Lakshman blessed Shrutakeerti at the other end with fraternal affection and could not but thank god for the blessings he had showered upon her in the form of this warm family. As they returned to the tents, Ram embraced Lakshman and forbade him to ever hurt Urmila again.

The family ate their breakfast and left for the Bhagirathi Tat barefoot, where Mother Ganga, the river goddess, smiled on them as they bathed in her icy waters. "Be happy," she whispered to the princesses in her cascades. The convoy left for Ayodhya immediately.

While they were still a few hours away from Ayodhya, Vindhya spied juicy wild berries growing in abundance on the way and requested Lakshman and Shatrughan to fetch them for her. The convoy stopped because Vindhya's wishes were their bidding. Lakshman asked Ram and Bharath to proceed towards Ayodhya while they went to the jungle to pluck berries.

"We shall catch up soon," Ram said.

Urmila and Shrutakeerti waited in their palanquins while Lakshman, Shatrughan and Vindhya went into the forest to gather the juicy green and yellow fruits which hung in clusters from leafy branches of the trees. As they pulled the laden branches down to their arm's length with bamboo sticks, they heard mysterious voices whispering nearby. Lakshman sensed that something was amiss and told Vindhya to run back to the carriages to check on Urmila and Shrutakeerti.

Vindhya was still nearly 100 yards away from the palanquins when she saw that Urmila and Shrutakeerti had been surrounded by a fierce tribe of demons, who had slain the royal guards. Vindhya silently melted back to the forest to inform the princes about the siege.

As the demons tried to break into the carriages, the Warrior Princess sprung into action. She took out her sword and felled the fiercest of the demons but some of them overpowered Shrutakeerti and held her captive.

The demons challenged Urmila, "We want Ram and Lakshman here. Their death awaits them."

Even after her marriage, Urmila sword kept her sword sheathed to her waist. She would never remove her sword.

"Are you afraid to duel with me?" Urmila turned out to be an obstinate opponent and slashed at the demon warriors with her sword mercilessly, inflicting deep wounds. One of the demons escaped to plead with their chief, Vakshasur, to save them.

Lakshman and Shatrughan ran back in alarm on hearing that the princesses had been accosted by the asurs. A battle ensued between Vakshasur and Lakshman.

Lakshman killed Vakshasur with his Brahmastra – Brahma's weapon.

But the fight was not over yet. The asur army was soon augmented by Markasur, Vakshasur's twin. While Lakshman and Shatrughan fought him, they were joined by Ram and Bharath, who had returned to Bhagirath Tat to find out if Lakshman and Shatrughan had resumed their journey onward with the princesses.

When he saw Lakshman at war with the asur demons, he threw in his might. Markasur attacked Bharath, who fell down unconscious from a powerful blow by the demon. The club-weilding Markasur towered over the princes.

While Shrutakeerti who was adept in the healing sciences of Ayurveda tended to Bharath's injuries, Ram, Lakshman and Shatrughan battled Markasur. Finally, Lakshman killed Markasur, along with the rest of the asur demons with his powerful arrows.

The chariots immediately left for Ayodhya, given the hazards of the journey through the ancient Kol heartland full of demonic tribes. In all, it took 6 days, 21 hours and 46 minutes for the convoy to reach Ayodhya from Mithila.

The Arrival of Four Kulvadhus – Brides

The wheel of time is the gateway to an epic set in motion.

Ayodhya was aware that the princes were soon to enter its boundaries with their brides. The wait seemed very long. As an impatient Ayodhya fidgeted, it heard the sound of the approaching royal convoy. It stood to its full glory to welcome the princes and their brides.

Urmila was fascinated by the grandeur of Ayodhya, one of the seven most important cities in Aryavarta. As their chariots negotiated the bustling streets, she was awed by its modernity and intelligent urban planning.

"It's so different from Mithila," she said thoughtfully. The River Sarayu and its banks dotted with shrines touched her soul with their tranquil beauty. Lakshman looked at her in humility, "You are home, Mila. What has been mine until now belongs to you too." She looked deep into his eyes, "I know *Swami*, and I can feel the warmth of your home."

The queens waited for them at the palace door. Raghukul's *kulvadhus* could pass through the carved ornate door only after performing the entry rites. Urmila's burning curiosity to meet the queens, especially Maharani Sumitra, revealed itself in her questioning gaze. She wondered which one of the three was Maharani Sumitra.

Kaushalya was one of the gentlest women Urmila had ever seen; a serene halo of light seemed to envelope her head. Ram resembled his mother.

Maharani Sumitra stood next to her. Urmila was amazed to see how much of her was mirrored in Lakshman. Her elegance and natural beauty drew Urmila to her; it was as if Lakshman was looking back at her. "You and Shrutakeerti are my daughters from now on. My joy and pride!" Sumitra said, holding Urmila to her bosom.

Urmila returned the affection with equal intensity. She felt the love of the mother she was missing for the past few days emanate from Sumitra like a warm glow, washing over her like a wave. "*Maa*, my dream has come true. I always wanted to meet you and god has blessed me with you as my mother. I cannot thank Gauri *Maa* enough." Happy tears shimmered in her eyes.

"You will take my place soon," Lakshman teased her. "*Swami*, I don't want to take your place, but I want to carve space for myself in everyone's heart." Sumitra smiled at their exchange and said, "Raghukul is blessed to have a *kulvadhu* like you, Urmila."

As they stood before Queen Kaikeyi to seek her blessings, Urmila understood why Maharaj Dashrath had a special soft spot for her. Kaikeyi's beauty was unnaturally fierce and shining. The strong face and the bold features were illuminated by an inner source of light. However, Urmila sensed a note of discord in her beautiful grace. Her face indicated her subtle displeasure at the sight of Ram and Sita or was it dislike for Sita? Urmila was hard put to make out. How could anyone dislike her older sister, a near-perfect woman? Urmila was intrigued.

Kaikeyi caught Urmila's bewildered expression.

Moving closer to Lakshman and Urmila, Kaikeyi put her hand on Urmila's head, caressing it, "I heard about your boldness and fierceness. I am glad to see you as Lakshman's wife. You two are a striking pair."

Urmila was flooded with gratitude. "I am grateful for your praise, *Maata*. I feel beholden to have met a warrior like you," Urmila said touching Kaikeyi's feet.

The palace refused to open its door to the brides till their luck quotients were tested.

The princesses were told to kick the *kalash* – a pitcher full of rice – and let the grain scatter on the ground. "The wider the grain scatters, the more is the happiness and prosperity for the clan," Shanta explained. The scattered grain filled the forecourt of the palace.

"Now, put your feet into the platter of *kumkum* and enter your new home," she said. Shanta assigned Vindhya to help conduct the rest of the entry rituals. Raghukul let its guard down to enjoy a light banter between the couples and their earnest attempts to win the ritualistic competitions until dinner time. But Maharani Sumitra precluded Lakshman, Shatrughan and Vindhya from it as a punishment against the prank they had played on Urmila on the way.

The pranksters left without arguments but they were hungry after a while. They looked for ways to satiate their growling stomachs. Suddenly Lakshman's eyes glimmered with mischief, "I have a plan. You both just follow me. Manthara *dadi* will give us food."

Lakshman stepped into Manthara's room quietly, "I have good news for you but it is a secret that should not be disclosed, *Dadi Maa*." They misled her into believing that Bharath would soon be made 'king' by Dashrath. Manthara, who always wanted Bharath to become the king of Ayodhya, was euphoric and fed them with her own hands.

Urmila, on the other hand, was disappointed at Lakshman's sudden departure. Sumitra observed the sullen faces of her daughters-in-law. "*Maa*, I do not have the heart to eat before him and more so when he might be hungry somewhere on his own." Urmila refused to eat without Lakshman. Shrutakeerti concurred with Urmila, following in her footsteps. They sat in a corner.

Sumitra was proud, "My sons are blessed to have you both as their wives. I exempt them from the punishment. Come, let's find them."

They searched for the trio all over the palace and eventually found them in the most unexpected place, Manthara's room, giggling over platters of food. Sumitra reprimanded Manthara but she in turn defended the princes, "Do not berate my children. They tell me what I always pray for. You have finally decided to make my Bharath the king of Ayodhya."

Maharaj Dashrath, who had accompanied Sumitra to Manthara's chamber, turned ashen.

"Manthara, Manthara, you will remain a fool forever. Only my Ram is the righteous heir to the throne, not Bharath," Kaikeyi laughed scornfully.

Manthara stood appalled, a crestfallen expression furrowing her wrinkled old face like crumpled leather. All of them mocked her aspirations for Bharath, but Urmila was filled with a strange compassion. She touched the old maid's feet with respect, along with Shrutakeerti. Manthara had tears in her eyes. It was the first time someone had shown her respect. Except for Ram, Lakshman and Shatrughan, everyone in Ayodhya looked down upon her, even Bharath. Manthara tried to remove her feet from Urmila's touch, "You should not be touching my feet. You are the princess of Mithila and the *kulvadhu* of Raghukul. I am just a maid here."

Urmila was a kindred soul. "How can you not be respectable for me when my husband calls you *Dadi Maa?* Hence, you are my grandmother, too. Please shower your love on me and my sisters just like you do on *Swami* and his brothers."

"Stay blessed for this thoughtfulness." Manthara put her hand on Urmila and Shrutakeerti's heads with humility in her heart.

Queen Kaikeyi was firm that the brides would sleep with their mothers-in-law till the *maha puja* – a rite to ensure nuptial bliss. The princesses were disappointed, but Raghukul was rigid about its wedding mores. They were about to leave for the queen's chambers, when Kaikeyi stopped Urmila. She led the princess aside by her hand.

"Urmila, I want to have a word with you. Daughter, I saw the way you looked at me for my unconscious reaction to Sita, my face showed it. I wanted to clear the air. No one can be more perfect for Ram than Sita even though she is an orphan. But I was hurt because it has always been my dream to choose an appropriate bride for Ram. Maharaj did not even consider seeking my opinion. And I consider you the true princess of Mithila." Urmila was silent. Even though she did not like Kaikeyi referring to Sita as an orphan, she realised it was best not to react.

Sumitra escorted her daughters-in-law to her chambers, where she fed them from a big golden bowl of sweet milk porridge, well-aware how hungry they must have been after the long journey and the entry rites.

Thereafter, she put one *kshaakh ke laddu* – sweet rice ball – into Urmila's mouth and *besan ka halwa* – sweet gramflour pudding – into Shrutakeerti's mouth. She said that the rice ball and the pudding were their husbands' favourite sweet dishes respectively.

The easy acceptance of the princesses from Mithila into the illustrious Raghukul left Urmila and Shrutakeerti speechless. Watching Sumitra sleep later, Urmila could not help but admire her gentle beauty and lithe frame that set her apart from the rest.

Sumitra, who had embraced the aggressive Warrior Princess from Mithila for what she was, not for what Ayodhya would like her to be, touched Urmila's heart.

The couples sat together for the *Maha Puja*. Gurudev Vashishtha led the sacrament, "Untie your partner's *raksha dhaaga* to mark the beginning of an uninterrupted marital life."

The couples untied their protection threads and sought blessings of their elders. "Before you embark on your journey as householders, we as parents have gifts for our clan brides. Sita, you are our Lakshmi because you are our eldest *kulvadhu*, hence we gift you Kanak Bhavan. Urmila, for your love of the colour blue and pearls, Lakshman's and your palace will be Moti Bhavan. Mandvi and Bharath will live in Ksheesh Bhawan while Shatrughan and Shrutakeerti in Kamala Bhavan," King Dashrath declared. The palaces were gifts from the Maharaj to his daughters-in-law.

The gift of palaces entrenched the status of the princesses as the regal mascots of Ayodhya, the royal daughters-in-law. The girls were touched by this gesture of generosity and respect.

Urmila mused over the events that marked the hectic day as she walked to the kitchen with Shrutakeerti. She admired the generous spirit of Raghukul.

They halted as Sumitra called out to them, "*Paakshaala* – kitchen – responsibilities will begin from tomorrow for you all. Today, all you have to do is cherish tender moments with your husbands." Both her daughters-in-law turned scarlet, blushing.

Sumitra took them to Shivalay (her palace) to calm their nervousness and help them to understand the significance of the first night spent together as husband and wife. She personally decked them out for it, embellishing them with silks and jewellery from her own collection, "My dear daughters, this day begins your new life as a women. The night helps you to appreciate each other as partners and connect you at a physical and emotional level. Don't panic. The fear will dissipate as soon as you feel your husbands' touch."

Sumitra herded Urmila and Shrutakeerti to their respective palaces.

Urmila's palace Moti Bhawan was colossal. Pearls adorned its massive doors, *rangolis* and earthenware lamps decorated the entrances and an enormous garden with colourful beds of flowers sported an ornate swing. Towards the left, the garden broadened into a wide green bank leading to the River Sarayu. The vista took her breath away. To the right of the large balcony was a king-size bed ornamented with sculpted flowers in full bloom that made her breathing uneven. Such opulence! Mithila was not a patch on the extravagant richness of Ayodhya.

Urmila lay on the bed, a trifle spent. Her subconscious energy was attuned to Lakshman's footsteps. The moment her heart missed a beat, she knew Lakshman had entered the palace. She opened her eyes to look deep into his eyes. Their gazes interlocked and without a word he reached out and unclasped her jewelled hairpin. Her tresses scattered around the pillow. He ran his fingers through them, "You take my breath away." Urmila rested her head on his chest, "I find peace here and the sound of your heartbeat is the sound I want to hear forever."

He held her hands in his, "I have yearned to feel you this close to me, Mila. Today, my fear that you will be taken away from me has been put to rest." Urmila wiped the tears that ran down his eyes, "I am yours. No one can ever separate me from you; we are bound in our souls." "You are yours first, Mila and shall always be. I love you for being you. You are not my possession but my pride." Lakshman kissed her eyelids.

"You are far too modest and gentle, my lord. The traits I noticed in you even when we fought brought me to you; made me yours."

Urmila matched Lakshman in his magnanimity – her love as wide as the milky ocean.

Lakshman hesitated just before he bent down to lightly graze her lips with hers. His touch was rough yet tender. It left her breathless. She let him kiss the tears that slid down her cheeks, "May I?" He sought her permission to finally make her his. "You do not need permission for what is yours, *Swami*."

Ayodhya hid itself behind the moon as Rajkumar Lakshman began his journey as Urmila's Laksh. Shesha floated in his ocean, Ksheera.

Life at Ayodhya

Passion scripts the complex politics of parting.

The morning after a consummate night is lazy, dreamy. Ayodhya feels the shy and quiet touches of love and pirouettes to its tune with gaiety as its royal scions begin a new chapter of their lives.

Urmila woke up in Lakshman's arms. Even in his sleep, he held her deeply. Looking at him, sleeping soundly, she wondered at the child-like innocence of his face and felt a tenderness consume her. His love for sleep and her dislike for it was often a matter of gentle fights and friendly potshots between them.

She wanted her first morning in Ayodhya to be exceptional. She skillfully managed to disentangle herself from him and prepared to get ready as Ayodhya's *kulvadhu*. As she put on her jewellery, she felt the touch of his familiar hands. He wanted to help her dress as his!

Is it really possible to love someone this much for it to become your strength yet leave you weak with its gentle fragility? Urmila, always a distinctively opinionated woman, only needed Lakshman's eyes to rest on her to melt into submission.

Lakshman slid a couple of gold bangles with colourful enamel inlay on her wrists and waited for her reaction.

"My first real gifts to my Mila! Their colours will always remind me of your laughter and how completely you fit in my heart," Lakshman was hesitant.

Urmila ran her hand lightly over the gold bangles and stood on her toes to kiss him with the same repose. He felt his breath leave him. How could a touch be so tender yet leave him so breathless? The arrival of a maid forced them apart. Kaushalya had called Urmila to her chambers. The queens were waiting for their daughters-in-law.

Maharani Kaushalya, the eldest queen of Kosala, sat on a delicately-sculpted bed surrounded by her maids. Dressed in white and gold, the serene beauty lived up to her reputation of sobriety, reticence and gentleness as the senior-most queen of Ayodhya and the mother of Ram.

"Ayodhya feels perfect with all of you here with us. We have been taking care of ourselves and the family, for a long time now. It is time for you youngsters to take the burden of responsibilities off our tired shoulders," Maharani Kaushalya smiled lovingly at the four new members of the royal family. The chirping princesses and the scions of Ayodhya quietened down; Kaushalya had a strange calming influence on them.

The two younger queens joined Kaushalya a little while later.

The Maharani delegated the responsibilities of running the palace to the princesses. The four sisters had to supervise the kitchen together. Besides the task of overseeing the kitchen, Urmila and Shrutakreeti who were proficient in Ayurvedic treatments, were assigned to take care of King Dashrath's deteriorating health. The king suffered from old age-related complications.

With the contentious task of apportioning house-holding chores settled, the queens introduced the princesses to their personal maids-in-waiting. They were old servitors, having worked in the retinue of the queens for more than 20 years. Sita was given Prabha and Seema, Urmila Tara and Shanti, Preeti and Jyoti to Mandvi while Kranti and Medha went to Shrutakeerti.

Urmila was helping the cooks plan lunch when Shatrughan barged into the kitchen with an urgent summons from the king, "You will have to come with me to the *Rajya Sabha*, *bhabhi maa*, the Maharaj seeks your immediate presence."

Urmila was embarrassed that Shatrughan, the prince and her brother-in-law, had taken the trouble to come to the kitchen to escort her to the court personally at the king's behest. She was also overwhelmed at the same time; she was not sure whether she deserved such respect.

"You could have sent someone else, you didn't have to come all the way to the kitchen," Urmila said with humility.

Shatrughan's eyes were full of affectionate respect, "You are a mother figure to me. How can a son send a maid to fetch his mother?"

Urmila and Shatrughan shared a unique bond. She called him her son and he loved her as a mother figure, even though he was Lakshman's twin. All through their lives, Shatrughan did not waver in his support of Urmila for she always remained his bhabhi maa.

Urmila walked into the court with uncertainty, fear lurking somewhere inside her. Her eyes scanned for Lakshman and as soon as she saw his smiling face, her nervousness vanished. King Dashrath introduced Urmila to his ministers, "Here is Urmila, the younger *kulvadhu* of Raghukul and my dear Lakshman's wife. She is an astute princess, well versed in the study of *dharma*. Her endorsement in the state affairs will benefit Ayodhya greatly as she is familiar with its functioning and governance in general."

"It will be an honour to assist you, Maharaj," Urmila accepted the responsibility with folded hands. But a few of the ministers were skeptical and wanted to test her skills and knowledge before allowing her to advice on governance.

The ministers posed a set of key questions to her.

"Between emotions and *dharma*, what should you choose?"

"*Dharma* is our foremost duty. It should precede everything else." Her reply found favour.

"What are the different *dharma*s?"

Urmila was forthright, "*Dharma* can be classified as *Samanyadharma* – ethical duties, *Varnadharma* – duties of the caste, *Aashramdharma* – duties of the stages in life, *Gunadharma* – duties of good qualities, *Nimittadharma* – duties of expiation, *Apaddharma* – duties during time of disasters, *Stridharma* – duties of womanhood, *Vyashtidhrma* – duties of dual lives, and *Rajdharma* – duties of kingship."

Gurudev Vashishtha and the ministers hailed her. Lakshman was quiet but his eyes shone with pride at her knowledge and statesmanship. Ayodhya was triumphant.

Lakshman was not interested in the affairs of the state, but Urmila was an extremely seasoned advisor. Having acted as Maharaj Janak's representative in Mithila, she found unequivocal adulation in Ayodhya for her wisdom and intelligence. The infusion of fresh ideas – and blood – from another illustrious line brought excitement to the court, fostering new hope.

Urmila's victory in the *Rajya Sabha* changed the mood in the palaces of the young scions. Till late in the night, Urmila, Lakshman and Ram discussed and debated the state of Ayodhya's political and military affairs. They even forgot to eat their dinner. The queens were worried that the trio would suffer from ill-health if they starved themselves to attend to the duties of the court.

"Do you want both my daughters to fall sick? Urmila has not eaten dinner yet. Come on, I shall feed you all," Sumitra sent a missive to Lakshman and Ram around midnight.

"Lakshman, your wife has not eaten anything since her breakfast," Queen Kaikeyi joined Sumitra. "Who will take care of her?"

Lakshman was angry. "Mila, why did you not eat your lunch?"

"How could I have had lunch without you? You are hungry too," Urmila was quick to remind Lakshman that she cared.

The mothers watched the two fighting each other for each other. They were so immersed in their innocent love tussle that they did not notice the rest leave the room quietly, one by one. Suddenly, Lakshman and Urmila realised that they had been left to themselves.

"Come, let's eat together," Lakshman took her by the arm and led her out. Dinner was a modest but warm affair in Sumitra's palace followed by a peaceful night of sleep. The princesses were worn out by their new roster of duties.

The next day, Lakshman planned a wonderful surprise for Urmila at night (when everyone slept), as a token of his thanks.

He took the big wooden ladder that was stowed away behind Maharani Sumitra's chamber and went to the stables. He needed a silent accomplice and this time the abettor came in the form of Vayusena, his favourite horse.

Well after sundown, Lakshman stealthily returned to his bedroom to wake Urmila up. "Mila, open your eyes, my love."

This was perhaps the first time she was in such a deep sleep. Usually, her sleep patterns were fitful. "Why are you still awake? Is something bothering you?" she wanted to know sleepily, but her voice was laced with worry at seeing him awake in the wee hours. Something had to be on his mind to keep him on his toes so late in the night. And she planned to find out what exactly it was.

"No if's, no but's! Please get up, Mila. I have a surprise for you," Lakshman was eager and firm at the same time. He could not let Mila spoil the little party that he had planned for her.

"Surprise at this hour of the night?" She was curious.

"Yes, I have to take you to a place where no one has ever been to. Please wake up," he pleaded.

"We can go later in the day," she murmured as she reached out for him, pulling him close to her. They both gazed into each other's eyes for a long time, and then he bent close to plant a kiss on her lips. But at the last moment, he pulled back leaving Urmila longing for the act of intimacy.

"No, Lakshman. You are a man on a mission. You cannot give in to her charms," he told himself audibly.

He made a sad face and turned to the other side. "Okay, then, good night," he said in a small voice. But he knew that he had broken through her wall – the barriers of sobriety and conventions.

"Okay, I am coming," she said. Urmila did want to destroy the romance of the moment and moreover, she loved surprises.

They sat close to each other. "Please remove your anklets or else you will wake up the entire palace, Mila!" Lakshman's proximity made her breathless.

She got out of bed, "But where are we going?" He laughed softly, "Ah! Now that is a surprise."

"What kind of surprise that I have to take off my anklets? I don't understand. It is considered inauspicious." Urmila, superstitious by nature, was wary about taking her leg ornament off.

"Why do you believe in such superstitions?" Lakshman was irritated.

"Because apparently, I love my husband to an extent that forbids me to take any risks!" she retorted. Lakshman rolled his eyes in mock disbelief but, smiled, nevertheless. She was worried about his well-being. He suddenly scooped her up in his arms, which earned him a small squeal of surprise and an angry glare.

He carried her as if she was a feather. Taking her down the ladder to a secret passage that led to the stables, he put her down. She glowered at him, once again. "Why did you have to carry me? I could have walked down."

"Yes, but you could have woken the entire palace with your anklets. What would you have answered them if we were caught?" he jibed.

"Fine, I surrender but only this one time," she said with a scowl.

Lakshman took her to the corner where his favourite Vayusena was tethered. "Mila, meet him. He is my secret keeper. I trust him the most." She caressed Vayusena. "Are we going riding?"

"Yes, we can enjoy being ourselves only during these hours when the kingdom sleeps. Don't ask me any more questions, I beg of you, my dear." Lakshman was ready to go down on his knees like a little boy.

A few supplies were tied at the end Vayusena's saddle in a cloth bundle and she wondered what kind of adventure he had up his sleeve. "Let us go," He said, helping her on to the horse and they galloped off in the darkness.

As they raced through the winding alleys between the palace clusters and their extended quarters – to the empty streets and the green fields, blanketed in darkness, Lakshman showed her the places he connected to the most, the landmarks of his childhood nostalgia.

She smiled at the enthusiasm with which Lakshman narrated the tiny anecdotes that tied him to each place. He took her to the streets where the four brothers distributed alms to the poor and destitute during the festivals. While looking back at his past, Lakshman's voice became wistful – subdued with sadness at what had been lost forever.

Urmila was touched by her husband's gesture. Her heart overflowed with love and respect for Lakshman's endearing and selfless persona.

"Mila, look!"

Her trance was broken by the soft murmur of his voice in her ears. She looked to where he pointed; at the secluded little knoll, mesmerised by its serenity. They were on the banks of a brook, gurgling like fluttering heartbeats in the silence of the hour when the sun was poised on the horizon washing the eastern sky in pale hues of pink and orange. The night star was still shining in the sky.

She sprinted to the edge of the brook and stood there with her eyes closed, facing the horizon. "Beautiful!" she exclaimed with a smile as the soft breeze of the dawn fanned her face. The birds chirped on the branches of the trees that covered the brook like a canopy.

"I know, my love," she opened her eyes to his smiling face, overwhelmed with love.

She blushed with an unfathomable desire.

"Mila, I wanted to share my past with you since you agreed to share your present and future with me. Tell me, did I do anything wrong?" He held her chin and looked at her intently.

"I am proud to have you as my wife. It is my *dharma* to give you a surprise, love. And stop punishing your lips for nothing. One of these days it will surely fall off! And I cannot have that!" He traced his thumb over her pink, swollen lips gently.

"No, I am fortunate to have you as my husband. I know I can be difficult and irrational at times but thank you for loving me as you do." She hugged him with all her might and softly kissed his heart. "Mila, when I say I love you. I love every part of you. Even your imperfections for they are you. And with each passing day I love you more." He closed his eyes feeling her. He made her sit on a rug which he had spread out near the brook under a huge, perhaps a 100-year-old banyan tree.

Urmila gently held his hand and urged, "Promise me you shall never leave me for I will rather die than lose your love. I cannot live without you." She touched her forehead to his and breathed in heavily.

"Leave you? I can barely work without seeing you through the day. How will I survive if you are not around?" He paused for breath and then continued, "Never! I will never leave you. Our love story is eternal, my love."

Sarayu Tat watched the lovers, blind to the rising sun, cocooned in their own world reaffirming their profound love for one another. Somewhere not far away Vayusena chomped at the tender green grass in peace. As the first rays of the morning light touched their faces, they retraced their steps palaceward to welcome yet another new day.

The First Wedding Anniversary

It had been a year since their wedding. Urmila mused over how quickly it had passed by. She felt a pang of melancholy in the bliss. She missed the moments that would never come back, the moments that took a part of her Saumitra with them every day, yet the day which brought them together had to be celebrated in an unusual way.

Thus, Urmila too planned a little tryst to colour the day in rainbow shades of romance. She was painting a scene of their wedding from her memory and making riddles – cryptic clues – about the moments that had brought them close. She was up and about since dawn.

"Mila," he searched for her next to him, but the bed was empty. He stretched lazily, when her voice brought him out of his languor. "My love, I am waiting for you. Find the clues lying around in the palace and get me. Get up, hunt for them," she exhorted him.

Lakshman was like a hunter at the scent of a prey. He liked treasure hunts.

The first riddle, written on a piece of parchment that was lying on the dresser read, "You hold me holding our first touch." Lakshman knew his wife was not a fool and began to contemplate. After thinking for a moment, he touched their favourite sword; the one Urmila had sent him as a gift. It bore their first touch.

He walked to the second riddle. The square palm shard placed carelessly in a corner of the terrace, said, "The first fragrance laced with my scent you felt on your breath." He did not need to think twice, he came back to the bed-chamber to pick out an orchid from the bunch of flowers in the vase that sat near the bed.

"My first gift of friendship to you." Lakshman smiled at the thought of the next riddle. The journey to their friendship was chaotic, he mused, but this was no riddle for him. He picked up a guava from the fruit tray. They had come out of the woods as friends that day.

He suddenly wanted to hold her. To have her in his arms, he had to solve more riddles. He moved on to the next that read, "I felt I was important to you."

She had been important to him ever since he has held her sword, but she did not know it then. He recalled every time he felt the rush of feelings for her. He could not make her respond because she did not know what he felt for her. Suddenly, it dawned on him and he plucked a blue lotus from the pool in the garden. He had saved her life in a pool inside the forest.

"My unspoken love tastes your lips." He fumbled over this one. He played and replayed the moments when he touched her lips. But each time, it was only after their love was disclosed. He pursed his lips to recall more such moments. "Ah, she means *malpua*," he had finally cracked it.

And ultimately, he came to the last riddle. It said, "We burnt for each other." As far as he could remember, he always had this insatiable yearning for her but when had she burnt for him? He paced around the chamber, while Urmila smiled at his unrest from behind the curtains.

He opened the cupboard, took out something, hid it behind him and picked up the last bit of folded parchment. "Mila awaits Laksh behind the curtains."

He went to the balcony where Urmila was hiding behind a pillar. She had a painting in her hands. "Happy Anniversary, my love." She handed him a small pot of vermillion which he put in the parting of her hair.

He looked at the painting which captured a moment from their wedding night in splashes of surreal colours. He felt the sting of tears in his eyes and kissed her forehead, "Happy Anniversary, my love. I am not me without you."

Lakshmila remained locked in each other's embrace for long moments inhaling the scent that enveloped them. Any existence without the other was insignificant to them and the thought of separation filled them with dread so deep that it almost threatened to suck out their life force.

Maharani Sumitra stopped at the door not wishing to intrude into their moment of perfect happiness. She found them wrapped in each other's arms. An unexplained wave of emotional contentment washed over her to see Lakshman happy and in love with his wife. It filled her heart with gratitude – for god who had been merciful and for the feisty princess from Mithila.

"God bless you both," she held a platter of *kshaakh ke laddu* for them. They touched her feet before embracing her and squabbling over the sweetmeats like children. Maharani Sumitra, Lakshman and Urmila spent some light moments together teasing each other, before the queen left Urmila's palace saying, "Shatrughan must be waiting for me. Get ready and join us for the *maha aarti* – the big morning prayer." She was on her daily rounds of the abodes of her children.

After the *maha aarti*, the couples walked barefoot among the subjects to seek their blessings and love in a customary *praja darshan* – meeting the subjects – ritual. Their support and acknowledgment touched Urmila.

You accept me in your prince's life so readily. I know what he means to you and I promise I shall never disappoint you, she thought, looking at the people of Ayodhya who had lined up to meet them, and then casting a furtive glance at Lakshman walking beside her. He seemed to read her thoughts and smiled, his eyes lighting up in gratitude.

She accepted him and what was his, this vast kingdom by the broad meandering river, so easily.

Just then, a little girl from the throng ran to Urmila, "*Pranaam* – greetings – Rajkumari. I want to be a sword warrior like you to fight for my land."

"God bless you, little one," Urmila said, picking up the girl in her arms. "The doors of my palace are always open to you. You will be the best warrior in Aryavarta some day." She blessed the child.

The subjects hailed her gesture of generosity – the *kulvadhu* of Raghukul – inviting a poor child to her palace to learn sword-fighting. They were amazed.

The girl handed a garland woven with scented white jasmine blossoms to Lakshman. She had especially wreathed it for Urmila.

"Rajkumar, can you please tie the wreath around Rajkumari's braid?" she demanded.

The crowd endorsed the child's plea even though Lakshman was embarrassed. But the happiness of his people was more important to him than his personal awkwardness at a public show of 'intimate affection' to his wife. He gently wreathed the string of white blossoms around Urmila's braid, twisting the strands so that they encircled the lustrous length like the *angavastra*.

Only his eyes reflected the pride and love he felt for his wife as he braided the garland in her hair.

A big surprise awaited them in the palace. The royal family of Mithila, accompanied by Gargi Vachaknavi, had arrived in Ayodhya to greet the couples on their first wedding anniversary. The reunion was steeped in powerful emotions; tears and laughter flowed together.

Urmila hugged Gargi, weeping profusely. Lakshman watched them quietly. Gargi looked at him in silent gratitude. He bowed his head in reverence to Gargi, and embraced Maharani Sunaina, who stood next to King Janak.

Lakshman had ensured that Gargi accompany Maharaj Janak and Maharani Sunaina. He knew the bond Mila shared with Gargi Vachaknavi. It was his unspoken gift to his wife on their first wedding anniversary.

Gargi drew Urmila close to her bosom. "I am here because he invited me," Vachaknavi said, pointing to Lakshman.

Urmila felt a surge of intense respect for the man who stood there with a shy smile. Someday, she would teach him how to express his love in words but until then she would remain engulfed in his silent overtures of love.

In the end, Urmila walked to her father Maharaj Janak who had been waiting patiently for his daughter. He looked hurt.

"It's been long, my child. I thought you would embrace me the first," Janak held Urmila to his heart. "Guru comes first, father. How could I acknowledge you before I met my *Maata*?" Urmila sought his forgiveness. Maharani Sunaina watched her daughter with pride, "You were always wise but now you have become humble too. Lakshman has changed you."

Maharani Sumitra set the remark in context. "Lakshman is a changed man with her in his life. She complements him perfectly. He has learnt how to love with her around. I am blessed to have your daughter as mine."

While the parents renewed their bonds, Lakshman and Urmila slipped way from the room to the open terrace. Together, they looked at the moon that shone so luminous and yet so silent. "We shall never give up on you, me and us," they said together to the moon. The orb seemed to glow brighter for a moment.

Lakshmila's love radiated like the moon – steady, white and selfless.

And the day slowly gave in to evening with blessings for another year as Lakshmila fell asleep in each other's arms.

Manthara's Plans

Time and tide flow to meet compelling prophecies.

Twelve years passed in the blink of an eye. Maybe the fear evoked in Maharani Sunaina by her astrologer's prophecy unveiled when everyone slept. Ayodhya stayed awake. Dread filled the air over Ayodhya. Fate was sulking in the shadows to strike its blow.

The love that struck tender roots to germinate into a leafy tree between Lakshman and Urmila had only strengthened in the last 12 years, a duodecennial of bliss. Every night, Lakshman and Urmila lay awake in each other's arms to confess their love with the moon as witness, "It will always connect us even when we are not with each other. Find me in its silver shadows Saumitra as I find you. It is and will be our mediator." Urmila ran her fingers through his hair to lull him to sleep. The white moon looked down at them with a sleepy smile.

Kaikeyi watched the moon, too, that night from her terrace. She suddenly wanted to say something, spill a deep secret that she hid very carefully in her heart. The queen called her maid Manthara to her side, "Manthara, may I reveal a wish which I have held on to since years to you today?" The moon was playing tricks with her head, making her feel light, open and a little 'conspiratorial'.

Manthara sat at her feet. "Have I ever not listened or understood? Go on!"

"I have loved Ram more than Bharath ever since the day he was born even though he did not come from my womb. And it is my heartfelt desire to see Ram become the king of Ayodhya after Maharaj," Kaikeyi sighed.

"You aspire for Ram but you have forgotten your own son, why?" Manthara was intrigued.

"Kaushalya *didi* worries about Bharath like she does about her own son. My love for Ram does not ever stand in the way of my love for Bharath, both of them are my sons," Kaikeyi said, remembering how she held Ram as a child for the first time. The queen was trying to convey a subtle message – but was leaving something important unsaid. An intuitive Manthara knew what she was driving at.

"Something here is not right. My sixth sense tells me," Manthara tried to provoke Kaikeyi, who carefully dodged the bait.

"Manthara, why do you dislike Ram so much? I don't approve of your attitude towards him. You seem to love Lakshman and Shatrughan more than Ram. Bharath has always been your priority, but why are you against Ram, railing silently against the one who is a perfect son, a perfect brother and a perfect husband, and even a perfect king." Kaikeyi insisted on knowing the reason.

She reached out to grasp the wrinkled arm of the old maid in a vice-like grip. The queen, however, kept her face averted from the maid and continued to stare at the moon. Her face shone with feline grace in the translucent light.

Manthara tried to free her hand from Kaikeyi's grip but the queen held on to it. "You will not leave before you answer me," Kaikeyi was unrelenting.

Manthara cried in exasperation, "I don't dislike Ram. But I don't trust Maharani Kaushalya. Kaikeyi, you are too gracious to understand that Maharani Kaushalya uses Ram against you because she is jealous of the fact that you are Maharaj's favourite wife."

"Manthara, you are mistaken. The queens have not ever discriminated against me. They love me as their own sister," Kaikeyi asserted, countering Manthara's ploy to divide Dashrath's wives.

"I am not trying to vitiate you against Maharani Sumitra. She is a simple lady with wise intentions but Maharani Kaushalya is a complex woman. I have a feeling that she is plotting to betray you soon. Mark my words, queen," Manthara incited Kaikeyi, sowing the seeds of doubt in her mind about Kaushalya's intentions.

"I do not want any further discussion on this. You may retire to your room, now," Kaikeyi ordered the maid.

"My words might sound bitter today, but very soon they will be vindicated," Manthara prophesied before leaving.

Manthara was angry at Kaikeyi's stoic defense of Ram but she had to protect Kaikeyi and her interest at all cost. If Kaikeyi did not redeem her boons, the divine plan would unravel; or probably she had been unable to gauge the way in which Kaikeyi's mind worked.

She believed that her Guru *ji* might help her and she fervently invoked him with her eyes shut, "Help me know who Ram is. He doesn't seem to be a normal being. Please, Guru *ji*."

Her Guru *ji* smiled and placed his hand on her head. She felt the reassuring grace of his touch, "See who he is, know him."

Narayan, the protector of the universe, stood before her with Ram's face. Manthara was suddenly enlightened. "Ram, Maha Vishnu himself. I must have done something good in my last birth to hear him call me *dadi* – granny." Her voice shook with wonder, gratification and penance, "I repent for my sins, my Lord. I shall serve you with all my heart hence on." She was in a daze with the light of her knowledge.

"No, Manthara. You cannot serve Narayan the way you want to because you are the chosen one," Guru *ji*'s voice was soft.

"How do you say such things?" How can I be the chosen one, when all I have done is to mistreat Ram? I seek Narayan's forgiveness." The old maid went down on her knees.

Her mentor smiled again, his benign aura surrounding her like a warm current. "Manthara, you do what you have set out to do. Let Ayodhya face the black hour for it is in this darkness that light will shine. Your Ram and Saumitra will have to leave the kingdom to redefine *dharma* and selflessness. Narayan wants you to be the inceptor of the plan." With his hand again on her head, he transmitted her into the future. A series of visions unfolded before her eyes; Manthara cowered in fear and reverence.

Tears flowed from her eyes. She was blessed to be of some use as a human being by her creator. Her hands trembled for a moment when she thought of how the world would hate her and yet to be able to help Lord Vishnu to fulfil the mission with which he had come to Aryavarta was more important than how she would be hailed by the epochs to come. Manthara's mind ticked at a ferocious speed, disseminating thoughts and the plan into a meticulous order.

Manthara needed allies, insiders she could trust to put her plan into action. It would not be easy to find friends who would be ready to 'betray' Raghukul but Mandvi could be a trusted ally. From what Manthara had gauged, Mandvi had a fond weakness for the trappings of kingship and the luxuries that came with the status of a Raghukul princess. Meshing her in her own material desires would be easy.

It was time to start sowing disagreement, doubts and treachery among the sisters. Even though Manthara was chosen by Narayan himself to carry out the plan, she was not comfortable with how vicious she would have to be if the mission had to get off the ground. Who would understand her pleas of forgiveness after the deed was done? That was the way the cosmos connived.

Manthara set out for Bharath and Mandvi's palace. At the door, Mandvi bent down to touch her feet but Manthara shrank from her touch. "Why should the queen-to-be of Ayodhya touch the feet of a maid?" she said, hinting at the future with a knowing smile. Mandvi looked at her in consternation and held her hand.

"I will tell you a secret today. Kaikeyi never speaks about it, but Maharaj Dashrath had promised Kaikeyi's father that her son would inherit the throne. In that case, you will invariably be the queen." The furrows on Manthara's face deepened as her smile broadened. This was the first time she had revealed the future of Ayodhya's succession to one of the new princesses.

"Can Arya be the king? But I wonder how? Ram *bhaiya* is the eldest and legitimately due to succeed Dashrath to the throne." Mandvi dared not hope though it floated like a light in the distance, tantalising and beckoning.

Manthara looked at Mandvi. "If I am not mistaken, you have always nurtured a secret wish to become the queen of Ayodhya, right? And why wouldn't you? You are the princess of Sankasya. You deserve more than that adopted daughter of Maharaj Janak," the maid said, adding grist to the simmering flame of greed, discord and sabotage. It had to rage like an infernal blaze.

"Maharaj could decide to make Lakshman *bhaiya* the king?" Mandvi wanted to check out every possibility.

"Maharani Sumitra's son will not ever make his way to the throne. Even though Maharani Sumitra is the second queen of the Maharaj, she is from Kashi which is not as wealthy as Ayodhya, Kekeya and Mithila. Why will the Maharaj make Saumitra or Shatrughan sit on the throne? He won't." Manthara's brutal description of Lakshman and Sumitra's 'royal pedigree' hit Mandvi, wounding her deep in the soul. Sumitra was her sisters' mother-in-law. She feared Narayan's wrath.

"You are right. I deserve more. Sita *didi* and Urmila have taken away so much from me. I won't let them do so now." Mandvi's arrogance resurfaced.

"You will become the ideal queen. You are perfect," Manthara reinforced, trying the drive the wedge further. Mandvi's smiled. The reason why she chose to marry Bharath was poised for fruition.

Narayan smiled. The seeds of betrayal had been implanted. Manthara would never be forgiven for her insidiousness.

As was the way of life inside the palace, the sisters often met to catch up on their personal well-being and trade gossip. The coronation of the prince-regent was uppermost in their discussion because the sweepstakes had been put in place. "Brother Ram will soon be crowned the next king," Shrutakeerti gushed in excitement.

"He may not be," Mandvi smiled secretively causing the other three to look at her in surprise. "Well, the Maharaj had promised Queen Kaikeyi's father that *Kaikeyinandan* will be the next king of Ayodhya," a naive Mandvi divulged with an air of self-importance.

"There you go again touting your baseless theories prompted by your greed to become the queen," Urmila lost her temper.

"At least, I have my priorities right. My husband or I do not run errands like servitors for Ram *bhaiya* as you and your husband do," Mandvi gloated.

Urmila was silent. Mandvi had failed to realise how deeply she had hurt her sisters with her inconsiderate and cruel words.

"I refuse to fall for your bait, Mandvi. What you say about *Sumitranandan* is unforgivable. It will be better if you stay away from my husband and me," Urmila excused herself from the conversation politely. She did not want to get into an argument with Mandvi before finding out more about her intriguing revelation.

An aggrieved Sita looked sadly at Urmila's receding figure because she was no stranger to palace conspiracies. Urmila was upfront in her stand against injustice; she had to master the art of tactfulness. Probably, time would teach her to be more restrained and astute in her reactions. Shrutakeerti glared at Mandvi, "Perhaps, it is your greed for the throne that drives you to say such. I am ashamed to call you my sister."

Mandvi left for her palace in a huff, but not before a few more harsh counterblows. Sita was desperate to pacify Urmila, but Shrutakeerti did not like the idea of mending fences now that the curtain had gone up on the subtle power play underway in the palace. She felt that Lakshman could best placate Urmila and set her doubts to rest.

Urmila was pacing up and down the terrace of her palace in anger when Lakshman returned late in the evening. She broke down at his gentle touch, her tears soaking his *angavastra*. At his persistence, she blurted out how Mandvi had hurt her with her account of the conspiracy being plotted to rob Ram of his inheritance.

Lakshman was not the least disturbed by the discord among the sisters. He smiled casually, "Who else but Ram *bhaiya* deserves to be the king? Ignore what she says. As for me, I am nothing without my brother and I have no qualms about it." He allayed her fears.

"Mila, you are such a crybaby. You have drenched my *angavastra* with your tears." He poked fun at her to change her mood. "No, I am not a crybaby. I apprehend trouble," she shot back. Their war of words ended in a cute flower and pillow fight. They fell into the bed laughing, happy that nothing untoward could happen to Ram.

After dinner, Mandvi tried to make up with Urmila, but failed to get through her bitterness to make her smile. Mandvi knew she had messed it up for good with her unthinking words. Unable to bear the uncomfortable silence between them, she hugged Urmila, "I am sorry, my *Rakshasi*. I hit out because Manthara had poisoned my mind with her wily plans."

Taken aback, Urmila stared at Mandvi. She refused to believe it but at Mandvi's persistence, she decided to let Lakshman know about the plot that Manthara was hatching – or perhaps fanning the fire that had been lit to destroy the clan. Urmila was pensive. Her mind ticked with the racing beats of her heart. She tried to probe the reason for Manthara's revelation but Mandvi could not throw more light on it. Urmila was not sure about the hidden forces at play.

Lakshman should know, she thought. Lakshman listened to her quietly and suggested that Urmila forget what Manthara had revealed because no one else but Ram would be the next king of Ayodhya; it was the order of succession.

Urmila was in a state of nervous disquiet; she could not shrug off the niggling worry at the back of her head.

Arya Sumantra interrupted the Raghukul royals at breakfast with an urgent letter from Yuvaraj Yuddhajeet, Queen Kaikeyi's brother. Maharaj Dashrath motioned him to read it aloud. Prince Yudhajeet wanted Bharath and Shatrughan to come to Kekeya soon as possible as Maharaj Ashwapati, Kaikeyi's father, was not well and was eager to meet his grandsons along with their wives before anything unforeseen happened to him.

It was decided that the younger princes with their wives would leave for Kekeya, the next morning.

Urmila felt a trifle sad and insecure to watch Shatrughan leave. Her son-like younger brother-in-law filled her with joy with his easy bantering and decency.

Lakshman hid his angst under the garb of frivolous sarcasm, "Enjoy Kekeya and the company of cousin Pritharth. Only you both have the strength to handle a hulk like him." Amidst ripples of laughter, Lakshman hugged his brother Shatrughan. For reasons unknown, he had this uncanny feeling that it would be a long time before he would meet his younger sibling again. Even though he brushed aside his misgivings with a merry smile, the uninvited tears in his eyes foretold of a tumultuous chain of events.

Bharath and Shatrughan departed with a heavy heart. They did not know that the Ayodhya they were leaving behind was to change forever. The very essence and roots of their ties would be swept away by a storm that would take 14 years to heal.

Dashrath's Sudden Announcement

The night of Ayodhya's undoing was also its redemption?

Destiny is often known to take sudden detours wreaking havoc since it is not always kind and Ayodhya was soon to learn this.

The day Bharath and Shatrughan departed for Kekeya did not augur well for Ram and Lakshman.

The weather was wet and sporadic rain doused the cheer that had generally pervaded the palace since the arrival of the Mithila princesses. The seers predicted a cyclone.

The palace was anxious for no apparent reason. Late in the night, a panic-stricken chambermaid from Queen Kaushalya's palace knocked frantically on the door of Moti Bhavan. Queen Kaushalya had summoned Urmila and Lakshman immediately to her living quarters.

The summons was unusual. Lakshman had a foreboding of a catastrophe and they ran to Shivalay. Ram and Sita were already present in the eldest queen's palace, when Lakshmila entered.

They were shaken to see King Dashrath in the throes of acute distress. He was breathing heavily and was in physical pain.

"*Maa*, what is wrong with father?" Urmila cried in fear.

"While we were returning from the *Rajya Sabha*, he fell down. His heart gave in," Ram was downcast.

While the family waited for the *Raj Vaidya* – royal physician, Sita and Urmila made an Ayurvedic concoction from herbs that the royal kitchen stocked. The potion rejuvenated the king, easing his breath and relieving his pain. The old king gradually opened his eyes.

"I have become old and weak now with death barely a step away. But, I know my children will not let death snatch me this early. They will always bring me back from the brink. You all go and sleep now. I need some time alone with your mother," Dashrath smiled feebly, thanking the princesses for their benevolence, presence of mind and acumen as Ayurvedic healers.

"I am here with him. You all can go. I will call you if necessary," a grateful Kaushalya urged them to leave. She was trembling in relief.

"Kaushalya, I do not have much time left on this earth. Before I go, I want to see my Ram sit on the throne of Ayodhya. His *Raj Tilak* – coronation – should take place as soon as possible," Dashrath said, resting his head in Kaushalya's lap.

"Yes, Maharaj. Let Bharath and Shatrughan return and your health improve," Kaushalya caressed his head with love.

"No, I do not have time until then. Kaushalya please help me fulfil my last wish," Dashrath closed his eyes.

"Hush…we will," Kaushalya lulled him to sleep.

At dawn even before the cock crowed to herald a new day, Dashrath woke up, slightly weak. He was firm in his resolve to perform Ram's *Raj Tilak* and convened an urgent meeting of his ministers, seers and noblemen in the *Rajya Sabha*. When the *Sabha* was full, he announced his wish for Ram and Ayodhya. Gurudev Vashishtha and the ministers were euphoric at the king's proposal. Ram was the perfect heir, they agreed.

The sooner Ram took over the reins from his father, the better and safer for Raghukul, the ministers concurred away from the king's sharp ears.

"Gurudev, since we have everyone's assent please set the nearest auspicious date for my Ram's coronation. I don't want to be as unfortunate as my father Aja, who died before I could sit on the throne of Ayodhya," Dashrath pleaded with regret in his voice.

"Let me look up the *nakshatra* – stars," Gurudev Vashishtha replied in a soft voice because he could foresee a tragedy, but he was under oath not to speak about to his father, Brahma Deva.

"Maharaj, Ram's *Raj Tilak* should be held tomorrow early in the morning. Arya Sumantra, please inform Ram and Sita, immediately." The seer sent Arya Sumantra to Ram's palace. Lakshman and Urmila were in Ram's palace when Sumantra arrived with the missive that King Dashrath wanted his eldest son and daughter-in-law to be present in the *Rajya Sabha* without delay.

According to custom, Lakshman and Urmila set out with Rama and Sita to escort them to the court, but Sumantra stopped them at the door saying that King Dashrath had sought only the presence of Ram with his wife.

"Forgive me, Prince Lakshman, I just follow orders. Only prince Ram and his wife have to meet the king," Sumantra explained to Lakshman. Ram was as bewildered by the secrecy of the audience as was Lakshman. He appealed to his brother and Urmila to be patient. Both Lakshman and Urmila were curious. Why had Ram and Sita been summoned to the *Sabha*? They decided to ask Queen Kaushalya about it.

The queens had flocked to Kaikeyi's chambers and when Lakshman walked in, the agitation on his flushed face was evident.

"*Maa*, do you all know why only brother Ram and sister-in-law Sita have been called to the *Rajya Sabha*?" he wanted to know.

"The Maharaj must have good reasons to call him and Sita," said Kaikeyi, baffled by Dashrath's strange behaviour. "Let Ram return," Sumitra tried to calm Lakshman and Urmila.

Kaushalya was quiet because she knew the reason but she chose not to reveal it without Dashrath's consent. Ram and Sita returned after nearly an hour.

They sought the blessings of the three queens.

"With your blessings, Maharaj wants me to inherit the throne of Ayodhya, Lakshman to become the *senapati* – commander-in-chief – and Urmila, the chief advisor of Ayodhya. Gurudev wants the *Raj Tilak* to take place tomorrow. The council of ministers has endorsed Lakshman as the commander-in-chief and Urmila as the chief advisor," Ram said.

Lakshman embraced his brother in an intense moment of love and joy while Urmila hugged Sita. Kaikeyi blessed Ram effusively, "My dream has come true. My Ram will be the king of Ayodhya." Kaushalya smiled while Sumitra blessed Ram and Lakshman for their good fortune.

Unknown to Urmila, Kaushalya and Ram had been observing Urmila's exuberance intently. "Has everything been done according to my instructions?" Urmila questioned the maids. "Yes, Rajkumari," the maids politely dispersed. "Urmila, you have not done all your work, a duty still remains to be discharged," Ram gently chided her.

"Which duty do you speak of, brother?" Urmila was clueless.

"Urmila, Shanta will not be able to be here for your brother Ram's *Raj Tilak*. You will have to perform the duties of a sister. Will you?" Kaushalya smiled.

"*Maata*, I will be honoured to. Ram *bhaiya* is the only older brother that I have. It will be my pleasure," Urmila felt self-conscious. Ram laughed.

***

Urmila performed her duties of a sister according to Gurudev Vashishtha's instructions. "Daughter, the *puja* is over now. You can ask Ram and Sita to grant you a wish."

Urmila joined her hands humbly in a *namaskar*, "Gurudev, I am younger than them. What can I ask for from someone who has already gifted me everything in the form of my Saumitra? All I want is their happiness."

"We knew you will not ask for anything. But we have a gift for our dear sister," Ram was always protective about Urmila and empowered her with a boon. "Urmila, I grant you a special ability. Hence on, you will be able to do three things at a time." Sita blessed her sister echoing Ram.

The night before the Rajyabhishek was long. Conspiracy and treacheries were weaving their way into the peaceful mosaic of Ayodhya. No one heard the approaching footsteps except Gurudev Vashishtha. While Ayodhya slept, the two sisters shared each other's joy.

"*Didi*, don't forget your little Urmi after you become the queen of Ayodhya," Urmila's voice wavered. A fleeting uncertainty took the firmness out of her voice; suppose she was thrown away to the sidelines in the sweeping turn of events?

"You are but a part of me. Sita is incomplete without Urmila," Sita was equally emotional.

"*Didi*, did *Maata* Gargi ever disclose that the day *Maa* became pregnant with me, she found you that very day? I am here because of you. Sita is the creator of Urmila. I love you," Urmila broke down. Sita drew her close, laughing away her tears.

Tragedy lurks in laughter. They did not notice the knowing look that Mithila exchanged with the moon that night, far away from Ayodhya.

Kaikeyi Goes To Kopa Bhavan – Grief Chamber

Gods always choose a vehicle to ferry-cart their will.

The whims of a beautiful woman can destroy lands, sometimes people, too. Ayodhya had mocked the saying until the very queen it flaunted became the destroyer of its peace.

An excited Kaikeyi told Manthara about the forthcoming coronation.

"Tomorrow, my Ram will become the king of Ayodhya. No one in Aryavarta can be happier than me at this moment," the queen gushed, handing the old maid a long list of requisitions for the ceremony.

The news came as a blow to Manthara. The maid panicked.

"Kaikeyi, come with me. I want to discuss something that cannot wait." The maid dragged Kaikeyi away from the unseen ears of the palace to the seclusion of her bed-chamber.

Kaikeyi was astonished by Manthara's aggression. "Kaikeyi, if you respect me as a mother then promise to hear me out without interrupting."

"I give you my word. Speak up..."

"Kaikeyi, it agonises me to say this, but you have been fooled by the Maharaj who you profess to love so much. He has only been playing with your feelings. Isn't it odd that Ram's *Raj Tilak* is happening in the absence of Bharath? Maybe he sent Bharath away in a deliberate gesture. Maharaj Dashrath had promised your father that your son will become the king after him but he conveniently forgot his promise after Ram was born. What vexes me is that you support him by loving Ram more than Bharath. Have you ever thought how your innocent son must feel at this humiliation? No wonder your son trusts Maharani Kaushalya more than you. In spite of warning you at the very outset that Kaushalya is the devil, you allowed Bharath to treat her as a mother. She hates your happiness. I am sure she planted the idea of a hurried coronation in the king's head. Kaikeyi, I forewarn you. Put an end to this *Raj Tilak*, else no one will be able to save your ouster from grace," Manthara said between sobs, waiting for Kaikeyi's reaction.

Kaikeyi was cornered. She swung between her loyalty to Ram and King Dashrath, and her aspiration for Bharath. Manthara may have been right in her intuition and observation. Manthara had friends in the most unexpected of places inside the palace.

"You may be right. It never struck me..." the queen faltered. "But how do I save Bharath's inheritance at this late hour? Help me, Manthara." Kaikeyi suddenly sounded desperate, her ferocious black eyes boring into Manthara as if trying to see into her soul.

"Well, I have a plan. Use the two boons Maharaj granted you at the time of *devasur sangram*. For the first, ask for Bharath's *Raj Tilak* and for the second seek Ram's exile for 14 years," Manthara advised.

The maid's sly ways troubled Kaikeyi. "...But Manthara, 14 years is too long a time to be away from the palace. I love Ram as a son," the queen protested.

"You cannot give in to sentimental love now. It is either Ram or Bharath. Or else, the throne of Ayodhya will be lost to Bharath forever, and history will remember Ram as the king," Manthara held Kaikeyi's hands to reassure her. "How can you think of Ram's well-being when Kaushalya back-stabbed Bharath?"

Kaikeyi, a mere pawn in Narayan's plans, agreed to do Manthara's bidding, "I shall go to Kopa Bhawan – the chamber of grief and atonement just now." The queen did not waste time.

Ayodhya was numb at this sudden twist of fate. Kaikeyi stood disgraced in its eyes. Ayodhya grieved it's loss of grace, unaware yet that Ram had to go away. The 'exile' had been decreed 'elsewhere', much before Aryavarta had drifted into its place from its parent cluster of continental mass.

The tremors of Kaikeyi's action, contrary to the natural flow of Raghukul's traditions, sent seismic shockwaves even before she could make her wish to the ailing king. Urmila wept in her sleep.

"Ram *bhaiya*, Sita *didi*, *Swami*, don't leave me alone. I will die without you, *Swami*." Urmila's plea woke Lakshman up from a nightmare that he was having.

"I am right here, Mila. I shall always be. I am not going anywhere." He held her close, choosing to remain silent about his own bad dreams.

Urmila clung to him tightly. "Do not leave me alone ever, Saumitra. I cannot bear to be separated from you." Lakshman hugged her tighter.

"We won't, Mila. Now go to sleep. Ram *bhaiya*'s coronation will be held early tomorrow. You have to perform several rituals," he lulled her. "...And when I am not with you, the moon will reflect my shadow, it will remind you that I am right here with you," he teased her to drive away her fear.

"Don't mock my love, *Swami*. Urmila is a body without breath if she does not hear her Saumitra's heartbeats." Lakshman wiped her tears and put her to sleep.

Maybe Urmila's subconscious mind knew what the 'conscious' had glossed over?

The morning was mellow. The sun shone through the stray cottony clouds tinted golden around their fluffy edges. The palace echoed with the sounds of celebration. Preparations were underway for Ram's *Raj Tilak*, which was to take place in a while. Since dawn, Urmila was busy with the ritual prayers that would run up to the actual coronation rite a little later in the day.

"The throne of Ayodhya awaits its new king and queen," the Warrior Princess declared. Urmila's happiness was bountiful.

"And don't you forget about Lakshman and yourself, Urmi. You both hold important positions from now on," Sita reminded her younger sibling.

"We will always be here to serve our king and queen," Urmila assured Sita.

Maharaj Dashrath could not take his eyes off Ram's face. The light of the sun reflected in his serene beauty casting an aural halo around his head. Everyone from the royal household was present at the *Rajya Sabha*, except for Queen Kaikeyi.

The king waited for her before flagging off the coronation ceremony. "Kaikeyi must be dressing up in her finery for her favourite son's *Raj Tilak*. Let me fetch her myself," Dashrath announced, beaming. He left for Kaikeyi's palace, barely a few furlongs from the coronation hall.

The doors of Kaikeyi's palace were closed. *Where can she go at this hour before the coronation*, an agitated Dashrath thought.

He called the guards, querying about Kaikeyi. They did not know. The king immediately summoned Manthara. His heart fluttered in fear. Manthara told him that Kaikeyi was waiting for him at Kopa Bhavan. He walked to Kopa Bhavan, chanting Narayan's name all the way. The chamber of grief and lament bore ill before an auspicious and important event like a royal coronation.

Kopa Bhavan was shadowed in darkness when King Dashrath entered it. The windows were heavily draped and no sunlight filtered into the little structure built like a cavern with a sanctum dedicated to the 'dark' gods, in the centre of the hall. Queen Kaikeyi, wrapped in a black *sari* – six yards of thick opaque body drape – with her face smeared in *kumkum*, lay on the floor, wailing in grief and beating her chest. She looked ghastly like a demoness in despair. Dashrath faltered as he walked up to her.

"Why do you lie here, my love? Ram is waiting for you at his coronation ceremony," Dashrath touched Kaikeyi on her shoulder.

"There will be no *Raj Tilak* if you are a man of your word," she lashed out in anger. This could not be his Kaikeyi; the king recoiled in horror.

Dashrath felt the sinking wave of doom in his heart and his face lost colour. "What are you saying, Kaikeyi?" he cried out, collapsing on the floor.

"Today, I claim my boons you granted me at the *devasur sangram*. Grant me Bharath's coronation instead of Ram's as my first wish and Ram's exile for 14 years as my second wish," Kaikeyi's voice was cold and emotionless.

Dashrath lamented in agony, "I cannot believe this is you Kaikeyi, the one I married, the one who loves Ram so much. My Kaikeyi can never be this cruel. Without Ram there is no Dashrath. My Ram is my life. Save me from this sin, the boons that you seek."

"Either you grant me my wishes or accept that Maharaj Dashrath's promise is meaningless," the queen was firm. The devil held Kaikeyi tightly in his grip, or perhaps it was god's strange will.

"I loved you as I have never loved any other woman but today I regret the moment I set my eyes on you. I disown you from this very moment. You are not my wife, anymore. I want you to think of Ram only. He respects you more than Kaushalya. What did my Lakshman do to you?" a tormented Dashrath lashed out at her in pain. The strain showed on his pallid bloodless face which was bathed in sweat.

"Don't you dare include Saumitra in your nefarious plan." Kaikayi was furious.

"My Lakshman is Ram's mirror. They look at each other in themselves, two in one. This betrayal will finish Lakshman as well." He got up from the floor where he had crumpled, on unsteady legs, to leave.

"You and Bharath cease to exist for me. Leave this palace right away. You are free to go to your father Ashwapati. I am ashamed of you. You are just like your mother, Kaikeyi...Evil!" the king said in disgust as he walked to the door of Kopa Bhavan.

"He who sells his own daughter calls my mother evil. I, Kaikeyi, the princess of Kekeya and the queen of Ayodhya, declare that even when *yuga*s − epochs − change, the world ends, there will be no Kaikeyi after me. I am and shall always be the one and only Kaikeyi." Her manic laughter echoed in the empty dark room.

Raghukul reeti sada chali aai. Praan jaai par vachan naa jaai − Raghukul stands firm in its words, life might end, but words hold, she mocked the king.

A distraught Dashrath tried to steady his wobbly feet. He felt the strength flowing out of his body and he held on to the wall for support. The king did not see Ram standing at the doorway of Kopa Bhavan, listening quietly to the bitter exchange.

"Ram, I don't know what she is trying to say," Dashrath sounded like an inconsolable child. The regent-in-waiting picked up his broken father, slumped against the wall, and held him close.

"Father, *Maata* Kaikeyi hasn't done anything wrong. No one would be prouder than me to see Bharath become the king of Ayodhya. And 14 years are too short a time to explore the forests," Ram was gentle.

Raghukul did not ever go back on its pledges. The words, unspoken, hung in the air. Ram had to honour Dashrath's boons to Kaikeyi.

"Ram, you can still call her your mother after the way she stabbed you? The woman who has ruined your life? I shall never forgive her," Dashrath could not stop crying. "Mothers never think ill of their children. If she wants me to go on exile, I will, for her word is my command," said an unperturbed Ram. Dashrath was overwrought, "No, Ram, you cannot go. Think about your mothers Kaushalya and Sumitra, and me. I cannot survive this loss."

"Queen Kaikeyi's words are my command. Wait till I return from exile," he bent down to touch Dashrath's and Kaikeyi's feet, "*Maata*, we brothers are in sync with each other. We understand that the past makes the present. We cannot escape it. Bharath will make a remarkable king because he has been brought up by you."

Kaikeyi stood quietly. No one knew what was going on in her mind at that instant because she had become a catalyst in Narayan's plan. But the divine scheme made in heaven had a steep price tag on earth. The mortal world would remember Kaikeyi as the plotting mother forever. Evil personified!

Lakshman Takes a Decision

Love tests strength like silver in the fire.

Gurudev Vashishtha was perturbed. He saw the undercurrents and wished he had not been reminded of what he had foreseen about Raghukulnandan 12 years ago. Was Ayodhya on the threshold of a tragedy? Ayodhya looked at him in despair, hoping it was not.

The court was in session for the coronation to begin. But Ram was missing.

He had gone to look for his father at Kopa Bhavan. The guests were impatient. They were relieved when they saw Ram enter the *Rajya Sabha*, but he was alone. Lakshman guessed something was terribly wrong at the sight of his brother's blanched face.

Before anyone could ask him anything, Ram went to Queen Kaushalya's throne.

"*Maa*, the coronation stands cancelled. *Maata* Kaikeyi wants Bharath to become the king." At Kaushalya's indrawn breath, the sound of which was so sharp that it was almost audible, he held her hands firmly. "…And a 14 year exile for me." There was grief in his voice.

Kaushalya turned white, the blood draining from her face as her head spun from the shock of the words which had come without any prior warning. She had no idea that Kaikeyi would choose this moment of coronation to redeem her boons. Lakshman held her. "No, this cannot be, you cannot leave me, Ram. Maharaj will never agree to this," Queen Kaushalya said.

"*Maa*, Queen Kaikeyi has sought these boons against a promise father made to her years ago. I will have to go to keep the dignity of the clan and my father's honour. The *shastras* – scriptures – say that a son who does not obey his father has no place in heaven. Please, give me your blessings and let me do my duty," Ram's voice was tremulous.

A hush descended on the *Rajya Sabha*. The exultation of the morning gave away to disbelief and despair. The guests and courtiers hung their heads down; Guru Vashishtha had tears in his eyes. Sumitra and Sita looked shaken while Urmila clutched Lakshman's hand to fill him with strength. She knew that he would not be able to bear Ram's misfortune and sorrow.

Her fears had come true as his hand tightened on hers in a gesture of helplessness and frustration. Lakshman had to hide his distress for the princes had been schooled early to restrain their emotions. He seethed silently.

Suddenly, Lakshman disentangled his hand from Urmila's and charged towards Kopa Bhavan, shouting, "Maharaj Dashrath, you are not man enough to stand up for what is right. At the behest of your vindictive wife you do what no father would ever do to his son." He threw open the door of Kopa Bhavan with his right foot, screaming, "Maharaj Dashrath, your *kaal* – time – has come. You will not be spared."

"I knew my Lakshman will come to undo your evil plans, Kaikeyi," Dashrath rushed to his son, but Lakshman pushed him aside violently. "No one except your oldest son is worthy enough to sit on the throne of Ayodhya. How can you consider Bharath, the most gullible of all, to bear the responsibility of Ayodhya? I beg you to reconsider your promise. And you want to send your own son away for 14 years. Is this justice?" he cried out in bitterness.

"The accusations are too harsh, my son. Do you think I will survive Ram's exile? He is my life. But I am helpless, betrayed by the very woman I loved the most." Dashrath pleaded with Lakshman.

Lakshman looked at Kaikeyi with hate. "*Maata*, you who loved him the most? Was it always a put on? Does it not break your heart to think of Ram in exile and Bharath on the throne? Do you think the Bharath you do this for will ever forgive you for this? He will not for he loves his brother more than he loves you. If *Sumitranandan* was taught to disrespect women, I would have banished you, but as a son I cannot do it except that I, *Dashrathnandan* Lakshman, curse you that the very son you do this for, will disown you."

"Urmila, take him away," Kaikeyi hit back. She was arrogant. Lakshman's accusations only served to fire her anger.

But Urmila ran to the rescue of an almost lifeless Dashrath, who was struggling to breathe.

"Father…" Lakshman stopped mid-sentence. Dashrath's health was sliding. The king was breathing heavily clutching at his heart. Lakshman turned to Manthara, who was sitting next to Kaikeyi in Kopa Bhavan and dragged her out. He knew that the old maid had incited Queen Kaikeyi against Ram, forcing her to seek the fulfillment of her boons to prop Bharath up on the throne. Her love for Bharath was known to everyone in Ayodhya.

"You are the plotter. You conspired against Ram *bhaiya* to edge him out of the throne. The whole of Aryavarta knows that you favour Bharath over Ram," Lakshman accused the old maid.

She denied the charges that he had hurled at her and told him to leave Kopa Bhavan. He let go of his grip on her.

"Fine, if you are not going to confess anything and *Maata* Kaikeyi does not take back her words, let me eliminate the very root of this chaos," Lakshman walked out of Kopa Bhavan towards the horse-stalls, where his chariot was parked.

Sensing that Lakshman was about to leave for Kekeya to bring Bharath back, Urmila ran to stop her husband. She stood between the chariot and Lakshman, "What would you gain by going to Kekeya? Bharath did not know what was going on here. It is not his fault. Will your hands not waver hurting your brother?"

"Mila, your concern for Bharath alarms me. Today, I regret having saved him from Markasur. I should have left him there dead," Lakshman was unmoved. "Lord, if not Bharath then think about Shatrughan. What is his fault? You know him. He will stand between you and Bharath. Shatrughan is as dear to me as my own child. I will not let you leave this place," she begged.

"Mila, Shatrughan will not be harmed. And, you are mistaken. He will side with what is right, and that is me, not Bharath," he persuaded her.

"No *Swami*, I will not let you go," Urmila did not move.

"Step aside, Urmila. You stand in the way of my duty," Lakshman's voice was distant and cold. Urmila cringed in fear for the first time. She realised that Lakshman was tied to royal *dharma*.

Urmila moved aside without a word and let him go. Lakshman suddenly felt like a stranger, his ruthlessness terrified and hurt her at the same time. She could not believe that it was the same man who called her Mila endearingly. In a flash, she became Urmila from Lakshmila, detaching herself from the united entity. He had not ever addressed her as Urmila in private, since the day they met at the Gauri temple.

Only Ram could stop a raging Lakshman bent on killing his own brother – fratricide was unthinkable in Raghukul.

"Ram *bhaiya*, please stop him. He is on his way to Kekeya to avenge your ruin," she cried in alarm. Ram ran after his brother, screaming, "Lakshman! Stop!"

"Don't stop me today, brother," Lakshman's eyes were misty.

"You want to kill our own brother for the throne? Do you forget our childhood, our love and our bonding?" Ram reminded him gently. "How does it matter which of us sits on the throne. We are one for all and all for one."

"I am not as humble as you brother. I am not speaking of my brother Bharath but the son of that evil mother Kaikeyi. I will not let her succeed in her intentions. How do you justify your action to these people?" he pointed to the crowd which was waiting for Ram's coronation.

"What do we say to the *praja* – subjects – who are waiting for Ram to take over the reins of the kingdom to bring about a Ram Rajya, a just state? Do you know how much they will hate Bharath when *Maata* Kaikeyi's conniving plans come to light? And with him, they will not forgive my innocent sibling Shatrughan as well. His fault was that he was born of the portion of the divine offering that *Maata* Kaikeyi had given *Maa* Sumitra to eat," Lakshman raged.

"Lakshman, calm down, nothing will happen," Ram said in a low voice shorn of all emotions. He had to bring the flaring tempers under control before moving ahead to fulfil Queen Kaikeyi's wishes.

"If you won't change your decision, then allow me to accompany you to exile for 14 years. Without Ram, Lakshman is incomplete. He is where you are brother. Take me, else see me on my death bed," Lakshman broke down.

A collective gasp of incredulity went up in the court. All those present in the *Rajya Sabha* could not believe that Lakshman had volunteered to accompany his brother to his exile.

"Lakshman, I shall never be able to repay you for this selfless act. I am blessed to have a brother like you. Ram is also incomplete without Lakshman. *Deshe deshe kalatraani, deshe deshe cha baandhavaah. Tam tu desham na pashyaami yatra bhraataa sahodarah* (one may have wives and relatives in every country but one cannot have a brother like Lakshman everywhere)," Ram enfolded his brother in a warm embrace. Peace had been restored for the moment with Lakshman's sacrifice.

"Let us go back to the palace. You must apologise to Urmila," Ram advised his brother.

Lakshman remained silent. "How do I face her with the wound I am about to inflict on her," he mumbled to himself.

Moti Bhavan was a picture of grief. The opulent palace was silent and dark when Ram and Lakshman walked in to find Urmila sitting huddled on the floor in a corner of her bed-chamber. Ram thanked Urmila for her presence of mind to send him after Lakshman. She barely smiled fearing for her destiny. Something told her that her nightmares had come true. The people she loved the most would desert her.

She tried to catch Lakshman's eye but he refused to look at her. He stared at her feet instead. "I am sorry, Mila. Please forgive me."

Before she could say anything he walked out. "I am going to *Maa*'s chamber. I want to speak to her."

Urmila stood alone in the empty palace drowning in a deluge of grief. She wondered about her karma, about what she had done in her past incarnations to invoke a fate as heinous and painful as this. The intense love that she nurtured for Lakshman blinded her to the dictates of another time, another world beyond this one.

Lakshman wept profusely at his mother's feet. "*Maa*, forgive me. I could not be the son that you can be proud of. But today, I have decided that I shall break you completely and kill my Mila."

To Lakshman's surprise, Sumitra did not break down. Instead she consoled her son, "I have always known that my son is an embodiment of *dharma* – religion. And today, his *dharma* says that he should be a shadow of Ram in the forest. I give you permission to accompany your brother and his wife to 'exile'. You have to be their protector now. And, you are mistaken. I couldn't have been prouder of you than I am now."

Sumitra, one of the most selfless women in Aryavarta, saw through Narayan's mortal form. She was the first one to recognise Ram as the incarnation of Lord Vishnu and also saw his Chaturbhuj Roop – four-armed incarnation – when Ram was a child. She also knew that her own sons were incarnations of Lord Shesha and Lord Sudarshana.

"What do I tell my Mila, *Maa*? How do I tell her that I will leave her alone for 14 years?" The pain of having to live without Mila was mirrored in his eyes. Emotions choked his throat and he felt shattered for the first time in 12 years. The years had been too short to live out the love – and passion – he felt for Urmila since the day he picked up her sword from the gift hamper.

Lakshman faced a conflict between his *dharma* and the call of his heart. His *dharma* clashed with his *prem* – love.

"Urmila is the Warrior Princess of Mithila, son. She understands *dharma*. I assure you, however much it breaks her, Mila will not flinch from her duty. Go to your wife. And I give you my word, son, that nothing will happen to her as long as I live. She is my responsibility from now on. You will find her the way you leave her on your return. Young, beautiful and pristine!" Sumitra pledged, standing tall in her strength, resolve and spirit of protection.

"Sumitra, I hail your greatness both as a queen and as a mother. You send your son with mine even though he could have been here. The world will remember your eternal sacrifice for the ages to come, worthy queen of Ayodhya. You are an epitome of selflessness and so are your sons, Lakshman and Shatrughan,"

Kaushalya and Sumitra wept together, holding each other. Only the heavens felt the grief of the mothers – their sorrow was beyond the realm of the mortal world.

Sumitra tried to retain her composure but her unsure smile was a sign of her anguish when Lakshman touched her feet, "*Maa*, for me, take care of your own self. I choose my duty and I leave my Mila behind. She will forever be your strength." He sought Sumitra's blessings, before moving to Kaushalya to pay his respect.

"My son, I know Ram is with you but do not forget to take care of yourself. I can get a son like Ram but I cannot get a son like you, my *lalla* – boy. I know you stand as Ram's shield. Narayan's *laddu*s will wait for you when you return," Kaushalya said, putting one into his mouth. The sweetness of the sugarball spread like stinging sorrow in his mouth.

Each step that Lakshman took to his wife in Moti Bhavan made him restless. Not having her by his side for 14 hours tore him apart, making him demented. But who could he share his anguish with? He went to Urmila, to leave a part of his self with her and take a part of her with him. But would she understand? He wiped his tears before he opened the door to the palace where she stood alone, trying to come to terms with the new reality.

Urmila Supports Lakshman

Passion seals parting.

Did they really have to part? Couldn't there have been a way that Urmila could have stayed with Saumitra? This question will always haunt the generations to come perhaps because when Narayan scripted his plan, he somehow overlooked the pain of Lakshmila's parting.

Urmila fell at the feet of her patron goddess, Gauri *Maata*. She looked at the goddess with tears in her eyes because she was certain that the time to part from her loved ones had arrived, "Why does it always have to be only me, *Maa*? I did not want to marry or fall in love, but you made me do so and now you snatch my happiness from me. How shall I love without whom I live for? You, who are my best friend, my confidante, who knows every secret of mine, wound me this severely? Please *Maa*, don't let it happen. Don't let my fears come true. Save us all, somehow, *Maa*. Remove this separation from my destiny. It will break me," her tears flowed without fetters, mingling with her prayers.

But the goddess was silent. How could she help Urmila when the tale was scripted by Narayan himself? Without the separation of the 14 years between them, how could Lakshman and Urmila prove that love transcended time, distance and was beyond physical presence?

Urmila found no consolation in the stony stance of the deity. She tried to assuage her trauma – the stark feeling of being ravaged – in many ways. She sang hymns, strung wreaths, changed clothes and sharpened her swords, but nothing really eased the piercing stabs of solitude that she felt at the mere thought of not having Lakshman beside her. She still refused to believe that they were to part.

It could not be!

And then suddenly her father's words echoed in her head, "Urmila, I have given birth to a Warrior Princess and warriors never give up. The one, who can fight death and come back to life, can fight anything. Always remember that when life puts you to the test, you should believe in your strength and face them. Prove that you only know how to win and no challenge can break you."

Remembering her father's words, Urmila wiped her tears and looked at the mirror, speaking in a soliloquy, "I shall stand with my Saumitra and make his exile easier for him, assured in the fact that these years will eventually end and he will return." Urmila was a firm believer in happy endings. But she was not sure whether Lakshman, being the man that he was, would take the separation kindly. He would always hold it against the dynasty of the sun.

She heard Lakshman's footsteps echoing in the arrhythmic beats of her heart and turned around to look at him with a passive smile. Lakshman was at a loss for words.

This unperturbed woman could not be his Mila.

Urmila rolled out the plan she had put together to keep up the charade. She could not allow anyone into the secret whirlpool of her grief; it could give away her weakness.

She was disdainful of Ram, ripping Lakshman apart with her words of contempt. His eyes mirrored disbelief when Urmila hit out at his brother, a man for whom she had great love and respect. "This is not like you, Mila. I refuse to believe in this farce. You have loved him more than I have."

"I don't. I never have. You believed in it because you wanted to. When will you realise that it is you who matters to me and it is for you I respect your brother? But you are so busy running errands for your brother that you fail to notice how it hurts me." Every word that Urmila said with deliberate 'disregard' for Ram broke her inside.

Lakshman was quick to anger. "It is enough, Urmila. You are worse than *Maata* Kaikeyi. You mock my love for my brother. I will not have it. I am not Maharaj Dashrath. You deserve to be left behind," he retorted.

She could barely control her tears as she heard him call her 'Urmila' again, the old formal address. Her fists clenched tighter, her nails digging harder into the soft flesh of the mounds on her palms. "As expected, I do not matter to you. Your older sibling always took the foremost place in your heart. I should have listened to you the day you told me your brother will always be your priority. I should have never married you. And, yes, before you planned to go, did you think for a moment about Sumitra, your mother?

"While your father lies on his death bed, your brothers are not here, you still want to leave everything behind and accompany your Ram *bhaiya*. He is not a child. He can handle the exile but who will take care of the family? Who will handle *Pitaji* after *bhaiya* goes? What about the promises you made to my father at the time of our wedding? You forget all but I cannot be like you. You are but your brother's attendant. I am a princess born to live in the luxuries of the palace and I will," she ended abruptly, before she gave herself away and broke down.

Lakshman knew that she had feigned the outburst.

"Then, I, *Sumitranandan* Lakshman, as of now, sever all ties with you *Janaknandini* Urmila. From now, you are a stranger to me!" His pride rankled and he left the palace hurt without even looking back at his wife. But he did not go away; Lakshman waited outside because he knew her better than his own self. He watched her collapse on the floor as soon as he left the palace. He let his tears flow unchecked, but he could not abandon her grieving all by herself and retraced his steps.

She lay on the floor in a heap – wounded, fragile and vulnerable. He pulled her tightly to him and crushed her in a protective embrace. "I am so sorry, Mila, for letting you believe I doubt you and using words that hurt you so," Lakshman sobbed. Urmila gave in. She rested her head on his chest and her resistance melted. She felt the strength drain out of her.

Was this really their last time together? The very thought scared them so that they clung to each other like children. Somehow, they wanted to run away from what was happening, wishing that they could stay with each other. But life does not work this way. Fate's knocks are often treacherous.

"Mila, how can I live without you? You always have the answers to all my problems. Help me find one today so that I can go away in peace, so that I don't have to yearn for you." The Lakshman that stood there looking at his wife was a humble man, torn between his duty and love. Something shifted inside Urmila as she gazed at Lakshman's helpless face. She became her old pragmatic self, hiding her grief under a facade of worldly wisdom.

"Love is weakness but duty is power. You can always choose between the two. Here, your *dharma* says you accompany your brother and his wife to the forest. That very *dharma* says I stay back and take care of *Pitaji* and *Maa* Kaushalya and *Maa* Sumitra. As the *kulvadhu*, after the older sibling and his wife leave, it is my duty to ensure no one feels your absence because I fill the void. Bharath and Shatrughan might find it difficult to handle the affairs of the state. Shatrughan may not be able to cope with your absence and Bharath may break down after knowing *Maata* Kaikeyi's role in the tragedy. Mandvi and Shrutakeerti are too young to handle this responsibility alone, so, I will have to be here. I know that with Ram *bhaiya* by your side, nothing can happen to you," Urmila reasoned.

"Mila, you have given a broken man some relief. But, I shall never forgive myself for leaving you alone," he was earnest in his lament.

"To live a life without you is better than to see you die every day if you abstain from your *dharma*. Whenever the world shall take your name as the ideal brother, I will stand feeling proud next to you as your wife," she said with a weak smile.

"I hope the world understands that the wife who stands next to the ideal brother is the one who sacrifices her laughter. She is his strength, allowing him to do his duty towards his brothers. Can you do me a favour, Mila, before I leave?" His eyes probed hers. "I don't want my *mirchi* to shed even a single tear till I return. Promise me not to cry ever till I come back."

She wiped her tears. "You have my word for it, *Swami*. Your *mirchi* will never have tears in her eyes till you come back from exile. But I too, want you to make two promises." He nodded in agreement. "Against the first promise, I want you to forget that I exist or that I am your wife. You will not ever think about me or utter my name or regret leaving me behind. It might take you away from your duty towards your brother."

"I am but you, Mila. How can I forget you when all I do is to think of you? You reside in my heart. The tears that flowed from Lakshman's eyes were leashed by Urmila; she made them hers. She kissed his tears away."

"Then hide me safely in your heart. Don't show me to anyone."

"I love you, Mila. I will wrap myself so tightly in your memories that the emptiness will not feel cold," he was tender. She closed her eyes in his embrace, drained of energy. "Now, for the second promise, give me your word that you will return."

"I will return, Mila. Death shall not touch me before you do. I give you my word. I will keep you hidden in me till I return; the world will not know that Lakshmila breathes inside me. No one will ever see the emptiness in my eyes. I give you my promise."

Urmila gently guided him to the temple inside their palace and lit an *Akhandajoyti* – the burning wick of life. "I will not let this blow out till you return. I hold my faith in this," she looked at him deeply with love in her eyes. The flame flickered.

"I leave my Mila in your care till I return. Protect her, god," his unspoken prayer echoed in the shrine as he knelt down in front of the deity with folded hands.

Love brings in its wake parting and renunciation.

Urmila went to the closet and pulled out a set of hermit's clothes, "How do I live as a *yuvrani* – princess – when my husband will live as a *sanyaasi* – hermit-in-exile? Though I shall reside within the confines of this palace, I will live as a hermit. I will not wear any other clothes and will eat fruits."

Lakshman held her face in his palms, "The thought of you living an austere life like me will torment me every moment. Don't do this to your Saumitra, Mila. I want you to enjoy the pleasures of life for me, too."

"There is no life for me without you," Urmila was firm.

She began to prepare Lakshman for his exile. First, she had to deck him up for his exile. And, she could not afford to cry as she was bound to his promise, and committed to it by her assent.

They both dressed each other in clothes made from barks of trees like the hermits in the forest. She removed his *angavastra*, jewellery and crown, replacing them with a coarse drape woven from tree fibres. She tied his dark brown hair into a *vanvaas kesh* – forest knot – above his head. He looked pale and yet handsome in the hermit's attire. The yellow *dhoti* with the orange *angavastra* and the beads of *rudraksh* around his forearms, wrists and neck imbued him with divine grace; he looked as if he had descended from another world.

For a moment, an indescribable feeling of having experienced this parting once before, somewhere deep in the mists of time, flitted through her head, dissipating instantly. The earth held Lakshmila powerfully in its bosom.

She disrobed slowly, shedding her palace finery and gold-threaded skirts for a simple yellow and orange *sari* under his gaze. She unpinned her jewellery but he forestalled her. "No, do not remove the gold of our passion, Mila," Lakshman whispered, holding her hands.

"The ornaments mean nothing to me. I wore it for you and now that you will not be here, I do not want them to adorn me anymore. My vermillion and the *mangalsutra* are my most precious adornments. Any other ornament will bring back the longing and hound me with the memories of the times that we spent together," Urmila replied.

Lakshman performed the last rite of passion. He picked up a pinch of vermillion from a golden pot and filled the parting of her open tresses with the red powder. He placed a wreath of white blossoms around her hair and put a small orb of sandalwood paste on her brow – the mark of a monk.

"Let this memory stay etched in my heart and mind. I want to remember my Mila as she is now," Lakshman said, looking at Urmila in her incarnation of a 'hermit' in the palace.

"Your Mila shall stay as you leave her," Urmila said, placing her lips on his forehead.

"Another thing I want to take with me is the scent and taste of your hands. I want to eat from your hands one last time," he closed his eyes when she put a small portion of a *maplua* into his mouth. "I shall never forget the taste of the food that you cooked for me. Pack me some food; I will remember you when I eat it."

He took a bit of the *malpua* from the same platter and put it into her mouth.

They found little moments of intimacies to cling on to. The simple acts of togetherness that would remind them of each other – the eternal bonding. Lakshmila sealed the void of their separation with bits of each other.

They forgot the world till Tara came to call them.

"Rajkumar, yuvrani *ji*, you both are wanted at Kanak Bhavan." It was time to go. Lakshman looked around his palace so familiar in its layout, embracing all the beautiful moments he had lived with Mila in its plush confines – its ornate and beautiful opulence. The Lakshman who walked out of Moti Bhavan was detached, cold and to an extent unfeeling.

Urmila walked with him to Kanak Bhavan holding his hand. She was smiling. The call of duty could not ever take away their love.

Destiny can destroy in minutes and resurrect in a moment. Two people who refused to give up on each other even for a day were about to let each other go for 14 years to attend to their call of duty, their responsibility towards their family, their people. Their love was beyond physical essence. They knew how to keep each other alive within themselves.

Judaii – Parting

Love is distance, love is parting, love is a rock.

Ayodhya felt as if its soul had been ripped out as it listened to the heartache that Lakshmila must bear silently for their dharma. It was shattered because only one of them would remain behind. It wondered if it would be able to bear Urmila's tears at night without Saumitra.

It was time to go. Sita did not know the reason for Urmila's makeover; she was appalled to see her younger sibling in hermit's clothes. Urmila told Sita that Lakshman would accompany them to the forest for 14 years, "Just as Lord Shesha is half-complete without Narayan my lord is not complete without my *bhaiya*. He will not survive without his brother. I am no one to take him away from his duty."

Sita was broken. She could not reconcile to the fact that her sister would renounce the life of a princess – and material comforts for 14 barren years, although she would live in the palace. She had made a difficult choice, one more severe and restrained than the one, which awaited Sita in the forest. The life of a monk for a young woman of royal lineage and rank inside the palace was the toughest test of purity, resilience and strength for Urmila. Sita was not sure whether her little sister should be put through such an enduring test.

"Urmila, how will you live without Lakshman all these years when you both cannot live without each other even for a few hours? If this is how it is to be, then allow me to seek *Raghunandan's* permission to take you along too."

But Urmila was insistent. "No, I shall stay here and fulfil my *dharma*. How can I go when everyone here finds strength in me? I cannot leave them pining for all of us, just to be with Saumitra. True love sustains across time and distance, it always follows *dharma*. We both stay without each other to stay within each other. He is in my heart, in every corner of this palace, in my memories. How can I be lonely, then?"

"Urmila, you are the true embodiment of a *pativrata stree* – chaste wife. The world will remember you for your unparalleled sacrifice. How shall Aryavarta ever compare any wife to a wife who sacrificed her love and accepted 14 years of separation from her husband?" Sita folded her hands to Urmila in reverence, feeling inconsequential in front of her sister.

Ram and Lakshman stood at the door of Kanak Bhavan, watching the sisters battle with their emotions – fighting each other for each other's happiness. Urmila touched her brother's feet.

"How will I ever be able to compensate for the years of companionship I take away from you, Urmila? I cannot look at you in the eye. I am ashamed," Ram was full of remorse.

"Do not shame me. My *Swami* does his duty, *bhaiya*. I do mine. Don't stop us from serving you." Ram blessed her. He had no words to extol her greatness.

It was finally time to bid *adieu* to Maharaj Dashrath, who was still semi-conscious in Queen Kaikeyi's chamber. Kaikeyi was still wearing her black *sari* that she wore to Kopa Bhavan, when Ram,

Sita and Lakshman entered her palace. Manthara stepped aside to allow them to speak to King Dashrath.

Dashrath's face turned ghastly pale on seeing them in hermit's clothes. "You cannot abandon an ailing Maharaj, your father, who may not live if you leave the palace," he pleaded, holding Lakshman's hands.

"Who will take care of him for 14 years if I don't accompany him?" Lakshman chided his father with love, wiping away his tears. "And what about your responsibilities towards your father?" Dashrath sobbed. "*Pitaji*, I leave your dear daughter Urmila behind. She is a 'prince'; she will take care of you like your son." The grief in Lakshman's voice was intense and apparent.

Could Lakshmila explain what was going on inside them when the fear that brought so much sorrow was set to become real in a few moments?

The trio touched Queen Kaikeyi's feet. The queen was still not sure whether Bharath would become the king and so she ignored the three and looked disapprovingly at Sita's jewellery. "Remove the jewellery before you leave, Sita," she said. "You are not a princess anymore."

The disdain in her voice cut through Sita like a blade. Sita removed her jewellery under Kaikeyi's chilly gaze, before stepping out of the palace. Manthara was in tears to see Urmila alone. Lakshmila's separation hung like a shadow of a catastrophe on her head, but she managed to hide her terror and hold back her tears at the injustice against Lakshman and Urmila.

Kaushalya's hands trembled as she performed the final *aarti* – prayer – before their departure. Sumitra helped her complete it. Kaushalya took Ram's and Sita's hands in hers, "Ram, take care of my Lakshman. Don't return if you let any harm come to him. He has sacrificed everything for you. Now, he is your responsibility."

"*Maa*, I promise you that nothing will happen to him as long as I am alive" Ram promised his mother.

Sumitra looked at the three of them tearfully, "Blessings to you my children. From now on, the forests will be your Ayodhya, you will lord over Aryavarta's lush wilderness, travel across the beautiful natural terrain of the land and make new friends and powerful allies but Ayodhya here will feel your void. The kingdom will not be the same till the three of you return. Do not drift from each other, for you will have only each other as family. The forests can be full of the unexpected at times, unity is strength on such strange bends," Sumitra slumped against a pillar, her words ringing in their ears. She could not watch Lakshman leave, the little boy who perhaps would never know how to live for his own pleasure – on his own terms.

It was Urmila who had to bid them farewell now. She stood at the altar of the goddess in the shrine of her palace, dressed in a monk's attire, holding a platter of flowers and sandalwood paste. Her smile was somewhat empty; it did not quite reach her eyes when she put a sandalwood and vermillion *tilak* – mark – on Ram and Sita's brows. She hugged her sister one last time, "I had no idea that a day would come when you and I would not be together, *didi*. Take care of my Saumitra for me," she whispered into Sita's ears.

Urmila could not take her eyes off her *Swami*, when she offered him her *aarti*. She lifted the platter of flowers and earthenware lamps to his head, and then brought it down to his chest – across his upper arms – in a circular motion three times like her deity, seeking blessings from the gods for his wellness and safety. She spread her palm on the wavering flames of the lamps, cupped the heat and the fragrance from the incense, and touched his face and head.

Its warmth spread across his face and warmed his soul.

Her eyes were dry. She could not shed even a tear. This could not be happening. What was Urmila without Lakshman? He did not allow her eyes to stray from him. His eyes held hers as intensely as they always did, oblivious to everyone's presence in the room. "I pray that you can find it in your heart to forgive me for what I do today, for this pain I inflict on you. I wait for the sunset that is to come after 14 years from now on," he muttered under his breath.

"Promise me that you will take care of yourself. Do not lose your temper. Stay calm and whenever you miss me, look at the moon. I shall be looking at it too. Talk to me through the moon. Feel no regret or guilt. My Saumitra is going to war, a war that will last for 14 years. I shall be here at this very door to greet my hero home. You shall find me as you leave me," she said, putting a *tilak* on his forehead.

Sumitra wanted him to put vermilion in her hair line one last time before he left. Urmila felt the warmth of his touch and her strength crumbled. He caressed her forehead tenderly, "Take care." She smiled at him and bent down to touch his feet. He knew that if he looked at her again, he would not be able to leave. He turned his back on her.

Desolation spread across Ayodhya like a grey pall. The hearths were cold. Not one kitchen fire smouldered in the homes of the grief-stricken subjects. The people blocked the path of the two princes and Sita as they walked to the main gateway leading out of the palace; but the trio was resigned to their fate. Allow us through, they wished silently, wending their way through the crowd that clustered on the thoroughfare.

On their way, they sought the blessings of sage Vashishtha, and climbed on the chariot that would drop them at the edge of the kingdom, where the forests began.

There was no respite in Urmila. How would she put together the heart that was falling to pieces?

She handed the platter of *aarti* to a maid and ran to the terrace of her palace to watch the trio leave. The charioteer wielded his crop and the horses neighed. The carriage moved out of the gateway of the palace, out of the purview of Urmila's vision. She stood watching his receding form in the chariot and could the feel his essence in the air of Ayodhya until he became a speck in the distance, a black head against a shining sun. She reassured herself, "Fourteen years without you? But I will wait for you, Saumitra. Come home soon!"

Her thoughts carried across the expanse of the terrace and the wide pathway outside of the palace. For just a moment, Lakshman turned around in response to the sound of her thoughts and looked straight at her, his Mila, who stood there forlorn, but with hope and faith shining in her eyes. He wanted to steer the chariot around and take her, his Mila, with him. He shut his eyes and let the tears flow.

Wiping them with his bare hands, he smiled, "I shall never be alone. I will carry you with me for 14 years, until we meet again, Mila." Their eyes locked before the chariot disappeared around a wide swerve of the road into the open forests beyond.

"Nothing will take away the pain from within me. But just as your love is mine, so is your separation. The world shall never see me broken or feeble. I shall forever keep my promise to you, *Sumitranandan*," Urmila thought, putting on a brave smile before she went back to the palace which would be her retreat for the next 14 years.

Who was to say what kind of love was greater, the love of the woman who lived with her husband in exile or the woman who lived in exile without her husband, for him? The debate continues.

Sumitra quietly drew Urmila into her arms. Their agony was mutual. The forlorn mother sought her son in her daughter-in-law. "I shall live with you in Moti Bhavan from now on. I see my Lakshman in you and by taking care of you, I shall feel him," the queen said. She had swapped roles from that of a mother-in-law to a mother.

Urmila traced the folds of Lakshman's *angavastra* tied around her wrist with her fingertips. The fabric carried his fragrance. "*Maa*, he is always with us. How can anyone take away Laksh from his Mila? The emptiness that he has left behind is a reminder that he is in me. I shall wait for him to fill it when he comes back." Emptiness, for Urmila, was also a tangible symbol of presence. Saumitra lived in her heart.

Sumitra and Urmila were bound together in grief; by the sorrow of parting from the one they loved the most. The same grief pulled Kaushalya into the common circle of heartbroken women – derelict and denied of their reason to live.

"I shall forever be indebted to Sumitra and you. How magnanimously you let go of your happiness for Ayodhya, for my Ram," Kaushalya's gratitude was one of lament. Urmila touched her feet, "*Maa*, he does his duty, I do mine. Ram *bhaiya* needs him as Ayodhya needs me." Kaushalya was speechless.

"Great are Maharaj Janak and Maharani Sunaina, who bore you," she whispered after a long silent minute.

Urmila shone like the brightest of the earthly divas, earning for herself and Mithila slots in immortality.

Moti Bhavan was mute in its testimony to the contrasts, destiny's queer twists. The sounds of Lakshmila's laughter followed Urmila's slow footsteps stalking the empty spaces at night and the silent tears that remained frozen on the palace walls, embedding in them like pearls.

Dashrath Breathes His Last

A curse comes true in a royal demise, the story moves on.

Ayodhya is in a shambles. It is desolate without the familiar presence of Ram, Lakshman and Sita. It keeps looking over its shoulder. It tiptoes its way to Urmila and covers her in a protective blanket even as it broods how it will manage to witness her pain of parting from Lakshman.

Dashrath was heartbroken with grief, an emotion that took its toll on his heart and weak body.

He still could not believe that they had left the palace for 14 years – and would not return. He knew that the people of Ayodhya would not forgive him for the injustice against Ram, Sita and Lakshman; but the king was helpless in his promise to a queen he once dearly loved. Urmila tried to console him by saying that he had been a worthy husband and a good father but the gloom did not lift from the old king's sagging shoulders. He wilted like a flower in the blistering heat, shrivelled and crumpled.

Sensing that his end was round the corner, Dashrath pleaded with Kaushalya, "Take me in, my eldest and my most obedient queen, to your palace. I do not want to die under the roof of the woman, who has snatched my Ram away."

Kaushalya, Sumitra and Urmila supported Maharaj Dashrath to Hari Kuntha, where he rested his head on Kaushalya's lap, sighing in despair, "Karma does not spare anyone. I am being punished for what I did years ago to someone innocent. Perhaps, the odious act of killing a son and his grief-stricken parents' curse has estranged me from my sons today."

Sumitra, who had no idea about the odious deed that the king had committed long ago, wanted to know about it. Dashrath took her hands in his, and reminisced:

"When I was very young, just a prince, once I went to hunt in the forest on the bank of the Sarayu River. As I went deeper into the jungle, I heard footsteps near a lake in the middle of the forest. Assuming it was an animal, I shot an arrow in the direction but when I heard a human cry of agony, I realised that it was not an animal, but a young man who had come to fetch water for his old and thirsty parents. I tended to the man but the shot was fatal. Before he died, he asked me to take water to his blind parents and tell them that their son will always be with them. I met his ageing parents. They sensed it was not him. When they asked me where he was, I had to tell them what I did. His mother could not bear the loss and died instantly, while his father cursed me."

Dashrath was repentant but one could not escape a curse. "His curse has come true. He said I will also die pining for my sons, and they will not be with me in my last days. And look, here I am, without any of my sons, now that I am ending my tenure on earth."

Kaushalya and Sumitra cried out in distress when they realised that the king was dying. Dashrath atoned for his misdeeds, "I have never been a good person, I have been a bad husband, and a worthless and cruel father. I took Shanta away from you. Will you ever forgive me? Will Shanta ever forgive her father?" His tears would not stop.

"Your daughter has never blamed you, father," Shanta said from the door where she stood with her husband Maha Rishyasringa. "She will always stand by you."

"Shanta, my daughter," he reached out for her. She embraced him, "It was not your fault, father. I did what I thought was right at that moment and would benefit Angadesh and Ayodhya. It was my decision."

"Shanta, you are trying to keep my heart. But here you are, my first child, my pride, a true Raghuvanshi, here with me, when I lie on my death bed," Dashrath was desperate to make up to Shanta, seek her forgiveness before he died.

You cannot cling on to moments even if you want them to live forever. Shanta was ecstatic. Her father gave her the love she had always yearned for. Dashrath was destined to die in the presence of his daughter; a daughter who did not exist in life. Shanta's happiness was short-lived.

Arya Sumantra returned to Ayodhya with news of Ram, Sita and Lakshman.

"Greetings, Maharaj. I have dropped the princes and the yuvrani in the safe areas of Dandakaranya." The ancient forest, where the trio was supposed to live the years of their exile, was in the kingdom of Dandak. It was a stronghold of the demon tribes and was known to have been ruled by the king of Lanka, Ramada's governor, Khar. Sumantra was worried about the fate of the exiled princes.

Sumantra, who had hurried to Kaushalya's palace after dropping off the princes and Sita, was shocked at the sight of the degeneration of King Dashrath's health.

"O, Sumantra, I was waiting for this news. Now, I can die peacefully," Dashrath gave in to his grief. Shanta beseeched her father to live; she wanted her father to live for her, for them, and till Ram and Lakshman returned from exile. But the god of death stood at the door, waiting to claim the king.

"My daughters Shanta and Urmila, promise me that you will take care of Ayodhya until Ram and Lakshman return from their exile. Take care of my wives Kaushalya and Sumitra, and son Shatrughan. And let me make a last wish, please don't allow Bharath or Kaikeyi to come near me or touch my body when I die, else my soul will never find peace." The king let go of his link with the mortal world. A collective cry of despair resounded in the palace. The lights of Ayodhya dimmed, announcing the end of Dashrath's wise reign.

Shanta and Urmila promised him that Kaikeyi and Bharath would not come near Dashrath in death. "My head will remain bowed in shame even after my death, my child, for I have not been able to keep my promise to your father. I could not take care of you." He folded his hands to Urmila in a gesture of prayer and apology – a dying king's homage to a mortal goddess, "If you can forgive this old father, child."

Urmila began to cry, "I am proud to be your son's wife, father, to be your daughter-in-law and will always remain so."

"Now, my heart finds relief. See, my Ram has come to take me to Narayan's abode. I have to go," Dashrath looked up at the sky and then collapsed on Shanta's and Kaushalya's lap. As the gates of heaven opened to let in the mighty king of Ayodhya, his kingdom on earth stopped breathing for a moment, anguished.

The queens wailed, beating their chests in grief. Shanta was heartbroken, but Urmila did not shed a single tear; the promise she had made to her husband had turned her grief barren.

As soon as Kaikeyi heard the news of the king's death, she ran to Kaushalya's chamber but was stopped by Sumitra, "Kaikeyi, don't! The Maharaj left us because you broke his heart. He loved you the most among us, so much that he did not once hesitate in making you his *Pat Rani* – chief queen, but you? You betrayed him when he needed you the most. You tore his heart apart, took Ram away from him. Why do you come here today? To scorn him in death?"

Urmila tried to calm her, but Kaushalya interrupted her, "Let her vent her anger. In all these years, Sumitra hasn't ever spoken a word."

"Forgive me for what I have done but do not take away my right to be with the Maharaj in his death. I implore you." Kaikeyi slumped on the floor, weeping hysterically.

Sumitra, a woman with a golden heart, gave in to compassion, yet again. She embraced Kaikeyi and allowed her to cry on her shoulder, "Kaikeyi, my sister, the Maharaj truly loved you. Perhaps it is our destiny that tricked us such. Don't be heartbroken. I am sorry for hurting you with my cruel words."

The queens had to ensure that peace prevailed in the palace. Any breach could spill on to the streets, whipping up ferment. Kindness and solidarity consolidated the foundations of an uncertain kingdom.

"No, *didi*, no words are harsh enough to punish me for what I did. I am the reason for this untimely death of the Maharaj. You are too humble, *didi*, for you forgive me not only for this, but also for how I snatched your portion of the offering during the *Putra Kameshthi Yajna*. Please, don't ever condone my conspiracies," Kaikeyi regretted.

She was ready to atone, but Kaushalya was skeptical. She saw the caprice in the weeping Kaikeyi and found it difficult to forgive her as effortlessly as Sumitra. But she chose to stay silent.

Gurudev Vashishtha mourned the death of the king, "Dashrath, my son..." he wept not for his Maharaj but for the boy he had been a parent to since Dashrath's father Maharaj Aja and Maharani Indumati's death.

"Arya Sumantra, send news to Kekeya to tell Bharath and Shatrughan to return to Ayodhya immediately. Until then, we will embalm the body in sacred oils." Gurudev motioned to Urmila to prepare the embalming oils of myrrh, honey, lavender, bitumen, basil, palm and the scented leaves and barks of the trees prescribed in Ayurveda to anoint the dead.

With the Maharaj gone, and no one named as the new king officially, Ayodhya dreaded the day when Bharath would sit on the throne where Ram was supposed to. It mused whether a brother would take what rightfully wasn't his or another sacrifice was on its way.

I Miss You

Farewell is a rite of passage to new arrival.

As Ayodhya prepared to bid farewell to its Maharaj, a silent tear slid down its cheeks. The kingdom looked sadly at the queens in their white clothes of widows, stripped of their grandeur and glitter.

Dashrath's body was preserved in Ayurvedic oils till Bharath and Shatrughan returned to Ayodhya.

Maharani Kaushalya was quiet while Sumitra remembered the days when the Maharaj would fill her head with vermillion every morning. A nostalgic Raghukul retreated into depression and then into complete silence.

Urmila consoled Sumitra, "*Maa*, you have to be strong. You have to live for us. *Maata* Kaushalya needs you more than ever. And you have some beautiful memories to live by." Urmila walked Sumitra to Kaushalya's chamber, where the oldest of king Dashrath's wives sat without a word.

Urmila noticed the fine lines of worry on Arya Sumantra's and Gurudev Vashishtha's faces. She asked, "Sumantra *ji*, Gurudev, what troubles you, so?" Arya Sumantra explained that the people of Ayodhya were up in arms and were threatening to disown the kingship, trying to bring it down.

"Gurudev, I request you to open the doors of the palace. Allow me to speak to them," Urmila appealed to Guru Vashishtha.

"No, yuvrani *ji*. We will deal with them. You do not have to worry," Sumantra was emphatic.

"No Sumantra *ji*, you forget that father has always treated the people of this kingdom like his own children and *Swami* left me behind to take care of crises such as these. It is my duty to fulfil the promise I made to my husband and my father," Urmila was determined to tackle the restive subjects and she sought the blessings of the queens before walking out of the palace to face the rebellious people of Ayodhya.

"My dear people, I appeal to you to maintain peace and help the royal family through these trying times. Ayodhya belongs to all of us and it is us, who have to ensure peace and harmony in the kingdom. With your Maharaj gone and your favourite prince Ram not around, I, *Janaknandini* Urmila, your Rajkumar Lakshman's wife assure you that whatever happens, I will always stand for you, by you and with you. I beg to you be patient till the future unfolds," Urmila implored the people with folded hands.

"What is happening today has happened because of Rani Kaikeyi. We want her to leave Ayodhya," the subjects clamoured.

"I will not hear of it. She is our *Raj Maata* – queen mother." Urmila was stern in her refusal.

"Yuvrani *ji*, how can you be so forgiving? If it were not for her, your husband would still be here," a woman countered, challenging Urmila.

"There is no greater deed than serving your elders. *Dharma* – duty – and *shastra*s – scriptures – say that our duty lies in taking care of the infirm and the old. While Saumitra went away to serve his older brother and his wife, I stayed behind to perform my duties as a daughter-in-law and wife. As a pupil of Gargi Vachaknavi and the daughter of wise *Rajrishi* Janak, this is the lesson I have learnt in my childhood and during the years of my adolescence," Urmila argued with gentleness.

The crowd looked at Urmila. Her arguments made them introspective – they wondered whether they had been wrong in accusing Queen Kaikeyi and disowning the kingship for its injustice to Ram. No princess had ever uttered words as 'wise, sane and reasonable' as Urmila. The people scattered, praising Urmila for bringing a semblance of calmness to the chaos. Urmila had been successful in her first task as a protector of Raghukul's honour in her brothers' and husband's absence.

Vashistha sighed in relief and lingering sadness. The responsibilities royal partings placed on fragile shoulders...

Urmila busied herself with Arya Sumantra for the rest of the day attending to the affairs of the state. Sumitra came to the *Rajya Sabha* late in the afternoon to take her back to the palace to eat a small meal, but Urmila refused to go. "How can I eat when he hasn't eaten yet?" she demanded.

Sumitra was taken aback. How did Urmila know that Lakshman was hungry and tired? Sumitra was possessive about her son and believed that she could feel his hunger and pain in her maternal cord.

"Our souls are connected, *Maa*. It tells me that he is still hungry and has not rested," Urmila closed her eyes and saw Lakshman smiling at her – the chimera of his aura was almost lifelike.

Sumitra's eyes misted with tears. "Urmila, I, his mother, cannot understand what he is going through and you just know it. Your love is beyond this world. My son is blessed to have you as his wife." Urmila had proven her worth – as a warrior, a statesperson, a woman with the power to advise and govern, and now, as a woman in love and a dutiful wife.

She had lived up to her soul connection with Saumitra, her other half.

Kaushalya, on the other hand, watched Sumitra and Urmila bond as mother and daughter, a familial love unfolding between them from a distance. She wished that her daughter-in-law Sita was there. She blessed both of them and urged Urmila to sleep with the queen mothers that night. But Urmila turned down her offer, "*Maa*, I am sorry but I want to spend this first night of our separation with Saumitra's memories alone."

And with that she left for Moti Bhavan. Every corner, every object and every small thing in the palace reminded Urmila of Lakshman. She heard the echo of his laughter in her bed-chamber. Her eyes fell on his clothes strewn on the bed, and she picked them up and held them close to her breast, breathing in his scent. For her, he was here, at that moment.

"A part of you is always apart from you, waiting and longing to be a part of you again," Urmila sighed, trying to find shelter. But she was restless. The moon beckoned to her and she glimpsed his image on its shimmering, milky surface. She moved to the balcony, looking at the moon – would it carry her messages to him? Did it carry vibes across time and space? She had always had this strange intuition that her love and life would flow and ebb with the tide of the moon – the celestial token of love, purity, sanity – and the vast stretches of the milky waters.

Urmila did not hear Queen Sumitra enter Moti Bhavan to find her staring at the moon, lost in her own world. "Urmila, come, let us sleep now. I shan't sleep in Kaushalya *didi*'s room. I cannot let you sleep alone. Consider my presence as a mother's concern for her daughter." Sumitra said, moving to draw Urmila to her lap.

"*Maa*, look at the moon. You will see your son's reflection in it." Urmila said, resting her head on Sumitra's lap. She was fatigued. Sumitra caressed her head, narrating tales about Lakshman's childhood. Slowly, Urmila's eyes become laden with sleep and Sumitra hummed a lullaby that she sang to Lakshman during his childhood.

In the forest, Lakshman stood near a pond that rippled silver in the light of the moon, and cried silently. He pined for his wife and his mother. He had not eaten anything throughout the day and Sita was worried about him. She asked Ram to go and feed him, but Ram hesitated. He could not bear to see his brother in so much mental pain. It made him guilty, "I see the angst of separation in his eyes. For the one who can't bear to be away from his wife even for a few hours every day, I cannot imagine what he will go through without her for these 14 long years."

Sita went to Lakshman, and stood quietly next to him. Lakshman was deaf to her approach and blind to her presence. He was floating in his own moonlit world, dreamy.

"I miss you, love. Today is only my first night away from you and I am breaking down. I wonder if I will survive these arid years without you. I talk to the moon as you wanted me to but it doesn't seem to whisper back your laughter or permeate your scented breath. Mila, help me ease this scorching ache," Lakshman mumbled to the moon.

Sita was moved to tears. Lakshman's audible conversation with the moon wrenched her heart. She admonished him for not eating and offered him some fresh berries, which he refused. "I will eat the food Mila has given me. It reminds me of her taste, *bhabhi*, the touch of her fingers. Please sleep, I will join you both in a while." He folded his hands in respect.

"My sister is blessed to have you for her husband. May your love shine and prosper." Sita caressed his ruffled head. Lakshman took out a *laddu* that Urmila had packed for him in a leaf-coiled basket which he tied around his waist. But before he put it in his mouth, he held the 'sweetmeat' to the moon, "Mila, I eat now with your permission. You may also eat and sleep peacefully now." The moon was their witness.

***

Back in Moti Bhavan, Urmila woke up to the rays of the sun filtering from the terrace. She turned around lazily and reached out for Lakshman. "Good morning," she whispered in a sleepy voice. Her hands groped for Saumitra in the pristine bleakness of the mat that served as her bed. Her greetings reverberated in the empty room and she came crashing down to reality.

Saumitra wasn't there any more; he had left Ayodhya for 14 years.

"I miss you, *Swami*," she kissed his *angavastra* tied to her wrist to remind her of his touch. The anguished cry of her mother from her door shattered her reverie, "Urmila, my daughter..." She looked at her mother Sunaina in a daze, and then rushed to her with outstretched arms. "*Maa!*"

Sunaina looked at the thin mat laid out on the cold hard floor, at her daughter's ascetic clothes, her pale face and sad demeanour. She sank to the floor in grief, "Why did he leave you? Wasn't there any other way? Your father and I gave him your responsibility at the *kanyadaan*. But he chose to go with his brother without a thought about your happiness?"

Sumitra was accusing Lakshman; her sorrow was tempered with anger and regret. A mother could not bear to see her daughter lead a monk's life while her husband was still alive. But Urmila stopped her, "*Maa*, why do you blame him? It was my decision to stay here. Wasn't it you who taught us sisters that an ideal woman of Aryavarta should honour her husband and in-laws? With *Pitaji* on his death bed, Bharath and Shatrughan in Kekeya, how could I leave the queen mothers alone and go away with them? My *Swami* followed his *dharma* and I am following mine. And don't you question his love for me. I know how deep it is. When he lives in me, how can you say he has left me? Nothing can break the bond between two souls who are connected to each other. No matter how long they are apart, no matter what happens, they are always connected..."

"There is no pain greater than the pain of separation from your husband and for a period as long as 14 years," Sunaina was frantic in her concern, "Come away with us to Mithila, my child."

Urmila held her mother's hands, "No *Maata*, I won't come to Mithila. Not without Saumitra. Ayodhya needs me. My Kaushalya *Maa* and Sumitra *Maa* need me. Sumitra *Maa* sees *Swami* in me. How can I deprive her of that bit of joy she finds when she looks at me? All these 12 years, she has been a mother to me and Shrutakeerti. I cannot leave her. And my Shatrughan, how will he handle the responsibility of governing Ayodhya all alone? Bharath will be distraught on learning the truth about his brothers' departure. *Maa*, allow me to remain with my family. In Moti Bhavan, I feel Saumitra's presence, his arms enveloping me and his warmth putting me to sleep. I cannot go with you."

Sunaina became emotional. Waves of guilt washed over her for neglecting her daughter's well-being in Ayodhya for more than 12 years, she had not even bothered to find out whether Urmila was happy.

Sita always came first, but the Urmila who stood in front of her mother was sheer power – tough, firm and resilient, a symbol of sacrifice. Her daughter made her proud.

Maata Gargi wanted to spend time with Urmila alone. Sunaina left them.

"I shall not ask how you are because I know how my Urmi is. She may be completely broken inside, but she will not let anyone know just how much she is hurting." *Maata* Gargi, who accompanied Sunaina from Mithila, embraced Urmila, "You may have taken birth from Maharani Sunaina's womb, but you are my daughter as well and I know for sure that you are not happy."

Urmila had never been able to hide anything from her mentor. "You are *trikaldarshi, Maata.* You can see the past, the present and the future. You know what is going on. I am not happy. Nothing will bring my Saumitra back. Every moment, I ache for him, the emptiness in my soul becomes more acute; but I hold on to the hope that he placed on my open palm when he left."

"I am proud of you, my daughter. I thank Narayan for considering me your godmother. Tough times baptise us by fire, my daughter, and I know that the Warrior Princess of Mithila will win this war against time, against the writs of destinies and the plots that the heavens and the earth draw up to test Lakshmila." Urmila felt strengthened in the presence of the wise woman.

A letter from Bharath and Shatrughan brought by messenger around mid-morning said that they were on their way back. "Bharath and Shatrughan might be here any day now. I wait for my Bharath for I know he will call back Ram and Lakshman. Ram will not be able to refuse his brother's plea," Kaushalya said with hope.

"My eyes yearn to see my son, Shatrughan." Urmila was happy for the first time since Lakshman left. The presence of Saumitra's younger brother was always a balm on the cruel wounds of fate.

An innate loneliness in Urmila gnawed at her and she often had to scout for ways to run from it. Shatrughan was her only refuge from the unbearable pain and hurt that hounded her.

Bharath and Shatrughan Return

Homecoming is but a piece in the big puzzle.

The air around Ayodhya was restless. It was heavy with the premonition of an approaching storm and another tragedy in the royal family. Though it still had not lost hope that someday soon, all the four princes would reunite and the empty portals would resound with the joyous laughter of the princes again.

The news of Bharath, Shatrughan, Mandvi and Shrutakeerti's homecoming spurred Urmila into a frenzy of activity. She ran to their palaces, ordering the maids to decorate the quarters for their arrival. Manthara, who was passing by, was relieved to see Urmila smiling. She begged for forgiveness from Lakshman and Urmila in silence, wondering if she had bailed them out of a destiny so tragic that it would have torn their mortal lives apart. But she could not have, for the story of Ksheera and Shesha had been written by Narayan long ago.

Urmila was touched by the tears in Manthara's eyes. "Why do you cry, *Dadi Maa?*" she asked, touching Manthara's feet.

The old maid hugged her, "These are the tears of happiness because my Bharath comes home today. But why do you still call me *Dadi Maa* when I am the reason for the exile your husband has imposed on himself?"

"We will always respect you. Lakshman loved you and we will not question your actions because there must have been a good reason for the way you acted." Urmila's tact and wisdom were not lost upon Manthara. The old servitor looked at the humble and wise princess who stood before her clad in saffron and white; a stirring of grudging respect somewhere deep inside her scheming heart brought a light of warmth to her eyes. She could not help but like the stoic hermit princess, who did not ridicule her. She blessed Urmila and walked away quietly, hoping someday everyone would understand that she was just putty in Narayan's hands.

Urmila walked to the kitchen to make Shatrughan's favourite sweet dish that he wanted to eat on his return, but Shanta stopped her saying fasting was a funerary ritual in the home of the deceased. The kitchen was shut for 16 days to mourn the dead. Urmila thought for a moment and found a way to solve the problem because she did not want to break her promise to Shatrughan.

Urmila ran to Shivalay. "*Maa*, there is something for which I need your permission." She knew that her mother-in-law, Sumitra, would not deny her the permission for what she wanted to do for Shatrughan. "*Maa*, you know I had promised Shatrughan that I would make his favourite *besan ka halwa* when he returned. But with *Pitaji's* demise, I cannot use the royal kitchen. May I please go elsewhere to make it?" Urmila pleaded with her mother-in-law.

Sumitra smiled for she could not ever deny anything to Urmila. The princess's eyes sparkled in glee as she rushed out of the palace to find a house in the city that she considered the best and the safest for her mission. She requested the lady of the house to allow her to make the sweetmeats in her kitchen for her brother-in-law. The lady recognised Urmila – the princess from the palace – and opened her kitchen to her.

People from the neighbourhood flocked to watch Urmila, the royal bride from Raghukul cooking in a commoner's kitchen. They were moved to tears at her fraternal love for Shatrughan and the endearing way in which she breached the walls between the high and the low in a city poised on an uncertain future. Urmila thanked the woman and invited her to the feast on Lakshman and Shatrughan's forthcoming birthdays.

The royal mothers demurred at Urmila's proposition to welcome Bharath and Shatrughan as their chariots passed through the gateway to Ayodhya for they did not have the courage to face their sons and break the news of Ram's exile, Lakshman's departure and Dashrath's death. Urmila was happily assigned the task of welcoming them – and escorting them to their palaces in the true manner of a king or a Warrior Princess.

Urmila waited for them with welcoming prayer lamps, sandalwood paste, flowers and sweetmeats in her hands at the door of the palace. Bharath and Shatrughan had this uncanny feeling that everything was not right at home. The subjects, who crowded the streets on either side of the streets to see the royal procession pass by, were unhappy. The hate and anger in their eyes reached out to the princes – an ugly agitation. The two princes and their wives looked at each other in fear and foreboding, wondering what had prompted the people of Ayodhya to resent their arrival.

As the chariots stopped in front of the woman in a monk's attire, the brothers felt the ground caving in beneath them. Urmila stood at the mammoth wooden door with an empty look in her eyes but she wore a bright cosmetic smile. Shatrughan experienced a twinge of fear.

Their instincts had been right that Ayodhya had been struck by a tragedy. After a brief welcoming ceremony, Bharath and Mandvi headed to Meghavan, Kaikeyi's palace, while Shatrughan and Shrutakeerti accompanied Urmila to Shivalay. Shatrughan glanced at his *bhabhi maa*, noticing her silence and the gaps in her laughter. She seemed to have changed in a month.

He hurried to his mother.

"*Maa*! When, how?" Shatrughan asked, in tears, at his mother's feet. The sight of Sumitra without jewellery, attired in a white *sari*, broke his tenuous connect with everything that he held precious and unshakable in life. His world crashed as he realised that his father had passed away. It was time for Sumitra to tell her son everything that shook Ayodhya when he was away. Urmila stood like a pillar of strength as Sumitra gathered the courage to reveal the truth about Bharath's impending coronation, Kaikeyi's demand at Dashrath's death bed, Ram's exile with Lakshman and Sita for 14 years, Urmila's sacrifice and the king's death.

"*Maa, bhaiya* did not try to stop Queen Kaikeyi? Why did he allow Ram *bhaiya* to go into exile? Why did father agree?" Shatrughan searched for answers.

"He tried, my son. He tried his best but could not reverse what destiny had written for him," Urmila cut into his train of questions.

Shatrughan's anger, much like Lakshman's, was slow to build up. "Manthara should be hanged to death! That evil woman is the reason why my brother is not with his wife, *bhabhi maa*. She has destroyed our family," Shatrughan lashed out. Before Sumitra or Urmila could react, Shatrughan headed for Manthara's chamber.

He dragged the old maid out and was about to strike her face with his palm, when Urmila screamed, "Shatrughan!" Her voice rose, "Let her go, immediately. Since when has it become legitimate to hit a woman in Raghukul?"

"My apologies, but a criminal has no gender. This evil woman has destroyed our family. How can you be so forgiving? Don't you realise that she is the reason for your separation from *bhaiya*?" Shatrughan glowered at Manthara.

"It was destined to happen. Don't blame her for it. Don't let anger override your etiquette. By punishing her, you can neither erase nor retrace what has happened. Step back and let her go," Urmila was unyielding.

Shatrughan looked around him. No one seemed to be willing to come to Shatrughan's defense in his tirade against Manthara. He released the old maid; Urmila gently took her aside and escorted her back to her chambers. The grief and fear on Manthara's face touched Urmila's heart and she was angry with Shatrughan for bringing shame on the family by venting his ire on a maid, an old serving hand. Before she could collect her thoughts, a servitor hurried to the room carrying an urgent message. She whispered something into Urmila's ears. The princess rushed to Meghavan, panting. As she reached the doors of Kaikeyi's palace, Bharath's lament stilled her in her tracks. She listened in fear.

"I did not ever think that my own mother would bring me so much shame. Just tell me one thing, *Raj Maata*," Bharath said with sarcasm. "Before you set out to destroy the man, who made you the *Raj Maata*, the sons who loved you as a mother, did your conscience not prick you? Did you even once think about me? But as rightly said, a son repents for the sins of his mother. I disown you as my mother, you evil woman, before I kill myself." An enervated Kaikeyi stood like a statue through his anger, bearing its intensity.

Urmila moved forward and held the sword that Bharath had whipped out to behead himself, "What is done cannot be undone but today I beg of you to forgive *Maa* Kaikeyi, not for you, but for *Bhaiya* Ram, who loves her the most. She does what she does out of her love for you. You are our last hope. Ayodhya needs you."

"But how will I face the people of Ayodhya? How shall I face *Maata* Kaushalya and *Maata* Sumitra? And you, I am the reason of your and Lakshman's separation," Bharath wept like a child.

"They have already forgiven *Maata* Kaikeyi and they await your presence in their palace. Cool your anger and do what is right," Urmila urged Bharath.

He looked at his mother scornfully one last time and yet with sadness before leaving for Hari Kuntha to meet Queen Kaushalya.

Shatrughan refused to perform his father's last rites because he considered Bharath, the regent incumbent of Ayodhya, the right person to do them. "Your father wanted you to perform his last rites. I implore you to fulfil his last wish, son," Sumitra pleaded with Shatrughan, who had no other option but to agree with reluctance.

As the family bid a tearful farewell to Maharaj Dashrath, an era in Ayodhya came to an end. It was beautiful while it lasted. But now it was time to learn how to live without the king's voice, his commands and his laughter. Ayodhya would never be the same again.

Meeting at Chitrakoot

Bodies return to the dust of creation's debri; souls remain bonded .

It had been 16 days since Maharaj Dashrath's last rites. Each day had been burdensome for Bharath since his return from Kekeya. He needed Ram's forgiveness. He sought repentance. But he had to find out where they were. He ordered Arya Sumantra to send the soldiers out to locate Ram, Lakshman and Sita.

Urmila encouraged Shatrughan and Bharath to speak to her to ease their anxiety and dump their woes on her. Shatrughan was troubled with the tumultuous chains of thoughts as he tried in vain to fill the emptiness left behind by his brothers. The fact that he was the youngest of the siblings made him feel helpless; he had been emotionally abandoned. He could not share his sorrow with Urmila.

They rested their heads on her lap like little boys and told her how much they missed their brothers. Bharath cried, blaming himself for their exile. Urmila ran her hands through their hair, reassuring them that 14 years would fly in a flurry of events, and all would end well.

Arya Sumantra came in with news of Ram, Lakshman and Sita.

"Where is my *Swami*, Sumantra *ji*? Did you see him? Is he well?" Urmila demanded to know in one breath.

The brothers and Sita were at Chitrakoot, on the other side of Dandakaranya, Arya told the princess. While Bharath and Shatrughan were ecstatic, Urmila ran to Goddess Gauri, the guardian deity of her palace. "*Maa*, keep my Saumitra safe. I entrust his life to you," she prayed fervently; possessed by fear, hope and the unquestioning faith in the power of the divine.

Mandvi, who followed Urmila to the shrine, blurted out, "We leave early in the morning to bring them back."

"I won't go," Urmila whispered.

"You are angry with us, else why wouldn't you go? There is no love greater for you than his," Mandvi insisted.

"No, Mandvi. I am not angry with you or Bharath. I cannot go because meeting *Swami* and then leaving him again will kill me. I will not be able to bear another separation from Saumitra."

How would Urmila explain to anyone what she would feel after meeting him and then letting him go again? Just as she was learning how to cope with life without him, the news that they were in Chitrakoot disturbed her hard-earned emotional equilibrium. She longed to meet him, but only to hold him forever; not to watch him go, again. She had no strength left for another farewell.

"Do you think Arya's love for his brothers will allow him to climb down from his pledge?" Mandvi argued. Urmila remained silent, for she knew in her heart that convincing Ram to give up on his word was impossible – promises were made in life and blood in Raghukul.

As they were arguing, Bharath, Shatrughan, Sumitra and Kaushalya changed the mood with news about their forthcoming journey to Chitrakoot but Urmila was firm that she did not want to go.

"Bharath, how can I leave Ayodhya? It is my *Swami*'s wish. And I cannot see my *Swami* go through the hardships of a life he is not meant to live," she tried to reason with her family.

Before Sumitra could console Urmila, Shrutakeerti erupted in rage, "Why are you acting so selfish when you are so selfless by nature? You constantly think about yourself, your agony. Do you forget that *bhaiya* also goes through the same pain of separation? Think about him, once. I know *bhaiya* doesn't express much, but if you do not accompany us, he will blame himself. He will consider it an indication of your anger and he will be heartbroken. But if he sees you, he will have a reason to smile. And, have you thought about how he will react when he learns about *Pitaji*? You know that a smile on your face can heal his wounds. He lives only for you. Please accompany us, *didi*, for his sake."

Urmila finally relented, but on the condition that Queen Kaikeyi went with them too. Bharath was reluctant but eventually he gave in to Urmila's request. However, he refused to look at his mother.

Early next morning, when the sun touched the horizon with its first golden light, the royal family of Ayodhya set out in an entourage out to meet Ram, Lakshman and Sita in Chitrakoot.

Kevat, a humble boatman and Nishad Raj Guha, a childhood friend of Ram and Lakshman helped the family cross the River Ganga. On the way to Chitrakoot, they met several great seers like Maharishi Bharadwaja, a renowned scholar, economist and eminent physician Bhagwaan Valmiki, Rishi-Munis like Atri Muni, one of the greatest Sapta Rishis of Aryavarta, who was the master of the Vedas and the father of the great saint Rishi Durvasa and Chandrama. He was defeated by Urmila in a debate when she was just a girl of 12! He advised the trio to stay in the beautiful forest of Chitrakoot, surrounded by lakes, trees and pretty birds. He said it was safe for a woman to live in the forest.

The family reached the hut where Ram, Lakshman and Sita were staying in the heart of the forest. They watched the three from a distance, unobtrusively – taking stock of their lives in exile. Bharath knew it is time to face their wrath for what his mother had done and decided to face them alone. He forbade Shatrughan to accompany him as he walked to the hut.

As expected, Lakshman was furious at the sight of Bharath approaching their hut. "How dare you come here? Ayodhya's crowned king, where is your army? Well, let me tell you that no plan of yours to harm my older brother and his wife will work as long as this brother is alive," Lakshman thundered.

"Lakshman, my brother, do not blame me for a sin I am not a party to. I regret Queen Kaikeyi's selfishness and the act of atrocity. Unfortunately, even though I have severed ties with her, I seek penitence for what she has done. Forgive me, brother."

Lakshman looked at Bharath with contempt and scorn. But Shatrughan could not control his eagerness to embrace his brother; he rushed out of hiding and held Lakshman tightly, "Brother, I seek forgiveness too, for I could not do anything to prevent *Pitaji's* demise."

Lakshman stared at his brothers in disbelief, shock turning his face into a chalky shade of white. It could not be! His father could not die. Bharath placed the pot containing Dashrath's ashes on the ground. Lakshman fell to the ground near the pot, his body quivering with tears of grief. The joy on Ram and Sita's faces at meeting their brothers disappeared the moment Shatrughan broke the news to them. The shade that had shielded them from the cruel blows of life had been taken away. The family huddled in the hut to grieve for the king of Ayodhya, their father, together.

The forest humbled the mighty royals as the gods looked down from heaven in benign sorrow.

Lakshman realised that life hadn't been kind to Sumitra. She looked aged, fine lines of grief and tiredness fanned out from her eyes in a spider net of wrinkles. He enfolded his mother in a gentle hug. Urmila watched them from afar, love shining in her eyes; she was scared to come out from the shadows of the trees, where she was hiding. Urmila was so caught up in the tearful reunion of Saumitra and Sumitra that she did not hear Sita walk silently towards her and stand next to her without a word.

"There isn't a moment when he doesn't miss you. He tries to hide it, but it shows." Urmila turned around to look at her sister sharply, and then sadly, torn by the revelation.

She emerged from her hiding place behind a tree, and walked shyly to Lakshman to touch his feet. She was startled when he ignored her touch and moved away. She immediately recoiled, hurt by his rejection. Lakshman walked away, out of Urmila's sight to wipe his tears. He was guilty of having put her through the heartache; he could not face her. Their love for each other tore them apart!

The family convinced Lakshman that Urmila could not ever be angry with him. She loved him and that was why she chose to stay behind to care for the family. It was a sacrifice of love, one that Aryavarta would always recant for centuries. They filled Lakshman with stories about her efficiency, courage, endurance, honour and good conduct in the palace. Shatrughan narrated how she had saved Manthara from his fury and had forgiven Bharath, stopping him from committing suicide by beheading himself.

Sumitra took her son aside, "A mother is blessed if her son gets himself a wife like *Janaknandini* Urmila. What more can I say?" The admission of her daughter-in-law's goodness from a queen as possessive and proud as Sumitra touched Lakshman, deep down.

He was still hesitant till Ram urged him to speak to Urmila, heal her hurt. "Lakshman, go and embrace her tightly so that her sadness disappears. You have been waiting for her since long, and today when she faces you, you turn away your face. Don't send her the wrong message."

Lakshman broke down in his brother's arms, "How can I face her, brother, when I am the reason for her pain? I failed as a husband. She might hate me."

Ram smiled calmly, "She loves you far too much to hate you. Meet her, she needs you."

Lakshman's pride in his Mila grew. He overcame his self-pity – and left the hut to meet Urmila. He found her sitting under a tree outside the hut in which he lived. He had made the hut – his little shelter – from mud, wood and thatch with his own hand.

"How do you know that I have made this?" Lakshman asked.

Urmila skirted a direct reply to his query. "You will not ever disturb your older brother and his wife," she said, avoiding looking him in the eye. She gazed at the little hut instead. Lakshman took her gently in his arms and they remain locked in each other's hold for timeless moments, or so they felt. The heavens sent a balmy breeze to cool the forest, the breath of relief by the gods that which had been decreed in the abode of Narayan would not hold the deities accountable for injustice on earth.

It was then perhaps that Lakshman and Urmila realised how helpless they were. They were jailed in their moral prisons of duties, responsibilities, faith and promises – on earth.

Urmila sensed a sublime sadness in her husband that struck a familiar vein in her. She wiped his tears gently, "Even when you are in the depths of despair, think of me and smile because you are the only reason I live for."

"But father, Mila...he would have lived had we not left," Lakshman put his head on her shoulders and wept like a child.

"He still is and shall always be with us. He lives in our laughter, in our conversations, in our strengths and our happiness. Why do you consider him gone?" Urmila ruffled his hair lovingly. Lakshman calmed down as always after listening to her. Her presence was like a salve.

She tended to his wounds, the bruises that the harsh life in the forest had marked on his fair skin, and fed him from a bowl of jungle fruits. This was the closest she could get to him in exile. He looked at her unable to take his eyes off her face – etching every line, every contour and every fold of her pretty face in his memory. He felt his hunger ebb. He could probably go through 14 years without regular meals after this day; he felt sated.

"You told me not to cry for 14 years and you are crying. This is not done, *Swami*," she teased him, when his tears did not stop flowing. "I told you not to cry because you are the strongest of them all. I am weak when it comes to emotions, you know..." Lakshman trailed off.

"But, *Swami*, you will have to keep your emotions in check. Remember what you promised me?"

After the family settled in the hut, Gurudev Vashishtha ordered the princes to scatter Maharaj Dashrath's ashes in the river. They floated the urn in the gushing waters of the Mandakini, weeping as they bid their father *adieu*.

Lakshman was embarrassed to face Maharaj Janak, Maharani Sunaina and *Maata* Gargi because the guilt of being unfair to Urmila was like a wound on his conscience.

Maharani Sunaina, who did not take kindly to Lakshman leaving her daughter alone in the palace, forgave him. She hugged him, telling him how proud she was to have a son-in-law like Saumitra, who had put his *dharma* before self.

"It has not been easy for me to come away without her, but I cannot bear to put her through a difficult life. My Mila deserves all the luxuries of life; she cannot survive barefoot in the forest. I will always be a culprit, but please forgive me if you can for not making your daughter happy as I had promised," Lakshman pleaded.

"You are the only one for her. There can be no one better for my Warrior Princess than you, and will never be," the king of Mithila said, allaying the doubts in Lakshman's heart.

The family remained strategically silent for two days before persuading Ram to return. On the third day in the morning, Kaikeyi ventured forth with her request.

"I seek your forgiveness, my son," she begged of Ram, "Let us go back to Ayodhya and fulfil the Maharaj's last wish. I have come to take you back, my son."

Ram could not be forced into breaking his oath, "I gave my word to my father. I shall only return after living out my period of exile. I was his pride. I cannot go back on my promise to him."

The family sought Maharaj Janak's intervention. After Kaikeyi's pleas fell on deaf ears, they looked to Janak to decide in favour of Bharath but Urmila knew that her father was an intelligent and wise man, who would always vote for *dharma* over personal interest and familial sentiments.

He looked at his daughter, drawing on her strength. "*Pitaji*, do what *dharma* prescribes. Don't hesitate to decide without bias because of my emotions. I want you to be fair and just," Urmila was rigid in her stance on justice.

"I know each of you trust me and expect the right decision. Today, I stand here not as a father, but as an objective listener and a judge. After hearing both Bharath and Ram, I seek your pardon if I have hurt your sentiments but I agree with Ram."

The silence in the air around them was more palpable than noise; it was as if nature had stopped breathing in shock due to Janak's verdict on Ram's exile. Bharath tried to reason with Janak but Gurudev Vashishtha told him not to press Ram to return. Bharath was as strong-willed as Ram and he was adamant that he would not go back to Ayodhya without his brothers. Eventually, he decided that he would stay at Nandigram, a village in the outskirts of Ayodhya, to do penance for the 'sins' against Ram, and Shatrughan would rule the kingdom for him.

Maharaj Janak and Gurudev Vashishtha had no choice, but to agree. Bharath was unflinching. "Lakshman serves you in the forest, allow me to do my duty towards you as your follower. Please give me your *paduka* − wooden walking shoes. I shall place them on the throne of Ayodhya. They will remind the subjects who is and will always remain their king. Only you are their king, brother Ram," Bharath announced. Ram cringed at the prospect of Bharath's quasi-exile. The humble request made by his brother for his shoes broke Ram to pieces. He held Bharath close to him and allowed him to take his wooden *paduka* as the new token of kingship. Finally, Bharath, Shatrughan and the rest of the royal troupe from Ayodhya and Mithila stepped into their chariots to return home.

The sun was setting on the distant hills.

The forest was covered in deep ochre shadows; the light of the late afternoon sun filtering through the thick canopy of trees in orange and yellow slivers. Lakshmila looked at each other in the light of the setting sun, for a long second, before they left, each to his own destination. The light played hide-and-seek on their faces, heavy with turbulent emotions. They would have to wait for another 13 years and 11 months to meet again. The thought was so terrifying. Urmila balled her palms into tight fists to withstand the physical pain of parting. Lakshman was tall and rigid in his stoic resignation to fate − but the hint of unshed tears in his eyes and his trembling hands gave him away.

Ram blessed Urmila, "My little sister, your sacrifice cannot be described in words. What you have done for Ayodhya, and for Lakshman, is not feasible for any woman. I promise you that I will bring your Saumitra back to you safely."

Urmila clutched at his hand that he placed on her head, "*Bhaiya*, I know my *Swami* will be safe in your care. But I worry about you."

Urmila stood in front of her Saumitra – memorising his smile, his tears, the lines on his face and even the trickles of sweat on his brow. Unknowingly, Lakshman did the same. His eyes caressed her mussed hair, her calm smile and the anguish in her big grey-blue eyes. "Take care, my love," he whispered softly. Their eyes mirrored their emotions.

Shatrughan hung around Lakshman, refusing to let go of his brother. Lakshman disentangled himself from his embrace and took Shatrughan back to Shrutakeerti's chariot, "Take care of my brother. He has not ever been alone without me, so perhaps he doesn't know how to live outside my protective umbrella."

"I will, *bhaiya*, always take care of your brother. And before you ask us, let me assure you, I will take care of your Mila too," Shrutakeerti promised Lakshman.

"Only you two can make her smile, apart from me. *Maa* told me that she smiled for the first time after I left Ayodhya when she heard that you were coming back, Shatrughan," Lakshman joined his palms in a *namaskara* to Shatrughan in a hushed voice. Shatrughan clasped Lakshman's hands in his and nodded without uttering a word. The family understood his desperate desire to see Mila happy, even without him.

Their feelings of guilt were tacit, running across in a silent refrain.

Could Lakshmila truly ever live without each other in their physical selves? They left their souls with each other in Chitrakoot.

Urmila Learns the Truth

Truths made in heaven are atrocities on earth?

Urmila had not been herself since her return from Chitrakoot. Had she left behind a part of her with Lakshman or had she brought a part of him with her to Ayodhya? But she had become quieter and more sombre. Her restlessness could be seen in flashes, at odd moments, but only in her eyes.

Bharath walked to Moti Bhavan and sat quietly next to Urmila. She was meditating. The Warrior Princess of Mithila sat in a lotus position with her hands joined in prayer at the top of her head. As she opened her eyes, Bharath touched her feet, *"Bhabhi,* I am leaving for Nandigram. I have come to seek your blessings. I will return only when my beloved brothers end their exile."

Urmila looked at Mandvi who stood behind her husband. Sadness had erased the lines of laughter on her face. Urmila saw her grief as her own. She blessed Bharath.

"Are you not taking Mandvi with you?"

"No, sister, she will stay here and perform her duties," Bharath was unrelenting.

"You need her more than us. The palace is full of people – three mothers, Shatrughan, Shrutakeerti and I. We can take care of each other, but without you, she will be lonesome. You should allow her to accompany you," Urmila tried to reason with Bharath.

"Bhabhi, I will only serve Ram *bhaiya*'s *charan paduka* – shoes – for these 14 years. My life with Mandvi will be on hold till my brothers return home from the forest. So, it is best that she lives here." Bowing in reverence, Bharath left Moti Bhavan. Urmila drew Mandvi close to her. She felt her sister's torment. Who could understand the anguish of separation better than her? She was powerless because she had not been able to protect her sister from the pain that she had been through?

"Urmila, do not let my situation aggrieve you. My pain is inconsequential compared to yours. At least, I am assured of my husband's safety. I can visit him and meet him whenever I want to. But you will live for 14 years in uncertainty, alone, without him around." This was the first time Mandvi was expressing her concern – for Urmila as a sister – an emotion that she had successfully managed to camouflage under her playful garb of barbs and sibling squabbles.

"Mandvi, your pain tears you apart just the way my pain shears me. Destiny has played mean tricks on us. If you want, you can live here with me in Moti Bhavan." Urmila's generosity brought tears to Mandvi's eyes, reminding her of the fights of their girlhood in Mithila.

"No, sister, let me find the strength to be alone without my *Swami* on my own. I have to learn to watch out for myself," Mandvi said, leaving for Ksheesh Bhavan. Urmila looked around her living quarters with nostalgia. She could not allow herself to indulge in the luxury of Saumitra's memories and soak in them. She mediated everyday to put Saumitra's reminiscences at the back of her mind – in a remote corner from where they would not torment her or intrude into her everydays.

Urmila opened her eyes to find Shatrughan sitting next to her on the floor.

"What is wrong, my son?" She asked Shatrughan.

Putting his head on her lap, Shatrughan whimpered like a little boy, "How do I handle Ayodhya, the affairs of the *Rajya Sabha*, alone? I can't do it without my brothers," he looked up at Urmila's face as she touched his head. "Since our childhood, we have always been together. But destiny has exile and hardship for them, while I stay here in the palace enjoying life's comforts?" According to Shatrughan, karma had been biased in its judgement and in arbitrating the destinies of the brothers.

"Why?" He wanted to know.

Shatrughan knew that his brothers did not take him because they wanted to shield him from the austerities of forest life. He was the youngest and the most loved and pampered. But he felt worthless; constrained by constant worry about his brothers' well-being. He could not govern the kingdom or run the household.

"Shatrughan, we will live together again. No eclipse hangs on the sun and the moon forever. But until then, you will have to be strong and take charge of the state," she said, staring at a statue of Lakshman she had sculpted. It resembled a deity.

"And what if I make a mistake? *Maa* told me how well you handled the affairs of the state in Ayodhya in our absence. Please continue doing so. I will assist you." Shatrughan said.

"No, son, I will spend these 14 years in meditation, praying for and to my Saumitra. You are capable enough. And this is your duty. You have to fulfil your responsibility towards your brothers and your land." Urmila was firm in her wishes for her youngest brother-in-law. She wanted Shatrughan to grow out of the shadow of his older brothers and feel confident of his own right as a regent in proxy.

The news of Kaikeyi's breakdown at Bharath's departure reached Urmila at noon, and she ran to Meghavan. The *Raj Vaidya* was there as were the two Maharanis.

They were told by the royal physician to keep Kaikeyi free from stress, else it could be fatal. The women posted vigil on Kaikeyi throughout the night to ensure that she slept without nightmares or attacks of anxiety. Urmila sat next to her as Kaikeyi, in her semi-conscious state, grasped Urmila's and Shatrughan's hands. "Ram, Saumitra, Bharath, don't leave me. Forgive your mother, my sons," the queen mumbled in her delirium.

Urmila and Shatrughan sat holding Kaikeyi's hand. She opened her eyes after sometime, ordering everyone except for Urmila to leave, feeling assured that with Urmila around no harm could come to her.

"Urmila, my child I do not know for how long I will live now. But before I break my silence today and reveal a truth to you, I beg of you to forgive me for causing you this pain and to promise me that the truth I unveil today will not be divulged ever," Kaikeyi folded her hands in an entreaty.

"A mother's hands are meant to bestow blessings on her children, not for anything else. I have somehow always known it, *Maa*. I had a feeling that you and *Dadi Maa* were hiding a dark truth from us and I promise you it will never be known to anyone else if you tell me." Urmila guided Kaikeyi's hands to her head for blessings.

Kaikeyi struggled to get up from her bed and with Urmila's help, steadied herself on the ground. She took Urmila to an enclosure near her bed-chamber where Manthara lay fettered on the floor at Shatrughan's orders. As soon as Manthara saw Urmila and Kaikeyi, she began to wail and tried to crawl to them, but the thick iron fetters held her back. She fell down, but before her head could touch the floor, Urmila put her hand under her falling head to cushion her from the hurt. She ordered the guards to unchain Manthara immediately.

"My child, how do I repay you for this kindness? You indeed are a devi. Now, I see it for myself. Guru *ji* was right. The gods of Vaikunth have come down to earth," Manthara paid her homage to Urmila with her eyes, which lit up for a moment in gratitude.

"Yes, it is true that Manthara provoked me, set me against Ram. But she forced me into it. This is the truth I wanted you to know. But there is more. *Maata* Saraswati herself appeared to me to reveal that Ram and Saumitra have been born to create a new world, free from evil. They can only do so when they are not bound to the Kosala kingdom. And to set them free, Narayan has chosen Manthara and me," Kaikeyi narrated.

Urmila did not know how to respond, her belief in supernatural scripts was laced with doubt that the truths crafted in heaven were wrought and undone by material concerns on earth. Could heaven and earth ever meet as one?

Urmila offered to free Manthara and take her back to her quarters but the old maid refused. She reminded Urmila of her promise, "You cannot reveal this truth to anyone. Freeing me may cause inconvenience to some people in the palace. I will stay here until Ram and Saumitra return. I will wait for Narayan and Shesha to take me home."

Urmila let her be because she could not ignore the wisdom in Manthara's request, "We will all come to take you back with dignity and honour, *Dadi Maa*. Until then, you will not face any difficulty here."

Urmila wanted Kaikeyi to stay with her at Moti Bhavan, but Kaikeyi was not comfortable with the idea. She could not accept Urmila's hospitality – her magnanimity pricked Kaikeyi's conscience.

"My injustice, however honest it may seem to my mind in the interest of my son Bharath, will always mock me and remind me of my treachery, if I stay with you. It will not let me live. Let me live my last days in Meghavan and repent for my sins." Urmila left her alone.

As the sun set over Ayodhya, Urmila took out her paint brushes and let the fine sable hairs flow in random strokes on the canvas in great dabs of colours. Art worked magic in Urmila's hands; the colours slowly began to melt into each other, taking definite shapes. She recaptured her wedding, her moments with Saumitra and the joy of those moments. As she painted, she spoke to him – a one-way conversation, "*Swami*, today *Dadi Maa* has unveiled why you had to leave. I hope you forgive her as I do. I look back on the day you..."

She heard his answering echo in the air; in the melting colours on her white canvas.

And every word she uttered transmitted to Saumitra. It was as if he heard. Souls that connect in the unconscious hear each other. They vibe on the same plane, and so did Lakshmila.

Nidra Devi Visits Lakshman

Sleep transforms, setting lives on paths unknown.

Ram, Lakshman and Sita felt empty after their families departed. They were paying for a crime they did not commit. The scriptures say the karma of the ancestors visit their children.

Ram decided to leave Chitrakoot after the royal visit because he was sacred that the people of Ayodhya might follow in the footsteps of the first family to visit their favourite prince. He did not want to draw attention in his exile, so he ordered Lakshman and Sita to pack their belongings and move on.

Lakshman, the quieter among the two brothers, noticed Ram walking barefoot among the stones out of Chitrakoot. He had given his *padukas* to Bharath to place them on the throne. Lakshman requested his brother and his sister-in-law to rest *en route*. While Ram and Sita sat under a tree, Lakshman crafted a pair of *upanah* – rough slippers – from light wood and bark ropes for his brother to wear for the rest of the journey. Ram blessed Lakshman in silence for his subtle and unspoken understanding.

They decided to visit Maharishi Kambuja's *ashram*. Kambuja was a Vedic scholar and the grandfather of Maharishi Paraspar, their niece Vindhya's husband. Lakshman smiled at the thought of meeting his best friend, his niece.

Maharishi Kambuja and his disciples welcomed the trio with warmth and ensured that they were comfortable and fed well. When Vindhya, who had now grown into a pragmatic householder and a happy retreat-dweller, came to know what had happened in Ayodhya, she sank into depression. The glorious recall of the other life, she experienced as a child in Ayodhya, was lost forever. The ache in her heart reflected in her eyes and in those of her confidant, Saumitra. The cheerful lad was an empty shell, consigned to his duties and *dharma*.

She sought time alone with Lakshman. Closing the doors of her hut firmly, she hit out, "Why did you leave your 'reason to live' behind? And did you not think of her, once?" Lakshman had no answers to her accusations.

Vindhya was angry with the man she had once idolised, who she thought was chivalrous and compassionate to women, "You disappoint me so." She could feel Urmila's pain inside her for she had been through the same heartache when her husband left her to meditate in the icy northern mountains.

"How could you do so? If your duty is to serve your older brother, your duty is also to take care of your wife and her happiness. Did you forget the promises you made to her and her father when you married her? You leave a woman who left everything behind to become your wife to chase after your brother in the forest. Have you ever thought about the torment you have put her through? This is an act of cowardice and selfishness." Vindhya did not spare Lakshman.

Lakshman was silent through the deluge of her fury. Tears filled his eyes as he put his thoughts into words, "You do not feel my pain? There isn't a moment I do not ache for her, but god had other plans for us. I had to leave her behind, for her own sake. I still remember I promised her a destiny different from my mother's. I vowed to her that she would live only in riches. How could I bring her with me to go through this difficult life? I am slowly dying without her by my side, but this is a punishment, I bear without complaints. And why do you all assume that if I am not with her in my physical self, I do not love her enough or by choosing to serve what is right means I choose my brother over her. No. Kingship is built on a different set of moral codes. A prince cannot afford to think with his heart. Responsibility is always greater than love."

The old friendship between the two friends kindled once again, even if for a day. Vindhya looked at Lakshman closely, waiting for his sorrow to reach out her. They had always been very close since she had first met him as a toddler; Lakshman was not only her uncle, but her brother and her best friend too. She had always understood his feelings without speaking a word. Why couldn't she see how much it hurt him to leave her behind? The connection was missing, probably broken by the strange turns of destiny.

Lakshman hugged Vindhya, "Why do you cry, my princess? You are right in your assertions but sometimes some decisions cannot be avoided even though they hurt. There is not a soul I love more than my Mila, yet I cannot be with her."

Vindhya held on to him till he regained his calm and composed himself. She finally began to understand love through its complex prism of emotions and actions. There could be no greater love than Lakshmila's, but doubts about the way it was fated to play out haunted her unschooled head. Vindhya was still very young.

Vindhya watched the trio leave the retreat with a heavy heart, hoping secretly to meet them again, soon. She longed for the joys of her childhood, the fun that she had in Ayodhya.

Ram decided to camp for a few days in a nearby forest. Lakshman gathered wood and hay to make a small shelter for them. The forest was dense and danger lurked in the form of sudden attacks by animals and tribes of demons. Lakshman stayed awake at night, watching over his brother, even though Sita insisted that he should catch up on his sleep once Ram woke up. But Lakshman refused to allow sleep to get the better of him. Sleep lulled the senses, he wanted to live the intensity of his hardship and suffer every moment for it.

Gradually, the lack of sleep began to tell on his nerves and strength. He was fatigued and his eyes were pools of darkness; but Lakshman was unrelenting in his war against sleep. In the heavens above, the gods gathered to solve the problem; and break through Lakshman's willpower. As Ram and Sita retired to their hut for an evening of prayer, meditation and a light sleep, the gods whispered to Nidra Devi, to visit Lakshman quietly.

"My dear son, I am here to warn you. You are suffering from severe lack of sleep. If you do not rest, your overwrought mind and body might lead you to your death," Nidra Devi, the Rig Vedic deity of sleep appeared to Lakshman, descending from the silver mist of the evening as a beautiful mother goddess, affectionate and tender like Lakshmi, Saraswati and Parvati, an all-in-one avatara.

"No mother, I cannot sleep because I have to follow my *dharma*. I want to sacrifice my sleep and serve my brother and sister-in-law for 14 years of exile," he pleaded with Nidra Devi.

"I am astonished at how dutiful you are, my son. Today, for you, I change the laws of sleep. Find someone who can sleep for you. What I mean is that you can only stay awake if someone else takes away your share of sleep. The person will have to sleep till you return to Ayodhya and only you can wake your sleeping counterpart on your return," Nidra Devi advised Lakshman.

Lakshman thought for some time. And the only one who came to his mind was Urmila. He knew she would not ever turn down his plea. Maybe, if she slept his sleep, it would calm his flustered head and help him stay alert at night. "*Devi*, I believe my wife will not deny your request."

Nidra Devi agreed to carry his message to Ayodhya where Urmila sat in the terrace, speaking to her Saumitra through the moon.

"Urmila," she called out softly from the air around the palace. Urmila turned around to see Nidra Devi coming out of the fine silver mist, shining as brightly as the resplendent Lakshmi as she stood in front of Urmila in her moonlit glory. "I have brought a message from your husband, my daughter," Nidra Devi said.

Chanting a *mantra*, Nidra Devi made Lakshman appear before Urmila in an aura of magical light.

Urmila looked at her Saumitra in a trance into which Nidra Devi had put her. Lakshman smiled at her and said, "Mila, I stand guilty for leaving you alone and causing you so much pain. But can I ask you for another favour, one that will also take away your angst? Please take a share of my sleep? I promise I shall wake you up when I return."

Urmila had tears in her eyes.

Was love really so selfless that it transformed mortals into angels? Lakshman, who loved to sleep was ready to sacrifice his sleep and Urmila who preferred to sleep only when necessary accepted it so easily? Was love the transmutation of desires and the essence of existence between lovers. A merging? The questions floated on the edge of Urmila's spiritual consciousness.

She nodded silently in assent. Emotions choked her voice. Before she could reach out to touch Lakshman's chimera, the apparition melted away into the misty moonshine. All she remembered was the sparkle of tears in his eyes.

Holding Lakshman's *angavastra* to her heart, Urmila slowly lay down on the cold stone floor of the terrace. As Urmila stretched out on the icy stones drawing her feet inward like a child, Nidra Devi was worried.

"Why do you lie on this frozen surface? You will catch a cold, my child," the devi said.

"Oh, Nidra Devi, if in the forest, my husband can sit on the damp grass and the icy stones through the nights to protect his brother, then how can I sit or sleep on a soft bed?" Urmila replied. Nidra Devi was touched by her selflessness, love and empathy for Saumitra. She chanted another *mantra*. And Urmila fell into a deep slumber, peaceful and dreamless, for 14 years.

Nidra Devi floated back to Lakshman, happy. She had stumbled upon true love – and lovers. She blessed him, "Lakshman, you and your wife are holy beings. Since you sacrifice your sleep and food, you will also be known as Gudakesh from now on, the one who did not eat or sleep for 14 years." The goddess smiled and disappeared into the wispy clouds fleeting around the silver moon.

Lakshman was restless without Mila; he chatted with the moon without a break, pouring out his heart. Yet, he was alone. The moon did not bring him back Mila's response or carry her voice. Urmila had fallen asleep. Sita noticed his restlessness and gave him a clay statue of Urmila, which she had sculpted during the day.

Lakshman wept profusely, holding the statue to his heart, "Forgive me, Mila, for how I hurt you. Pray that these years without you will pass in the blink of an eye, and I can come home to you, alive."

Sumitra came to Moti Bhavan late in the morning, when the sun was mid-way in the sky. She wanted to speak to Urmila about something important, but Urmila was not in her bed-chamber or in her temple. After a thorough search, Sumitra found Urmila asleep on the terrace. The queen found it odd because Urmila was neither too fond of sleep and nor did she sleep at unusual hours during the day. She woke up early. Sumitra tried to rouse her from sleep up but nothing worked. Urmila was in a deep 'trance-sleep', beyond consciousness.

A frightened Sumitra summoned the family. Something was seriously wrong with Urmila. The queens and Shatrughan sought out Gurudev Vashishtha – to find out the reason for her sleep. Or was it unconsciousness? Sumitra was on the brink of a breakdown.

The royal seer pacified them, "She is just asleep." Sumitra sighed in relief, along with the rest of the household, but at the same time could not help but weep.

Urmila had been blessed by Sita that if she wanted she could do three things simultaneously at the same time. As a result, her spirit or mind could travel and work in three places at a time in 'out-of-the-body experiences' even when she was in her transcendental sleep.

The trance travel took place during phases of light sleep, hypnosis, trance or deep yogic meditation – or at times during stressful sleep which led to the dissociation of the conscious mind from the unconscious.

Somewhere in the sleep-heavy recesses of her head, she felt the wetness of Sumitra's tears. Urmila lifted her hands in a slow sweeping motion and wiped the tears off Sumitra's eyes, in her sleep. "*Maa*, please don't cry," she whispered. There was a stunned silence in the palace. The sleeping princess could move her hand and speak too even when her brain slumbered and the eyes remained shut.

It was time for the truth to come out, the story of the 'divine visit' which Urmila slowly narrated in her sleep. Every one sitting by her on the floor cried as she revealed the boon of sleep granted by Nidra Devi and her pledge. "I will sleep my Saumitra's sleep for 14 years," she said. Somnolent and peaceful!

"Urmila, blessed are the parents who gave birth to such a jewel. Indeed, Raghukul is grateful to have you, my child," Kaushalya wept.

Sumitra and Kaushalya decided to live in Moti Bhavan to guard Urmila in her trance. They wanted to make sure that Urmila was taken care of and did not wake up from her sleep till Lakshman returned.

Urmila was alone in her sleep as much as Lakshman was in his wakefulness. Everyone understood their pain, and their strange 'condition of being'. Lakshmila had to live their own destiny.

Incomplete Without You

Fire tests, purifies and strengthens.

Lakshman eventually settled down to the loneliness of exile without Mila, even though she was vivid in his every breath. The moon still reminded him of her every night, but he had learned to accept her absence.

It was Lakshmila's wedding anniversary – the first anniversary that Saumitra would be spending by himself in the wilderness. He sat under a tree in silence, his eyes spanning the deep green cover of the forests and the sudden glimmer of water bodies, in-between, stretching like a painted landscape into the distance. He was silent because he was sad.

He whispered to himself, "Happy Anniversary, Mila. I miss you, my love." Tears pricked his eyes, shining like pearls on his lids.

Sita watched him from her hut, a few yards from the tree under which Lakshman sat daydreaming. She was helpless, she yearned for Urmila and Lakshman to meet, but she knew that a reunion was not possible in the near future. She saw the barren exile spread like a desert before her and tried to think of a way out of it – to intersperse the barrenness with snatches of laughter.

She prayed to *Kama Dev* (god of love), seeking his help to lift Lakshman out of the mire, into which he was sinking. Kama Dev knew about Lakshmila's selfless love for each other and agreed to help him. Transforming himself into a pigeon, he became Lakshman's messenger.

Ayodhya had reconciled to Urmila's boon of sleep. It was a waking sleep. Even while she was sleeping, she could perform all her duties because of the special power given to her by Ram and Sita. The gift allowed Mila to handle affairs of the state with Shatrughan, teach sword-fighting to children from across the city and oversee family matters – even in sleep.

Urmila's eyes were shut, but she could see everything. The only thing she could not do was to rouse herself from the deep trance. Sumitra watched over Urmila day and night. She sang Shiv *bhajan* – odes to Lord Shiva – to her in the mornings and lullabies at nights.

The family could not take away Urmila's grief on her wedding anniversary – their first after the separation. She had planned a surprise for him like every year, but destiny had disrupted the little adventure she had in mind for Saumitra. The year before had been a one-on-one – intimate.

"This year, all I wanted was to feel your warmth on my skin, your heartbeat against my ears and your touch on my soul. But fate has taken you so far away from me. I miss you love, Happy Anniversary," she connected to Saumitra in her sleep on the morning of their anniversary.

As Urmila spoke to Saumitra in her sleep, Kama Dev disguised as a pigeon flew into Moti Bhavan. He removed Urmila's anklet, without her knowledge, and carried it on his beak to Lakshman, but Kama Dev was unaware that Urmila knew of his presence and the gift he took as a memento to her *Swami*.

The pigeon fluttered over Panchvati, the sacred forest where the trio was staying, and flew down low over Lakshman's head to drop the anklet into his lap.

He went into a fit of ecstasy at the sight of the delicate gold trinket, encrusted with jewels. It was his birthday gift to Mila. He kissed the anklet and slid it around his wrist.

Time flies like streaks of lightning – like the touch of spring after winter and before the scorching summer.

Amid the confusion, regrets, little conflicts and also the great calm of nature, 13 years flew past in exile. Ram and Lakshman killed many demons from the rakshasa tribe in the forest, freed several sages held in captivity by the demons, met many scholarly saints and learnt from them over the years. But Urmila in Ayodhya was resolute in her dreams of Saumitra; she prayed to her gods for her lord to appear to her every night. She counted the days of exile and separation even in her even in her trance.

Mahadev was said to have instructed Goddess Yogmaya to take control of Urmila's dreams and show her in a vision that Urmila was the reincarnation of Devi Ksheera.

On the other hand, Lakshman's respect for women did not go down well with Indra Dev, the Vedic god of thunder, rain and war. The arrogant and aggressive god, who liked to cavort with beautiful divas and celestial nymphs, was often humiliated by his pantheon because of Lakshman. The gods matched Indra's arrogance against Lakshman's gentleness, humility and reverence for women – comparing the contrasts between the two.

An angry Indra decided to test Lakshman's purity one day. He ordered apsara Kumudh, a beautiful nymph, to go to Panchvati deep inside Dandakaranya and seduce Lakshman. But Lakshman, as usual, did not dare look beyond her feet. He remained immune to her beauty and charms because the only two women he had ever looked at in the eye were his mother and his wife. He held on to his moral values, chastity and self-control. He sharpened the tips of his arrows, reluctant to give in to the charms of the apsara as she pranced around him, showing off her grace. Sita came out of her hut at that moment to see Kumudh, moving like a dancing bird around Lakshman. The apsara was ingenious. She left a strand of her hair on Lakshman's shoulders and disappeared.

Misunderstanding the situation, Sita was quick to judge Lakshman, "My innocent looking brother-in-law, I guess you have found your second wife in this beautiful forest of Dandakaranya. You, who profess to love Urmila so much, break your vows of a husband so easily. It amazes me." Lakshman was mortified because he had promised that he would remain faithful to Urmila all his life – and even after.

Sita's callous accusation pierced his soul like an arrow. He did not utter a word in self-defense. The only way to prove his innocence was an *Agni Pareeksha* – trial by fire. He walked away to gather wood for a fire.

Ram was extremely angry with Sita for her brashness, but words once uttered could not be taken back. Ram tried to drive sense into Lakshman, warning him not to go ahead with the fire rite but his brother ignored his pleas. Lakshman was broken and ashamed. Ram watched helplessly as his brother stepped into the fire, fearing for his safety.

"If my love for my Mila is true, if my hands and eyes have not touched anyone else other than my wife and mother, if I am chaste as a man, I pray to the god of fire to let me pass through unscathed, else scorch me in the flames of the underworld," Lakshman folded his hands and prayed to Agni Dev as he walked through the bed of smouldering firewood.

Sita stood there humbled. Her head hung in shame as Ram cried like a child for his brother, looking for him amid the pile of blazing wood but he could not see even the shadow of Lakshman in the inferno. The dry wood crackled and exploded as they caught fire, the tongues of flames licking the air high above. The trees wavered in the shadows cast by the fire. Ram felt terror gripping his heart like icy talons, when two strong hands carried Lakshman out of the blazing pyre to safety. It was Agni Dev. He took Lakshman to Ram, cradling him like an infant.

"There is no man more holy and chaste than Lakshman. He is an ideal husband. There is no one else in his heart except his wife, *Janaknandini* Urmila. The world will always remember him for his selfless love." The flaming god vanished. His words echoed in the air of the forest and in the burning remains of the woodfire.

Sita asked Lakshman to forgive her, but Lakshman smiled and sought her blessing instead.

"May I remain true to my Mila."

How could Sita forget his love for her sister? How could she forget his one-woman vow just like his brother? Was it the effect of the morbid jungles that played a trick on her mind or was it something else? Narayan may be paving the way for something big.

Lanka's Princess Meenakshi

Evil is about to be redeemed by the hand of god.

Finally, the reason why Narayan was born as Ram was set to unfold. The reason stood looking at Ram and Lakshman in the eye! Maybe they had not seen it yet but they had begun to hear the footsteps of a bad omen in the air around them.

Jatayu, a very close friend of late King Dashrath, watched over Ram, Lakshman and Sita in the forests of Panchvati. He was the only noble being in the forest who commanded trust.

Danger loomed over Panchvati in the form of Khar and Dushan, Raavan's relatives, who wanted to see the royal exiles out of the forest, which they treated as their fief.

Khar and Dushan found a willing ally in their kin Meenakshi, also known as Chandranakha or Surpanakha. She was the only daughter of sage Vishrava and his wife Kekasi of the rakshasa tribe. Meenakshi had been a raving beauty since childhood and as she grew, her wild beauty flowered like a wild blossom, radiant and passionate. She was loved by everyone in her family and clan, barring her mother Kesaki, who considered her a curse.

It was believed that Meenakshi had nails like the moon and hence she got her other name Chandranakha. And since her mother was a Rakshasi, she had asura blood in her veins, which gave her the power and the ability to change herself into anything or anyone she wished to.

Of her three brothers, Kumbhakaran, the giant who woke up once every six months, doted on her. Kumbhakaran was married to Vajramala with two sons, Kumbha and Nikumbha.

No one in the family, not even her father Vishrava, had ever tried to protect Meenakshi from her mother Kekasi because she was known to be ferocious. Kekasi could kill anyone.

When Meenakshi was in her twenties, she met Vridhutjivha, a *daanav* – demon man – who pretended to be in love with her.

The cunning demon man wanted to snatch Raavan's kingdom, to which she belonged, and take Raavan as a prisoner and slave.

Since the tribes of the daanav and the asura were born enemies like the snakes and the eagles, Raavan was against the union, but eventually his wife Mandodari convinced him to let the two marry. Raavan set a condition that Vridhutjivha would have to stay in Lanka after he married Meenakshi.

Meenakshi gave birth to a son called Shabhra Kumar. When Shabhra was 12, Vridhutjivha tried to kill Raavan for his kingdom but the demon king cut off Vridhutjivha's tongue for lying and gouged out his eyes for harbouring carnal designs on his sister. He later killed Vridhutjivha.

Unable to bear the pain, Meenakshi vowed to avenge her husband's death. This fire of revenge awakened the demoness in her, Surpanakha, which was Meenakshi's ugliest form. She grew a big belly, her eyes became protuberant and her hair changed colour to a metallic shade of copper each time she became Surpanakha. Her voice became gruff and frightening. But she did not lose her power to interchange into any of her three forms – Meenakshi, Chandranakha and Surpanakha – at any time.

To teach her son the art of warfare and make him strong enough to fight Raavan, Meenakshi began to live in Dandakaranya with Shabhra Kumar. She sent her son to the sages in the jungle to study *Brahma vidya* and gain as much knowledge as possible because his dead father Vridhutjivha wanted his son to become a knowledgeable man – as well as a brave warrior.

But destiny had other plans. It waited in the wings to deal Meenakshi a blow.

One day when Shabhra Kumar was out hunting, he spied Jatayu, the great and the wise birdman, sitting on a rock outlying the forest. Thinking that Jatayu was a normal bird, he attacked the feathered giant that looked like a cross between a vulture, eagle and a human. Lakshman, who saw Shabhra attacking Jatayu from a distance, shot an arrow at the boy to save his father's old friend. The demon prince fell down dead.

Moving closer, Lakshman saw that the hunter was a mere child. He felt sorry for the 12-year-old boy but he could not bring him back to life. Lakshman placed a few wild roses near the boy's dead body and returned to his hut.

At sundown, Meenakshi began to panic. Her son has not yet returned from his hunting safari in the forest. She sent out people to find him. An hour later, they returned with Shabhra's body. The princess of Lanka was inconsolable with grief. She suspected that it was Raavan's doing and her hate for her brother grew stronger, fuelling a zeal for vendetta. He had not only widowed her, but had made her childless as well.

She ordered Khar and Dushan to find out her son's killers. After a couple of hours, they returned with full information and accompanied Meenakshi to the hut of the Ayodhya princes.

They pointed to the princes who were sitting in the thatched shade of their huts, from a distance. The princes were attired as hermits. "The one with the lotus eyes who feeds the pigeons is Ram," Khar said. "And the one with dark brown eyes and a skinny frame is Lakshman. He is the one who killed Shabhra Kumar," Dushan said with fury in his voice.

The human mind and heart work in mysterious ways, more so in the presence of divine beings.

A demoness, who went to avenge her son's death, suddenly began to feel like a woman upon seeing Ram and Lakshman. She lusted for the princes and thought of ways to tempt them, "What beautifully sculpted bodies they have! What if I can get one of them to marry me?" The demoness in Meenakshi worked in sync with the primal instincts of the forest – wanton and heathen.

Can a mother feel no pangs of remorse for her dead son? Can she really take a man who has killed her son in cold blood as a consort? The answers are elusive. Was Meenakshi's lust deliberate? Meenakshi had an inkling that the hermits were not seers but warriors in disguise who could avenge her husband's death and destroy the king of Lanka, Raavan. Probably, they could also be better husbands.

She went to Ram and Lakshman after performing the last rites of her son, disguised as a beautiful woman in her Meenakshi avatara. She knocked on Ram's door first. "Is there anyone here who can help me?"

Ram was warm, "Beautiful lady, how can I help you? With your petite waist, charming face and eyes like pearls, you look like an apsara."

Meenakshi blushed at the compliment. "I am Meenakshi, the younger sister of Raavan, the king of Lanka. I have lost my heart. Will you help me find it?"

"Greetings, dear princess of Lanka, I am Ram, the prince of Ayodhya. I am living here with my wife and brother. The man must indeed be blessed to have captured your heart," Ram teased her.

Meenakshi was surprised to learn that Ram was a prince and hinted that she was enamoured of him. Ram politely turned her down, "Pretty lady, I apologise for breaking your beautiful heart. I am a married man bound by a one-woman vow. But, my brother Lakshman is there," Ram pointed at Lakshman. "He is here without his wife. He is handsome and I can assure you that he will make a good husband."

A mischievous Ram laughed, throwing Lakshman a covert look, hoping that his prank would bring a smile of happiness on his brother's sad face. He had not seen Lakshman smile once in the last 13 years of exile. Meenakshi tried to flaunt her charms in front of Lakshman, but he refused to look at her.

"It is futile. No woman other than my wife holds any fascination for me. You waste your time here, princess of Lanka."

"You are a married man? But your brother said you are single. Anyway what difference does it make? Princes have many wives. You can have one more." She tried to lure him with her words – and her offer of freedom.

"No, as my brother says, I am just a servant of the lord. Would you like to spend your life as a maid? You deserve someone like my brother," Lakshman was angry.

Meenakshi recoiled as the insult found its mark, the thought of living as a maid made her furious. She went back to Ram, but Ram rebuffed her in a firmer tone and joined Sita, who had come out of the hut to watch the little play. Thinking that Sita was the only obstacle in her path, the demoness Surpanakha inside Meenakshi came out and sprung on Sita to kill her.

Sita, in a fit of revulsion and rage, ordered Lakshman to teach the demoness a lesson.

Lakshman chopped off her breasts, ears and nose with his sword. Blood spilled all over. As soon as Lakshman saw blood gushing out of an injured Surpanakha, who writhed on the ground in intense pain, tears of guilt filled his eyes. This was the first time he had been savage with a woman, even if she was a demoness.

But Ram set his remorse to rest.

"Do not be upset, Lakshman. What you did was necessary! Even after the eras pass, epochs change, people will always remember this. Intentions matter. And you did what you had to do, else it would have been Sita lying dead here," Ram said.

The demoness was insane with anger.

Not to be vanquished, the humiliation and hurt only served to strengthen her plan to destroy Raavan. She plotted to get Khar and Dushan out of her way. She incited them to challenge Ram and Lakshman to avenge her slight. Khar and Dushan dared the princes of Ayodhya to a battle – and were killed.

Meenakshi rushed back to Lanka and narrated what had transpired in Panchvati, but she skipped the part where she tried to seduce Ram and Lakshman, the prime reason for Dushan's and Khar's death. A livid Raavan pledged to kill the Ayodhya princes. Wily Surpanakha told him about Sita, Ram's beautiful and virtuous wife, instigating her brother to wage a war against them and teach them a fitting lesson for hurting a woman little knowing that the world would remember Surpanakha not as a woman or a sister wronged, but as an accursed mother and demoness, who lusted for her son's killer.

In Lanka, Raavan began to plot revenge.

The war was just a catalyst in heaven's big plan. Raavan's revenge was destined. How else would Raavan, the fierce lord of the rakshashas and an

*ardent devotee of Lord Shiva fight Ram, the incarnation of Narayan? Raavan
had to be taken out of Aryavarta. Or was it Raavan's redemption that he had
to die at the hands of a mortal god?*

Where Is Sita?

The rape of virtue is beginning of an epic battle?

*Raavan and Lanka were frantic. The southern isle, once decreed invincible
like a magical realm, had been challenged by Ram. His sister, whom Raavan
took pride on, had been attacked viciously. Lanka, however, did not know that
each step it took closer to revenge changed the destiny of Aryavarta.*

Akampana, an asur and a lieutenant in Lanka's army,
and Raavan's uncle, sowed the seeds of Sita's abduction from
Panchavati. He put the idea in Raavan's head that if he kidnapped
Sita rather than killed Ram and Lakshman, it would teach the
brothers a fitting lesson for maiming Surpanakha.

Raavan warmed up to the idea and summoned his uncle
Mareecha, a wily sorcerer and a *yogi*. They had to find a way to
kidnap Sita. The king of Lanka and Mareecha decided to visit
Panchvati in disguise and whisk Sita away by trickery. Mareecha
transformed himself into a golden deer and tempted Sita to catch
him. Sita, who was fond of frisky pets, sent Ram to the forest to
capture Mareecha. Ram ordered Lakshman to guard Sita before
going to the forest in search of Mareecha.

It was a stumbling block in Raavan's plan. He could not abduct
Sita with Lakshman around; he had to remove Lakshman from
her proximity to execute his plan. Mareecha came to his nephew's
rescue again.

Mareecha, who had the power of magic to transform himself
into anything or anyone with the power of *maya jaal* – the mesh
of illusions – mimicked Ram's voice, calling out to Lakshman for

help. Sita panicked and requested Lakshman to find out whether Ram was safe inside the forest. Bound by Ram's order, Lakshman refused to listen to Sita. He said he could not obey her because his brother had forbidden him to leave Sita alone.

A depressed and an angry Sita lost her temper and snapped at her brother-in-law, "You are but a man without character, Lakshman. You want to stay here with me when your brother is calling out to you for help. You wish death upon him so that you can carry out the nefarious designs that you have on me. I will not let it happen. I will let no harm come to Ram. I will protect him myself. You stay here. But beware, for I shall tell your brother about your bad intentions once he returns," Sita walked out of the hut in a huff.

Sita's words were like stabs of a sword in Lakshman's heart but he understood why she was angry. Despite the misgivings, Lakshman decided to flout his brother's words of warning.

The forests were unknown; dangers lurked like shadows at every bend. What if Ram was in real trouble? Prompted by concern, Lakshman broke his promise to his brother. He told Sita to stay inside the hut as he picked up his quiver and bow to venture into the forest to help Ram.

"I will go after him at your order, but your safety lies in your hands. Take care of yourself until we return and do not come out of the hut under any circumstances." He chanted a *mantra* for Sita's safety, instructing her not to take a step out of the four walls of the hut.

The reason why Sita considered Lakshman frivolous not once, but twice, even after proving his innocence with an Agni Pareeksha is not known. She was aware of how much he loved Urmila. His decision to leave his wife behind for 14 years to watch over his brother in exile may have made her suspicious?

As Lakshman went deep into the jungle to search for Ram, Raavan, disguised as a *rishi* – holy man – came to Sita's hut. He stood at the door begging for food. Sita was torn between sending a hungry sage away without alms and Lakshman's warning not to step outside the hut. Raavan's insistence that the virtuous woman hand him food lured her into his trap. As soon as Sita stepped out of the hut to offer him food, Raavan returned to his 'demonic' avatara – as the fierce king of Lanka – scooped Sita up in his sturdy arms and flew off to his oceanic isle.

"Leave me alone, you fiend, I will not go anywhere with you... Take me back," Sita's feeble cries fell on Raavan's deaf ears as he carried her over the forests, rivers and the seas; beyond the great landmass of Aryavarta. Panchavati remained a mute and distraught witness to the heinous abduction.

Raavan could not go inside the hut and force Sita out as he had been cursed by Rishi Patni, his wife, that if he entered a married woman's home, he would be burnt to ashes. So, he had to coax Sita out.

An unwitting Lakshman was drawn into the depths of the forest where he met Ram by a grove of bamboo and evergreen trees. Ram had slaughtered Mareecha. He was alarmed at the sight of Lakshman because he sensed unforeseen danger. Mareecha's 'occult' magic had been found out – and Ram could see portends of something even scarier in the tempting run of the asur-turned golden deer. Ram and Lakshman hurried back to the hut, leaving the dead Mareecha in the jungle.

Sita was not in the hutment. The brothers looked for her everywhere frantically, but she seemed to have disappeared without a trace.

Ram nearly lost his sanity; he knew that something terrible had happened to Sita. While the brothers combed the forests for Sita, they came across a wounded and bleeding Jatayu, who had tried to rescue Sita from Raavan. His wings had been sheared by Raavan and his life was ebbing. Before dying, Jatayu revealed to the brothers how Sita had been abducted by the king of Lanka – and the only way to reach his kingdom was through Shabri's hut.

"The road to Lanka will lead through Shabri's humble home," the dying bird gasped.

Lakshman took over as Ram broke down at Jatayu's death. Lakshman had once told his brother that someday he would care for him like a mother. They abandoned the hut in Panchvati and travelled for several miles barefoot till they reach the shores of Lake Pampa. Hidden in the overhangs that skimmed the blue-green waters of the lake was the hermitage of sage Matanga, who had died many years ago. A woman, with a face like a wrinkled palm sheath and hair like white fleece, sat outside Matanga's hut. She was 205 years old, and was hailed as one of the most fervent devotees of Narayan.

Shabri believed that Lord Narayan and Lord Shesha would visit her abode one day.

The old woman, who had decorated the hermitage with wreaths of fresh flowers, greeted her guests by touching their feet. Tears flowed in cascades from her old and dimming eyes, "Lord, you have finally come!"

She took in the tired faces of the princes and knew they were hungry and thirsty. She offered them black berries that grew in abundance around the lake. Not a single berry was sour, which made Lakshman suspicious that the old woman must have tasted each one of them, and they were 'tainted'. Ram nibbled at the plump little fruits with relish while Lakshman hesitated to put even one in his mouth. Noticing Lakshman's reluctance, Ram ordered Lakshman to eat them – an order that Lakshman could not defy.

Happy, Shabri showed the brothers the way to Lanka before immolating herself to join her mentor Matanga in heaven.

The next stop was Kishkinda, nearly 11 miles ahead, in the lair of the lord of the monkeys, Hanuman, Ram's staunchest devotee and ally. Hanuman looked upon Lakshman as his older brother. Tears of gratitude flowed from Hanuman's eyes as Ram and Lakshman stood before him. He carried Ram and Lakshman on his shoulders to his brother Sugriva, the king of the monkeys, deep inside the heart of Kishkinda, where he reigned as the king with his wife Ruma.

Sugriva, the king of monkeys, lost his kingdom and his family to his evil brother Bali. Ram helped him get his kingdom and wife back. In return, Sugriva accompanied by Rikshraj, Jamvanta and Hanuman, helped Ram rescue Sita and destroy Lanka.

Ram, Lakshman, Sugriva and Hanuman drew up a strategy for a war on Lanka. Before embarking on their mission, they tried to find out where Sita was being held captive and whether she was safe. Hanuman sought permission from Ram to go to Lanka to locate Sita. His flight to Lanka was difficult, because he had to overcome several obstacles in his way. He killed rakshasis Sursa and Lankini before alighting in Ashok Vatika, where Sita was held in custody under the watchful eyes of Raavan's demon maids.

Hanuman was confused when he saw three beautiful women in the *vatika* – garden.

The three women were Mandodari, Sita and Sulochana. Mandodari was Raavan's wife and Sulochana was Raavan's son Meghnaad's wife.

Finally, Hanuman identified Sita from the way Ram had described her. He hid on the tree under which Sita sat, speaking to Sulochana. "*Maata*, can you narrate the *Ram Katha* – story of Ram – today?" Sulochana asked Sita. Sulochana had been visiting Sita everyday ever since she had been brought to Lanka.

Sita remembered nothing of her life as a goddess in Vaikunth, so, she did not recognise Sulochana but Sulochana knew who Sita was.

Sulochana also knew Lakshman and Urmila were her parents and Ram and Sita were Narayan and Lakshmi.

Sulochana wondered when she would meet her parents from 'another lifetime' as she chatted with Sita. It had been 50 years since she had met Lakshman and Urmila as Shesha and Ksheera and she longed to feel their loving hands on her head. Sita was naturally attracted to Sulochana – she felt deeply connected to the pretty young woman but she could not understand what bound her to Meghnad's young wife.

Hanuman, who had been eavesdropping on their conversation from a tree, could not restrain himself. "I shall narrate the Ram Katha to you," he said in a deep lilting voice.

Sulochana and Sita gazed up at the Ashoka tree – the tree without sorrow – to find the ape lord sitting on one of its leafy branches. His face was red and his muscled body glowed golden in the light of the sun. As Hanuman chanted the *Ram Katha* in his deep musical voice, they realised that he was a messenger from Ram and immediately knew why he was in Lanka. Taking the cue, Sulochana ordered the guards to leave Sita and herself alone for some time. After the guards dispersed, Sita commanded Hanuman to climb down the tree and show himself. Hanuman came down the tree and introduced himself by offering Ram's engagement ring as proof of his identity to Sita, "The lord of Ayodhya has sent this to you. He sends word that he will be here in 10 months to rescue you."

The guards, who had retreated to a distance at the far end of the garden, suddenly spotted the monkey lord. They rushed to Hanuman with their lances and attacked him. The demon guards were led by Sulochana's 16-year-old adopted son, Akshay Kumar.

Akshay Kumar was the youngest son of Raavan, who was raised by Sulochana. Since Sulochana hadn't been able to conceive after several years of her marriage to Meghnad, Mandodari gave birth to Akshay Kumar for them.

Akshay Kumar refused to listen to Sulochana's pleas of not fighting Hanuman. The boy was rash and headstrong. He wanted to prove his strength as a warrior to Raavan. He challenged Hanuman and died in the battle, crushed by the monkey lord.

Akshay Kumar's death left Sulochana heartbroken; she knew that Lanka would be destroyed soon. She mourned the boy's death for days, warning Raavan that the end of Lanka was near.

"Why do you grieve for the one whom you didn't even give birth to? Look at Mandodari, is she crying?" Raavan's heartless words hit Meghnad and Sulochana like blows from the mace that he carried, tearing at their hearts and breaking them to pieces.

"O, king of Lanka, a child is his mother's heartbeat whether she gives him birth to him or not. Akshay Kumar was my child! And I warn you, just like today I have become childless because of your arrogance, that day is not far when all the mothers in Lanka will become childless!" Sulochana raged like an inferno.

The fire spread across the kingdom – the flames of fury and revenge. Ashok Vaatika was completely destroyed by Hanuman when a frenzied Meghnad attacked the giant ape with the Brahmastra to avenge Akshay's death. Hanuman did not retaliate because he was also a devotee of Brahma's. He bore the brunt of the fireball that Mehgnad hurled at him, but survived because of a boon he had received from Brahma. He flew away with Sita's ornament as proof to Ram that Sita was alive and he had managed to find her.

Lakshman failed to recognise Sita's bracelet, "I have never looked beyond her feet. How do I know if they belong to her? Had it been her anklet, I might have said something in acknowledgement."

Ram, however, recognised the ornament as Sita's and confirmed his decision to attack Lanka, but a war on Lanka was not easy. The first step was to cross the vast expanse of water that stood between Aryavarta and the isle of Lanka.

The army could not reach Lanka any other way than by land or sea. Lakshman suggested that a bridge be built over the southern sea but they needed Samudra Dev's permission for one. Ram performed a 20-day rite to appease Samudra Dev, the keeper of the seas, but he did not respond to Ram's penance. Finally, Ram lost his temper, "Show me a way to Lanka else I, *Dashrathnandan* Ram, will dry up every ocean on this earth with my arrow."

Lakshman tried to quell Ram's anger and pleaded with Samudra Dev to relent before it was too late. Finally, the deity of the ocean appeared to show them the way to Lanka.

The causeway bridge to Lanka had Ram's name written on every stone. Since Ram had measured the land by his bow to calculate the distance between their position and Lanka, the site took the shape of his bow and was named Dhanushkoti.

A great devotee of Mahadev, Ram decided to inaugurate the Ram Setu by performing Shiv *puja* and built the Rameshwaram temple to honour the god.

Ram, Lakshman, Hanuman and the army of apes crossed the ocean to Raavan's kingdom. As they were about to enter the boundaries of Lanka, Lakshman felt that someone he knew very well was waiting for him there. A sense of detachment from all that stood for Ayodhya and the mission to rescue Sita haunted him, in those rare moments of déjà vu.

He was about to meet his daughter Sulochana, from another life, a connection that would withstand time and births!

Sulochana and Her Natha – Lord

Gods on earth face their kin in the isle of magic.

The news of Ram and Lakshman's arrival at Lanka with their army spread throughout the kingdom. Sulochana yearned to see her father but she could not, for they were Lanka's enemies and she was Raavan's daughter-in-law.

Sulochana implored Vibhishan to join Ram's army and help him win the war as it would be a victory over evil.

Vibhishan, who loved Sulochana like his own daughter, Trijata, agreed to defect immediately. He knew that she was the daughter of Shesha and Ksheera, the closest allies of Narayan.

Vibhishan was an ardent devotee of Narayan and Shesha.

Before switching allegiance, Vibhishan tried to convince Raavan to seek Ram's pardon for abducting Sita and set her free. Raavan was furious and ordered him to leave the palace for taking Ram's side.

Vibhishan went to Ram and pleaded with his eyes downcast, "O, prince of Ayodhya, I am the younger brother of Raavan. If you consider this a reason to throw me out, I shall not refute. I come here to seek shelter under you umbrella for I am a follower of *dharma*. I want to join your army to fight for what is right. I want you to forgive my brother for his sins."

Ram granted asylum to Vibhishan and allowed him to become a part of his army naming him 'Lankapati'.

When Ram, Lakshman, Hanuman, Sugriva, Jambvant and Vibhishan sat together after dinner that night, Ram wanted to know about Vibhishan's family. Vibhishan told them about Sulochana, "Among the seven sons of Raavan, Meghnad is the eldest and the dearest to my brother. He is named Meghnad because his first cry at birth sounded like the rumbling of the clouds. He was very sharp and intelligent as a child and possessed all the celestial weapons. Now, he makes his own magical weapons. He is a scientist, too, and is even more powerful than his father. Meghnad is married to *Naag Kanya* Sulochana, the daughter of Shesha and Ksheera."

At the end of the story, Vibhishan looked at Lakshman pointedly.

Meghnad was the incarnation of Lord Shesha's 1001th hood. Once Lord Vishnu felt that the 1001th hood of Lord Shesha was moving to the path of adharma, he cut it off with his Sudarshan Chakra to keep him on the right path. He is said to have given him a boon that he would be born in every yuga and marry Shesha's daughter, Sulochana, who will bring him to the path of dharma.

On hearing about Sulochana, Lakshman was filled with a seemingly undefinable restlessness. The connection of the past life bound Lakshman to Sulochana with a misty chord, one which he did not remember, but felt in his soul. The power of *yogbhram* – yoga that erases karmic memory – had wiped out Sulochana's memory from his present consciousness. *Yogbhram* was a power used by the gods to make the soul forget its previous birth.

Even the gods could not escape it.

"Do you know more about Devi Sulochana, Vibhishan? Can you tell us about her?" Lakshman was eager to know more about Sulochana.

Vibhishan understood Lakshman's restlessness and his natural pull towards Sulochana. He agreed to narrate her story:

"At the end of the Satya Yuga, Devi Ksheera gave birth to a beautiful girl, *Naag Kanya* Sulochana or the one with the beautiful eyes. Sulochana was a pampered child, Lord Vishnu's favourite for she filled the void left behind by his daughters Amaravalli and Sundaravalli, who were married. Sulochana was very close to her father Shesha, who protected her from all external influences and harm. But Sulochana was abandoned by her parents when she was very young – barely five years old. They had to leave Vaikunth to accompany Vishnu and Lakshmi to earth to be born as mortals. Vasuki, Shesha's younger brother, agreed to stand in as Sulochana's guardian and vowed to Shesha that his daughter will marry the man she desired."

One day, when young Sulochana was playing in the garden of Naag Lok with her friends, Menka and Nitara, they lost their magic ball. The girls went in search of the ball across the vast garden, each in a different direction. Sulochana found the ball lying near a tall man, who stood quietly behind the trees admiring her. He was none other than Meghnad, who was on a *Trilok Bhramarh*, a journey across the three worlds of heaven, earth, and the underworld. The tall and handsome man with a sharp profile from the asura clan charmed Shesha's daughter.

Sulochana fell in love with Meghnad at first sight. "I have been searching for someone as powerful as my father Shesha. I see him in you. I think I have fallen in love with you for I have never known a feeling as overpowering as this. My father has given me the freedom to choose my own groom and I choose you. Will you marry me?' The Naag maiden was forthright in her confession of love and offer of marriage.

A proud Meghnad spurned her love saying she was a fool to believe in love, but he would marry her. He mocked her, "O, *Naag Kanya*, I am the mighty Meghnad. I have met thousands of women like you who want me as their husband."

Her mind was set. "I have already accepted you as my *natha*. Accept me as your wife. It is only you in the entire *Brahmanda* I wish to marry."

But Meghnad again scoffed at her idea of love.

Meghnad was a sharp asur but he was arrogant. He considered women insignificant. Having grown up surrounded by evil women like Kekasi, Tadka and Surpanakha, he looked upon women as devils. Even though his mother Mandodari was gentle and polite, she remained silent fearing Raavan's wrath.

Sulochana decided to win his love with her gentleness and patience. She had faith that if her love was true, he would come to her. Her confidence left an indelible impression on him. He decided to stay in the garden at Naaga Lok. One day, he confessed that he was in love with her. He held her hand and proposed to her.

"Sulochana, I want to marry you."

A euphoric Sulochana ran into his arms and clung to him; she was vindicated that her love had been reciprocated and happy that she had found someone she could call her own after so many years.

Vasuki, on the other hand, wanted her to marry Indra Dev, the god of thunder and war. She did not like him. "He is lusty by nature. He has tried to molest me once, but I managed to escape. Please do not send me to him, uncle. I will die if you force me to marry him," Sulochana begged her uncle, who sang praises of Indra every day.

When Sulochana told Meghnad about Indra Dev's lusty overtures, the demon prince erupted in rage, threatening to kill the god. He left the snake kingdom to take the deity out of his abode and challenge him to war.

Meghnad is said to have attacked Indra Dev but just when he was on the verge of killing him, Brahmadev intervened and asked him to spare Indra. Bestowing the name 'Indrajit' on Meghnad, Brahmadev agreed to grant him a boon. Meghnad asked for immortality because he did not want his wife to become a widow. But Brahmadev refused, "Dear Meghnad, immorality is not possible. One who takes birth on earth has to die. Instead I give you a boon that only a Gudakesh will be able to kill you, the one who hasn't slept, eaten and had any physical attachment to a woman for 14 years."

Empowered by the boon, Meghnad returned to Naaga Lok to seek Sulochana's hand in marriage. Vasuki opposed the match. He considered an asur unworthy of his niece. Sulochana defied her foster father, who, in anger, held her captive in a dungeon without food and water for 10 days to break her powerful will.

Despite her trials in captivity, Sulochana refused to succumb to Vasuki's pressure to marry Indra. The grapevine had it that Vasuki had even secured Vaikunth's approval for the alliance.

"Rivers may stop flowing but rain will never stop pouring. In the same way, my *natha*'s name is like a rain of nectar to me. How will you stop it? I have already accepted him as my husband in my heart, body and soul. And I know that my *natha* will come to take me away from this jail," Sulochana's faith in Meghnad was rooted in the knowledge that the fierce asur prince loved her and was willing to fight the mightiest of the warriors in heaven and earth for her.

Just then, Meghnad attacked Naaga Lok to rescue his beloved. He descended like thunder to fight Vasuki, armed with powerful celestial weapons. Before dying, a humiliated Vasuki cursed Sulochana, "Your own father will kill your husband in this birth and in the next birth, both of you will not marry each other. Sulochana, you shall remain unmarried in your next birth." Her uncle's words cut her like a knife but she accepted her fate.

Sulochana and Meghnad got married in a Vishnu temple. She took the idols of her parents for the rituals and asked the priest if he could bless the idols as her parents were not with her – and neither did she have a brother who could give her away.

Since Shesha and Ksheera were omnipresent, their blessings were considered given. After the seven vows, Meghnad filled Sulochana's hairline with vermillion and put the sacred thread around her neck. He took her to Lanka and built a Vishnu temple inside the palace. Though praying to Narayan was prohibited in Lanka, Meghnad understood his wife's devotion to Narayan and stopped his father from entering his palace so that Sulochana could pray to Narayan.

At the end of the narrative, Vibhishan breathed in a big gulp of air; his audience was still under the spell of his story.

Reactions were belated – the emotions surfacing after a long silence. Lakshman was angry and distraught at the same time at Sulochana's strife. His tears did not stop. "The poor child. How could her uncle Vasuki put her through so much anguish when she was his responsibility?" He wanted to meet her, but restrained himself for she was a member of Lanka's royal clan on which the Ayodhya princes were going to wage a war.

Ram sighed in sorrow while the rest were silent.

Lakshman was angry with Vasuki.

That night, Lakshman looked at the moon again to connect to Mila. He told her about Sulochana.

In the palace at Lanka, Sulochana tried in vain to explain to Meghnad that Ram and Lakshman were divine beings, incarnations, but Meghnad did not believe her and told her to sleep. He said he wanted to rest before the war the next morning.

My Lord Is Safe

Heroes on earth clash in mortal combat, hearts grieve in heaven.

The war began next morning with the unfurling of the standards and the blowing of conch shells and horns on either side.

By mid-day, Lanka suffered heavy losses as it lost its great warriors, one after the other. Raavan's sons Atikay, Narantaka, Devantaka, Trishara, and Prahasta fell to Lakshman's arrows. All except Meghnad, who was still breathing and plotting bigger assaults.

Sulochana grieved for her slain brothers-in-law and tried to convince Raavan to let Sita go, but Raavan was firm in his stand; driven by manic hate and an insane anger. Wanting to inflict the same pain on Ram, Raavan commanded Meghnad to kill Lakshman with the deadliest of the weapons, Vaasvi Shakti. Lakshman was the king of Lanka's most dreaded and hated opponent because he had defeated Raavan twice on the war turf and moreover, the demon king knew that Lakshman was the source of Ram's strength. Winning the war would not be possible for Ram without the aggression and the survival instincts of Lakshman.

Unable to refuse his father and knowing the fate that awaited him, Meghnad left for the battlefield. Lakshman came to know from his network of spies that Meghnad had set out for the war zone and he vowed to kill Raavan's son and surprise Ram with the news of Meghnad's death.

When Meghnad faced Lakshman in the battlefield, he hesitated. Knowing that the strapping prince, who was not much older than him, was his wife's Sulochana's father Shesha, Meghnad knelt down to pray to the serpent lord silently.

He apologised to Lakshman for doing what he was about to do. Meghnad fired every weapon in his kitty, but none of them felled Lakshman – the Brahmastra, the Vaishnavastra, the Varunapasha and even the Yamapasha dropped off like pebbles mid-air.

Left with no recourse, Meghnad invoked the Vaasvi Shakti and aimed it at Lakshman. As the flashing missile travelled through the earth's atmosphere towards Lakshman, he began to feel restless. His intuition told him that something ominous was going to happen to him – the premonition of a disaster. A wave of intense heat surrounded Lakshman, swirling like a spinning funnel, and a flash of light nearly blinded him.

Meghnad's *maya jaal* – web of magic – had trapped Lakshman and the missile found its mark. It hit Lakshman just above his right chest.

"Mila," Lakshman cried out before falling down to the ground in a faint.

Urmila heard him scream in agony, far away in Ayodhya. She reached out to him in her trance and shielded him with her spirit. "I am right here. Nothing will happen to you, *Swami*." Her soul entwined with his, giving him strength; protecting him against the fatal Vaasvi Shakti, the weapon of Indra. Both their souls fought Indra's power – as one. Meghnad had been ordered to carry Lakshman off into the walled city of royal Lanka to claim victory over him, but Urmila's soul held her husband tightly in its grasp. How could anyone touch Lakshman when his Mila stood by him, not even death? Urmila's soul remained with him till Hanuman arrived. The monkey lord was scared at the sight of Lakshman in a swoon. He carried the prince back with him to Ram.

"Get up, Lakshman. I order you to. You cannot leave me alone. We came here to rescue Sita, not to lose you. I may be able to replace Sita, live without her, but there can be no other brother for me. You are my life. Get up, brother. We have to go," a grief-stricken Ram urged Lakshman. Sugriva and Hanuman tried to console him but Ram was inconsolable.

The thought of losing Lakshman was inconceivable.

"What will I tell Urmila, Lakshman? How will I look her in the eye when she asks for you? If not for me, wake up for her, brother, Mila is waiting for you. She has been waiting for the last 14 years. Sumitra *Maa* and Kaushalya *Maa* await our return, they will not let me enter Ayodhya without you. Don't try my patience, Lakshman. Let's finish what we have come for and leave." Ram nudged Lakshman desperately; shaking him, pressing his heart to revive the beats and – chafing his pulse to pull him out of the death swoon.

As the news of Lakshman's 'death' reached Sulochana, her first impulse was to run out of the palace to the battlefield to be with her father in distress, but her duty towards Lanka stopped her. She was torn between her love for father Shesha, and her loyalty to her husband Meghnad. The astute Sulochana decided to work in secret.

Sulochana summoned her chief maid-in-waiting Malati and directed her to inform Ram about the royal physician, *Vaidya Raj* Sushena, Meghnad's most efficient and trusted doctor.

Vaidya Raj Sushena's healing skills were outstanding. Meghnad had a habit of trying all his heavenly weapons on his own self to ascertain their impact before using them. Sushena could heal him, effortlessly.

Hanuman went out in search of *Vaidya Raj* at Malati's secret advise which she carried as a missive from her lady, Sulochana. The doctor initially refused to treat Lakshman saying Ram's sibling was his enemy, but Hanuman was determined to take him to Lakshman. After much coaxing and cajoling, Sushena agreed to visit Lakshman. He prescribed the rare Sanjeevani herb from Donagiri hill in the icy northern region of Aryavarta, the abode of the snow, to heal Lakshman. Hanuman flew like lightning to the abode of snow, but was confused about the herb in the lush wilderness. What if he carried the wrong herb back to Lanka and it killed Lakshman!

In his confusion, he picked up the entire mountain and carried it on his palm to Lanka. He held the mace in his other hand to ward off enemies on the way.

On his way back to Lanka, he flew over Ayodhya. In the outskirts of the capital, Bharath spied him from Nandigram and mistook the mace-wielding Hanuman for a demon. He shot an arrow at him. Hanuman fell to the ground, crying, "Ram, Ram."

Bharath was alarmed. The monkey seemed to be a *Ram Bhakt*- a devotee of Ram. Bharath tended to Hanuman's wound and found out about him. Surprised at having met Bharath, Hanuman narrated Ram's, Lakshman's and Sita's plight to him – about the war on Lanka, the fight against Meghnad, Lakshman's injury and his death-like condition.

Bharath plunged into despair, blaming himself for their suffering. Hanuman requested Bharath to allow him to meet Urmila before leaving Nandigram. Bharath took him to Ayodhya. The shocked family suffered from trauma on learning about Lakshman. Sumitra, the most stoic and patient of the queens, suffered a nervous breakdown.

Urmila, on the other hand, was unperturbed. Hanuman wondered at her serenity, but understood why Ram respected her so much when she said, "God bless you, my son."

The monkey god touched her feet.

"*Maata*, I promise you that your husband will return unharmed" he said.

"Hanuman, I know my *Swami* is safe with Ram *bhaiya* to watch over him. Saumitra was now resting peacefully in his brother's lap. He is extremely weak because he has not eaten or slept for the last 14 years. But take care of my older brother because I know he feels the pain of *Vaasvi Shakti* more than my Saumitra and is blaming himself for his brother's injury," Urmila comforted Hanuman.

Hanuman was struck by Urmila's 'other-worldly powers'. "*Maata*, nothing can happen to a man who has a devoted wife like you. You are an ideal wife. I am blessed to meet you, *Maata*," Hanuman hailed her.

Urmila was worried about Sumitra, who broke down, weeping profusely, "*Maa*, why do you cry? Have faith in your eldest son. He will bring Saumitra back. And look at this *Akhandjyoti*, it is still burning. Your son will return home safely. He has promised me and I know he will never break his promise," Urmila consoled Sumitra.

"Urmila, I am alive today only because of you," the queen held Urmila's hand in gratitude.

Hanuman saw another solitary figure hiding behind the curtains, crying. It was Shatrughan, the youngest of the four brothers.

Shatrughan pleaded with Hanuman to take him to Lanka saying he could be useful in the war but Hanuman could not do so without Ram's permission. He turned down Shatrughan despite Queen Kaikeyi's pleas that the youngest of the Raghukul princes go with Hanuman to Lanka.

"Just a matter of a few days mother, your sons will return home safe," he sought their blessings before continuing on his journey, but Kaushalya stopped him. "Hanuman, take a message to my son. Tell him he is not welcome in Ayodhya if he returns without Lakshman."

Hanuman nodded, bowing his head in respect. Just as he was ready to take off, Urmila called out to him, "O, son of Anjani, please convey my message to Saumitra. Tell him that he has to wake Mila up from her *nidra*." Hanuman looked at Urmila in surprise – only the sentient beings and the gods had the power to sleep-talk and 'work' with their spirits in *nidra*. For a moment, Urmila shimmered like a diva from heaven, bathed in a white light.

Hanuman bid them goodbye and returned to Lanka with the Donagiri mountain. The royal physician identified the plant, uprooted it, and crushed its leaves and roots into a paste and potion to anoint Lakshman's wound – and feed him as medicine.

Slowly, Lakshman revived.

He called out to Mila as soon as soon as his lids fluttered; she heard Lakshman across the seas and knew that he had been saved from near death. The news of Lakshman's recovery spread across Ayodhya.

Sumitra thanked Lord Shiva for reviving Lakshman and sent a message to her father, King Kushasthan, informing that she would make a pilgrimage to Kashi after the brothers returned home to seek Mahadeva's blessings in the shrine on the banks of the Ganges.

Lakshman's brain began to focus through his stupor, almost after an hour. Ram swam into the periphery of Lakshman's vision in the fog that clogged his head. The *Vaasvi Shakti* was said to stop the functioning of the brain – and kill the conscious mind.

Ram's face became distinct, floating inches above his own. Lakshman opened his eyes wide and smiled at his brother. Ram admonished Lakshman gently for being foolish and reckless with Meghnad in the battle.

Hanuman interrupted the siblings with his description of Urmila and how he had met her in Ayodhya. The brothers were perplexed because they did not know how and when Hanuman had met Urmila. Urmila? Hanuman filled them up on how Bharath mistook him for a demon and shot him down and then took him to meet the family in Ayodhya.

"How is she?" Lakshman's quiet voice stopped Hanuman's flow of words. He was desperate to know about Mila.

"You are blessed to have her as your wife, brother. She was calm even after hearing about your injury in the battle against Meghnad. She cannot afford to become agitated or else the family will collapse. She is a pillar of strength for Raghukul even in her sleep," Hanuman was fulsome in his praise for Urmila.

"Yes, my Mila always had to sacrifice her own happiness, position and comfort to make room for other." Tears filled Lakshman's eyes. Hanuman and Ram sensed his disenchantment – and perhaps Lakshman's regret at having to choose duty over personal happiness. Lakshman had been forced to fight a war that he had not ever been a party to; the battle of *dharma*, karma and *bhatri prem* − religion, duty and greater loyalty to the brotherhood.

"She awaits your arrival, brother. She wanted me to tell you this, when you opened your eyes," Hanuman passed on the message.

Lakshman was occupied with his thoughts and drifted into semi-consciousness. All that he wanted to think of was how his Mila had been waiting for him for the last 14 years. Her laughter, her joyful chatter, her frolicking ways, mischief and the sword fights reeled in his mind like an opera − in a spiel of images, and he longed to go back to her with an intensity that overrode all other concerns of the moment. He held his brother, sobbing like a child.

Hanuman earned his reward from the Raghukul royals. Urmila named him *Sankat Mochan* − the one who warded off disaster by saving Lakshman's life.

Meghnad Attains Moksha − Salvation

Son lies in death at father's feet, mankind fetes victory.

Late at night, the news that Lakshman was still alive reached Lanka. Meghnad tried to convince his furious father that Ram and Lakshman were no ordinary human beings and Sita must be given back to Ram.

Raavan ridiculed him, "What kind of a son you are, Meghnad? Don't you feel ashamed to ask me to pull out of my pledge − to climb down from my stand? Look at Ram, who honoured his father by spending 14 years in exile so that he did not fall from grace, and you trying to show your own father in a loser's light. I was so proud when Brahmadev called you Indrajit, but today, I regret calling you my son."

Meghnad could not bear his father's arrogance and rejection. "I implore you, father, to take care of yourself after I am dead," he reminded his father with sorrow. He went to his mother's palace and bowed his head in respect, "O, Mother, take care of your self. Don't cry after I am dead because I am going to be killed by a god. I am blessed having married the daughter of Lord Shesha and now, I am ready to die in his hands. I will attain *moksha* – salvation."

"Son, why do you fight the war when you know they are gods and you will be killed by them? Stay here with me," Mandodari cried in anguish.

"Mother, I can't. I cannot disobey my father's order; he is the king of Lanka. Loyalty to my father and loyalty towards my kingdom mean everything to me. I know I will die peacefully," he wiped his mother's tears.

"The world shall always remember your sacrifice." Mandodari defied her husband, scorning him, "O, powerful king of Lanka, look at my brave son. He may be just a warrior for you but for me he is my son, my pride, the *kohl* in my eyes that doesn't fade. Even if my son dies today, he will be immortal!" She embraced Meghnad and bid him to the battlefield with stately grace.

Meghnad dreaded breaking the news to Sulochana but he had to take formal leave of her. Sulochana greeted him with a smile, which Meghnad found strange knowing her intense love for him, "You know that I may not return tonight, but you still greet me with a smiling face."

"My lord, you have always been a winner to me. You may lose as a warrior today, but you will be victorious as a son. Your unswerving loyalty towards your father shall be remembered and will serve as an example in the coming eras. I smile because I know if it be your last day in the world; it will be mine too. I am happy that we can leave the world together."

Sulochana was torn between her father and her husband because she knew that Raavan would lose the war, maybe his life as well, but it was useless trying to make him see sense. His end was destined. But she did not want to lose Meghnad to a preordained destiny.

Meghnad, in a desperate attempt to save himself, decided to perform a *yajna* – rite – at Nikumbhala Devi's temple for he had once been granted a boon that if he successfully completed a ritual invocation of the deity at the temple, no one would be able to defeat him.

But before Meghnad could complete the *yajna*, Vibhishan sent word to Ram about the boon. Ram was aware of the implication of the rite and he ordered Lakshman to kill Meghnad immediately, before he could step out of the shrine.

Lakshman stormed into Nikumbhala Devi's temple, accompanied by Vibhishan and his army. He found Meghnad praying to the goddess, alone.

Lakshman ordered his army to stop the *yajna* and waited for Meghnad to challenge him. He forbade the army to touch Meghnad because *dharma* dictated that a battle between two great warriors should be one-on-one.

Meghnad felt let down seeing Vibhishan with Lakshman and lashed out, "I lost my brothers and uncle Kumbhakaran because of you. I wish no family has a member like you that destroy its own clan. You are a shame, uncle Vibhishan."

He attacked Vibhishan with the Brahmastra but Lakshman stood between the weapon and Vibhishan. The Brahmastra rebounded, together with all the other weapons that Meghnad used, making him even more furious with Lakshman for saving Vibhishan, each time he tried to kill him.

"O, mighty Meghnad, if you are so sure of your bravery; then fight me. I challenge you," Lakshman dared him to battle.

Meghnad and Lakshman fought for three days and three nights. Lakshman sustained several wounds on his shoulders and chest.

At last, Lakshman took out his Indrastra – the divine sword – and prayed, "O, Indrastra, if Ram the son of Maharaj Dashrath has never strayed from the path of truth and *dharma* and is second to none in power, go forth and destroy Meghnad." The sword, one of the weapons blessed by the god of storms and lightning, found its target with divine power and struck with the force of rumbling thunder and blazing lightning.

Meghnad begged of Lakshman, "I fought for my father, for my land, but dear father-in-law, if I have been a good husband to your daughter Sulochana, bless me to that I may revel in your affection in my next birth."

Meghnad thought about his wife and her smiling face one last time, silently seeking her pardon as the thundering weapon streaked through the air, beheading the mighty prince of Lanka. A deep remorse swept through Lakshman for killing a man so young and brave. He became melancholic when he thought of Sulochana.

Lakshman paid tribute to Meghnad's courage, carrying his severed head to Ram, "I have beheaded this son of Raavan with your blessings, brother." He sent the headless body to Lanka. Ram praised Lakshman, but he noticed the expression of pain on his face. Unable to hold back his agony from his brother, Lakshman spilled the reason for his grief, "My heart goes out to his poor wife. She is too young to be widowed. And, the thought that I am the reason for her husband's death breaks my heart for some reason. I cannot put it into words."

Sulochana's Sati – Immolation

Sulochana reunites with Meghnad in soul bonding.

Dharma struck yet again and Lanka stood devastated. This time, it had to pay a huge price for its king's ego. It lost Meghnad, the most precious and bravest of all princes of Lanka, at the hands of Lakshman.

With Lakshman's permission, ape commanders Nal and Neel allowed the Lankan army to take Meghnad's body. A huge black cloud spread like a shroud over Lanka and stormy winds lashed the island, the sea rolled in billowing waves that threatened to swamp the kingdom and the battlefield.

"The winds bring a bad omen. What could it be? Why do I feel nervous?" Sulochana wondered.

Malati, her chief maid, burst into her chamber. She was out of breath and her face was pale. She looked at Sulochana with tears in her eyes and the realisation dawned on Shesha's daughter that Meghnad had fallen in battle. She crumpled on the floor, the anguish of losing her brave Meghnad coursing deep in her blood. It could not be! He could not leave her without saying goodbye. The fact that she was still breathing was evidence that Meghnad was alive.

But destiny mocked her, laughing at the irony that the father who protected his daughter from every blow in life had taken away her joy. Was Lakshman really to be blamed? The only person responsible for Meghnad's death was his father, Raavan, and she had to confront him, seeking answers.

"Lankeshhhh," Sulochana cried in impotent anger as she stood facing him in the *Rajya Sabha*, "O, mighty king of Lanka, don't you feel any shame at pushing your sons to death to feed your ego and *adharma* – faithlessness? My husband would have been alive if it were not for you. You abused his devotion to you by sending him to battle Shri Lakshman. I pray that no son gets a father as cruel and heartless as you."

When Kekasi, Raavan's mother, reprimanded Sulochana for the way she spoke to her father-in-law, Sulochana was sharp in her retaliation, "No, mother, today I am only a wife whose husband has been brutally killed by this demon, whom my husband called his father."

"Pramila, I stand as aggrieved as you. The man you call your husband has been dearer than life to me. How can a father take his own son's life? It is Lakshman who killed my Meghnad!" Raavan tried to reason with her.

Scriptures have it that Raavan called Sulochana Pramila because Sulochana was the name given to her by Narayan. Raavan, who had a running fued with Narayan across lifetimes because of his devotion to Shiva, did not want to call her by this name.

"Don't pity the boy you never loved as a son, else you would not have sent him to his death. My husband fulfilled his duty towards you but you failed as a father. You are waging the war to wrest Sita from Ram, have you managed to bend her to your will? Your lust has destroyed the clan. Had anyone else killed Meghnad, he would not have attained *moksha*. I thank all the gods in heaven that *Shri* Saumitra slew my husband."

Sulochana continued, "I cannot do anything against you as I am your son's wife and, somewhere, he has been wrong to side with your evil plans, even though he has tried to reason with you several times. So, today, I curse you Lankesh that the day you die at the hands of Ram will always be celebrated as Ram's victory – a victory of *dharma* over *adharma*, in Aryavarta. People will burn their ego in your effigy on that day every year to remember that ego ruins emperors and empires just like it destroyed you. *Yuga*s will pass, *kalpa* will change but the earth will not ever see a more egoistic man than you, Lankesh."

Sulochana's curse is the reason why every year the effigy of Raavan is burnt on Dusshera.

Mandodari silently watched Sulochana curse Raavan because deep down she knew Sulochana was hitting at the right place – Raavan's pride.

The court was shocked into silence when the guards marched in a sombre procession carrying Meghnad's headless body. Mandodari rushed to remove the shroud off Meghnad's corpse as Sulochana stood frozen in disbelief. The strapping Meghnad looked shrunken and frail in death; it smote her heart to see the brave young man reduced to an inconsequential mass of flesh.

Her lament echoed through the court; the dirge resounding across the swathe of the emerald isle, "You cannot leave your Sulochana behind, my lord. You are *Atimaharathi*, you are Indrajit. How can the one who fought Indra and defeated him not take his wife with him? Death cannot take away Lord Shesha's son-in-law, the husband of *Naag Kanya* Sulochana. Wake up, my lord." In her head, Sulochana knew that Meghnad had gone forever, but her heart was not ready to believe it.

The court was mute. No one had the courage to console Sulochana as she grieved for her husband. Sulochana stopped Raavan from touching his son's body. "O, Agni Dev, if I, Sulochana, the daughter of the serpents is a chaste and a devoted wife, if I have always been devoted to my husband with all my heart, body and soul, then burn this idol of ego, Lankesh, the moment he touches my husband's body." She knelt by Meghnad's corpse, folding her hands in prayer.

A thunderous Raavan screamed in indignation and disbelief, "Pramila, you overstep your limits. You blame me for a crime I have not committed and nor do I have any way to prove my innocence. But, yes, I can do something to prove my love for my son and that is to kill the reason for this tragedy. I will kill Sita right now."

"King of Lanka, how many more sins will you commit? Are you not ashamed of your endless wrongs, of breaking Devi Vedvati's penance, killing your sister's husband, abducting Sita, playing with the lives of your sons, and now this? Mark my words, Lankesh, the very Mahadev who you worship every day will also not save you from your death when the time comes."

Sulochana walked out of the court in a trance, the way ahead covered in a dense colourless mist of sorrow. Mandodari tried to stop her, but she was firm, "I have to get back my husband's head for the last rites."

Raavan was furious at her demand. "Pramila, have you gone mad? Ram and Lakshman are our enemies. You cannot fetch Meghnad's head from them!"

"The one whom you call our enemies are my own. Ram is my uncle, Narayan and Lakshman are my own father, Shesha," Sulochana revealed in a fit of rage.

"Oh!" Raavan said, stung by the information. "Then why did your father not feel any remorse while killing his own son-in-law and spare his life?" the demon king mocked Sulochana.

"Look, who says this? Lankesh, it is you who is responsible for my husband's death. My father follows his *dharma* and faith does not discriminate between their own and aliens," Sulochana could not bear this tirade against her father. Handing over the responsibility of embalming her husband's body to Mandodari, Sulochana went to meet Ram and Lakshman in their camp.

Sulochana's trepidation grew as she walked towards the enemy quarters.

Her hands became clammy and cold in nervousness and with the anticipation of meeting her father, Shesha. She wondered how he would react to her in this life on earth.

Lakshman was uneasy. He felt as if someone familiar was calling out to him from the stormy waters – from the dark emptiness of the mayhem around. A guard informed him that Raavan's daughter-in-law, Meghnad's wife, had come to meet him.

The moment had arrived, fraught with powerful emotions for Sulochana. She could not hug her father because she had been incarnated as Meghnad's wife on earth. "*Shri* Saumitra, this is *Maata* Urmila's love for you, which won today! My oblation to you, dear princes of Raghukul, I am Sulochana, daughter of Lord Shesha and *Maata* Ksheera, and the wife of Mandodari's son Meghnad. I request you to return his head to me so that I can perform *sati*." She knelt at their feet.

Lakshman agreed to return the head. Sulochana tugged at his heart, but Sugriva interrupted, "How do we know this is the real Sulochana and not Raavan's illusion?"

Ram and Lakshman looked at Sulochana, who pleaded with them to fetch her husband's head to prove that she was the real Sulochana and not *maya* – magic. "My lord always smiles when he sees me. Bring his head and let me see if he can recognise me." Vibhishan corroborated her claim and asked Hanuman to bring Meghnad's head.

As soon as the severed head set his open eyes on Sulochana, he smiled.

Sulochana drowned in a sea of grief – the void hounding her soul. The same mischief and love shone from Meghnad's open eyes. And then the tears flowed, forming a pool around her.

The head turned towards Sulochana and his mouth opened. "Don't cry, my love. Who will wipe your tears, now? My hands are tied elsewhere," she heard Meghnad's voice floating in the air; and she knew that this was the last time she was hearing his voice – laughing, teasing, gentle as ever. Lakshman looked at Sulochana's crumpled form bent over the head like a child, and his heart went out to the bereaved woman. He moved away from her path so that she could take Meghnad's head. She sought her father's blessings before leaving, "Bless me, father before I burn in the same pyre with my husband as *sati*. May I be reborn as your daughter again."

Lakshman flinched at her words, fearing to bless her because he could not recollect the memories of previous birth. The warmth of paternal affection stirred in his heart – followed by an instinct to protect the child from the twists of destiny, but he could not understand its source.

Sulochana was heartbroken.

Heaven was guilty; the unease was palpable in the sanctum of the trinity. The creator of the universe, Brahma Dev, sensed it was time to reveal the truth about his identity to Lakshman else Sulochana's restless spirit would stalk Aryavarta forever.

He suddenly appeared to Lakshman surrounded in a great halo of light, and changed the prince of Ayodhya to his original avatara of Shesha, the myriad-hooded serpent Sheshnaga. He showed Lakshman his past life in Vaikunth, Vishnu's home, his marriage to the Goddess Ksheera, the birth of Sulochana and events that led to their abandoning of the infant – leaving the child in his brother Vasuki's care.

"My daughter," Shesha's voice was tremulous. He suddenly recognised his daughter whom he had left behind 50 years ago. He ran after her and pulled her into his arms. She broke down in her father's warm embrace, mourning the loss of her childhood and every moment that she had lost out on his love.

"Forgive your father, my daughter, for leaving you behind with brother Vasuki and for being the cause of your grief," Shesha apologised.

"Father, please don't blame yourself. It is my destiny. I am proud to be your daughter. Time has come to bid farewell now, I will have to prepare for *sati*," Sulochana was calm in the face of her self-imposed death.

Lakshman was distraught. He pleaded with her to return to Ayodhya with him and live with Urmila as their daughter. Urmila would not ever forgive him for leaving Sulochana behind.

However, Sulochana was firm about immolating herself on her husband's pyre because the call of *dharma* was stronger than the ties of blood, "No, father, I cannot. I cannot live with you because the reason why you had to leave me in Vaikunth to incarnate on earth is incomplete. People on earth will know that you are a god born here and I am your daughter. It cannot happen and without my lord, I am only half alive. I have no desire to live anymore."

The gods sided with Sulochana because her *sati* was a victory of *dharma* on earth. Brahma Dev agreed with her, "Yes, Shesha, let her go. But today, I grant Sulochana a boon that in every *yuga*, whenever you and Ksheera descend on earth in your mortal incarnations, she and her husband Meghnad will also be reborn. I bless her to return to Lakshman as his daughter in this life, Lakshman *Putri* Somada, after 12 years and Meghnad as Rajkumar Devansh." He then turned to Sulochana, "O, daughter of the serpent, for your pious loyalty to your husband, the world shall always remember you as *Sati* Sulochana," he blessed her and disappeared into the clouds.

Lakshman did not want his daughter to go yet, and accompanied her to Lanka. The sense of desolation raged like a wildfire through Lakshman, rendering his mortal will barren. For some time, the work that he had set out to accomplish in Lanka seemed futile. He did not have the heart to go through it.

Sulochana summoned the courtiers to attach the severed head to Meghnad's body and then build a pyre of fragrant sandalwood to lay the body on. Sulochana decked up in the pristine red clothes of a bride and stepped on the pyre to sit with Meghnad's head cradled in her lap.

The sight of Sulochana sitting in *sati* with the valiant Meghnad shattered Lakshman; for a moment the world seemed to fall apart, spinning in grief. Tears ran down his cheeks. What Shesha had not bargained for was the strength of his daughter Sulochana; it shook the coiled serpent king inside him. Lakshman, the distraught father, battled with his duties as a mortal warrior committed to the service of Raghukul and his *dharma*.

He trembled, seized by a violent spell of disorientation, feverish confusion, palpitation and an unnamed fear from another lifetime beating like a drum inside his heart as he picked up a flaming sandalwood log to light his daughter's pyre. He knelt by it, weeping like a child.

The flames engulfed the pile of wood criss-crossing the pyre in a dense web, filling the air with the incense of sandalwood. The heavens opened up. Showers of flowers mingled with the flames, carrying Sulochana's spirit up to her gods in Vaikunth, borne by the columns of the curling grey smoke.

Sulochana was a woman of great substance. A sati by choice! She gave up her life willingly for her husband and fulfilling her commitment to stand by her husband in death as in life. The gods wept in heaven.

An inconsolable Lakshman planned vengeance on Vasuki for ill-treating his daughter and wondered how he would tell Urmila about Sulochana and her tragic fate.

Lakshman collected the ashes of his daughter in an earthenware urn to take back with him to Ayodhya to immerse in the Sarayu. The river wept in grief and vowed to redeem Sati Sulochana.

Sati Sulochana was one of the Mahasatis — one of the pious women in Hindu spiritual mythology. Sati Anusuya and Sati Savitri were two others, who are still venerated as 'deities'. Mahasati means a very chaste woman and a virtuous wife. These women are true Pati Vrata Strees — women who devoted their whole lives to their husbands. There are no greater women than these. They are always labelled as 'Sati' before their respective names. In Sanatan Dharma, there are four Mahasatis — Sati, the first consort of Mahadeva, Sati Anusuya, the consort of Atri Muni, Sati Sulochana, the consort of the great warrior Meghnad and Sati Savitri, the consort of Satyavaan.

The war went on despite the personal trials because the Ayodhya princes had no way to pull out of it without rescuing Sita and defeating Raavan. The war continued for several days and nights till Ram took out the divine arrow – the dreaded weapon of Brahma – and shot Raavan in his navel.

Ram and Lakshman vanquished Raavan, one of the most learned and feared kings of the Treta Yuga. Before dying, Raavan paid homage to Ram, happy in the knowledge that he had been killed by Narayan and would find a place in heaven.

According to some religious texts and the Jain Ramayana, it was Lakshman who killed Raavan, not Ram.

After Raavan's death, Vibhishan was crowned the king of Lanka and he married Mandodari soon after.

Sita returned to Ram but once the news of the victory reached Ayodhya, the subjects began to question Sita's virtue and Ram, as a king, was under pressure to prove her chastity to his subjects. He asked her to stay back either in Lanka or go to Mithila to live with her parents. A shocked Sita lost her faith in Ram and vowed to go through an *Agni Pareeksha* to tell the people of Ayodhya that she was 'pure'.

Her karma was coming back to haunt her. Once, because of her allegations, an innocent Lakshman had to go through Agni Pareeksha to prove his virtuousness. Now, it was her turn.

Lakshman tried to convince his brother that the purification was not necessary and it could rebound on Raghukul later but Ram was ashamed that Sita was under a cloud of suspicion. He had to prove her innocence. She walked through the fire unscathed; her innocence proven and intact.

Just before their departure from Lanka, Lakshman urged Ram, "Dear brother, if what Brahmadev says is true and you are Narayan and I am Shesha, then bless me that I am born as your older brother in the next incarnation. I want to take care of you."

Ram smiled, his ever so calm smile and granted him the boon, "My dear Lakshman, you are no less a father to me for you have always taken care of me like a child. You stand by me, so do not forget that Shesha is Narayan's support system and Ksheera is Shesha's. I bless you, my brother."

Lanka bowed to the footsteps of Ram and Lakshman, one last time, as they readied to leave. The land had been blessed by their holy presence even though it would always be known as the enemy's turf.

Can't Wait To Meet You

The moon ends vigil, love sings in the hush.

The long years of pain and suffering were coming to an end for Urmila. It was time to return. Ram and Sita were happy; Lakshman was scared, frightened of being happy after 14 years, of falling in love with Mila, again.

The war over evil had been won by the righteous. Ram, Lakshman and a taint-free Sita were eager to return to Ayodhya as soon as possible; they did not have the time to take part in the festivities that the new king of Lanka, Vibhishan, had planned.

Vibhishan arranged for the Pushpak Vimana – flying chariot – to ferry them home in safety.

Ram instructed Hanuman to return to Ayodhya before their arrival to tell Bharath not to do anything rash or put himself in danger. Ram was on his way home.

Lakshman, on the other hand, was extremely quiet. Nothing of what was happening around him made any sense to him because his thoughts were channelled to Mila. The thought that he would be able to see her, feel her and touch her sent him into a trance – swinging between intense euphoria and extreme uncertainty. Every moment that he had spent without Urmila in the last 14 years had been like an eternity to him.

He wanted to accompany Hanuman but he could not desert Ram at the last moment. Hanuman flew to Ayodhya with the joyous news of the trio's impending return. The royal household felt rejuvenated after 14 dark years and Ayodhya prepared for the brothers' homecoming. Away from the din and dust of the rebuilding and preparation in the palace and in the city, which had been in hibernation for 14 years, Kaushalya planned a tender reunion for Lakshman and Urmila.

She hurried to Urmila's quarters to convey the happy tidings but Urmila remained silent even after hearing the news of Ram's homecoming.

Only the tightening of her fist and clenching of her jaw showed how the news of their return affected her mind even in her state of deep trance.

Kaushalya gently caressed Urmila's hair, trying to ease her turmoil, "It is time to rejoice, my daughter. Your Saumitra is on his way back. The sacrifices you both have made and the pain you have borne are incomparable. Ram and Sita were with each other for all these long years, while you and Lakshman had to live in physical separation, existing only in your thoughts. Ayodhya will never be able to repay you for the hardships you both have suffered and for your sacrifices, my daughter."

Urmila calmed down for a moment. Her sisters, Mandvi and Shrutakeerti, insisted that she opened her eyes, but her sleep was beyond that of the mortal world.

"My *vanvaas* – exile in the forest – is still not over. It will end only my husband wakes me up." Tears streamed down her sleep-weary eyes, and Shrutakeerti wiped them. Her sister had borne so much and so wonderfully with such regal grace and humility. Shutakreeti wanted to be a part of the happiness that would surround Urmila when Lakshman's footsteps echoed in the palace. "Let us decorate Moti Bhavan like a wedding venue."

Mandvi melted. For years, since her childhood, Mandvi had been jealous of Urmila because she was always at the forefront of events. But today, perhaps for the first time, Mandvi felt the bonding of womanhood with her sister. Bearing Lakshman's loss for 14 years with such dignity and strength had put Urmila on a pedestal. What a great sister to have…

"I want nothing to stand between us today when he enters the portals of the palace. If your decorations take away his eyes from me, I will be jealous," Urmila smiled, but she could not brush aside the streak of possessiveness. After 20 days, the family learned that Ram, Lakshman and Sita were to touch down at Nandigram in their *vimana* from Lanka – a distance of nearly 3,000 kms from Ayodhya.

Sumitra offered to stay back with Urmila, but grand-daughter Vindhya accompanied by her brother, Rishyaksh, who had arrived to take part in the family celebrations, insisted that Sumitra go with the family to Nandigram to welcome the trio. The queens were stunned to see Vindhya after 26 long years, grown up and mature. They showered her with affectionate kisses. Vindhya was bursting with information and she regaled the queens with stories about her meeting with Ram, Lakshman and Sita in exile.

Vindhya and Rishyaksh stayed back to watch over Urmila.

Maharani Sunaina, Chandrabhaga and *Maata* Gargi refused to accompany the rest of the family to Nandigram to care for Urmila – and to oversee preparations to welcome the trio to the palace.

According to the Purans, Maharaj Dashrath was reborn as Rishyaksh. It was his way of atoning for casting Shanta away.

The family – comprising mostly of the royal menfolk from all over Aryavarta with the queen mothers from Ayodhya – gathered at Nandigram.

The flight was long and slow – spinning, tumbling and racing through the great banks of clouds, lightning, gusty winds, towering forests and mighty rivers – from across the sea in the southern-most tip of Aryavarta. As the sky chariot hovered over Ayodhya, Lakshman whooped in joy like a boy, ready to jump off the *vimana*.

"Here, I am home, Mila," he shouted inside his head in glee. The smile on his face broadened.

Ram looked at the smile on Lakshman's face with sadness, the first real smile in 14 years. He knew how desperate Lakshman was without Urmila.

The chariot bent earthwards, its nose dipping in a straight descent and settling on the ground gently with a small bump. The trio looked at the welcoming party on the open field with tears – the mothers had aged, deep wrinkles grooving their faces from the corners of their eyes and mouth; their bodies were thin and weak. A wave of protective love washed over Lakshman at the sight of his mother.

Sumitra chided Ram for losing so much weight, scolding him for not eating enough and caring for his personal well-being.

"How could I? We had to fight a war," Ram replied in a whisper.

The moment was happy and yet sad. The changes of the last 14 years stood between them!

Sumitra clasped Lakshman to her bosom, "My son, my heart has ached for you for the last 14 years, but I am so proud of you. I am blessed to have borne a brave son like you."

"How can you be proud of a son who has failed, both as a son and as a husband?" Lakshman jabbed his mother gently. The regret in his words was apparent, flowing across to touch Sumitra, who held on to him for a long moment.

A mother and her child are said to understand each other's heartbeats, each other's anguish and happiness.

Lakshman touched Kaushalya's feet, and then paid his respects to Kaikeyi. Remorse had turned her face ashen over the years, the greyness touching her hair. As he paid his oblation to her, Kaikeyi clutched him to her frail bosom, "Forgive me if you have the heart to condone this old queen, it is because of me you had to sacrifice your life of safety and comfort to take care of Ram in the forest, stay away from the child who sleeps in the palace waiting for you. Endure agonies and the traumas of war and pain of separation from your mother and wife."

Lakshman consoled her that with time, hurt faded and became a distant memory and healed.

Shatrughan noticed his brother's inner disquietude and whispered into his ears, "She is waiting for you in the palace. You are to wake her from her *nidra*."

"I missed you so much, brother," Lakshman embraced Shatrughan tightly.

"Not more than me. You had Ram with you, but my own brother wasn't there with me. On every birthday, Holi – the festival of colours, on the full moons and the new moons, on the days of special prayers and festivals, on every normal day, I went through the pangs of solitude – of being left out of the flow of your destiny," Shatrughan, the softest among the four, broke down.

"I will make it up to you for every moment you have been alone, brother." Lakshman patted him on the head fondly and looked at Bharath, the shadow king of Ayodhya, who was waiting to welcome him.

"I would have never forgiven myself had something happened to you," Bharath choked on his tears.

"Nothing happened. We have returned and you must stop blaming yourself for Queen Kaikeyi's wish for you – father had to redeem his pledge and grant her what she sought as a boon," Lakshman's compassionate reasoning brought the brotherhood back as one, again.

"May we leave for Ayodhya now?" Shatrughan sought permission from Guru Vashishtha. The convoy left Nandigram.

Lakshman was lost to the world. His heart fluttered for Mila.

"Has Mila become more beautiful? Will she be the same fierce Mila, who fought with me every day, have the years changed her? Will she be angry with me or will she come running into my arms?" Lakshman's thoughts were as wild as the royal charioteer's run through the countryside towards Ayodhya.

The palace burst into life as the chariots entered through the ornate gates of the capital city, decorated with flowers and earthenware wicker lamps to greet the princes and Sita back from exile; a single lamp burned brightly at the shrine in Moti Bhavan – the *Akhandjyoti* that Urmila had lit on Lakshman's departure 14 years ago.

The flickering light of the *Akhandjyoti* was like a ray of hope in the darkness of the new moon – touching Urmila's heart like a flame and waiting to erupt into a blaze. "Why do you take so much of time, Saumitra? Each moment is an agony, please, step into the palace now." She looked around at the once-plush quarters in her semi-conscious state. The palace looked unkempt with the last 14 years of neglect, old and yellowed.

"Get ready to welcome him back. Our life returns, my Saumitra returns," Urmila whispered to the walls around her.

Moti Bhavan, which was said to possess a divine life of its own like a breathing being, turned crimson. The scarlet core of the *Akhandjyoti* painted the walls a deep shade of red. The rani had finally spoken to the mute palace, ordering it to spring back to life and for the flowers in the garden to bloom, once again.

"O, dear eyes, get ready to see the new world where no separation exists. Lovers live together forever. O, dear hands, get ready to hold him tightly such that he can never leave. O, dear lips, get ready to touch his in a beautiful kiss, one that will cast a spell on him forever. And, O, dear moon, it is nice that you have hidden yourself. You have finished your long hours of duty, my friend," her thoughts spilled – blurring, crashing, and incoherent – delirious with happiness.

Lakshmila's Reunion

Moon hides in shame in the ardour of Lakshmila's love.

For 14 years Ayodhya did not sleep or eat. Ram, Sita and Lakshman's arrival rekindled the lights in the kingdom's soul, filling it with a hunger for feasting and revelry.

Queen Sumitra knew what her son was searching for in such earnestness, since his return. His eyes scanned every room in the palace, darting to every corner, scanning the throngs that had assembled to welcome them to the palace – the multitudes of relatives, royal courtiers, servitors, guards, maids and important subjects.

"Lakshman, the one you seek is waiting for you in sleep. She will not open her eyes unless you wake her up. Release her from the tough penance, she has performed on your behalf for the past 14 years," Sumitra implored Lakshman. The most-awaited event of the day for the clan was the reunion of Lakshman and Urmila because their forced separation was the most barbaric atrocity on two innocent lives – and yet the most poignant in the history of Aryavarta: keeping of the royal *dharma* by a prince and his consort at the cost of their personal happiness.

The people of Ayodhya had virtually stopped breathing – in anticipation of the reunion. They wanted to see a wrong righted, they refused to leave the forecourts of the palace till Lakshman and their most-admired yuvrani – the Warrior Princess – made a public appearance. King Janak and Queen Sunaina of Mithila felt a sense of secure well-being at the subjects' love and loyalty to Mila; it eased their fears of a portend that Lakshmila might be cast off in the melee of new kingships, new orders and in the grand designs of imperial expansion.

Lakshman walked to Moti Bhavan with unsteady steps. The thought of touching Urmila made his hands tremble; he was so lost in day-dreaming about how he would face Mila that he did not realise the warmth of another pair of hands holding his tightly.

He looked at the person beside him. Vindhya smiled, "How could I not be beside you now? I hold your anxiety, my best friend, while you walk to your love."

Just as he was about to open the ornate door of Moti Bhavan, the one leading to Urmila's bed-chamber near the terrace, Ram stopped him. He wanted to meet Urmila before Lakshman, who stepped aside to make way for Ram.

Ram entered Moti Bhavan and walked to where Urmila was sleeping peacefully. With folded hands, he bowed his head, "Goddess Urmila, my brother's most devoted wife, forgive me for causing you pain. Forgive me for being the reason of your separation from your husband. You are a goddess and should be worshiped by everyone for you have redefined love. I bless you today, my dear Goddess

Urmila that every unmarried man who seeks a wife like you will be blessed with one if he fasts on *Jaya Ekadashi*, your birthday. Goddess Urmila, I ask you to bless every mother to have a daughter-in-law like you. Raghukul will forever remain grateful to you for your sacrifice." Ram touched Urmila's feet.

The happy-go-lucky mischievous Warrior Princess from Mithila was transformed in that instant into a deity for seekers of love and marital bliss.

Ever since that day Jaya Ekadashi is considered Urmila Patni Vrat. Suitors do not eat or drink water for 14 hours. They pray to Urmila and offer blue lotus, orchids, guavas and mangoes which were her favourites and wear blue or white clothes. The Purans say Lord Krishna and Balram had also fasted on Jaya Ekadasi for their wives Rukmini and Revati.

Fourteen years on, not much had changed in Moti Bhavan; the nooks and the crannies were still the pale shimmering pearl like the gemstone after which the palace was named. One earthenware lamp cast wavering shadows on the walls, dancing in the light breeze from the terrace.

The moon was nowhere to be seen but the open terrace adjoining the bedroom was translucent. Mila slept on the cold stone and terracotta floor, which warmed and cooled with the passing seasons. "Mila, my love, my reason for living in the last 14 years," Lakshman cried in rapture – at the same time, with the acute grief of the separation that punched him like a fresh blow in his heart at the sight of his sleeping wife.

The much-awaited reunion was like a searing pain in his breast.

She was as beautiful as ever. "The moon is nothing compared to your face, and betel stain is shamed at the sight of your lips, nectar is bitter at your words, and your touch, the feel of your skin is cooler than water for my parched soul. Your feet are still soft like the white lotuses in the pool, wake up Mila and cover your body in gold and silks. Remove this hermit's cloth, the saffron and the wooden beads from your body," Lakshman whispered. He sat on the floor next to her quietly and kissed her forehead without making a sound.

Still, she did not move. Lakshman was terror-struck. Had Yama's sister, Nidra Devi, put her into eternal sleep? He ran to Vashishtha, the clan guru, seeking guidance. The sage asked Lakshman to pray to Nidra Devi to rouse Urmila from her slumber.

"O, goddess of sleep, Nidra Devi. I have returned to Ayodhya. Please, give me back my sleep and wake up my wife," he prayed focusing all his energy to invoke *nidra*.

Nidra Devi appeared to Lakshman in folds of gossamer light from the opaque darkness of the new moon; lulling and sweet. "I understand your agitation," she allayed Saumitra's fears. The goddess of sleep chanted *mantras*, and Urmila slowly turned in her sleep. Shivering, she sank into a delirious stupor.

"Who are you? Why are you here? You are trying to accost a young and helpless creature like me who is fragile. If my father or my brothers-in-law hear of this intrusion, you will be killed. Indra is ugly because he chases another's wife, Raavan lost his life because he kidnapped Sita and yet you chase me? Don't you have a sister at home?" Urmila babbled, unable to register Lakshman's identity in her head.

The goddess vanished as silently as she came. Desperation, a helpless grief and fear gripped Lakshman. "I am Ram's brother, Maharaj Janak's son-in-law, Sita's brother-in-law. Don't you know me? Wake up from your sleep, Mila, for I have returned to you after 14 years," Lakshman's tears fell on her cheeks.

Urmila was in deep trauma; caught in a time-warp. Her clock had stopped moving the day she fell asleep in lieu of Lakshman's nights of vigil in the forest. "Saumitra is in exile in the forest," Mila wept.

"Fourteen years are over, Mila. Since the day I left you behind I have neither eaten nor slept. If you do not acknowledge me, I will kill myself," Lakshman was firm in his threat.

Lakshman pulled his sword out from its scabbard ready to kill himself. Time – *kaal* – relented at Saumitra's daring resolve. The forgetfulness of 14 years fell off like the old bark of a tree, unpeeling in layers from Urmila's head. She opened her eyes to rest them on her husband's face. She lifted one thin hand to trace the outlines of his bony face, eyes, nose and lips.

"Lord, you are back. Are 14 years over?"

Lakshman embraced her as if he would not ever let her go. Tears coursed down her eyes – the pain of 14 years. She lay in his arms inert, listening to his uneven breath, content. Lakshman tenderly lifted her face from the crook of his shoulders and took his fill of her with longing. They cried, smiled, laughed, teased and hugged each other, simultaneously.

"Will you give me something to eat, Mila? My stomach churns in hunger. I have not eaten anything for 14 years," he tried to break off from her hold. Her eyes lingered on his lips.

"Were they still as soft?" she wondered. He caught her gaze and without letting her eyes deviate from his, lowered his lips to hers and took them in raw hunger. She sighed in fulfillment and deepened the kiss. The kiss tasted warm and salty. Her lips felt as soft as he remembered them to be. Her body felt as fragile as it had been. "The nights without you were barren, Mila. The touch of your soul grazed me every night until I could no longer think."

Before their touch became a raging and all-consuming fire, she moved out of his embrace and urged him to the main entrance of the palace.

Lakshman was reluctant to go because his life was there in that moment where she was. She took him to the shrine of Gauri *Maata*; picked up a platter of flowers with the *Akhandjyoti* and touched his head with the offerings in oblation – her homage to Adishesha. She offered him sweetmeats from the plate, sating his hunger. They laughed in memory of the nightmare when she touched Lakshman on the spot right above his chest where Meghnad's *Vaasvi Shakti* had hit him.

At the memory of Meghnad, Lakshman suddenly became quiet and gloomy. Urmila sensed a change in him and she was curious to know the reason. "Meghnad's wife Sulochana is our daughter, from our previous life!" An expression of disbelief and utter incomprehension flitted across her face. She had no recollection of her previous avatara. Lakshman summoned a guard to fetch the pot containing Sulochana's remains, which he collected from the *Sati-Stahl* – the place where *Sati* Sulochana was consigned to flames. He showed her the ashes and the bits of embers – narrating to her the story of Sulochana and her death. He told her about what Brahma Dev had revealed.

Urmila's heart ached for the child. The memories were misty, buried in the distant recesses of time. "I wish I were there to meet her. How was she?"

"As beautiful as her mother. You will meet her for she shall be born to us again in this life," he consoled her. They mourned Sulochana's death together in the prayer room, pleading with the gods to keep her happy in heaven – with Meghnad.

The mother in Urmila pined, the wife in her smiled.

Lakshman picked her up in his arms and put her on a low seat in front of the mirror on the dresser. He chose her shellac comb from the holder and ran it through the mess of her tangled hair – unravelling the knots of 14 years.

"I remember how you loved it when I combed your tangled tresses. I loved doing this more than you because I can smell your fragrance, this close," he teased her. Urmila blushed.

The sounds of heavy footsteps forced them apart. Queen Sumitra entered their chamber to bless them and to escort them to Smriti Van, the garden of memories, where the clan waited for them. Urmila ran into Sita's arms, "I missed you, sister! A day hasn't gone by where I did not wish for your presence by my side." A silent Sita hugged Urmila tighter.

Lakshman introduced Urmila to Hanuman who feted her both as a goddess and as a sister-in-law. Sumitra's son had been an older brother to the monkey lord in the forest, guiding and protecting him. Amidst the blessings and the reunions, Gurudev Vashishtha announced that Ram's coronation ceremony would be held in two days. Lakshman would be the commander-in-chief of the army and Urmila, the chief advisor to Ram. The clan celebrated the announcement with the invocation of Devi *Maata* in the temple.

At sundown, Ayodhya, sparkled with rows of little earthenware lamps in every home and flaming torches that hung on every street – *Dipawali* – to ward off the dark years and ring in light and the rule of the just, the bright and the righteous.

Urmila felt nervous like a new bride. She had felt the same on the first night she spent with Lakshman after her wedding. She was dressed in royal finery and Saumitra was attired like a prince. She kept her eyes to the floor. In the dancing lights of the lamps, she heard his soft voice, very close to her.

"I have a gift for you, Mila."

She looked up startled.

He began to take off her heavy jewellery. She allowed him to remove them one by one, the slow rhythm of his hand driving her mad with longing. He picked up a silver tray laden with heavy floral wreaths – strung and crafted like many-stranded necklaces, earrings, amulets, bracelets, finger rings, tiara, waistband and anklets. He put them on her, decking her up like a flower girl, a forest nymph.

"Mila, I made these for you at night, when I stayed awake in the forest guarding Ram and Sita," Lakshman whispered. He slowly picked her up in his arms and carried her to the garden outside Moti Bhavan, ablaze with flowers in bloom and earthen lamps. He put her on a swing. "Close your eyes," he ordered softly.

Urmila closed her eyes and opened them, minutes later. She saw herself reflected in the crystal pool near the swing. She was silhouetted in the water, shimmering in a golden sheath of light from the lamps like a celestial being – an exquisite flower girl, an apsara.

"This is beautiful," she stuttered, love flushing her cheeks with a warm rosy hue. The flowers of the forests still held their fragrance. She rested her head on Lakshman's chest. "Mila, you know each time I missed you, I looked at the moon and made these flower wreaths while *bhaiya* and *bhabhi* slept. I know you love wearing flowers," Saumitra smiled.

"Yes, but not more than you, my love," she smiled as she kissed his heart. Lakshman dragged her into the pool to frolic in the water like two nymphs.

Lakshman pulled her closer towards him and sprinkled water on her. He traced the profile of her face with his fingertips. The two lovers remained locked into each other for what seemed like an eternity. The night was as calm as the peace inside both of them; they were finally reunited. Passion flared as the emptiness and longing of the 14 years of separation swamped them in its primal tide.

Ram's Rajya Tilak – Coronation

Boons in divine gift packs; heaven comes to earth to right a wrong.

Ayodhya rejoiced because it was to receive a new master. The brightest scion of Raghukul was being returned his rightful place.

A day before the coronation of Ram, Urmila pointed out that the royal family had sinned against an old woman, who was perhaps not guilty of a crime for which she had been punished. She could have been merely a pawn on the chessboard.

"Before the *Rajya Tilak*, we need to do something that we have forgotten. We have to apologise to Manthara *dadi* and free her from captivity. She was a cog in the gods' plan to rid the earth of demons, she was penalised for a crime that was destined to be perpetrated. She was a mere pawn in Narayan's hands, but she will not accept freedom from the shackles unless Ram and Saumitra fetch her personally from her prison cell," Urmila was firm in her request.

The family was repentant. They went to the little enclosure next to Sumitra's bed-chamber in a posse, where Manthara was chained. Lakshman was mortified at the sight of the bent and wrinkled woman, who was ailing. Manthara wheezed, breathing loudly from her mouth. She was well past 90. He touched her feet, "Forgive me, grandmother, I was a fool not to have understood."

"I am but the culprit, Saumitra, the reason behind your separation and pain. Don't be gentle with me. I do not deserve your kindness and compassion," she shrank back from his touch.

"No, grandmother, if you would not have advised Queen Kaikeyi to redeem her pledge, Aryavarta would not have been free from Raavan's terror and tyranny." Lakshman was grateful that the old maid was astute and devout enough to see into the future – and to understand Narayan's plan. Ram removed the chain from her arms and feet. "Your place is in the palace with us. You have done what was required of you. Let us repent for our sins, now," he persuaded Manthara to go to the palace with them.

After atoning for all the follies and setting right all the wrongs, the *Rajya Sabha* was finally ready for a historic change. The grand hall was decorated in regal finery. The kingdom was ready to anoint Ram as the new king of Ayodhya – and raise the curtain on Ram Rajya.

Ram wanted Lakshman to become the king of Ayodhya but Lakshman refused.

The gods and goddesses from heaven also looked down on Ayodhya in beneficence – putting their seal of approval on the celebrations.

Ram's crown is said to have been especially designed by Lord Vishwakarma, heaven's engineer, who built the shrine of Siya-Ram, Lakshmila, Bharath-Mandvi and Shatrughan-Shrutakeerti.

Urmila oversaw the preparations for the ceremony with Mandvi and Shrutakeerti. The day was significant in many ways, not only for Ram but also for Lakshmila, who were instructed by the queen mothers to wear clothes that had been sent by Lakshman's maternal grandmother, Maharani Bhargavi, Queen Sumitra's mother, from Kashi.

Lakshman's maternal grandmother secretly regretted Queen Sumitra and Lakshman's sacrifice and pain – and her daughter's subservient standing in the late King Dashrath's hierarchy of power and influence in Ayodhya.

An hour before Ram's *Raj Tilak*, the rite, in which the king was to be decorated with the sacred mark of kingship on his brow and the crown – Lakshman was inducted as the commander-in-chief of the army and Urmila was sworn in the chief royal advisor.

"Today, I *Sumitranandan* Lakshman, in the presence of my people and with the blessings of the ancestors of Raghukul, vow to always guide the army. The Raghukul flag will flutter high as long I am alive."

Urmila was given the sacred scrolls of Raghukul, a notebook and a special peacock feather quill meant to write *dharma*. She pledged, "O, great ancestors of Raghukul, I *Janaknandini* and Lakshman *Patni* Urmila vow to always direct my king to *dharma*. I will not let *adharma* breathe in Raghukul, as long as I am alive." As the chief advisor to the king, Urmila was summoned by Shanta to crown Ram as the king of Ayodhya together with clan sage Vashistha and King Janak.

The crown was blessed by six deities from heaven, some of whom came down to earth for the coronation ceremony – Mahadev, Brahmadev, Narad muni, Samudra Dev and Rishi Kashyapa.

An overwhelmed Ram asked every member of his family to seek a boon from him. The first in the order of rank was Urmila. Ram requested her to stand next to Lakshman, but she refused to do so. "Thank you for the honour, dear brother, but how can I be where my husband isn't? Just as he considers it his duty to serve your lotus feet, bless me too to always remain at your feet and serve you just like my Saumitra," she bowed in reverence.

Ram was moved to tears by her humility, reverence and generosity. "Urmila, today, I bow down to you in respect and grant you a place in my heart. You shall always reside in it just like your husband does. O, dear incarnation of the goddess of milk, Goddess Ksheera, also known as Vimala Devi, I bless that you will always remain at my right feet in the form of *ksheera*, which is very dear to me. Whenever my devotees will pray me to, they will be given *ksheera* as the ceremonial offering. In Kali Yug, your shrine will be right in front of the main temple, built by Lord Vishwakarma dedicated to Lord Vishnu, at Jagannath

Puri. You will be worshiped as Vimala Devi or Devi Ksheera. People will invoke you to be blessed with an ideal wife and a daughter-in-law, just like you," he said, touching her head with the open palm of his hand.

Even today, the Vimala Devi Temple in Puri is very famous. The wishing tree next to the Temple is blessed by Lord Shesha and Goddess Ksheera. If a married couple goes round the Temple seven times, Ksheera and Shesha bless them with marital bliss.

Ram granted Mandvi eternal togetherness for all their lifetimes with Bharath. Shrutakreeti sought that the hermit's attire and the *rudraksh* beads worn by Ram, Sita and Lakshman during their exile should be worshipped as 'icons of divinity' in Ayodhya and in Aryavarta. Ram blessed her, consenting.

"I have everything; just allow me to always serve you," Lakshman appealed to Ram.

"Even if I won't allow, I know that you will serve me. O, Lakshman, you are an ideal brother, a brother any man will want. Remember you asked me for a boon in Lanka? I give you a boon that from now whenever I shall incarnate in Aryavarta, you shall take birth as my older brother and I will serve you as you have served me," Ram embraced Lakshman.

Bharath pledged to serve Ram throughout his the life whereas Shatrughan wanted an opportunity to prove his abilities and work for the fraternity's welfare at the cost of his own survival and comfort. Ram granted him both.

The three queen mothers expressed their desire to become grandmothers and live in peace with their grandchildren. Ram happily granted them their boons. The coronation over, the clan gathered for a lavish feast of traditional Raghukul delicacies in Queen Kaushalya's palace.

Life Moves On

Ferment robs the spirit of amity among sisters.

The guilt of maligning Lakshman's character stayed with Sita even after she became the queen of Ayodhya. She knew that it was time she owned up to her sister. Gathering courage, Sita called upon Urmila, "Today, I come here to own up to something I did when we were in exile. I hope you can find it in your heart to forgive me."

Urmila looked questioningly at Sita.

"I maligned your husband's character not once, but twice. I know he has not ever spoken about it to you, but he hurts inside. I have not been able to calm the turmoil inside me and the guilt ever since, I should not have insinuated his covert desire for me when he hesitated to go to the forest to rescue Ram, who was out to trap a magical golden deer for me. The apparition was Raavan's decoy to abduct me. I told him that I was suspicious of his motives." Urmila listened with a wounded expression on her face.

The stories of the forests were as dark as their undercurrents.

That allegation that Sita doubted Lakshman's chastity was too severe for her to bear. "Just as I trust Saumitra completely, I trust you whole-heartedly too. I have always known you to be the wisest, the most serene of us all. If such words have come out of your mouth, I am sure he was not doing his duty, perhaps straying from the path of *dharma*. Don't demean me by apologising." Urmila did not allow her heart to run away with the emotional churning inside her. An accord had to be maintained, at all cost, for the safety and prosperity of Ayodhya. And for Ram to flourish as the king.

"I don't know why I forgot how much Lakshman loves you. I do not know what made me utter those callous words, doubting his integrity. Was it my anger that he left you behind or was it my own impatience with a life of hardship and austerity that made me unfeeling? I was feeling insecure. I know the heavens will not forgive me for hurting someone as righteous as Lakshman. Maybe, that was why I went through the *Agni Pareeksha*."

Sita began another narrative on the back of the one she had just ended – the one of Lakshman's test of virtue by fire after she accused him of cavorting with apsara Kumudh. Urmila broke down in fear and grief at what could have happened and what Saumitra was forced to undergo.

"Agni Dev carried him in his own arms through the fire unscathed," Sita said, recalling Lakshman's *Agni Pareeksha*. The sisters cried together, hugging each other.

"Karma does not take revenge on someone like you. There is no one in the world I will consider more holy in thoughts and actions than you, sister. You were forced to denounce the luxuries of the palace – and you gave them up willingly – to stand by your husband for 14 years. As for Saumitra, he is your younger brother first and then my husband," Sumitra consoled Sita, reassuring that she empathised with Sita's violent reaction to Lakshman's reluctance in leaving her alone in the hut.

"No, Urmila. There is no greater pain than the agony of separation from someone you love as much as life, and yet you bore it silently for him, for us. How can I ever compare my pain to yours? I walked all these years with my husband; you lived for your husband and yet without him in a forced sleep. Sita stands small in front of Urmila's sacrifice," Sita embraced her sister fiercely.

"You make me proud," she said.

The princesses might have been different in their births – one from the earth and another born to the palace, but the bonds of sisterhood and shared parentage went beyond those of the flesh; binding Sita and Urmila in common grief, lament and relief. Sita, the wise daughter of the earth, looked at the Warrior Princess Urmila in wonder, as if seeing her for the first time.

Urmila was extremely angry with Ram for forcing Sita to go through the *Agni Pareeksha*; she recoiled in shame and helplessness at not being present with Sita during that tragic moment when Ram left her in spirit. But she kept quiet about it because she did not want her sister to look back at the trauma of walking through fire to prove her chastity. Sita was as chaste as any loyal and obedient wife in Aryavarta.

The days were no longer the harbinger of sad news to Ayodhya, after a long time. The nights were quiet and peaceful for they witnessed only love and companionship that had been returned to the royal clan; the sisters could not think of threatening the fragile amity – the 'mirage' of peace.

On one such bright and sunny morning, the brothers and their wives sat together in Moti Bhavan to reminisce about the good old days.

They looked at the paintings Urmila had made after Lakshman left. The paintings depicted moments dear to Urmila from her childhood till the day Nidra Devi put her to sleep. Her wedding, Ram lifting the Shiva's bow, mentor Gargi's retreat, Lakshmila's wedding dinner and many more...They marvelled at her extraordinary talent. Lakshman looked at her because he knew the intensity of her feelings behind each painting. He knew that she was recreating him in images while he was away, to keep his memory alive.

Her love enriched his very essence; it was the very breath of his life. He dreaded to think of life without her and knew he did not have the courage to be separated from her again.

At night, Urmila teased him, "Do you also wish to paint?" Lakshman studied the painted images with the concentration of a seer – he wanted to carve every line in his memory.

Lakshman pulled her closer, "If I had to draw a warrior, she'd have your eyes, if I had to sketch a healer, she'd have your hands, if I had to paint a goddess, she'd have your face." He picked up the paint brush, and began to paint Mila.

They spend the night painting each other's portraits in raw splashes of colour and reliving memories. The next day brought movement.

Sumitra's little camp comprising Lakshman, Shatrughan, Urmila and Shrutakeerti prepared to undertake a sacred journey – pilgrimage to their maternal kingdom of Kashi – to fulfil Sumitra's pledge to pray at the Mahadeva temple after Lakshman returned from exile. Sumitra did not want to slip on her promise to Mahadeva, her mascot deity, and her family. They would travel more than 100 miles – for more than a week across the country and the riverine lowlands, for the first time as a family in 14 years.

"I have so many fond memories of Kashi," Lakshman remembered as their chariots entered Kashi. Urmila looked around in amazement at the glorious temples that dotted the city and its bustling lanes. Sumitra insisted that they stop at the Mahadeva temple on the bank of the Ganga first, before going to the palace, her home.

Kashi has always been known as the city of Mahadeva. Maata Gauri and Mahadeva were married in Kashi.

They were welcomed like heroes in the temple and later in the palace – where Sumitra, her sons and their wives spent nostalgic days, filling each other in on their childhoods, memories and bonding with relatives.

After they returned to Ayodhya from Kashi, Urmila was preoccupied. She wanted to become a mother but she did not know how to convince Lakshman about it.

At night, when Lakshman and Urmila retired to Moti Bhavan, Urmila snuggled close to him on the terrace, under the starlit sky; a canopy for the deepest secrets of her heart. "Lord, I want to cradle a prince or a princess like you in my arms, I want to embrace motherhood," Urmila whispered into Lakshman's ears.

Lakshman drew her closer to him, "Very soon Mila, we will plan a child very soon. My only desire in life now is to see you young once, all over again, and live the years I have missed. I wanted to be here so that we could grow up together."

Sleep eluded them that night. They made plans for the future like planting rose-beds in the garden, adding new ones and seeking the fragrances of the blooms that they did not notice in the mist of the last 14 years. They dared to think of a life with children of their own and their Sulochana reborn.

The morning was full of happy tidings. The palace was abuzz with the news of Sita's impending motherhood. The subjects celebrated.

While tending to Sita, Urmila sank into a swoon one day. The maids helped her to a mattress in a corner of Sita's bed-chamber; fanning her and sprinkling cold water on her face. The royal physician rushed to examine Urmila for she was the *dharma* advisor to Ram, the king of Ayodhya – and was an important court official. The physician announced the forthcoming arrival of yet another baby – Lakshman and Urmila's. The sisters broke the news to the queen mothers and to the rest of the women in the palace on the same day.

Urmila was shy to tell Lakshman about her pregnancy. When he entered Moti Bhavan at the end of the day, Urmila hid in the shadows, waiting for Lakshman to seek her out. When he dragged her out from a shadowy corner, she took him to the terrace, smiling slightly, to look at the moon strung like a silver orb in the night sky. She gently took his hand and placed it on her stomach. A curious expression crossed Saumitra's face before the implication of the gesture dawned on him.

"I cannot believe it, Mila. Are you sure?" Saumitra asked in a daze.

"Yes, lord."

He hoisted her high up into the air like a child, exclaiming in joy. Then, he ran to the Shiva temple, holding her hand.

"I wish Maharaj was here to celebrate the beginning of our new generation with Ram and Lakshman's children." Kaushalya remembered Maharaj Dashrath fondly when Lakshman told her that Urmila was expecting a child.

The palace was ready to welcome the next generation. Days later, Mandvi and Shrutakeerti announced their pregnancies as well. The queen mothers called the maids to spread the word in the city with generous gifts of jewels, coins and sweets to the natives of Ayodhya.

A special prayer – the baby shower rite – to celebrate the imminent motherhoods began in the palace in which the mentor of the princesses, Gargi, revealed her power of *Yogmantra*. She predicted that each of the princesses, including Sita, would give birth to twins. Ayodhya would witness the birth of eight children.

Urmila refused to go with Janak to Mithila for the childbirth. She could not bear to be away from Saumitra, even for a day, now. She wanted Lakshman to see the child grow in her. Sita, following in Urmila's footsteps, told her father that she too would stay in Ayodhya. They needed their husbands more than ever – and their husbands had a right to see their children being born.

Sita's Exile

People's writ in Ram Rajya, the king hides in his shell.

The sisters were almost into their sixth month of pregnancy. Each had her own routine. Urmila spent most of her days reading spiritual books and practising the art of using weapons because she wanted her children to be brave.

Lakshman gradually donned the mantle of a caring father as he took up the task of responsible house-holding – to prepare for the arrival of Lakshmila's child. He made a few basic changes in his life; the biggest of which was to put a leash on his anger. He learned to sync his mood with Urmila's swings to take care of her fragile health.

The women rarely moved out of their quarters. Contingents of maids attended to their needs during the day – at night, their husbands comforted them. The royal physician came every week to check their temperatures and monitor the growth of the babies in their wombs. Life flowed at a slow pace. Ayodhya basked in the joy of Raghukul's good fortune.

But tongues did not stop wagging; the grapevine in the palace and the city was full of strange speculation. The women folk, instigated by a section of washermen, wondered if Raavan had not ravaged Sita in Lanka during the 10 months when she was held as a prisoner; hinting that the children might not be Ram's, as Sita was making them out to be. The clan smelt a conspiracy. Ram came to know of the gossip doing the rounds among the working folks and drowned in grief.

His *raj dharma* – duties as a king – clashed with his *patni dharma* – duties to his wife. He could not bear anyone mongering rumours about his virtuous wife, who was about to become a mother; but as a king, he could not ignore his people's fear and doubts. He sank into depression, building walls of pensive silence around himself.

An astute Sita, who was in synergy with Ram's emotional twists, soon found out the reason for his pensive moods and arrived at a decision that in a strange way was also a denouement. She decided that she would go way from Ayodhya and no one would ever know where she was.

She went to Moti Bhavan quietly and revealed her plan to her sister, who was as agitated as Sita with the taint that was being cast on her virtues; she could not believe that anyone could gossip about Sita. She had proved her innocence with an *Agni Pareeksha.*

"I have to leave, Urmi. No one will ever know where I am. I have come to meet you today to request a favour from you. Take care of your brother when I am not around." Urmila was speechless with shock – at the crushing blow of destiny and the terse end to Raghukul's brief tryst with contentment. Her sister could not leave the kingdom when life was just beginning to fall into order.

The Valmiki Ramayana says the reason for Sita's vanvaas during her pregnancy was grounded in a visit to a seer's retreat when they were children, aged around 4 and 8 respectively. While they were playing in the garden, Sita accidentally killed a crane, whose wife was with chicks. The stories vary. The female crane was in her 6th month of pregnancy and hence, it was believed that it was Sita's destiny that she had to be separated from her loved ones just as she had taken away one bird from the other.

"I do not agree with your decision, sister. Running away is not the answer to such fatuous gossip. We will face the rumour-mongers together. Your children have to be born in safety. They deserve a palace, not the harsh life of the forest. I am the chief advisor of Ayodhya, I am the Warrior Princess of Mithila, let me stand up to this injustice. I will not let *adharma* – anarchy – prevail in Ayodhya." Urmila said in anger.

Sita pleaded with Urmila not to do anything rash. She made Urmila promise that she would not ever blame anyone for Sita's exile because it was her own decision. Urmila gave in with reluctance. The palace played host to yet another heart-wrenching drama. Ram called Lakshman in his capacity of the commander-in-chief of the royal army and ordered that he drop Sita 'to a safe retreat in the forest without anyone's knowledge'.

A stunned and distressed Lakshman refused to obey the order. A humiliated Ram tried to ease Lakshman out of his position for defying him. "You will have to leave your post in the army if you dare defy me. I, the king of Raghu kingdom, command to you step down as the commander-in-chief," Ram was cold in his whip. The firmness of his command shook Lakshman.

"Oh, brother, do not disown me. The reason for my birth is to serve you. I prefer dying than staying away from your lotus feet and not obeying you," Lakshman cried in outrage and fear when Ram ordered him to relinquish his army post.

"Then leave your queen in the forest as I command you to," Ram ordered Lakshman once again. Lakshman could not disobey the king's order any longer, and left with Sita right away.

Urmila could not bear to watch her sister go. She held on to Sita until the last moment, "We will always wait for your return even though you claim otherwise. The foreheads of my children will always stay bare without their *Badi Maa's tilak*."

Sita hugged her tightly, "My children may never know of their father but they will always know about their aunts and their cousins."

"Dear husband, leave my sister in the safest area of the forest," Urmila entreated her Lakshman. With tearful eyes, everyone in the palace bid Sita farewell.

Ram did not look at Sita's receding figure while Urmila watched the chariot till it disappeared around the bend. Before leaving Ayodhya, Sita vowed never to return to Ayodhya and in deep anger towards the people, she cursed that the city of Ayodhya would always remain unhappy for the pain she had to undergo.

Sita asked Lakshman to stop near the Valmiki *ashram* because she wanted to continue her journey from that point all alone. She was adamant. She took out an arrow from the quiver and drew a line, "Lakshman, this is Sita *Rekha*. You will not cross this boundary."

"O, dear mother, have a safe journey. I have always considered you my mother. I am bound to obey your order but please let me visit you with my wife sometime, at least for her sake because her condition might worsen." Lakshman felt like a beggar – small and selfish – standing in front of Sita.

"Son, you may come just for Urmi," Sita wept.

Lakshman was distracted on his way back to Ayodhya. He headed straight for Ram's chambers, where the king waited for him anxiously. He was overrun with compassion for his brother. However, protocol prohibited Lakshman from showing his grief, anger and discontent; guilt hounded him like a beast of prey.

Lakshman told Ram that he had done his duty, but was ambiguous about Sita's destination. No one would know, except Lakshman, that Sita was at the Valmiki *ashram*.

In the evening, Lakshman returned to Moti Bhavan; his face darkened in despair. How could he face his Mila? Urmila rushed into Lakshman's arms as he stepped inside, "Lord, I know I will have to be courageous. But I cannot make my heart understand this. It grieves for the loss of my sister – my soul and my lifeline."

Lakshman held her, sobbing like a child. He cried for the crime that the subjects had committed against Sita, Raghukul's fate and Ram's 'heartless' *raj dharma*. "Mila, don't ever forgive me for what I have done. During the *vanvaas*, I left her alone in the hut one day at her insistence and today, I deserted her again. I deserve to be punished."

Urmila allowed him to weep and then wiped his tears. "No, lord, it is not your fault. It is your duty to serve your king. My brother's pain runs deeper than he shows but he did his duty as a king. What happened was so wrong but we cannot be judgemental. We have to listen to the subjects, keep them happy. But how will Ram ever come out of this grief? This is the time to stand by him and help him out of his anguish, so we have to be strong, Saumitra," Urmila tried to fill him with strength. Lakshman could not find any thread of reason in Raghukul's chain of karma. But life had to move on.

When they were eating their evening meal, a servant came running with the news that Ram had collapsed in his palace. Ram lay disconsolate, almost lifeless. How could Ram, who couldn't live without his Sita even for a moment, survive without her?

Ram looked for Sita in Urmila's eyes – to find if her shadow was reflected in them. He looked at her searchingly. His expression was loaded with unspoken queries. He held Urmila's hands and broke down, "I can never be forgiven for the agony I have put Janaki through. Urmila, do you see these walls, this chamber, this Ram?" Urmila shook her head; she refused to drown in Ram's grief.

Ram insisted, "Then why don't I? I see yet I feel nothing. I live yet I am dead. The king Ram lives and Ram, the gentle prince, the husband, is dead. Only I know what I have lost."

Urmila invoked the goddess of destiny to spare them, but maybe Ayodhya was paying for its past karma.

Lakshman stood there watching Ram and Urmila, the two people who meant the world to him. He made a promise to himself to take Urmila to meet Sita after she gave birth, but he chose to remain silent about it. He planned it as a surprise to her.

They put Ram to sleep and tiptoed out of the room. This became a daily routine for Lakshman and Urmila, every sundown. They brought Ram out of his grief with their nurturing care – and consolation. The three sisters – Urmila, Shutakeerti and Mandvi – cried for their lost sibling, and the wanton days of their childhood.

But Ram was adamant and so was Sita. The decision was not one-sided any more. Perhaps that was the way Narayan wanted it. Sita would not ever return to Ayodhya.

The Birth of Angad – Chandraketu

Children breathe life in desolation, Ayodhya hopes

Everyone except Ram gradually learnt to live without Sita. His brothers and their wives tried their best to calm him, especially Urmila, but Ram was always restless, grieving Sita's exile.

An unusual silence sapped the life out of the palace soon after it erupted into a flurry of sounds and revelry to celebrate the imminent arrival of the new prince lings. Nothing good ever happened in Ayodhya and neither lasted long!

In that grey atmosphere of gloom when even the sun seemed to have fizzled out of the sky behind a steely curtain of clouds, Urmila surprised the despairing clan with her strength and resilience. She attended the *Rajya Sabha* every day as the chief advisor to Ram, despite the fact that she was in her last month of pregnancy. She believed that her involvement in the administrative decisions would inculcate a sense of good kingship in her unborn children and help them become able rulers in the future.

One day, a few sages from Madhupuri – a village not far from Ayodhya – came to meet Ram in the *Rajya Sabha* to seek protection against a demon, Lavanasura, the king of Madhupuri (known as Mathura now). He was Raavan's cousin. The seers said the demon had made their lives miserable because he wanted to avenge the death of his brother Raavan, the king of Lanka.

Shatrughan offered to fight the asur king of Madhupuri and sought Ram's permission to go with the seers. Shatrughan, the youngest and the most protected among the siblings, sensed in the siege on Lavanasura an opportunity to prove his strength to his brother Ram and to the people of Ayodhya as a worthy warrior. The family wished him victory.

Ram advised him to use the Narayanastra against Lavanasura. Lakshman told him to visit Valmiki's *ashram* on his way to seek the seer's blessings before going to Madhupuri.

Urmila, who was listening to Ram and Shatrughan intently, blessed the youngest member of the Raghu clan, wishing him good luck. As the chief advisor to the king, Urmila had no power to decide on the wars that the brothers waged against their enemies. Lavanasura was an old and powerful demon and an old enemy and Shatrughan had to defeat him. Moreover, Shatrughan had to carve out space for his family – and descendants – with a kingdom he could call his own.

"I would like to meet the king of Madhupuri when you return. Don't come as a loser but as a victor," she said, with tears in her eyes.

"I will. But take care of yourself, *bhaabi maa* – sister-in-law," Shatrughan assured her.

His mother, Queen Sumitra, promised to take care of his wife, Shrutakeerti. The princess was in tears when Shatrughan went to take leave of her. "I want to cry but I know that my husband is great warrior. I am confident that he will win. And don't you worry about your children in my womb. Nothing will happen to them as long as *bhaiya* is around," Shrutakeerti said. Shatrughan looked at her for a long time and left.

The sage and his followers were celebrating the birth of two beautiful boys in the retreat when Shatrughan arrived at the gate. He was welcomed with affection by Valmiki, who asked him to bless the newborns. They were the children of a retreat dweller, Vandevi. Shatrughan held the twins in his arms without knowing that the infants were his own nephews – Ram's twins – and Vandevi was Sita, the exiled queen of Ayodhya.

Ram and Sita's twins, named Luv and Kush, were born in the month of Shravan, Shukla Purnima – on the full moon. This day is also celebrated as Luv-Kush Jayanti.

Shatrughan won the war against Lavanasura, who was said to be more powerful than Raavan. But the demon king was no match for Shatrughan because he was the incarnation of Sudarshana, one of the most powerful weapons of Vishnu-Narayan. The people of Madhupuri hailed Shatrughan as the regent incumbent of Madhupuri. He returned to Ayodhya victorious but said he wanted to be crowned the king of Madhupuri only after Urmila, Shrutakeerti and Mandvi become mothers.

The royal entourage from Mithila arrived in Ayodhya as Urmila neared her date of labour. They were embarrassed about Sita – her exile weighed heavy on King Janak's heart with anger, guilt and humiliation. The king, however, could not refute the allegations made by the subjects of Ayodhya. *Raj dharma* prohibited defiance of people's wish – and their demands.

Away in the confines of Moti Bhavan, love bloomed deeper between Lakshman and Urmila, who had grown closer during the months of Mila's pregnancy, awaiting impending parenthood. Lakshman understood her better than before, bending to her minutest change of mood. In his head, Lakshman was ready to die with Mila, if fate so commanded.

Exactly 10 days after the birth of Luv-Kush, on the *tithi* – date – of *Shravan Krishna Paksha Navmi*, Urmila suddenly screamed in pain. Searing cramps made her head reel. Lakshman panicked. Tears welled up in his eyes as he watched Mila writhe in agony on the open terrace; he picked her up in his arms and ran to her bed-chamber in the palace, ordering a maid to fetch his mother and a midwife.

"Urmila has gone into labour," the older maids whispered to one another, assigning a younger one the task of informing the queen mothers and the courtiers' wives. The retinue of royal women from Ayodhya and Mithila rushed to the palace, accompanied by queen mothers Sumitra and Kaikeyi. Urmila cried like a demented woman, in pain, struggling with the exertion of giving birth.

Kaikeyi ordered Lakshman to leave the chamber till she gave birth to the babies. "She carries twins; she will experience a long labour," Kaikeyi said to Lakshman, who was swinging between terror and wild happiness. Twins! The revelation shook him to the core; he held on to the wall for support.

"He, who deserted his wife, has been blessed by Narayan," Lakshman's mercurial thoughts overlapped into each other, racing with happiness.

Urmila clutched at his hand. "No, mother, don't send him away, I cannot do without him. I will die if I don't see him. He is the first person I want to see after my children are born." Urmila's eyes scanned Lakshman's face in her semi-conscious haze.

"Stay right here. Don't go anywhere," she commanded Lakshman.

The usually brave Saumitra quaked in fear; a feverish trembling seized his body as he watched the streams of sweat pouring down Mila's flushed face, red with suffused blood and the strain of labour.

"She is our Warrior Princess, don't worry, son, she will win this war as easily as she fights with her emotions, her sword, and the unexpected turns in life. She will give birth to your children," Maharaj Janak reassured Lakshman with a smile.

Lakshman held on to his strength, "I know, father, but I cannot see her in such pain."

After almost an hour of Gargi Vachaknavi's rhythmic chants from the healing Vedas to ward off the pain and the evil spirits, hot and cold compresses on Urmila's feverish brow, continuous fanning by the maids, and her own inhuman efforts at pushing the infants out of her womb and by god's divine benediction from heaven, the first child made an appearance and a few minutes later, the second.

Lakshmila heard the first wail of their twin sons through a mix of tears and joy. Queen mother Sumitra picked up the first infant and placed him in Urmila's arms and Queen Sunaina of Mithila put the younger one in Lakshman's arms.

Sumitra looked at her son while he looked at his children. She was emotionally content, watching Lakshman feel the same as she had felt years ago when he was born. She was ready to leave the world without remorse.

Lakshmila beheld their children and then looked tenderly at each other; their love becoming deeper in that very instant. Their soul connection was the bundle of twin joy in their arms.

Lakshman wanted his newborns to see the light of the world; he sought Mila's permission to take them outside. She assented. Lakshman picked up the swathed bundles of linen and fine silks – smelling lightly of rose water – to show them the grandeur of their lineage. He placed the twins in Ram's arms in the *Rajya Sabha*, where the king had been waiting eagerly with his subjects for news from Urmila and Lakshman.

"Your sons, my older brother," said Lakshman in a low voice, pointing to the infants.

Ram began to cry like a child; the joy of holding his nephews was dimmed by the sorrow of the absence of his wife – and his twin sons, whose births had not been revealed to him.

"Had Janaki been here…" Ram's voice had a wistful note to it.

Lakshman understood his brother's emptiness but he could not do anything about it. A strange warp of destiny and duty enchained the siblings. Ram overcame his trauma and instructed Arya Sumantra to distribute jewels and clothes among the people to celebrate the birth of the royal heirs.

Urmila opened her eyes at sundown after a whole day of sound sleep. Lakshman sat beside her patiently. He looked at her lovingly, "Mila, today you have made me whole, I am grateful to you."

"No lord, I should thank you and the gods for them. They are ours," she cried.

Urmila held the babies close to her chest. An indescribable feeling of happiness filled her whole being. The thrill of holding her newborn was so pure and the joy of motherhood so euphoric she felt tears of joy welling up in her eyes.

The palace came back to life with the newborns despite the tribulations of the last 14 years. Repeated wars had rendered the coffers of Ayodhya depleted, but the king and his brothers went out of their way to keep the subjects and the common people of the kingdom happy – and the household running. The days passed in a whirlwind of activity and the signs of revival were seen in the fields and the farms which were once again lush with harvest and in the gathering pace of trade and commerce.

The family was worried about Mandvi's and Shutakreeti's labour schedule. Exactly after 10 days, Mandvi gave birth to Bharath's sons and then after another 10 days, Shrutakeerti became the mother to Shatrughan's twins. The princes and the princesses missed Sita; she stayed in their minds through the day, and more fiercely at night, when they feared for her safety and shed tears in private.

The naming ceremony of the little heirs of Ayodhya was held with zeal and fervour.

An auspicious day was chosen from the full moon calendar to give the children their names. After an elaborate prayer in the temple and a little *yajna* to invoke the deity of bounty ad prosperity, sage Vashishtha began with Lakshmila's twins. After reading their birth charts, he proclaimed with a smile, "Your sons, combination of Ayodhya and Mithila, will be great scholars and warriors. The elder one, a little on the angry side, just like his father, should be called Angad, whereas the younger one, as charming and innocent as the moon, will be known as Chandraketu."

Shesha and Ksheera completed their circle of love on earth. The heavens smiled. "Angad, Chandraketu!" Everyone hailed the infants, blessing them.

Urmila looked at her younger son with a rush of protective affection. He was a crybaby; the child wailed as soon as his mother left him.

"My Chandra!" Urmila whispered to the smiling baby.

Bharath's thoughtful twins were named Taksh and Pushkal; whereas the youngest and the mischievous-looking heirs of Raghukul, like their father Shatrughan, were named Subahu and Shatrughati.

Ayodhya went on with its life without Sita. The gurgling laughter of the newborn scions echoed in every heart.

Secrets Revealed

Pranks, mischief; everyone is a child again.

The corridors of the royal palace of Ayodhya echoed with the sounds and antics of the six little princes. The little boys twisted everyone around their little fingers, including Ram, who doted on them. It was only Ram, who could make them eat – khichdi – rice porridge – which the toddlers hated.

Lakshmila's twins took after their parents. While Angad was quick to anger just like his father, Chandraketu was soft like his mother. Even though Urmila loved Angad almost as much as she loved Chandraketu; she had a softer nook in her heart for her younger son.

When the princes were seven years old, Lakshman decides it was time to begin their training in the martial arts. After Angad and Chandraketu got into a fight among themselves, Lakshman made a silent note of their aggression and their natural body language of warriors. The boys were destined to fight and rule.

"It is time your mother began your sword-fighting lessons." Lakshman said to them. The boys were shocked to know that their mother would teach them to fight with swords; they stared at their father in curiosity.

"How will mother teach us? Shouldn't you teach us, father?" Angad urged.

"Why will I teach you when you can have the best swordsperson to instruct you in the art of sword combat? She has even defeated me a number of times and don't you know she is the Warrior Princess of Mithila?" Lakshman teased Urmila in the presence of his sons. "And, it is time you return to your passion too. It has been years since you held a sword," Lakshman offered

Urmila the freedom she had been craving for. The overture was spontaneous; Lakshman's natural wish to see Urmila empowered, once again.

"Don't you think it is too soon? The boys are still young and they might hurt each other inadvertently while practising with the sword," Urmila tried to stagger the decision about their sword-fighting lessons. She worried about Chandraketu's safety more than Angad's.

"You were well-versed in sword-fighting at eight. No, they aren't young any more. I think we should begin to inculcate values of kingship and skills in them." Lakshman had made up his mind.

"I am sure *mall* – the wrestler – will agree with me," Lakshman ribbed Chandraketu, who was showing an early flair for *mallya-yuddha* – wrestling.

Angad and Chandraketu had unusual fighting skills. Angad came to be known as the best archer of his times. He is said to have defeated even Ram, who was considered the best in the Treta Yug. Chandraketu grew up to become the best wrestler of his era, defeating Hanuman many times.

The Ayodhya princelings trooped in early in the morning, a day later, to begin their training on a field adjoining the palace. Their *guru*, Urmila, took a headcount before commencing with the lesson – Angad-Chandraketu, Taksh-Pushkal and Subahu-Shatrughati stood in order of their seniority, armed with swords. The daily lessons were made of 'war games' and basic grounding in *dharma*.

Six months later, they were ready to put their lessons to test, but on a condition. The children demanded that Lakshman and Urmila first fight each other before their tests began. The clan cheered. Urmila, however, agreed with reluctance.

The stage was set for the tie – a decorated arena where Lakshman and Urmila were going to link their blades to clash – even if in goodwill. The fight was a return to the days of yore, when they loved each other a little more through their sword fights.

"Warrior Princess of Mithila, I challenge you to win against me in this fight. Can you?" Lakshman challenged her, his eyes dancing with a merry light. He adored the thrill of watching Urmila's fiery disposition unravel in her dancer's gait as she fended off moves by the opponent. She was an elegant fighter; it brought out the romantic and 'wild' in Lakshman.

He tries to inch closer to her and graze her cheeks with his, but Urmila was smarter. The point of her sword immediately touched his neck and she whispered mischievously, "Prince Lakshman, you try and work your way through the fight by enticing me, but it won't help you win. Today, the clash is between our swords."

Lakshman was mesmerised all over again by her fighter's charms. He silently thanked the children for allowing him to watch Urmila in battle gear. After an hour-and-a-half, Urmila won the fight by pinning Lakshman down to the ground with the tip of her sword.

An excited Chandraketu ran to congratulate Urmila while Angad sulked. He was disappointed that his father had not won; Lakshman ruffled his older son's hair with a gentle explanation about the essence of Lakshmila, "Your mother and I are one. Her victory is as mine as my defeat is hers."

Angad looked at Lakshman with a strange expression in his eyes; at once wise and yet distant. He intuited the compartments in love – his father's for his mother and for the children.

The boys filed in to show off their skills; they were nervous to face the crowd of subjects and the clan. Angad, the eldest, emerged from the test unscathed with exemplary performance while the others performed fairly well.

Taksh and Pushkal did not exhibit much affinity to weapons; they were introverts who loved to spend time with musical instruments. Bharath's twins did not get along well with Angad and Chandraketu, who found Taksh and Pushkal callow and boring. Subahu and Shatrughati, on the other hand, idolised their Lakshmila cousins. The princes, despite their disparate natural instincts were bound by a thread – Urmila's commands – which they held as binding. They looked upon her as a symbol of affection, compassion, strength and resilience.

When the boys were ready to fence with the 'Urmi Sword', one of the heaviest and the sharpest swords in the clan's armoury, a tense Urmila broke into a sweat. She clenched her fists when Angad exhibited his skill with it. The child's tremulous smile touched her heart; she wished him well. He came out a winner; the love of a mother can move mountains for a child.

Along with training, Urmila enforced culinary discipline in the royal kitchen in the absence of Sita. Lakshman, indulgent to the point of pampering, allowed the children to gorge on sweetmeats throughout the day, but Urmila insisted on delicately curried vegetables, rice porridge and milk for their balanced nutrition and growth.

At dinner, Angad and Chandraketu made faces when the platters of food were placed on their mats. "We don't want to eat this bland and tasteless food," the boys said, looking at the pale rice porridge and vegetables balefully. The boys were joined in their tantrums by Subahu and Shatrughati.

Lakshman and Shatrughan remembered their childhood while looking at their sons. They did not upbraid the children, tacitly supporting their revolt over the food.

An exasperated Urmila, together with Shutakreeti, warned their husbands not to step into their chambers till they coaxed the children to eat; the boys by this time had marched into the royal kitchen with their platters demanding that fresh and more spicy food be cooked for them.

The cooks, who had been instructed to ignore the naughty princelings, looked the other way. Queen mother Sumitra watched them from a distance with tears in her eyes, remembering Lakshman's and Shatrughan's childhoods. The fathers chased the boys as they ran through the palace in protest against the fare. They were finally stopped in the long passage ways by the panting servitors, and brought them back to the dinner mats to eat. Ram, Lakshman, Bharath and Shatrughan entertained them with stories about their childhood as they ate.

The children of Raghukul were as natural as any other kids.

Meeting with Vandevi – Deity of Forest

Reunion is also a farewell, Raghukul moves to power mode.

Destiny wanted a reunion of the sisters! It played out Lakshman's wish, made years ago, through Angad and Chandraketu.

The nights were warm and blissfully long in Moti Bhavan, heavy with fragrance of the white blooms wafting in from the gardens outlying the palace. The moon was midway up in the sky, surrounded by a black cloak woven with tinsel stars.

Angad and Chandraketu tended to their father's aching muscles after a hard day's work; and then helped their mother Urmila rearrange the clothes closet. The parents were curious about the boys' compassion – their unexpected rush of tender care for their parents. At the inquisitive look from their parents, Angad and Chandraketu put in a soft request, "We will like a gift from you on our birthday, this year. Will you give it to us?"

Chandra implored his mother, "Please, *Maa...*" Before Urmila or Lakshman could reply, Angad followed it up, endearingly, "Please, we want to go for a picnic. This is the only gift we want this year."

Urmila tried to persuade them to go to Mithila to celebrate their birthday in their grandfather's palace, but the boys were firm. They wanted to go somewhere else, somewhere they had never been to. Lakshman remained quiet through the exchange; he was preoccupied with thoughts of his own. At Urmila's exasperated look, he broke into a doting smile, "I think they have a very valid point. We should see new places, Aryavarta is so big. Okay, Angad, Chandraketu...We will go to meet someone special this year, someone you three will love to meet deep inside the forest on the edge of our kingdom."

Urmila looked at him searchingly, probing, but he avoided meeting her gaze. "It's a surprise," he said.

Since their birthday was barely a week away, Lakshman spent the morning preparing for the picnic. The journey would take them four-and-a-half hours from the capital city on a horse-drawn chariot. He informed Ram about the excursion, seeking leave of absence from the court and the barracks for a week — and spread the word in the palace, but only in half-truths so that the destination and the person they were going to meet were not revealed or discovered by the secret network of listeners.

A week later, they left quietly in the evening when the sun was low on the horizon in a chariot commanded by one of Lakshman's faithful and trusted horsemen. The children were excited as the chariot exited the main entrance of the palace and sped across the countryside through the villages the lush fields and the wide river, broken by large sand banks.

They reached the Valmiki *ashram* — the retreat of the seer — after a journey of nearly 50 hours, stopping at various inns in the little settlements and the tiny hamlets, where the subjects lined up on the mud tracks to see the royal party.

Lakshman told the charioteer to stop near the Valmiki *ashram*, away from the gate and directed his family and a small coterie of guards to walk with him barefoot for the rest of the journey. Urmila was suspicious, but kept her mouth shut in fear. Superstitious, she crossed her fingers but refused to let her mind wander.

The boys, who were looking forward to wild adventures on the way, were in an irritable mood by the time they reached the *ashram*. They brooded all the way. "Why here?" They whispered to each other, trailing behind their parents.

Urmila was happy to meet the wise old seer again, her face glowed. She bent to touch the seer's feet; he held her gently and said in a low voice, "My daughter, someone special is waiting to meet you in her hut. She had been waiting for years." He pointed to a thatched dwelling in the farthest corner of the retreat.

Urmila looked at Saumitra for a long time, and then she held the hands of her boys and marched to the hut with brisk strides. She knew who it was!

She stood at the door of the hut which was half ajar, looked inside the shadowy living space, half-lit by the sun from a courtyard behind it. She began to cry. Sita, her sister, her soul mate, was sitting on a mat, weaving bark threads.

Urmila sniffled like a child. Sita turned around at the noise. A look of utter disbelief crossed her face – before crumpling into intense grief and at the same time awash with tears of joy on meeting her sister, her closest kin. Her hands trembled with the emotions that raced in her heart; they ran like concentric strings, each circling into the other and then dissipating. She had no power over her thoughts. The tears threatened to burst into a flood. They hugged each other as if they would not let the other go.

Angad and Chandraketu were dumbfounded. They had never seen their mother as emotionally wracked as this.

"*Maa*, who is she?" The precocious boys were scared for the first time.

Before Urmila could tell them the truth, Sita stopped her, "I am Vandevi, sons. I am your *Maa's* soul sister."

"Our *pranaam, Maa*," they touched her feet.

Sita bent down and hugged Angad and Chandraketu, who barely reached her waist. They heard Lakshman at the door.

"*Maata...*" he cried and fell at her feet.

"God bless you," Sita ran her hand through his hair, tousling it lovingly and picked him up from the ground. Lakshman and Urmila looked around, searching for their nephews.

Lakshmila recognised the twins as soon as they came bounding in; Luv was Ram and the one that resembled Sita, Kush.

Luv and Kush greeted Lakshmila with warmth and respect. They seemed to know their uncle and aunt very well. Urmila looked at her sister in confusion.

"They know about their family and clan?" Sita smiled. She had made it her sole mission in the years of her exile to educate her sons about their lineage and family, except for the identity of their father. The task had been difficult because the children were full of questions about their father, but she feigned grief at his early demise. They stopped asking about him, eventually.

"God bless you, my sons," Lakshmila was overwhelmed.

The cousins bonded immediately over stories that they traded about the lives and the games they played in the forests surrounding the retreat. Luv and Kush took Angad and Chandraketu on a tour of the sprawling *ashram*. Lakshmila were alone with Sita.

"Sita *didi*, I have been quiet because the children were around, but I want an answer. Why didn't you tell them about Ram *bhaiya*? Don't the boys have a right to know who their father is? And why do hide your identity from them. Why do you call yourself Vandevi? Don't you miss us?" Urmila plied Sita with her quiverful of questions, which sounded like more like allegations born of outrage.

Sita calmed Urmila. She was wise in her argument that she had not revealed the identity of their father because she did not want Luv-Kush to resent their father's decision, his compulsions as a king over his role of a father.

"It was the subjects' fault, not *Raghunandan*'s. But they are too young to understand this. They might never forgive him. And as for missing you all, I miss you every moment but I cannot do anything because it has been my destiny at birth to part from all of you. Over the years, I have learnt to live like this, without *Raghunandan*."

Sita was sad and stoic, resigned to her fate.

"Ram *bhaiya*'s torment gnaws at my heart for he does not say anything; he just aches for you every moment. He yearns to know about his children. They are the heirs to the throne of Ayodhya," Urmila cried. Sita looked at her with a mysterious light in her eyes – it was as if Goddess Lakshmi was paying her personal tribute to the generous and expansive Ksheera, the vast resting place of Vishnu-Narayan.

Sita avoided speaking about Ram; she kept her longing for *Raghunandan* under wraps because it was too deep. She inquired about everyone in the family and Urmila filled the gaps in information about each one in detail. She entertained Sita with stories about Bharath's and Shatrughan's offspring, and the little fights among the children in the palace.

Time flew as the sisters caught up with the years that they had missed out on. Lakshman took stock of the state of law and order in the jungle fiefs inhabited by several asura tribes, who troubled the sages, Valmiki's devotees and the students, in the retreat. He spent time with Sita trying to know about her plans for the future, he told her about the kingship, but stopped short of describing Ram's achievements and his life in the palace.

He beseeched her to return but Sita turned away her face. He felt the reticence, the hurt and confusion that shuttered Sita's eyes – and her soul.

"The time is not yet right," Sita did not elaborate.

The farewell at the end of the three-day forest safari – meeting with Vandevi – was tearful. Sita made Angad and Chadraketu promise that they would not talk to anyone about their 'adventure' in the palace or outside.

"Let Vandevi be your secret, Angad and Chandraketu," she laughed at the boys. They understood the undercurrents, but could not completely grasp the implications of the pledge. They were still not old enough to understand the compulsions of Ram Rajya. They stared at Sita for a long searching moment. Sita emptied her head of thoughts so that her sorrow did not reflect in her eyes.

Lakshman and Urmila sought Valmiki's blessings before leaving. Valmiki made a prophecy, "Lakshman, Urmila, take good care. Very soon, you will be blessed with an unusual and extraordinary daughter. She will make you proud as parents and the world will remember her for all the eras to come."

The boys did not know about their connection to Vandevi. They were happy to have found a new set of brothers. They pledged not to speak of the picnic, ever.

The Ram Katha – The Story of Ram

The galloping warhorse finds its true riders.

Ayodhya silently hid the memories of Sita deep within its forest, almost inside its own self. The kingdom knew that Ram searched the nights for clues about Sita, where she was and how she was.

Ram decided to perform the *ashwamedha yajna* – horse sacrifice ritual – when the princes were 12 years old, on Lakshman's advice. Ram wanted to free himself of the guilt of killing Raavan, who was supposed to be a learned Brahman, and establish his imperial might even beyond the boundaries of his kingdom.

But the *yajna* could not be conducted without the queen. The elders in the court – senior ministers, older relatives, the priests and even the queen mothers – advised Ram to remarry because he was still young. Ram spurned their words of conventional wisdom, saying he belonged to Janaki in his heart and body even though he sat alone on the throne like a dutiful king.

After considering every option, including sending secret word to Sita to return to the palace for the ceremony, Ram came to a strange solution. He handed Sita's gold jewellery to a sculptor of repute in the kingdom and commissioned a golden statue of Sita. He was firm in his requirements: the statue had to look exactly like Janaki Sita because it would sit next to him at the *yajna*, shimmering like a golden queen, in place of the real queen.

After the white stallion with black spots was consecrated with holy waters from the Sarayu River on the first day by the king, queen and the priests of Ayodhya, it was set free in a north-easterly direction and was gently prodded to gallop wherever it wanted to, for a year. Shatrughan was assigned the responsibility to follow the horse. The kingdoms through which the horse ran – without being challenged – become part of Ayodhya naturally; else the owner-king of the horse had to fight the rival, who stopped the horse.

A year later, when the horse was on his way back to Ayodhya, Luv and Kush spotted the beautiful mount in the forest and stopped it.

"That is a majestic war horse. We must not let it go," Luv whispered to Kush, watching the horse graze in a meadow not far from Valmiki's *ashram*. An expert in taming wild horses and equestrian war games, the brothers challenged the horse and lassoed it.

Shatrughan tried to reason with the boys, but the youngsters held on to the horse saying they wanted to own it. Reluctantly, Shatrughan picked up his bow and arrow and dared the boys to fight. The youngest prince of Ayodhya, said to be an incarnation of Sudarshana, was trounced by the 12 year olds, who scattered the royal army commanded by Bharath, Sugriva and Hanuman, with their arrows.

When the news that the horse had been stopped by two boys from Valmiki's hermitage reached Ayodhya, Ram was dumbfounded, and worried at the same time. Who were these boys to have the temerity to challenge Ram and the mighty army of Ayodhya?

Finally, he summoned Lakshman and ordered him to take charge of the retreating army. Lakshman was perturbed because he knew who had stopped the horse. But Lakshman was compelled by his *raj dharma* – royal duty – over his karma, as a thinking, feeling and an affectionate human being to lead a bigger army against his nephews.

The 12-year-old Luv and Kush were his own kin and he would be forced to fight his own children for the sake of Ayodhya. What if the two had been Angad and Chandraketu, in place of Luv and Kush? The war had to be fratricidal in nature because Lakshman was accompanied by his son Angad.

Kush charged at Angad from his hiding place, making Lakshman lose his paternal restraint. He was quick to anger because no one was more important to him than his sons. On the other side, Kush hesitated to face Lakshman and Angad, but a war was a war. The boys knew they could meet the king of Ayodhya only if they defeated Lakshman. They forced Lakshman and his sons to retreat in a tactical war.

In the capital, a furious Ram prepared to march against the boys with an even bigger army the next morning. Urmila was disturbed because she did not want Ram to confront his own sons on the battlefield. She sent Chandraketu, her younger son known for unusual ability to resolve conflicts with his wise discourse and trouble-shooting, with Ram to the war against Luv and Kush. She advised Chandraketu to bring peace among the warring boys, their father and uncle.

When Ram and Chandraketu reached the site where the boys were locked in combat with the army of Ayodhya, Chandraketu pleaded with Ram to allow him to meet Luv-Kush, before they took on their enemies in the morning. Arya Sumantra took Chandraketu to meet Luv and Kush in his chariot.

Chandraketu paid tribute to his brave cousins. Bowing his head, he pleaded with Luv and Kush, "Brothers, I, *Urmilanandan* Chandraketu, want to congratulate you on your bravery. I am shaken by the display of your mastery in warfare. The way you have defeated every esteemed warrior in Ayodhya leaves me speechless. Please accept my regards."

"Wise prince of Ayodhya, you are bold and heroic yourself. I am equally impressed by your attributes," Luv returned the compliment gracefully.

"Please consider me your younger brother and allow me to take the liberty of the relationship to find out the reason for your refusal to return the *ashwamedha* horse," Chandraketu was polite in his request.

"The reason is simple, brother. Kush and I have wanted to meet King Ram of Ayodhya for a long time but we couldn't. We consider our king our father because, unfortunately, we do not know our father. We have high regard for him. Then, we came across this horse. We were disappointed that the King Ram we think so highly of is so arrogant that he considers himself supreme enough to force other lands to surrender to him by a mere rite. We wanted to meet him and convey to him our regret," Luv replied with a wisdom that defied his 12 years.

"My grandmother says my *Jaysht Pitaji* – elder father, uncle – is the lord of the universe. And the king, whom you think of as arrogant, is extremely considerate and humble. You paint a wrong image of him in your mind. Moreover, do not consider yourself fatherless as there is someone who longs for his children too. Let me tell you the tale about Raghukul, of my *Jaysht Pitaji* Ram and *Jaysht Maata* – elder mother, aunt – Janaki today," Chandraketu's voice quivered with unshed tears.

Luv and Kush offered an emotional Chandraketu water to console him.

Meanwhile, Ram was becoming impatient and ventured out in search of Chandraketu. Ram feared that he might have been wounded. Ram saw him speaking to two other boys of the same age, away from the battle zone.

Chandraketu ran to Ram, on seeing him, and touched his feet. "Chandraketu, come here and embrace me, my son. Calm my anxiety with your innocent warmth," Ram hugged Chandraketu tightly. Tears flowed from his eyes.

"Is everything well with you, my son?" he asked with concern.

"Do not be concerned because I am well, and unharmed. This young boy Luv has immaculate qualities and I request you to look upon this eminently brave warrior with equally affectionate eyes as me, or perhaps even more." Chandraketu commanded innocently with a flourish of his arm.

At Chandraketu's words, Ram blessed Luv. The boys were curious about the identity of the king and Ram introduced himself to them. They liked him but refused to return the horse. Just before the war cry was sounded, seer Valmiki ran out of his hut with an order for the boys not to fight the king of Ayodhya.

Luv and Kush could not disobey their teacher's orders and returned the horse in dismay. They kept their eyes downcast and refused to look at the king of Ayodhya, his brothers and their cousins. Chandraketu and Ram returned to Ayodhya, victorious, with the horse, to complete the *ashwamedha yajna*.

After the army left the battlefield near sage Valmiki's retreat, the seer, in consultation with Sita, narrated to the boys the tale of their birth, the identity of their father and the reasons why Sita was forced into exile.

The brothers were broken and humiliated.

"We will have to tell the people of Ayodhya the truth about our mother and her worth," they vowed and left the retreat.

After a few days, Luv and Kush were found sitting by the thoroughfare near a shrine with a *dholak (*drum), singing the *Ram Katha* in sweet voices to the beat of the drum. So melodious was their chanting that people flocked to the streetside to hear them.

Word reached the palace and the king invited the boys to the Raj Bhawan to narrate the *Ram Katha.*

Luv-Kush, who were used to the cosy cloister of Valmiki's retreat, missed their mother. Upon seeing Urmila, they ran into her arms.

"Mother, we know the truth," Luv cried. Urmila kissed the boys on their cheeks.

The twins had let the people of Ayodhya know about their mother's sacrifice.

Ram was shaken on learning that Luv and Kush were his sons, who were born in Valmiki's retreat in the forest, but he could not open his heart to them. They reminded him of Sita and he yearned to reunite with her, see her, touch her and live with her happily.

"I will have to fetch Sita to atone for my dilemma and injustice against her," Ram told his brothers and sisters-in-law, confiding about the events that took place 12 years ago. The family was aghast.

He collected his little brood from the palace and journeyed to Valmiki's *ashram* to plead with Sita to return to Ayodhya. Sita was wise in her refusal; she said she could not climb down from her moral ground. She was chaste and she would rather die than allow the people of Ayodhya to see that she had lost the battle of honour – and truth.

"My lord, take only Luv and Kush. I cannot go back," she said. A distraught Ram, humbled and shattered, took the twins back with him.

Sita was free of her earthy chores; she had completed her duty.

She wanted to return to her mother's arms; to the depths of the earth from where King Janak had picked her up as an infant. It was karma. She bade farewell to her family, handed over the responsibility of her sons to Urmila, dredged up courage to take the difficult decision to bury herself alive and basked in the goodwill of the hermitage dwellers, the seers and the pious folks – a day before she prayed to her mother to accept her back into her earthy womb.

She dreamt of the smiling Goddess Bhumija – the deity of plenty and prosperity – holding sheafs of ripe cornstalks in her hand.

"Take care of the boys for me. Urmi, you are the support system and strength of our family. Always remember that it is only you who can tie our family in one single knot and keep it tethered. God bless you, my sister. After I leave for my heavenly abode through *paatal* – the underworld, I know you will add a new member to our family, who will be exactly like your sister Sita," Sita said in her prophetic farewell to her sister.

Urmila was mystified because she could not believe that Sita would not be with her and the rest of the family, a day later.

"Where do you want to go?" She asked Sita.

"To the deepest parts of the earth," Sita replied with an air of mystery. Urmila tried to cajole her out of her decision to return to earth, but Sita was unmoved.

The night was lonely and sad. It watched Ram and Sita together for one last time, listening to each other's silence. It wished that it could stop their separation but was as helpless as it was years ago, when Lakshman and Urmila had separated.

Early in the morning, Sita prayed to Mother Earth to draw her into her depths. The soil cleaved into a deep gorge; brown, wet and dark, revealing the face of *paatal*.

The people, along with the army of Ayodhya, who had arrived in large numbers to Valmiki's retreat, begged her to reunite with Ram and live happily ever after. Sita's eyes were far away; she had already drifted to another world.

Urmila seethed in rage because she could not bear the agony and the emptiness in Ram's eyes, the shock in the eyes of young Luv and Kush – and the grief of the family – watching Sita enter her grave in the chill of the early morning. When the same washerman, who had spread rumours about Sita's chastity during her stay in Lanka, broke down at her feet pleading that she reunite with Ram and not commit suicide by self-burial, Urmila's fury erupted like the lava from the bowels of the earth.

"Aren't you the same man who questioned my sister's purity? Aren't you the same people of Ayodhya who forced them to separate? Aren't you the same people because of whom these innocent children were forced to stay away from their father and family? End this hypocrisy now. Let my sister go. Set her free. She has been disgraced enough. A king is the father of the kingdom and Ram became king at the cost of his own happiness, but you could never become his children. You questioned your mother's purity?" Urmila screamed at the silent audience as Sita stepped into the pit.

She crouched inside the earth like a fetus – as the baby that her father scooped out with his golden shovel. The earth shifted back into position, like two plates from either side, to cover the crevice.

The people of Ayodhya stood with their heads hanging, tears of shame streaming down their cheeks.

Sita's karma, her reason to be born on Aryavarta, was over. She returned to Vaikunth through Paatal Lok. A bit of Ram died too that very moment. But his karma still remained on Aryavarta.

The Birth of Lakshman Putri Somada

A happy fairy weaves magic of the future.

Ayodhya changed after Sita's departure. It felt as barren without her as a child feels without its mother. It often wept at night for her, but stood tall and majestic every morning so that no one could see how remorseful it was at what happened to its queen within its boundaries.

An unpropitious silence hung in the palace through the day. The nights were eerie, haunted by shadows of premonitions – the sounds of Sita's footfalls echoing in the empty corridors of Kanak Bhawan. Ram rarely spoke. He had even forgotten to smile, and had lost the *joie de vivre* – zest for life. It was as if his body was a hollow shell without a soul that had left with Sita. Shatrughan and Shrutakeerti visited Ayodhya often from Madhupuri, which was now Shatrughan's kingdom. The three mothers were forlorn, having given up their desire to live with their grandchildren happily in their twilight years. They merely wanted to see the younger generation safe.

The children, perhaps, were most graceful in their acceptance of fate. They welcomed Luv and Kush as their older cousins and spent most of the day practising arts of warfare, learning the basics of *dharma*, playing in the lush gardens and exploring the city. In the midst of these changes, Lakshmila had fragmented into Lakshman and Urmila somewhere along the way.

Urmila could not forgive the subjects – for allowing Sita to consign herself to her grave, but pretended to be strong as she plodded through her day's work. She cried behind closed doors, without letting Lakshman know. The humiliation was deep – desecrating the pride which Mithila had in its princesses. Urmila was ashamed to face the court, at times. She felt demeaned in the eyes of the people and she often suffered from a strange paranoia that unseen eyes were monitoring all her moves, assessing her conduct and measuring her virtues. She worried about Shutakreeti and Mandvi constantly.

She became a mother to Luv and Kush. Mandvi's and Shutakreeti's twins called her '*badi maa*' – older mother. Urmila took on the mantle of the 'palace mother', drifting slowly into the role of caregiver for the children, responsible for their upbringing.

Lakshman stuck to Ram, trailing him like a shadow. He did not ever let Ram out of his sight because he was concerned about his older brother's health and sanity, for the king of Ayodhya was often on the brink of breakdown; crying, nervous and delirious in private. In the court, Ram was impassive as though set in stone.

The distance between Urmila and Lakshman grew. Urmila began to spend almost all her time with the children, tending to their needs, playing, eating and sleeping with them, especially with Luv and Kush. She did not notice Saumitra waiting for her till late in the night day after day.

Lakshman misunderstood her indifference, thinking she had not forgiven him for Sita's 'self-sacrifice'. He was scared that she would leave him and return to Mithila to live with her father and mother. Uncertain, he gradually turned his back on her. Lakshman and Urmila were so caught up with their emotional turmoils and conflicts that Angad and Chandraketu began to feel insecure. They tried to bring their parents back, but they came across two people, who loved each other desperately, but could not express it anymore.

They missed the old laughter, banter and the togetherness – and ended up groping in the empty spaces for the old familial connections. They could sense their mother's selflessness, but could not break through the cordon that she had thrown around herself. They saw the sadness in her eyes and realised how patient their father had been but they were too young to mend the cracks in the Lakshmila romance.

Luv and Kush consoled their younger brothers. It was futile because the family was slowly breaking apart and there was little the boys could do about it. They fell asleep with tears in their eyes.

Urmila happened to hear the conversation between Angad, Chandraketu, Luv and Kush. Their innocent exchanges about Lakshman's and Urmila's indifference towards each other broke her heart, how could she not feel her Saumitra's pain? She had been so callous that the very man, who was life itself to her, was the one who was now farthest from her life. Urmila wallowed in remorse, cursing herself, as the realisation hit her that she was bringing the illustrious Raghukul down on its knees by her emotional meanderings.

She went to the boys' bedroom quietly and kissed the sleeping children on the foreheads. She wiped the tears from their cheeks, whispering, "I am so sorry for hurting you, my children, and also perhaps your father. You will have your wish granted. Your parents will be as they were."

She swallowed the lump that hurt like sore tonsils in her throat: the combined grief of losing Sita, her sister, and her distancing from Lakshman. Exactly a month later, she took her first tentative steps to go to Moti Bhavan after a long hiatus, both physically and mentally.

Sensing her arrival in the bed-chamber, Lakshman turned around. He looked gaunt and thin; the circles under his sparkling eyes stretching like dark pools of agony. The colour had drained off his hearty face. She winced at the familiar ache in her heart and she ran into his arms, clinging to each other like two children. They said nothing. The silence enveloped Lakshmila like a feathery quilt, drawing them into its warmth. It was heavy with the sounds of unspoken words and emotions.

The days apart felt like an eternity in the salt of their tears as they kissed, softly at first and then with a fierce hunger to feel, to believe and to hold on to what was left – that Lakshmila had not ever parted. A conversation was long overdue.

"Forgive me, Saumitra. In my anger, I hurt you much. I have not ever blamed you for her suffering but I could not – and still cannot – get over her passing away into another world. She did not have to die that way. Somewhere, sometime, I began to walk alone leaving you behind," she shivered as the words poured out of her mouth like a garbled waterfall.

"No, Mila, it was my mistake that I left Sita there," Lakshman did not forgive himself.

"No, neither were you to be blamed nor was it Ram's fault. It was my sister's destiny. I am finally at peace with myself. She had to go, she had completed her earthly duty," Urmila said, looking back at Sita's sacrifice and the events that led to it.

"But, Saumitra, we did not realise that Angad and Chandraketu have been suffering more than us for the last one month. I saw them cry today and heard their conversation with Luv and Kush. I felt broken," Urmila said, narrating to Lakshman all that she had heard and seen. Lakshman was silent.

"The children are growing up. But do not worry for they are maturing beautifully. We will have to take care of their feelings from now on more than our own. As for Sita, well, she was a pious soul who wished everyone happiness, most for her sister, Urmi. Let us try to see her presence in Luv and Kush," the father in Lakshman peeped from behind the facade of the hard-boiled army commander and the brash young man.

"Before Sita left she had hinted that we could become parents again and this time to a beautiful princess." Urmila was suddenly shy, Lakshman held her, "Very soon, my love, sooner than you think." The mischievous light flared in his eyes for a moment. They still found solace in each other's arms.

The next day, Lakshmila walked in together to the nursery to wake up their children. The boys were in the seventh heaven to see their parents smiling down on them in the early morning light. They sat together on the bed, speaking about the little things that delighted them – from the day's meals to the games that they were going to play. Chandraketu, the more intuitive and delicate of the two boys, kept looking at his mother and then slowly whispered into her ears, "*Maa*, you are going to gift me a sister?"

Urmila looked at him in stunned silence. Now, where had this knowledge come from? She wondered in utter terror, for a second. Were the boys so big, so grown up?

"Now that you both are not so angry with each other, please bring us a sister from somewhere. Can you?" Angad reinforced what Chandra said. And Lakshman and Urmila smiled, looking at each other with a secret message in their hearts from above the heads of their children.

Urmila learned about her pregnancy after two months. The family was jubilant on receiving the news; the queen mothers called it the 'rain after a long drought'. Urmila became the centre of everyone's attention and affection; the sounds of celebration resounded in the empty corridors, again.

Ayodhya felt cheerful again. After a long time, the kingdom wanted to dance in joy for it knew what the world did not. Urmila had conceived. Soon, another familiar soul would descend on Aryavarta!

Urmila was well into her seventh month of pregnancy when Ram exhorted her to go to Mithila for the childbirth. "I think you should allow your father and mother to pamper their daughter – you – and the newborn. They were completely broken after Sita left us. They will be happy if you stay with them for a while. Your responsibility is not only towards your husband and his family, but also to your parents."

Urmila looked at her older brother-in-law through a shower of tears, unshed. She was in a dilemma because she did not want to leave Ayodhya.

"And do not worry about the boys. We will manage. If you want, take Angad and Chandraketu with you. I will send the news of your arrival to your father Janak."

Urmila had not ever said no to Ram. She left for Mithila in a week without the children. A lonely Lakshman spent most of his time with his mother in Urmila's absence – and checking on the boys in the evening when they returned home from the day's routine of study, training and games. His mother's feeble health saddened him. He knew that she had to depart from this world someday and the thought troubled him. The thought of life without his mother transported him back to his childhood, when he had felt lost without his mother. He put his head in Sumitra's lap; crying for all that she had borne for him over the years.

A secret lament like an insidious tongue of fire licked his heart; he could not offer Queen Sumitra the glory of being a *Raj Maata*.

In Mithila, the days were like a trance – cold and fragrant from the wilderness of herbs growing around the palace, lulling Urmila to sleep now and then. One day, she received a missive from Saumitra that read:

My dear Mila,

Days without you mock me, and nights laugh at my restlessness. Need I say, I miss you terribly and wait for you and my little princess to be back soon? Your little boys are doing just fine. They are to come to Mithila soon. They fill my empty days with laughter that sounds just like yours. Everyone here is doing fine. Shatrughan and Shrutakeerti are visiting Ayodhya. *Maa* misses you and sends you her love and *kshaakh ke laddu*s. This is our last separation. Now, no more can I bear to be away from you.
Always yours,
Saumitra

Urmila read and reread the letter several times in a day. And opened the basket of sweetmeats to tuck one into her mouth in secret, everyday.

His words touched her like his physical self. It was in her last month of pregnancy that her sons came to Mithila to stay with her to welcome the new addition to the family.

On the day of *Magha Shukla Ashtami* – the eighth day of the full moon in the Hindu month of *Magha* – Urmila gave birth to a beautiful daughter. "Your daughter is not a normal human being, Urmila. She is a Gandharvi," *Maata* Gargi pronounced as she placed the newborn in Urmila's arms.

Gandharvi was a celestial woman. Since Somada was a rebirth of Sulochana she was extremely beautiful.

Lakshman was by Urmila's side as usual, even in Mithila. Urmila looked at Lakshman as he held the newborn. Lakshman felt the sting of tears in his eyes as he gazed at the serene face of his daughter. His thoughts went back to his meeting with Sulochana; she was finally here. He held her tenderly feeling the same warmth, the same rush of protectiveness and love. The daughter from his previous lifetime was back.

Both Angad and Chandraketu held their little sister too. They caressed her soft cheeks and marvelled at how tiny she was, "She is so small!"

The birth of Lakshmila's little princess was the harbinger of happiness. The royal family of Ayodhya gathered at Mithila to fete the infant, and Lakshman named the princess in a pious ceremony. "She is no less than a slice of the moon, and hence, the world will know her as Lakshman *Putri* Somada!" He hugged the child close to his chest.

Lakshman's world felt complete. It was for the first time in years that he felt there was nothing more he wanted from life or from Narayan.

Grown-Up Princes

Old order fades, paving the way for new one.

Life at Ayodhya which had settled to a peaceful routine was restive that day. The city was once again racked by the same anxious nervousness on the day it had felt years ago when the four princes of Ayodhya had to return home from the Gurukul.

After Somada's birth Lakshman established a new kingdom, Lakhanpur, at a distance of nearly 135 kilometres from Ayodhya. He travelled back and forth between Ayodhya and Lakhanpur with his wife Urmila. They managed both the kingdoms with extreme diligence and discipline.

Lakshman watched his daughter grow into a magical little girl, who charmed all those she touched. The family doted on her, especially Angad and Chandraketu for whom life without Somada was unimaginable. But soon, the young princes prepared to leave Ayodhya for the *Gurukul* to receive formal education. With a heavy but a hopeful heart, the mothers and the grandmothers bid farewell to the boys.

Ayodhya was at leisure to enjoy the elfin games of Somada for this was the first time after Shanta that Raghukul had a princess.

The years flew by like the wind.

The city was dressed in colours of all shades to welcome the princes back from their *Gurukul*. Strings of yellow and white flowers hung at the entrance gates and festoons decorated the temple spires and the palace roofs. Flaming torches lit the streets.

Somada ran around the palace, beseeching her uncles and father to take her to the main gate of the city to welcome her brothers home the next morning. Raghukul, which had held aloft its ancient conservatism like a standard – the chief among them of not allowing women to go to the city gates with the men – broke its rule to allow Somada to accompany Ram, Lakshman, Bharath and Shatrughan outside the palace to the city.

Ram gave in to her whim only to see her smile, and earning for Somada the title – *Rule breaker of Raghukul* – from Gurudev Vashishtha. Chandraketu scooped little Somada up in his arms.

Urmila burst into tears at the sight of the eight strapping princes. She watched Luv and Kush bend down to touch her feet, the tribute reminding her of the days when Sita enveloped her in her arms whenever Urmila was distraught. How much like her sister Kush looked! The ache of Sita's absence was like a physical pain in Urmila's heart. Luv was the younger version of Ram.

Taksh and Pushkal had nothing of their mother in them; they were as sincere as Bharath. Subahu and Shatrughati had grown tall, and manly. A rush of maternal affection warmed her soul as she stared at them. They winked at her with mischievous twinkles in their eyes, Urmila laughed spontaneously. The boys were so like Shatrughan; full of laughter and mischief.

Lastly, she set her eyes on her own boys. Angad, who resembled her Saumitra, was perhaps the most handsome among them. He bore his father's smile and wide-eyed innocence. She looked at Chandraketu for a long time, who returned her look as if reading her expression as always. *He was still as loving and selfless as ever*, she thought.

Lakshman hugged his sons tightly. They made him proud.

Angad was the great archer, and Chandraketu, an accomplished wrestler. He couldn't have been more content knowing that both of them were assets on the battlefield.

At the end of the day, Angad and Chandraketu sought a quiet moment with their mother for they had not heard her wonderful and exciting stories for years. The boys wanted to relive their childhood. The evening was spent celebrating, first in the court and then in the palaces. As the darkness deepened, Lakshmila quietly spirited their children away from the rest of the clan to the privacy of their terrace in Moti Bhavan. The moon showed her bright white face from behind a curtain of summer clouds.

Angad and Chandraketu put their heads on their mother's lap while Somada lolled in her father's arms. The family sat on a feather rug under the pale light of the moon, which played hide and seek with the silver-rimmed clouds. Lakshmila spent the night, awake, laughing with their children, listening to their stories about the *Gurukul* and filling them in with anecdotes about life in the palace, when the boys were not around.

They fell asleep only when the dawn sneaked in from the eastern horizon and a light breeze ruffled the flowers in the blooming garden, below the terrace. The first rays of the sun smiled at them letting the quintet dream well into a sunny day.

The family woke up around mid-day.

Life rolled on in the silos of family traditions – daily chores, house-holding, prayers, rites and the duties of the *Rajya Sabha*.

Now that the boys were in the prime of their youth, Lakshmila began to hunt for suitable brides for them. They had to handle responsibilities of the state and house-holding. Like their forebears, the princes vowed to remain one-woman men.

Soon, the eldest of the princelings, Luv, married Sumati, the princess of Angadesh, and Kush married Lord Shesha's younger brother Takshaka's daughter, Kumudhwati. Love and gratitude shone in Ram's eyes as he looked at his sons on their wedding day. Not even once during these years had there been a moment when he had not sought her presence next to him or ached inside with longing. Janaki would have been so proud today of her sons.

Had it not been for Urmila, they would have grown up yearning for their mother's love; an emptiness hounding their souls.

Urmila had been the cementing force in keeping the illustrious Raghukul together.

Lakshmila stepped into their role of in-laws with grace because they had been preparing for this phase in life for a long time. Urmila remembered her promise to Chandrarashi and Malvika, her best friends from childhood and she invited them to the wedding of Kush.

She played the match-maker by making Angad and Chandraketu meet Padmini and Chandrika, her friends' daughters, whom she wanted to bring to Raghukul as her daughters-in-law. The plan worked!

Urmila's well-crafted 'accidental' meetings which put the boys in the frequent company of the princesses prompted Angad and Chandraketu to fall in love with the daughters of her mother's friends. Their wedding took place at Kalinga, Padmini and Chandrika's native turf. Lakshmila completed their circuit of happiness – bridging the generations with weddings and spreading their wings with new alliances across Aryavarta.

Taksh and Pushkal married Kalika and Chanchala, and Subahu and Shatrughati, Menaka and Kamala. The clan was flush with hope – with the hint of new beginnings and warm bondings. The youth took away the torment of twilight, the old and the frayed were regenerated by novelty.

A few years later, Padmini and Chandrika gave birth to Lakshmila's grandchildren, Kamakshi, Ashwath, Chandrakanta and Dharmaketu. Angad and Chandraketu were crowned the kings of Angadaya and Chandrakanta near Mithila, to take care of their mother's kingdom, which Urmila inherited in natural order from her father Janak.

Ram, on the other hand, divided Ayodhya into two parts. He made Luv the ruler of the northern terrain, Shravasthi and Kush, of the south, Kushravati.

Bharath's sons Taksh and Pushkal were crowned the kings of Takshshila and Pushkalavati, near Kekeya.

Taksh, a scholar, was later known to have established the well-known Takshshila University.

Shatrughan made his elder son Subahu, the king of Madhupuri and his younger son Shatrughati, the ruler of the kingdom of Vidhisha, previously Shankasya, which became his inheritance after King Kushadhwaja passed away.

The maharanis were old and frail now. One by one, the clan bid goodbye to the three queens who died of old age.

Lakshman and Urmila sat on vigil throughout the night, a day after the death of Maharani Sumitra, looking back at what she had bequeathed to them and what they had lost. She was a mother to Lakshmila, their pillar of strength since childhood.

An era came to an end in Aryavarta. The older orders in Ayodhya and Mithila – two of the most illustrious kingdoms of ancient India – passed away to make way for the new ones. The deaths of Queen Sunaina first, and then of King Janak, drew the curtain to a close. Lakshman, the son of Mithila, performed Queen Sunaina's last rites.

Some scriptures say that Maharaj Janak was alive during the Mahabharat war whereas some scriptures like Garuda Purana say that he passed away the day he heard about his wife's demise. But Maharaj Janak wasn't a Chiranjeevi – immortal – hence, it would not be right to say that he was alive during the Mahabharat. There is no mention about Maharaj Janak's death in the Valmiki Ramayana and the Kamban Ramayana.

Time began to rewind itself. What comes always goes and that is what Ayodhya learnt through the painful goodbyes.

Lakshmila Breathe Their Last

Nearly 11,000 *treta* years after the consecration of Sita to *bhumi* – earth – the golden Goddess Lakshmi visited Lakshman and Urmila one night, in their dream.

"O, dear Shesha and older sister Ksheera, it is time for you two to come back to Vaikunth. The place seems empty without the two of you. It has been decided that you both will depart from this earth together. Ksheera, since you are the support system of Vaikunth, you will walk into the Sarayu River before Shesha, who will follow in your footsteps. Lord Narayan shall follow you both, soon after. The time to return home has come," Lakshmi prophesied, smiling.

The heavens were appeased.

The next morning, Lakshmila was sad because they knew the time for them to leave Aryavarta was near. They decided to spend their last days with their children; they had no regrets about their years on earth because they had led a rich life, barring the 14 years of exile, when they were separated from one another.

Urmila called her children from Angadaya and Chadrakanta to Ayodhya on the pretext that she was feeling nostalgic and lonely in her old age, and she longed to meet her sons and their families. She was worried about their well-being. Angad and Chandraketu arrived within a week, filling the palace with their raucous chatter and laughter.

Urmila fed them *ksheer* with her own hands and sang the same lullaby that she used to sing when they were toddlers. Somada did not move from her father's side for she had a foreboding of a tragedy that was waiting to strike.

Perhaps, she knew that Lakshmila would not be around much longer as she snuggled close to her old father at night, demanding that he tell her stories. Lakshman began his story – softly – about a day when the gods went to Vishnu-Narayan's abode, in Vaikunth, to find a way to purge the earth of demons with his help.

Halfway through the story, Somada fell asleep.

The city of Ayodhya had aged, along with the palace and its inhabitants. The old stones had gathered layers of green and black moss, the terracotta had greyed with time, the woods flaked off in rotting patches and the marbles were chipped. Time was tolling the curfew hour in the city.

Since morning, the sun refused to show through the blanket of clouds. A mist, unusual for the time of the year, overran the city in wispy patches of smoke after a light rain. The kingdom shivered with a sudden chill. Maha Kaal – the keeper of time, strode into Ayodhya dressed as a holy man with dreadlocks – tall, muscular and stately, clad in robes of saffron and red, to seek a private audience with Ram.

He was stopped by the guards at the gate of the palace. Kaal called out to Lakshman for help, who took him to the *Rajya Sabha* to meet Ram. At the entrance of the *Rajya Sabha*, Kaal told Lakshman that he wanted to speak to Ram alone. Lakshman was hurt but he kept quiet.

Kaal made Ram promise that anyone who interrupted their conversation would be killed.

Ram ordered Lakshman to guard the door. Lakshman had a faint idea of what was about to happen but he did not move from the door. Kaal spelt the end of *karmic* cycles.

Inside the court, Maha Kaal assumed his real avatara of a fierce god and asked Ram to return to Vaikunth. Ram could not dissent because time was the king, the final arbiter of human destiny. He sought Kaal's counsel on how he should return to Vaikunth, when sage Durvasa arrived at the court to meet Ram. Lakshman, who was guarding the entrance, forced the aggressive sage to wait for a while saying that Ram was in a private audience with Kaal and he was under an oath not to interrupt the two. Durvasa, in a fit of rage, lost his cool and cursed that Ayodhya would be burnt to ashes for his humiliation.

A terrified Lakshman had no choice. He was ready to sacrifice his own life to save Ayodhya. He entered the court to inform Ram about Maharishi Durvasa's arrival and his angry curse.

Ram, tied to his vow that he made to Maha Kaal, had no alternative but to kill Lakshman.

"But this will bring a further curse of fratricide on Ayodhya. The curse will visit our children who might kill each other in battle," Ram said in fear. Suppose, the boys butchered each other to grab more land and expand their kingdoms. He saw them lying in pools of blood in a sudden vision – and trembled.

And, how could Ram allow his own brother to die? He summoned an urgent meeting of his courtiers in the *Rajya Sabha*, in the presence of all his children and grandchildren. Urmila was furious at the thought of Kaal trying to harm Saumitra; she could not allow the crafty wheel of time to touch Saumitra with its murderous fingers.

Urmila ran to the *Rajya Sabha* in a frenzy of rage and shouted, forgetting her regal restraint, "O, king of Ayodhya, before you pronounce capital punishment for my Saumitra, I, *Janaknandini* Urmila, Lakshman *Patni* Urmila, Raghukul's daughter-in-law, disown this clan. I vow to leave Ayodhya forever – and end my life with that of my husband's."

Ram looked at Urmila, helplessly, feeling as powerless as the moment when Sita courted death by burying herself alive. How could he make them understand that as a brother he loved Lakshman the most, but as a king he could not retract his pledge – or renege on his *dharma*. His *dharma* as a king came first.

"I cannot award my own brother capital punishment. I disown him as of now. He has to leave Ayodhya instantly." The catch in his voice gave away the agony of his verdict.

"I lose today again to you, rules of Raghukul. One day, you took away my heart and today you take away my soul," Ram lamented like a demented man, beating his chest, flailing against destiny and time.

Lakshman, as always, obeyed his brother without a word. "I have to go," he declared in a quiet voice.

The family bid a tearful farewell to Lakshman and Urmila. Their three children, Angad, Chandraketu and Somada, hung on to their parents' hands; they could not believe that Lakshmila had to go.

Ram blamed himself and his children pointed fingers at him. "You are weak as a human being, father. You could not defy time. Kaal proved to be mightier then you. What a shame...the great scion of Raghukul, born to the dynasty of Iskhvaku," Luv and Kush lashed out together. Hate shone from their eyes, they exhaled rushes of hot air.

The children had always seen their parents stand selflessly for dharma and for what was right and just. Even this day, the family was somehow trying to come to terms with the fact that Ram, for whom Lakshman was his life, was giving up his brother because as a king he had pledged to do so.

What the world didn't understand was that Lakshman was an incarnation of Lord Shesha. In Hindu mythology, Lord Shesha holds the world on his 1,000 hoods irrespective of the pain he endures. How could Lakshman be anything but selfless and sacrificing?

Shatrughan and Bharath, Mandvi and Shrutakeerti watched their childhood walk away for ever with Lakshman and Urmila's departure. They could not save the two, they were helpless.

Ram did not have the courage to face his brothers. He locked himself in his palace and refused official audiences. He even stopped going to the royal court. Every member of the family, from the oldest to the youngest, broke down when it was time for Lakshman to go.

A helpless anger raged in his soul against fate – and a deep grieving hurt against his brothers. He could not walk out of Ayodhya without taking formal leave of Ram. He kept glancing at Kanak Bhavan, hoping that Ram would come out, but the king had shut himself in darkness. The wickers had been snuffed out and an inky shadow drowned the interiors of the usually-glittering Kanak Bhavan – the palace of gold.

The brother who he had served all his life with unflinching loyalty was the 'brother' who did not stand by him at a time when he was courting death to keep his honour. A flashback of the day when he left the palace for 14 years with Ram and his late *Maata* Sita crossed his mind like a scene from an old painting. He had not dithered then, and neither would he hesitate now. Death was passé to Kshatriya kings!

The people of Ayodhya refused to understand Ram's helplessness and blocked the entry points to the city to hold back Lakshmila. They refused to disperse from the main gate.

The ire of the *praja* against Ram broke bounds, threatening to erupt into a revolt. Angad, Chandraketu and Somada stood up for Ram and begged the people to let their parents go to their self-imposed exile and death, in peace and silence. The people of the city placed their hands – with their palms open – on the ground like a human carpet for Lakshmila to walk during their last journey out of Ayodhya.

Urmila, who had been silent all the while, turned around to look at her children for a long time, imprinting their faces in her heart. They ran to her one last time. Somada pleaded that she accompany them, but Urmila gently reminded her of her responsibilities in the palace, "When the time is right, we will call you where we go. For now, stay here. And, do not worry about your father, I have always been there with him, and I shall always be. He and I are never alone with each other." Somada wailed like a child.

The people of Ayodhya followed Lakshmila in single file as they walked over the human carpet to the bank of River Sarayu, which waited for the two in full spate. The waters were placid, somber and crystal clear – blue along the edges and grey-black mid-river where the fathoms plumbed unknown depths.

Kneeling, they prayed on the bank, looking up to the heavens to give them courage.

Lakshmila waded slowly through the blue shallows till they reached mid-river. The waters that lapped at their ankles at the bank, were now chest deep. They looked back at the crowds milling on the banks, the thousands of people who stood with their hands joined in oblation.

Lakshmila lowered themselves, head-down, into the depths of the current. It pulled them in. Somada watched their *jal samadhi* – immersion – from a great distance. Her world spun for a second and then drowned in tears.

She slumped to the ground in distress, when suddenly Lord Shesha and Goddess Ksheera appeared to her in her daze. "O, dear daughter, you are Sulochana, our own daughter. You will live on this earth for some more days and then we will come back to take you along with us."

"I shall wait for both of you to fetch me," she folded her hands in a *pranaam*. They blessed her, laughed and disappeared. Lakshmila's soul left for Vaikunth through Sarayu.

In the dark and cold palace, Ram's world crashed. He felt the fleeting swirl of water around him at that very moment when the current pulled Lakshmila into its depths. Life was meaningless without Lakshman and Urmila, two people he had trusted more than his own self, at times.

He decided to end his life the very same day and in the very same way by immersing himself in the River Sarayu, right where Lakshmila had entered its deep waters.

Ayodhya spilled on the banks of the river as Ram folded his hands in a *namaskara* to the setting sun, before drowning himself.

Bharath, Shatrughan, Mandvi and Shrutakeerti followed in Ram's footsteps the next morning. Every single person who took part in Narayan's plot to save the earth left with them. Sarayu welcomed Dashrath's children and their wives with open arms.

Hanuman was put in charge of safekeeping the children and singing the glories of Ram till the end of the Kali Yuga.

There are two Sharad Purnimas in the Hindu calendar. One is the day Lakshmila ended their lives and the other is the day when Ram ended his life; barely 8 hours separate the two dates.

According to the Valmiki Ramayana, every citizen of Ayodhya including the animals left the kingdom with Ram, except their children.

The people of Aryavarta could not speak of anything else, but recanted the lores of Lakshmila's love for centuries. A love as intense and majestic as Lakshmila's was hard to find in the epochs.

Epilogue
Somada's Letter

Every evening, a lissom Somada, pale and beautiful with her flowing black tresses and big doe eyes, sat at the Lakshman Ghat – the stretch of the Sarayu bank where Lakshmila had prayed before the river took them home to Vaikunth.

It took her closer to her parents and held her warm in their memories as she cried for them.

Somada picked out the quill from a quiver of inky dye that she carried with her, along with the roll of parchments, to write letters to her parents. Tonight, Lakshman Ghat was pensive. Maybe it was her sadness that echoed in the silence of the night or the spirit of Lakshmila that haunted the lonely arc of land.

And she began to write.

Maa, Pitaji,

Today, yet again, I am missing you both. But then there is not a moment when I don't miss you or think of you. You were not only my parents, but also my mentors, my gurus. You taught me how to live even under the most difficult circumstances and, however empty my life feels without you, my heart glows with the memories of your love. You reside in my heart and will always be there. Do you know that I often look back on your love for each other as my strength whenever my love for my *Natha* wavers? I want to remember you, us and our life together on this earth in my last days. I want to write my story and I want you to become a part of every moment I share with this world. I stand humbly before you today and thank you for bringing me to this beautiful world, and letting me feel all that I have felt and have been feeling through these years.

Forever yours,
Lakshman Putri Somada

Thus began her long narrative in epistles.

Vaikunth looked down on the beautiful girl sitting alone along the Sarayu with benediction and sadness. She had to live out her span till her time came...

Acknowledgements

The night of 13 November 2018 changed my life. Narayan came to me and made me realise that I am none other than my *Maa-Pitaji*'s i.e. Lakshman *ji* and Urmila *maa*'s daughter and gave me the task to make the world realise their importance of being an obedient daughter to my godparents.

And on Thursday, the day of Narayan, 15 November 2018, I began my journey as my *Maa-Pitaji*'s daughter.

I would not have been able to depict the true emotions of Lakshman *ji* and Urmila *maa* without the presence of Narayan and Lakshmila themselves. Every night I sat down to meditate, they both came to me and narrated what happened to them, how they dealt with it.

Dear You, *you* are the Laksh to this Mila, I wouldn't have been able to complete *Lakshmila* without you. Thank you for bringing out the best in me. All the strength and motivation I have is from you. *Lakshmila* equally belongs to you as it belongs to me.

I am fortunate to have such open-minded and supporting parents like my Mumma and Daddy who have never cared what the world said and have always encouraged me to achieve my 'Laksh'. In those two years of writing *Lakshmila*, I realised that no one can love and support a child except parents.

A special thanks to my best friend, Mumma, for being the big pillar of strength for me. I cannot express in words how much my Mumma has supported me throughout. To my bundles of joy, my siblings Tanisha and Vyom, for being my research tour partners and always bringing a smile to my face when I was sad after writing an emotional chapter.

A special thanks to my Mamta *didi* at the Brahma Kumaris' retreat for being my best friend, sister and mentor. Thank you for teaching me meditation and being there with me every time.

I would like to thank my TEAM LAKSHMILA without whose collaboration *Lakshmila* would not have reached this level today,

I thank my literary agent Dipti ma'am of Word Famous Literary Agents, who has been the sweetest person I have known in this literary field. Thank you, ma'am, for wishing the best for *Lakshmila*. I remember my (late) astrologer A.P. Uncle for helping me with all the *nakshatras* and dates. I hope you're happy watching this from heaven...Wish you were here today.

Thank you to the lovely team at Om Books.

I thank Shantanu Sir, the editor-in-chief of Om Books, for trusting my writing and hand-holding me throughout the publishing process and my Quora and Instagram families for being a part of my various surveys over the years.

I thank all the friendly people at Geeta Press, Gorakhpur, for being so cooperative and helping me with all my research.

The people of Ayodhya and Mithila (especially the priests) for being so cooperative and welcoming.

A special mention to all the references from which I sought help.

Amongst the 28 lakh versions of the Ramayana in this world, there are many I had read and referred to. Every version has its own perspective. But, the basis of this book are the south-Indian versions of the Ramayana which make extensive references to Lakshman and Urmila and the Valmiki Ramayana, the original one at the Asian Library, and the one at Geeta Press. This book also contains references from the Kamban Ramayana – Maharishi Kamban, *Uttararam Charitra* – Bhavabhuti, *Meghnad Badh Kavya* – Michael Madusudhan Dutt, *Padma Puran* and *Vishnu Puran* – Maharishi Ved Vyas *ji*, *Gauri Stuti* – Goswami Tulsi Das *ji*.